## THE GHOST OF AUTHORITY

When Jack and his men pulled up to the National Guard Armory, they weren't certain of what to expect. But as they assaulted its doors with a thundering crash and paced its long corridors without interruption, something was becoming apparent: they were alone. And when they found that what they were looking for—the weapons cache—was undisturbed, the Armory took on an eerie air.

Within a matter of hours, the men hoarded their loot into the M-113A armored personnel carriers, fueled up, and drove home. And they carried out this mission with tenacity and speed, as if the ghost of authority loomed over their shoulders. But it was just that. A ghost.

And all along the way back to Henderson's Corners, the men saw no one. It was as if everyone had simply gone home to die. . . .

**MORE FANTASTIC READING FROM ZEBRA!**

GONJI #1: DEATHWIND OF VEDUN (1006, $2.95)
by T.C. Rypel
Cast out from his Japanese homeland, Gonji journeys across barbaric Europe in quest of Vedun, the distant city in the loftiest peaks of the Alps. Brandishing his swords with fury and skill, he is determined to conquer his hardships and fulfill his destiny!

GONJI #2: SAMURAI STEEL (1072, $3.25)
by T.C. Rypel
His journey to Vedun is ended, but Gonji's most treacherous battle ever is about to begin. The invincible King Klann has occupied Vedun with his hordes of murderous soldiers—and plotted the samurai's destruction!

CHRYSALIS 9 (1077, $2.50)
Edited by Roy Torgeson
From astronauts and time travelers, to centaurs and telepaths, these tales of the inexplicable and the bizarre promise to astound you!

SURVIVORS (1071, $3.25)
by John Nahmlos
It would take more than courage and skill, more than ammo and guns, for Colonel Jack Dawson to survive the advancing nuclear war. It was the ultimate test—protecting his loved ones, defending his country, and rebuilding a civilization out of the ashes of war-ravaged America!

*Available wherever paperbacks are sold, or order direct from the Publisher. Send cover price plus 50¢ per copy for mailing and handling to Zebra Books, 475 Park Avenue South, New York, N.Y. 10016. DO NOT SEND CASH.*

BY JOHN NAHMLOS

ZEBRA BOOKS
KENSINGTON PUBLISHING CORP.

ZEBRA BOOKS

are published by

KENSINGTON PUBLISHING CORP.
475 Park Avenue South
New York, N.Y. 10016



Printed in the United States of America

*Dedicated to my beloved family and friends who gave me the support and encouragement I needed.*

# A NOTE ON CHINA

As originally planned, this novel would use only the modern Pin Yin renderings of Chinese words that have become the official usages in all Chinese documents, rather than the more familiar Wade-Giles usages. However, the result was considerably less successful than anticipated, with commonly recognized Chinese words becoming unrecognizable in the process. For example, China becomes Zhongguo, Canton becomes Ganzhou, and the reader becomes confused.

Thus, in order to avoid confusion, Pin Yin has been used wherever the correlation between it and Wade-Giles is clear, and the more familiar Wade-Giles wherever the correlation is less clear. Hopefully, no insurmountable problems will arise for the reader.

## A MESSAGE TO THE READER

This novel has its genesis in fact.

The results of actual studies available to the public indicate that nuclear exchanges of as many as ten thousand megatons will not eliminate the human race, as so many books, both fact and fiction, suggest.

Instead, civilization as a whole will revert to a level equivalent to the late nineteenth century. And civilization's recovery from this setback will be rapid, as only the total elimination of every last tangible trace of its vast body of knowledge could slow it down.

While serious studies are being made on "thinking on the unthinkable," and while these studies impress the public with the feasibility of surviving an exchange of ten-thousand megatons, the likelihood of such an exchange is increasing. We can only wonder what the classified studies show.

It is a matter of historical record that the Soviet Union has never hesitated to go to war when the political leadership believes that such a war will protect the national interests and be winnable. The examples range from the Polish-Soviet War of 1920 to the present day occupation by force of nations bordering on the Soviet Union. Since its formation, the Soviet Union has the unenviable record of having been at war with or attacking every one of its European neighbors, and most of its Asiatic neighbors as well.

China is a helpless giant today, relying more on masses of men to hold off an invader than the use of sophisticated technology. Coupled with this is the fact that China is presently desperately seeking to replace its aging Soviet supplied or designed equipment with something more modern. There is a genuine irredentist bent to Chinese policy, and since the Soviet Union holds extensive areas of former Chinese territory, there is a definite source of friction, just as there is a definite reason for the Soviets to want to nip Chinese expansionism in the bud, while the battles will still be relatively easy, due to superior weapons and training.

Furthermore, Europe has never been weaker in the face of a Soviet threat. Because of this weakness, the tactically and strategically bankrupt Allied Nations are coming to rely more and more on the stocks of tactical nuclear weapons scattered in dumps across West Germany. Use of such weapons will make escalation into a more dangerous situation much more likely.

# BOOK ONE: ANTEBELLUM

## PROLOGUE

### I

General William Bryant slouched deeper into his plush chair as he listened to the president give his customary pep talk, the same one which had preceded every meeting that Bryant had ever attended. The usual stream-of-consciousness monologue fell from the president's lips with its accustomed inanities.

"Yes, gentlemen," the president said, "the world situation is grave, but not yet serious . . ."

Bryant thought about the elections which had swept the previously unknown congressman from California into the White House and shook his head. It was hard to believe that the electoral process could have ever selected such a mediocrity for the most sensitive job in the world.

Why, the man didn't even look like a national leader.

If one word could describe the man, that word was gray. His hair was gray, his face was gray, and his politics were gray, without form and without direction. His policies had become more and more devoted to reacting to outside events than to acting decisively to avoid problems.

Now, new elections were coming up, so perhaps the nation would wake up and get rid of the man once and for all. It would certainly be a pleasure to have someone in authority who could make decisions, not someone who trekked all over the world aimlessly and retreated into the fastness of Camp David for weeks to plan his next moves. The droning voice was finally winding down to a close as Bryant pulled his attention back to the reality that confronted him.

"... and finally, gentlemen, let us remember the great ideals of our great country and move forward cautiously in this time of great peril.

"I thank you all."

## II

The scene in the huge concrete bunker complex buried in the trackless forests north of Vladivostok was a study in contrast with the lethargy and boredom that filled the Washington conference room.

The brightly lit corridors were crowded with men walking back and forth carrying bulging filecases from office to office, while the grim-faced guards, in full combat gear, carefully watched everyone who came close to the doors opening into the auditorium.

Inside the doors, the auditorium resembled some large college lecture hall that had been filled with crisply uniformed men and their ever-present aides. Behind the podium was a huge computer map display, built with Western technology, and now serving the needs of the Red army.

All noise of conversation and movement ceased as the officers rose to respectful attention when an aged, bent man in a heavily bemedaled uniform walked into the room and climbed up behind the podium. With a curt gesture, Marshal of the Soviet Union Feodor Denisovitch ordered the men to be seated. After waiting for a moment while the sound of rustling uniforms died away, the old man began to speak.

"Comrades, you have been ordered here to listen to the results of my recent journey to Moscow. To you, my corps and divisional commanders, I have the pleasure of saying that our political leadership has approved the final plans for 'Operation Motherland', our campaign against the Chinese enemy!"

The marshal halted his prepared speech for a moment as a stir passed through the room. Each man there knew instinctively that the moment was historic, but only the most perceptive realized just how historic a moment it was. Each of the men knew about the border provocations along the Sino-Soviet border. Some of them had been staged by units under their command or by Soviet commandos who infiltrated the Chinese lines, while the others had been genuine. They had been going on for almost six weeks, starting even before the snows had fully disappeared or the ground had dried enough for the armored vehicles or trucks. Their attention was called back to the podium by the rapping of a gavel. The marshal continued his lecture.

"As you know, there have been a number of border incidents creating great tension along our border with the People's Republic of China. Some of you have more intimate knowledge of these actions than others.

"Suffice it to say, the incident just one week ago was the ultimate insult. The ungrateful Chinese, backed in their warlike actions by the West, attacked several of our villages along the border and kidnapped or killed the people living there. Our country can no longer suffer such insults to our national honor.

"Yesterday, our reconnaissance satellites confirmed the real reason for these incidents. The Chinese Second and Fourth Field Armies, a force of over sixty divisions, are poised on the border of our gallant ally, the Democratic Republic of Vietnam. We expect, from the results of this surveillance, that an attack will be launched within a matter of days.

"As you can undoubtedly appreciate, the border incidents were designed to indicate to us that the Chinese would fight if we should go to the aid of our allies. Our political leaders have determined that we must teach the Chinese a harsh lesson for their arrogance."

The marshal paused for a moment and drank from a glass of water. The only sound in the entire room was one of the officers coughing. Denisovitch resumed speaking.

"We have no doubts that our Vietnamese allies will be able to hold the Chinese in check. Their defense will be aided by the fact that the Chinese, in their previous incursions into the Democratic Republic, have destroyed the very roads and bridges they would depend on in any future attack during their withdrawal.

"After the previous attacks, our military assistance command in Vietnam devised a plan of operation in the event of future Chinese attacks.

"The Vietnamese will withdraw into their country, letting the Chinese advance without serious resistance, and once the Chinese are fully committed, the Vietnamese will strike, and hold the best Chinese divisions locked in combat in the south, while we attack in the north.

"Our plan is basic, and involves two inescapable facts. The first is that the Chinese are militarily weak. They are unable to keep their weapons in full operating order, and are trying to secure new weapons from the West. We cannot allow this.

"The second fact is that the bulk of Chinese industry and raw materials lie in Manchuria. Our nation and our allies, the Mongolians, surround the area on three sides, creating a huge salient that may be pinched off, just as our gallant forefathers did to the Nazi beast after the Battle of Kursk.

"Thus our plan, to cut off Manchuria from the rest of China, eliminate the fighting forces of China before they become strengthened, and incorporate the captured areas into our own Far Eastern territories."

The sounds of men murmuring to one another interrupted the marshal, as the officers in the auditorium expressed their shock and surprise. He allowed them to speak for only a minute, then rapped again for attention. The officers obediently settled down.

"Our operations will take the form of two main thrusts and a single air insertion.

"The first thrust will consist of a force of forty divisions operating from the Mongolian People's Republic, with the Mongolian army guarding the flanks. This force of Soviet units will strike out along the axis Ulaan Baatar-Beijing-Tianjin, and will form a cover across the base of the salient, cutting Manchuria off from the balance of China as soon as the lead units reach the sea. Further, we will gain the considerable political advantage of capturing the enemy capital. Once the initial objectives are obtained, the forces will move southward to the arc Huhhot-Taiyuan-Tianjin to make certain that the enemy will be unable to break through our defenses.

"Our second thrust will be launched simultaneously with the first, but will be operating out of the Vladivostok area and strike south along the axis Vladivostok-Changchun-Shenyang, through the heart of the Chinese industrial areas and southward to link up with the first thrust. Obviously, such an attack will serve to disrupt or eliminate most Chinese industry.

"Our aerial insertion will be directed against the city of Lanzhou, the center of Chinese nuclear capacity, and be directed toward securing or interdicting all those installations in the city. The force will consist of two airborne divisions, leaving us three further airborne divisions in reserve.

"Detailed operational plans have been prepared and printed and will be issued to your troops as soon as possible. We plan to strike decisively in two weeks, on the first of May.

"Are there any questions?"

"Yes, comrade marshal. Given the large numbers of Chinese troops we will undoubtedly encounter, how will a force of sixty divisions be able to cope with the problem?"

"General Varonovski, you have raised, as usual, a most important point that is covered in your operational orders; I am going to take the opportunity to deal with the problem now, to make sure that there are no questions or misunderstandings on this matter.

"Our political leadership has approved the use of chemical and tactical nuclear weapons, which are even now being issued in quantity to the appropriate units. Since it is a well known fact that the Chinese lack almost all protection against modern chemical weapons, we should have an easy, and casualty-free, time flushing them out of their tunnels."

"Comrade marshal, I have a question."

"Yes, Belinski?"

"If we attack the Chinese, what response can we expect from the Western Allies? After all, we will be eliminating one of their choice sales areas."

"Our newspapers and television are already setting a major information campaign under way, readying everyone for the crescendo which will come the moment the Chinese cross the Vietnamese border. We will stress facts to make the West forget that the Vietnamese have ever been the aggressor, so their own people will be far too busy picketing for peace to let their governments react in time to the crisis.

"Besides, the Western economies are completely disrupted as a result of the latest OPEC oil embargo. Their factories are empty and their armies and air forces almost without fuel.

"In fact, we have obtained a copy of a report by one of their top generals that states that the only chance the USAREUR had of delaying our attack is to litter the roads with the wrecks of its own destruction!

"We need not fear the political twit who holds power in Washington or any action that he may contemplate. We can almost guarantee that he will react to our actions only after long and careful deliberation. By the time he finishes deliberating, we will be parading through Paris!

"Yes, comrades, we plan to remove the Chinese threat from our rear, then turn west, removing all threats from the frontiers of our beloved motherland, forever! The process of proletariatization begun in the streets of Leningrad in 1917 shall reach its culmination in the peace that we shall dictate in Washington, DC.

"Because the Western Allies are so gullible, we have already informed them of our preparations for war. We have told them that we shall conduct extensive maneuvers in the German Democratic Republic, and under cover of these maneuvers, we shall complete the forward deployment of our armies and air forces.

"Comrades, in less than a month, the political face of the whole world shall change. It shall change so much that no observor shall ever recognize what once was!

"Victory shall be ours!"

## III

Colonel Jim Dawson watched with silent amusement as his chief, "Bad Boy" Bryant, lived up to his reputation. His head had suddenly snapped back after almost falling on his chest, just in time for the end of the latest in a long series of boring presidential blatherings. Jim was very careful to hide the smile that almost appeared on his face, though. Ever since the last assassination attempt had almost gotten the president, the security guards had tightened down hard on everybody admitted to the Presence.

The attempt had surprised nobody, since it was the latest in a series of eighteen attacks in the last year. This one had been the worst, though. While the president and vice president were attending a diplomatic reception, about a dozen, some said as many as thirty, waiters suddenly threw aside their trays and opened fire. Before they had been shot down, a couple of dozen men were dead, including the vice president, and a lot more wounded.

It had all been brought on by the presidential failures that plagued the administration. Jim really couldn't see how anyone, least of all the supposedly intelligent men who formed the cabinet and the military men who had access to the president could believe the man and trust in his judgment. Since he had been elected, more political doublecrosses and dumping of allies, domestic as well as foreign, had taken place than in any previous administration. It had all been done in the name of "political realities". Jim doubted seriously that the president would know a political reality if it came up and bit him!

The relationship with General Bryant had been much more solid than any attachment Jim felt for the president. The general was more than just a commander for all these years, he had become a friend of both Jim and his twin brother Jack. It had all started years ago, back when all of them were in the Green Berets.

It had been Colonel Bryant and Captains Dawson

then, when they had been assigned, along with a dozen other men, to pick up the pieces after the Cong had overrun a special forces base up in the highlands. They had gone in and were almost immediately ambushed, losing their radio and radioman in the first second of the battle. The only thing that saved the men was the counterattack by the tribesmen who had been driven out of the base.

The tribesmen were simple people, living at a level little higher than their ancestors had lived for the last thousand years. The only real difference was that now they carried modern rifles into battle. Their real loyalty was to the man who commanded them, not to an abstract like country and justice. The Cong, though, offered them only death, as they had so amply demonstrated on their helpless prisoners. When the Americans returned, they acted as a catalyst for the revolt.

By the time the tribesmen had finished off the Cong ambushers, all but six of the Green Berets had been killed. Bryant had taken over immediately, and organized the tribesmen to march out of their homeland and head for the coast, where they would link up with more American units. Everybody, from the tiniest babe in arms to the incredibly wrinkled grandparents, had set out, hoping to find safety somewhere beyond the mountains.

Marching through the jungles is one of the toughest forms of walking possible, and especially when the enemy was soon in hot pursuit. Luckily, the Cong couldn't call in aircraft to spot the marchers, so they avoided traps, but there was nothing they could do to avoid the attacks from friendly aircraft.

During the march, they had to cross the Ho Chi Minh Trail, one of the most heavily defended areas on earth. They had waited until they saw an American air attack on the enemy antiaircraft defenses and attacked as soon as the planes flew off. The big old lumbering Spads had done their usual efficient job, so the attack was easily pressed home, but even so, they lost the other three Americans.

In the hell-fire glare of burning trucks, exploding ammunition, and combat, the tribesmen had walked across the Trail in good order, stopping only long enough to loot the enemy of guns and ammunition needed to keep on fighting. The NVA troops had finally gotten their act together enough to use their antiaircraft to attack the fleeing refugees. The flashes and trails of tracer fire from the ZPUs and ZSUs made fiery necklaces through the air, and killed wherever they hit.

The Americans and some of the tribesmen had charged the nearest gun positions and taken several of them, then turned the guns on the NVA. That seemed to even the battle up a little, because the enemy fire slackened, then stopped. In a short time, the colonel had ordered them out to check out the enemy gun positions. Inside the log bunkers, they found the NVA dead or wounded, and took their time about blowing up the guns and ammunition.

Finally, as they pulled out of the area, they had detonated the demolition charges. The results were more spectacular than they had expected. The whole hillside had exploded into a mass of red, yellow, green, and purple tracers as the network of bunkers went up. Enemy missiles in the blaze caught fire and went snaking across the ground like fireworks gone wild and exploded. That had been what killed the other three men.

After they crossed the Trail, the tribesmen and Americans had marched on and on, finally getting into contact with other Americans having a captured radio set. The Americans refused to believe they were real. All through the march, the colonel had grown closer to his two subordinates by the simple fact that he needed someone he could talk to whom he could trust. The colonel had almost become a third Dawson brother.

Finally, with less than thirty kilometers to go, their luck had run out, and they had run into an ambush. They had lost their entire lead party in a vicious two-minute long firefight. The ambush cost them time and men, and allowed the enemy following them to catch up.

In desperation, the three Americans had led a close assault on Charlie's roadblock, firing RPG-2 rocket grenades into the brush, and following up with their own close-range rifle fire. In the swirling battle that followed as they closed to hand-to-hand combat range against the enemy, knives, machetes, entrenching tools, even fists were used to bludgeon their way through. The NVA finally broke under the pressure and fled, the tribesmen pursuing them with whoops and battlecries.

The bulk of the families were hustled past the roadblock. Behind the families came the rear guard, fighting hard to protect their families. The three Americans managed to gather enough men together to set up an ambush for the NVA to cover the retreat.

In a lull in the battle, the tribesmen carefully concealed themselves in the underbrush, and put on the uniforms of the dead NVA over their own black pajamas, readied the enemy machineguns, and waited.

The NVA walked into the trap, after calling out to their "comrades," and having a tribesman who had been educated in French Hanoi answer them in their own familiar accents. The result was chaos as the NVA were mowed down in a deadly crossfire from their own weapons.

Officers and men alike were chopped down and killed by the machinegun fire, and finished off by the mortar bombs that the tribesmen dropped into their shattered ranks. In a couple of "mad minutes," the tribesmen had fired off all the ammunition they had brought with them and all they had captured. All of the ammunition had been obligingly supplied by the NVA; now, the butcher's bill was settled.

As the tribesmen ran out of ammunition, they abandoned their weapons and fled through the jungle to the road and discarded their NVA uniforms along the way. They had been ordered to get away as soon as the ammunition was gone, since even the toughest soldiers without ammunition are helpless. The colonel and the two Dawsons led the sniper party which stayed behind to cover the withdrawal.

They knew that some of their people had made it back to friendly lines when an M113 armored personnel carrier came rolling up, supporting them with fire from its machineguns. They were sure they were safe at last when the airplanes arrived and turned the jungle into a cauldron of flying fragments of undergrowth and blazing napalm, all accompanied by the *a capella* choir of screaming enemy soldiers.

After their hospitalization for exhaustion and wounds the three men had been promoted and separated. Jim and the now-brigadier general stayed behind to command the tribesmen, while Jack was sent off to Europe. Jack had been the unlucky one, because after he had been in West Germany for a while, something had happened that cost him his family. He resigned his commission after staying in the hospital for a time and went back to run the family farm. Even Jim couldn't find out what had happened.

The sound of General Bryant's voice pulled Jim's attention back to the conference. Bryant was, as usual, trying to get the president to understand that there was a reason for the Chinese build-up along the Vietnamese border, that there was a reason for corresponding Soviet build-up along the Sino-Soviet border and in Manchuria, and that the maneuvers in East Germany could very well be a blind.

Just as he always did, the president dismissed the evidence with the now all too familiar words: "... but General Bryant, you must appreciate the political realities ..."

Jim sighed and thought that if he heard that phrase one more time, he would explode!

## IV

Cal Lundgren was one of the Secret Service agents who had been assigned to the presidential bodyguard after the latest assassination attempt. Now, because he was lucky enough to have a high security clearance, he stood in the conference room where world-shaking decisions were made.

Unfortunately for Lundgren, his enthusiasm wore off too quickly for his own good in the face of the realities of the situation. Now he stood in the room and spent his time trying to stay awake. The heat in the room usually built up without control, now that even the White House had to submit to energy rationing. Of course, the actual living quarters were fully cooled. Sacrifices do have their limits, he was told.

The heat didn't make it any easier to stay awake with the constant flow of words from the president, his short choppy gestures, and whining voice. If he wasn't wafting he was stumbling over himself. The man was boring!

Lundgren studied the people in the room. One of the men who stood out was the dapper General Bryant, a tall man, his athlete's body still neatly filling his uniform, even though his black hair was beginning to gray around the edges. His darkly tanned face formed a setting for the bluest eyes Cal ever saw, so blue they almost had no color, a real "black Irishman", that one! Lundgren almost laughed out loud as the general's head suddenly snapped up when he woke up to give his speech.

Behind Bryant stood Jim Dawson, one of the few men Lundgren knew well. His house was just five doors from Lundgren's own, and their kids played together regularly.

Jim was a bull of a man, almost six six tall, with the bulging muscles of the professional wrestler or weight lifter, yet with enough grace that he regularly beat Cal at basketball when they played with the older kids. When he talked to you, you could see his eyes twinkle and you could feel the personal magnetism of the man, a real leader.

The man was a near genius and had graduated near the top of his class at West Point, and then went on to pile up graduate degrees, win a Congressional Medal of Honor in 'Nam, and to climb up steadily in the military intelligence agency. He even wrote books, under an assumed name, to provide his family with the luxuries that they wanted.

If anything shocked Cal, though, it was Jim's simple statement that his brother Jack was better than he was at everything. Cal had had his curiosity raised enough to try to check it out.

The file that he had gotten showed a photograph of a man that looked exactly like his brother, and showed a record that was, indeed, better than Jim's, but there the story ended. All the records showed after that was that he had been assigned to Europe, and later resigned from the service, after hospitalization. Even Cal's sources couldn't penetrate the curtain of secrecy that masked the man.

As Lundgren kept his eye on the president, he saw the man make the secret signal that the meeting was over. Cal stepped over and opened the doors, letting the hot air out and the cooler—but not much cooler—air rush in, while the president used the distraction to scuttle out his private door.

*I wonder what he'll do if someday they don't turn around when the door's opened,* Cal thought.

# ONE

## I

The shrill, strident ringing of the alarm clock shook Jack Dawson out of his sleep which had been filled with the usual terrible dreams. He lay there, soaked in sweat, as he tried to calm himself after the terror that the dreams brought.

Finally, he got out of bed and crossed to the bureau, picked up his pipe and filled and lighted it. He sat down on the easy chair that took up part of the room.

The dream was the same one that had haunted him for almost five years, ever since that terrible day in Munich.

Jack, Lori his wife, and their two children had looked forward to his assignment to West Germany for a number of reasons, not the least being his own return from the dead.

They had settled down into a nice apartment in a new complex in Munich. Jack had always believed that the best way for him to polish his language skills was to live with native speakers. Since Lori spoke the language well, it was a double bonus for all of them.

Jack had been placed in a counterintelligence post and had been running a network of agents in East Germany for almost two years before the first arrests had started. The networks dated back to the end of the Second World War, and had been assembled after certain men realized how dangerous a threat the Soviet Union was in Europe. The original recruits had come to the Americans because they hated the Soviets and what they were doing in the east. They soon supplied the Americans with volumes of data that surprised even their own intelligence operatives.

As the years passed, the agents grew older and recruited their own replacements. Sons, daughters, even grandchildren were joined into the network. Now, though, agents on the other side of the wire were picking their people up off the streets and taking them away for questioning and the agency wanted to know why.

Jack was given the herculean task of finding out who the traitor was and eliminating him.

Jack was forced to move quickly and soon narrowed the list of suspects down to either of two people of high rank in the local station. He had set up a plan to expose the true traitor by setting up fake rendezvous with pseudo agents, supposedly high-ranking Soviet officers who wanted to defect. Jack knew the Soviets would have to act on the information while it was fresh, and whichever rendezvous was interrupted by the Soviets would tell them who the traitor was. Jack had only to sit back and wait for the traitor to hang himself.

On that last horrible day, Jack had taken Lori and the children out to dinner, and had come home late. As soon as they walked into the apartment, Jack knew that something was wrong, but really couldn't put his finger on any hard evidence. He was to regret that moment's hesitation for the rest of his life.

The moment he walked into the apartment, the door slammed behind him and a crushing blow fell on his head. Dimly, just as consciousness faded away, he heard his wife's long, despairing scream.

When Jack woke up, he was lying in a hospital bed, his head and back swathed in bandages. Jack buzzed for the nurse and found that he was in the base hospital, and that after the people attacked him, they had shot him in the back, directly over the heart, with a small-caliber, silenced pistol. Only Jack's enormous muscles and the small caliber of the pistol had prevented the assassins from killing him.

As it was, they had killed his family.

Officially, the assassins were Palestinian commandoes who had attacked his apartment by mistake, rather than that of the prominent Jewish activist who lived next door. Jack knew better.

The moment Jack heard and digested the news, he got out of bed, pushed his nurse to one side, and began to get dressed. By the time he had his pants on, a burly male nurse had been called into the room to stop Jack. The nurse might as well have tried to stop a landslide for all the good it did him. Jack simply knocked him unconscious and threw him into a corner.

Jack walked out of the building and hailed a jeep to take him to his office. Inside the building, he found the report that he had been waiting for on his desk. He knew who the traitor was, and the fact that it was a man made a wolfish smile cross Jack's face.

Jack picked up the .45 caliber pistol that Lori had given him, a specially accuratized version of the M1911, designed for combat shooting. Jack walked down the hall to the traitor's office with his pistol in his pocket, brushed the man's secretaries aside and kicked his private office door open.

"You're a traitor, Williams. I have all the evidence I need. You're going to go to jail for a long, long time. The only thing I want to know is why did you order my family killed, you bastard? You know even if you got me, some person here would have found you out."

"I swear to you, Dawson, that I didn't do that. I have a family of my own, and I'd never do anything like that!"

With those words, the man jerked a pistol out of the desk drawer in front of him and brought it up to bear on

Jack's chest. Jack hadn't wasted time, but had watched the man, looking for the telltale movement that would reveal just when the man was going to make his move. Jack was even ready to let him have the first draw. The two men fired simultaneously.

Jack's combat-honed accuracy was better than the traitor's, with the soft-lead bullet catching him square in the chest and bouncing him off the wall behind his desk, then throwing him sprawling as his body convulsed in death. William's bullet, on the other hand, missed Jack and went through a wooden office partition, striking one of his own secretaries. The building security guards entered the office just in time to see a screaming, bleeding secretary running out of the office, and a man standing in the door of an office, his head wrapped in bloody bandages, and a smoking pistol in his hand, lift up a bloody man's body in the private office.

Without stopping to question what was going on, or even to shout a warning to Jack, the guards opened fire. Luckily for Jack, they were armed with .38 caliber pistols with light loads, so that the wounds, though serious, weren't fatal.

Afterward, in the hospital for the second time in less than twelve hours, Jack explained to his superior exactly what had happened, even to the point where he told him that he had gone there to kill Williams. Once Jack had recovered from all his wounds, he resigned his commission and returned to his boyhood home.

As Jack sat there, puffing his pipe, he thought back on all that had happened, that still haunted him after such a long time. He knew his dreams were making an emotional cripple of him, yet he still couldn't seem to shake the conviction that there had been something he could have done to save his family, yet he knew there had been nothing anyone could have done.

Despite the logical argument, the doubts still tormented him.

## II

Mario Ginetti stood on the empty streetcorner in the cold wind and waited for the delivery of his latest drug buy from his dealer. A swarthy boy of just seventeen, he didn't look the part of the leader of the Demons, the gang which had killed off or absorbed every other gang in the city. Even more, he didn't look the part of the boy who had been almost completely successful in driving the organized crime people out of their own business, and taking them over.

In just two years, he had climbed to the top of the garbage heap, killing, torturing, and stealing all along the way. His own record was clean; he was far too smart to do anything that would give himself away. Even more important, he had never allowed even his closest companions on the way to the top to get too close to him. Nobody, not even his family, knew what drove him.

Even something as dangerous as a major narcotics buy wasn't trusted to subordinates, so that was why he was standing out in the cold sunlight on a deserted corner. He trusted the guards whom he scattered around to warn him if anyone tried to break up the buy or double-cross him.

Mario thought about the empire he was building up, an empire which was starting out slowly, just like that of another Corsican almost two hundred years ago. Napolean would have thought the empire of murder and terror, drugs and prostitution, gambling and loan-sharking small potatoes and probably would have been disgusted to see the boy who was in charge, but Mario liked to call himself another Napoleon. He always promised his subordinates their marshal's batons and cash for rewards.

The cash was there in plenty, for Mario was almost totally in charge of all the former exclusive mob-run rackets in the whole city. Even though few of the mobsters knew it, they had been beaten at their own game by a teenager. If they ever found out that a mere kid had broken their hold on the city, they would have fought back, hard, but then, even at his worst, Mario was never "mere."

Finally, Mario saw the car which was carrying his drugs pull into the vacant industrial development where the meet was to take place. The bare countryside gave an incomparable view all around and gave him enough warning of treachery.

Mario picked up the battered old duffle bag containing almost a million dollars in small, untraceable bills, and walked toward the curb. As the car glided closer, Mario's heart leaped up into his throat. There were three men in the car!

Mario turned and ran, dropping his million dollar bag. The car behind him suddenly roared into action, shooting gravel out from under its tires and bouncing over the curb. Mario leaped for a clump of grass and hugged himself against the dirt.

Behind him, Mario heard the sound like the high-pitched vibration of jack-hammers or cloth ripping, but greatly magnified. The men Mario had placed to guard the meet were firing the M16s that they had stolen from the National Guard armory and were cutting the organized crime hitmen to ribbons.

Mario, like Napoleon, rarely made mistakes.

## III

Jim Dawson and General Bryant had been carefully

studying the computer-enhanced photographs of the Sino-Soviet border areas which covered their table top for many hours. There was absolutely no doubt about the situation. The Chinese, after invading Vietnam yet again, were suffering heavy casualties in the south, and were drawing combat-ready troops off their mutual border with the Soviet Union to reinforce their offensive. They had begun filling in the gaps they had themselves created by calling up militia units.

Worst was yet to come, because of the photographs of the Sino-Mongolian border. At least thirty-five, and possibly as many as forty Soviet divisions had gathered in the area, and were moving into their attack positions. Matching the Mongolian build-up was the build-up further to the east, around Vladivostok, where at least another thirty divisions were massing for the attack.

Throughout the Soviet Far Eastern provinces, the airfields were becoming jammed with aircraft, loaded with weaponry, and the air was becoming filled with coded transmissions. The transmissions were in no code that the agency had yet penetrated, but from the amount of traffic, and the locations plotted by the radio-direction finding units, the traffic was but a prelude to a full-scale assault.

In Europe, the situation was equally bad, with abundant evidence pouring in that the Soviet "maneuvers" weren't really maneuvers at all, but covers for the advance of units into their attack positions. Further, huge quantities of military supplies were being openly moved into East Germany and known military installations were being dispersed. Most alarming was the number of line-crossers who were coming across the border into West Germany, staging many serious incidents.

"Jimmy," the general said, "I want you to take the family and everything you can take with you and go visit your brother for a few months.

"I think we're going to get into a shooting war soon, and there isn't a damned thing that you can do here. I want you to take a copy of all this stuff—no, on second thought—better make it two copies, along with you. Give one set to Jack and have him hide it somewhere out there. Get home while you can, Jim, and get your family to safety."

"What about you, sir?"

"I'm alone, Jim, you know that. I plan to get in to see the president as soon as I can and try to make that fool see what's going on. I've tried to get an appointment with him for the last two days, and those damned fool secretaries of his keep saying that he's busy.

"I don't think those turkeys could find their own rear ends with a compass and a road map. I finally talked to one of them who showed some sense; that Mrs. Hunter he keeps as his private secretary. She heard me out and got me an appointment for the day after tomorrow. Four days might be too long to wait, but we've got to risk it.

"Jimmy, I want you on the road tonight, before I actually go up there. The White House has gotten awfully scary since the latest assassination attempt, and I think some mighty strange things are going on up there. I want you to be able to cover my ass if this thing should blow up in my face, Jim. Besides, I want to make sure that somebody I trust and care for gets out of this mess with a whole skin, even if I don't.

"Now," he said, handing Jim two bulging envelopes, "take these files and get out of here. I've already made arrangements for somebody to drive your car home, because I have a truck waiting for you at the gate. It has some, um . . . well, presents inside for you.

"Don't let anyone, not even Jean, look inside. I had another truck and a crew of moving men go to the house to remove everything.

"Now here's some cash, you'll probably need it. Here

are some military priority papers that'll guarantee you fuel and passage through any roadblocks. Tell Jean and the kids that I love them, and say hello to Jack for me, and get out of here. Good luck," the general said, shaking the younger man's hand. "Please don't waste time."

## IV

Virginia Henderson Schroeder stood in front of her board of directors and carefully detailed exactly what she expected of them for the next quarter. Standing there in her navy blue suit, she made a startling contrast to the high-powered executives who hung on her every word. Barely two inches over five feet tall, blonde and slight, she didn't look the type to run a multi-million dollar corporation. Looks, however, seldom tell the whole story.

She had been raised on her grandfather's farm after her parents had been killed in a plane crash, and had grown up used to physical labor. She spent at least an hour a day exercising and had taken up karate as a hobby, a hobby that paid its costs back a thousand fold after she had beaten off a rapist who thought she was an easy mark.

Mentally, she was even stronger, having graduated from the university in record time, and capping her college career off by marrying the only son of a wealthy family, bringing with her a small boy of her own.

Her husband and her parents had survived just three years after the marriage, having been killed in an auto crash, leaving Ginny with two more children to raise and a business to run. Running the business was made more complicated by the fact that the family managers had decided to break and loot the company.

The young woman had not only successfully defeated the managers' plans, but had expanded the company into a major corporation, with interests in everything from agriculture to electronics, and from banking to baby foods. The company was finally breaking into the major world markets in time to be seriously hurt by the OPEC oil embargo. Things were serious, but Ginny wouldn't let anything stand in the way of her family's success.

Even so, Ginny loaded her family into her private plane twice a year and flew off, out of town. Where she went, no one knew, but when she came back, she was relaxed and refreshed, and had the type of tan that no self-indulgent lolling on a beach could duplicate. Nobody but her private secretary knew where she went, and he was impossible to bribe. Everyone had his own pet theories about the mysterious absences, ranging from drunken orgies to some sort of religious retreat, but not one came close to the actual truth.

Ginny and her family went back to the tiny town where she had been raised and had worked for her grandfather in his store and on his farm, just as she did when she was a girl. Ginny tried to make the pilgrimage home at least twice a year, and enjoyed every minute of the visit, especially as no one knew she was anything but the same hometown girl who had gone away to the big city and gotten married.

The time spent on the farm gave Ginny time to get things back together and reminded her that despite all the money she accumulated, she was still a small-town girl at heart. With the ever more serious international scene, Ginny had delayed her traditional visit to call this special meeting and stay in Chicago for some time to keep her business on track.

She planned to go home in just about a week.

# TWO

## I

Jack Dawson had been carefully following the news for the last several weeks, especially since the Vietnamese border incidents with China. The Chinese invasion had gone in with great success at first, then seemed to bog down in a confusion of propaganda from both sides. Since both of the combatants were traditionally given to heavy-handed propaganda, the whole picture wasn't clear to anybody except the American and Soviet military intelligence experts, and probably they weren't too sure what was really happening.

Jack knew that the situation was bad, since that crazy radio message that his brother sent the day before. Jack couldn't believe that his brother was coming back to the farm of his own free will, yet that was what he had said.

Jack shook his head and smiled to himself. His brother certainly had the right to come to the farm any time, since they both owned it after their parents' death, but the only reason even Jack had come home was to recover from his own family's bloody death. He had figured that the job of managing the huge farm would keep his mind off the unthinkable.

The time hadn't been wasted, though, since he had done some work that had needed doing for the last forty years. He had acquired some Bureau of Land Management leases for grazing, and bought out some other farms and ranches, finally winding up with forty thousand deeded acres and another twenty thousand acres under BLM lease.

The herd and the cultivated acreage had both been increased to the point where they were the same as in his great-grandfather's day, and then had gone the old man one step better. Jack had dammed off several creeks that ran through the property to provide some badly needed irrigation water, and had put small hydroturbines in the dams to give him his own free electricity. Instead of being a net electrical consumer, Jack became a net electrical producer.

With the OPEC oil embargos, Jack had converted all the trucks, cars, and tractors to alcohol fuel and had rebuilt the big old still that had been on the farm ever since the Great Depression when fuel was equally hard to come by. Now, everything ran on alcohol, and Jack had his own "green gas".

With the radio news finished, Jack hurried to finish off his cup of coffee, pulled on his boots, and got up from the kitchen table to go to work.

Outside, the land was finally shaking off its white wintery coat and even the high mountains were losing their blanket of snow. The farm was wet from the meltwater and some of the fields too watersoaked to plow. There was a farewell nip in the air as winter reminded everyone that it was just waiting to come back, just as it did every year.

As Jack walked away from the house, he turned back and looked at the huge stone pile that he had been born in. His great-grandfather had built the place like a fortress, back when men needed stronger protection from their neighbors than from the elements. The house even looked like a fortress, but still and all, it was home, and Jack loved every inch of it. Attached to the house were the additions that every generation of the Dawson family had seemed compelled to add, some sign that they had also lived in the house. Each of the additions was built in the same style, just as each of the other buildings on the farm had been built. It seemed that building for eternity was a dominant feature of the Dawson family.

Jack figured that his brother would be back at the

farm soon, and wanted to make sure that all the chores were done or underway. If he didn't keep after his hands, they tended to loaf. Before Jack had taken over, he and Jim had always gotten fat checks from the manager whom they had hired, and now Jack had pretty much cut them back to nothing. Jim knew why Jack was doing it, to buy all the land that the family had sold off; both of them had dreamed of returning the farm to its old extent for years, ever since they were boys.

Another quirk, almost an obsession, was being self-sufficient. The water turbine had been built in Jack's own shop, and installed to provide electrical independence. Back in the twenties, the family had bought one of the windmill power generators, using it until Roosevelt's rural electrification program made the installation too inefficient. Now that the government had instituted such wide-ranging power controls that brown-outs were commonplace everywhere, and regularly scheduled blackouts of certain areas were the norm, Jack's farm could use electricity in its normal fashion since he was considered a self-provider.

The alcohol fuel situation was also a blessing. With the latest OPEC oil embargo in full effect against the United States and Europe, the use of fuel for almost everything was forbidden. The result was that farmers and ranchers everywhere were forbidden to use their tractors except for certain specified times of the month, and heaven help them if they couldn't finish their work in that time. That was one of the reasons why rationing was in effect in the United States.

One of the things that made self-sufficiency possible was the fact that Jack had simply cut off Jim's profit-sharing checks from the farm, and had plowed his own money back into the operation. This gave Jack enough capital to buy things that weren't really vital to the farm's operations, like the tractors and tools, but which could be used to build things that would be useful. The water turbine had been built using tools bought this way, and cut the farm's electrical bills from about $2,000 per month to nothing. The same for the alcohol still. It provided all the fuel the farm needed to operate normally at almost no cost. That saved thousands more every month.

The money saved from just these projects went into developing other self-sufficiency projects. The farm's stock of food was raised from its normal winter's supply to two years' worth of freeze-dried foods, enough for everyone on the farm and a number of other people as well. Finished steel, ready for machining, was stocked against some need in the future, and the farm shop was expanded to the point where it could rebuild any piece of machinery on the farm without hiring out the work and the supply of spare parts on hand increased to cover four or five years' normal repairs.

Self-sufficiency wasn't without its drawbacks, though, since the isolated farms and ranches tended to attract people out for an easy buck. Jack knew several farms in the area which had been raided over the last five years by marauders looking for whatever they could steal. Jack had spent a fair amount of his spare time clearing away underbrush around the farm, filling in pockets where men could hide as they sneaked up on the buildings, and setting up passive traps. The defenses had been tested once already when a motorcycle gang tried to take over the farm for the winter. The survivors had been only too glad to get away, leaving thirty of their people behind, dead.

Nothing worth having, though, is without a price. Three of Jack's people were killed in the defense of the farm.

Jack knew that his brother would be along soon with his family, and he would be glad to see what all the money taken for the farm had accomplished. The fat checks that the two of them had always gotten from their manager had been nice, but the money now was serving a better purpose. The excess money was going to buy back all of the land that the family had been forced to sell off over the years since the Dawson family farm was founded. Both of the men had had boyhood plans to restore what had been theirs, and now Jack had the way and means to do it.

Jim would be satisfied with his brother's work.

## II

"Mr. President," General Bryant said, gesturing at the wall filled with photographs behind him, "we know what the results of the Chinese invasion are; they're stuck and trying desperately to extricate what troops they can. The photographs show that they're pulling troops out of the Sino-Soviet border areas and replacing them with half-trained militia.

"These photographs, here, show the extent of the Soviet build-up in Mongolia. These units are in attack positions right now, ready to go. They're not there for manoeuvers.

"As for the situation in Europe, we have positive proof of the actual purpose of their manoeuvers. They have issued eight days ammunition and fuel to the low-level units, and have another sixteen days' worth of ammunition and almost a month's worth of fuel in the middle-level units. They've moved their supply dumps forward and dispersed them.

"What's even more important, they're moving units forward from the interior. We've intercepted signals from units which were deployed near Moscow, but even that source of data was cut off when the Soviets imposed communications controls on their units and sealed the whole of Eastern Europe off from news reporters.

"The Soviets have also stepped up the infiltration of agents and saboteurs into West Germany and Italy. Why, just last night, a West German destroyer intercepted a convoy sneaking along the coast near the Kiel Canal. They had a real firefight going there for a little while, but finally the West Germans sank or drove off most of the boats. One was driven ashore by its crew.

"The West Germans sent a motor launch in to capture the crew and the equipment the boat was carrying. As soon as the motor launch closed with the enemy boat, there was a flurry of small arms fire from both boats, then the whole thing exploded when the Soviets on board the stranded boat set off their cargo. They must have been carrying a couple of tons of explosives, since there was nothing left of either boat but a few burnt fragments.

"Sir, we have a real reason to worry about this crisis. There aren't enough men, or ammunition, or fuel in Europe with our forces right now to seriously delay a Soviet strike into West Germany. Even worse, the men we do have in the country are so demoralized that they aren't really capable of fighting a serious war. Most of the men are in a state of mutiny, just like they were at the end of Vietnam.

"Mr. President, it is my opinion that the Soviets are planning an attack in the West, and have it scheduled for some time in the immediate future."

"General Bryant," the president said, interrupting the general's flow of words for a moment, "don't you believe that you may be overreacting? I agree that the Soviets are sending a threat-signal to the Chinese, but I have been acting on the request of Premier Wing to arrange some reconciliation between the Chinese and the Soviets. I believe that the special relationship I have with Premier Davidov will carry the day.

"Why, I believe that where you see threatening moves

on the part of the Soviet forces in East Germany, I can see a positive signal to us to remain inactive while the Soviets pursue their policies in the Far East. You do see that, general?

"After all, you must have as firm a grasp on political realities as I myself do to appreciate the full implications of the Soviet activities. They don't want war, they just want peace for their Vietnamese allies."

*Special relationships and political realities my ass!,* General Bryant thought. *Every American president since Roosevelt believed that he had some special insight into the Soviet mind. That made Roosevelt give that bloody-handed murderer Stalin control over all of Eastern Europe. Every one of the presidents since then had been fooled by that old line and never realized how badly they've been fooled.* The general hesitated for a moment, making a diplomatic choice of words that belied his nickname.

"That is indeed a possibility, Mr. President. If so, the signal is also telling us to stand aside while the Soviets deal with their Chinese problem in their own fashion. They can equally be telling us that they're ready to use force against us in Europe if we make any move that they don't approve of.

"Sir, you've spent the last week trying to placate the Chinese and the Vietnamese, but nothing has come of it. The Soviets have every military and political reason to strike now against China, since the best Chinese divisions are tied down firmly in Vietnam and are bleeding themselves white.

"The Chinese have always planned on taking higher casualties than we allow, but now they're losing their men at an even higher rate than they planned. So are the Vietnamese, and they're not likely to be willing to lose as many men as they have without a firm Soviet promise of an attack on the Chinese rear.

"The Chinese are withdrawing men from their divisions along the Sino-Soviet border and replacing them with militia. That couldn't play into Soviet hands better if the Chinese leaders were traitors, since the borders are now weakly defended at best. I . . ."

"General Bryant," the president snapped, "I believe that the Soviets are not so foolish as to risk a general war just to rescue their allies.

"Why, Premier Davidov himself is planning to visit with me here in Washington as soon as the May Day festivities are over. He should be here that afternoon in fact.

"I choose, let me repeat that *I choose*, to believe that you're wrong. My instincts tell me what is fact. I believe that you are overwrought, sir, and should take a vacation. In fact, I order you to take a vacation, general!"

"Sir," General Bryant replied, his words heating up just a little as he approached his flash point, "I can't really see how you can believe that the Soviets aren't stepping up their activities in Europe as a prelude to war! The attack on the V Corps headquarters was no accident. The Soviets blew up the whole damned block of offices and that takes a hell of a lot of explosives, tons of explosives like the tons that the West German Navy intercepted last night!"

"That was the single terrorist act of the German People's Liberation Front, general, and had no connection with any Soviet action. Why, we have a letter from the head of the Liberation Front that says so!

"Now, general, I think our conversation is at an end."

Without waiting for a reply, President Matthews rose out of his chair and angrily walked out of the room, slamming the heavy door behind himself, and leaving an equally furious General Bryant behind in the room.

Bryant shook his head in despair as the president disappeared and began to gather his materials together, putting them in the security attache case on the conference table. When he finished, he sat down and lit a cigarette. Taking a deep drag, he blew the smoke out in the direction of the portrait of Lincoln that hung on the wall. *I wonder what you'd have thought, Honest Abe, if one of your generals warned you about what lay ahead at Bull Run?*

The general stood up and pushed his chair back, ready to leave the room. The door that he was reaching to open swung open in front of him and admitted a Secret Service agent.

"General," the agent said, his face and voice both falsely smiling, "the president's compliments, sir, and he would like to invite you up to the Camp for a rest. He feels that you need a rest, and he wants you to get it in the best possible surroundings. I'm supposed to escort you up there.

"Now, if you'll just hand me that heavy case, general, we can get going."

"I don't want to go up to the Camp, and furthermore I don't need you to carry any case. Now, if you'll just get out of my way . . ."

"Sorry, general," the agent said, blocking the door, "but the president ordered my men and me to take you up to the Camp, and, by God, you're going to go!" With that, another four men forced their way into the conference room.

"All right, but what about my wife? Let me call her and tell her to meet me. I'll go along with you if you let me do that."

"Your wife's been dead for the last eight years, general, so let's stop the nonsense and get a move on."

"*NO!*" the general shouted, pulling away from the men, "I'm not going anywhere! Let me alone!" Bryant turned and tried to open the presidential door, only to be tackled from behind by one of the agents. The struggle lasted for only a moment or two, as an agent, wielding a hypodermic, injected a massive dose of sedative into one of the general's arms.

## III

President Matthews had stopped his flight from the disastrous conference with General Bryant only long enough to order his secret service agents to arrest the man and take him up to the Camp, where he could be put on ice for a while.

Once that job was done, the president had composed his outer appearance and walked down the corridor toward his private office, head down and ignoring everyone he met. The pressures from the latest OPEC oil embargo, the stagnating economy, and the political opposition within his own party were building up high enough without having to listen to some crazy general besides. With unemployment at fifteen percent already and expected to climb past thirty percent by election day, the economy needed all his attention, certainly more time than he could devote to events in some far-off lands that he never really understood anyway, let alone the paranoid suspicions about events in Europe as well!

The Chinese had gotten into this mess on their own by invading Vietnam again, and would have to get out the best way they could. Their army had stalled less than twenty kilometers from Hanoi and the bloody defensive fighting that was flaring all along the front was creating tremendous Chinese casualties, even more than the manpower-rich Chinese could easily afford. Now, Premier Wing realized that he was about to be attacked in the rear by the Soviets and he was pressing the president to do something about the situation.

Premier Wing had obliquely asked for him to arrange

some sort of cease-fire, but the Vietnamese had refused to even listen. Perhaps there was something in what Bryant was saying after all. No matter, though, for the president planned to discuss the matter with Premier Davidov as soon as Davidov arrived in Washington. Perhaps a few words right into the Kremlin's ear would get the results that he hoped for, despite the fact that the diplomatic pressure the United States could bring to bear any more was very small.

The buttress of the clout should have been the armed forces, once proudly trumpeted as the best in the world, but now, as the neglect of the seventies and the disaster of the all-volunteer army came to a head in the eighties, the president was faced with a particularly stark reality. Many of the men were barely literate, and all were poorly trained, since training, especially with live ammunition, costs money, and the budgeteers had eliminated most live training. The equipment they did have available was among the most technologically sophisticated in the world, but the men just weren't capable of using them because they couldn't understand their equipment. The army had always gotten a secret—and not so secret—laugh out of the Soviet tanks having to manoeuver by the follow-the-leader system in the Second World War; now the situations were reversed, and it was the American tankers who were barely able to use their own tanks.

The insurrection in Puerto Rico was proof of just how bad the situation was, since even the elite 82nd Airborne Division was just barely able to fend off the partisan attacks, and the 82nd was supposed to be the best division that the army had. Since that mess had started, most recruiting for more soldiers had come to a grinding halt, and in the last two years, only about ten percent of the required men had come forward, and congress still refused to act on a draft bill!

Diplomacy was the sole remaining option, of course, just as it had been for the last twenty years. Now, though, the bottom of the diplomatic barrel was in sight. The United States had too few allies or good will left in the world to do much good. Too many allies had been double-crossed and too many had been abandoned when they were put under pressure by some tiny group, all in the name of political realities. Of course, those governments collapsed when their main ally threw them to the wolves; they couldn't help but collapse. The fact of the matter was, except for the president and a few others in Washington, there was nobody in the world who seriously believed that America was a "Great Power" any more.

The President brushed past Mrs. Hunter, his private secretary, without a word. She had been with him long enough to know what that meant. She quickly cancelled all his remaining appointments. There would be no contact with him that day.

In his private office, Frank Matthews sat down exhausted, his head hammering from high blood pressure and the almost constant pain which came from the cancer which was killing him. If word of the cancer ever got out, he knew that his party would never have a chance of getting back into the White House. It had only been after the total deadlock that had nearly destroyed the party had been broken by his compromise nomination three years before that his party had managed to get back into the White House.

After sitting for a few minutes, he took a deep breath and opened the bottom left-hand drawer of the ornate desk which he had inherited from a previous administration, and pulled out the bottle he always kept hidden there. *A few inches of good Kentucky bourbon ought to ease my problems,* he thought.

As he uncorked the bottle, his hands began to tremble, spilling the amber fluid over his blotter; only a few drops managed to make their way into his glass. Without hesitation, he tilted the bottle to his lips and drank a long, deep swallow. The bourbon tasted terrible to him, but it had become a part of the image that he projected, of the homey, all-American, folksy president. He hated the stuff, but loved the release from his tensions and pains that it gave him.

The day passed by unnoticed by the president as he sat behind his desk. Finally, the sunlight that filled the room was replaced by the reflected bluish glow of the night security system that had been installed to protect him from the many assassins he knew lurked in the bushes outside.

Matthews was roused from his drunken stupor as the door of his office opened, sending a splash of light across his face. For a moment, he stared owlishly at the doorway, trying to focus on the intruder. Finally, he recognized her.

"Hello, Mrs. Hunter. I suppose you're here to try to make me eat some dinner?"

"Frank, I've been with you since you were the junior congressman from California, and I think I've earned the right to worry about you just a little. I know you're drunk again, Frank, but you're going to have to listen to me and try to understand what I'm saying.

"It's the reporters, Frank. They're starting to get restless, and even the press controls that you forced through congress aren't going to stop them from wondering and collecting information, and you know what that means. You were here in town when Nixon was destroyed by the papers and the TV reporters.

"Frank, you just can't brush past congressmen and other people waiting to see you as though they weren't even there and not expect some comments to be made. There's far too much trouble here at home and overseas to just try to sweep this under a rug and forget about it. The time for presidential rug-sweeping has just about come to an end, and the buck is stopping in front of the White House door. You've got to stop the pill popping and boozing, because people are starting to notice that you don't act like you're all there anymore. That fund-raising dinner last week was an absolute disaster. We got out of it by saying that you've been up late trying to patch up some agreements between the Chinese and Vietnamese, and that the doctor gave you a sedative to slow you down, but we're not going to be able to use that story much longer. Even worse, if word about your cancer gets out, the party will be split so badly that we'll never get back together. You're the only one who can hold the party together, and if you fail, we all fail. Please, Frank listen to me!"

"Mary, I know that you're doing this for my own good, and the good of the party. You're right, absolutely right.

"Mary, I just had to order the arrest of a man for trying to tell me the truth, and I'm afraid, really afraid, that I'll have to do even worse things behind the scenes before this mess gets straightened out. There's going to be a war between the Soviets and the Chinese, and there's nothing I can do to control it, let alone stop it.

"Here at home, things are almost as bad; you know it as well as I do. Power brownouts, unemployment soaring out of sight, and the economy grinding to a halt as it runs out of fuel, and just to top the whole thing off, the revolution down in Puerto Rico getting worse, not better.

"I swear that if I had known then what I know now, Mary, I would never have accepted that nomination when the committee came to me while the deadlock was on. I would have fought that nomination, first because I'm totally unqualified to run the country, and second, because I'm afraid I was elected just to preside over the breakup of the United States. That's something that I don't want to do."

The president stopped talking for a few minutes and sat still, his head slumped on his chest. Mary Hunter thought he had fallen asleep, but then saw his fear and pain wracked face move. Finally he spoke to her.

"Dammit, Mary, have a drink with me! That's a presidential order!"

"Frank, if you're saying something like that, then I know the situation's serious. I'll break a rule and have one with you. Frank, do you suppose that there's any danger in Europe? That's where my Bill's stationed, you know."

"I don't think so, Mary. He's probably as safe there as anywhere else. I don't think they're out to stir up trouble, especially with Premier Davidov coming here day after tomorrow to visit with me."

The two sat there in the blue-lit darkness, drinking in silence, all words torn from their minds, each thinking their own deep thoughts. Once, long ago, they had been more than boss and secretary. After Mary's husband had been killed testing a jet and Frank's wife had divorced him, they had been lovers. Now, after the fires of their passion had been almost drowned in the waves of Frank's ambitions, they were friends.

## IV

Comrade Company Commander Hsin Piao reached out to shake hands with his wife as they stood together there on the railroad station platform. He wanted desperately to hold her and kiss her goodbye for one last time, but even in post-Mao China, public displays of affection between even man and wife were frowned upon. He, as company commander, was a special example to his men. Besides, his political advisor was watching everyone carefully.

So he shook hands with his wife as they stood on the ground-level platform of the grubby wooden train station, the best this poor village could afford. Even now, more than thirty-five years after the formation of the People's Republic, they had not replaced the Japanese station that had been built on the ruins of a brick railroad station.

Behind him, he could hear the puffing and panting of the steam locomotive which would carry him and his men off to the frontier, where they were to guard their borders against the incursions of the Soviets. Even the locomotive which steamed behind was a left-over relic of the past, since it had been built by the Baldwin Locomotive Works, of Eddystone, Pennsylvania, USA. Hsin Piao knew that was the truth, because his father had been the locomotive driver of that very engine before the Red Guards tore the builder's plate off the firebox in an attempt to wipe out all trace of foreign devils.

What was more important to him than anything else was that his battalion of militia was being called up to reinforce the border after regular units had been pulled out of the lines. On this day, of all days, the day before the great May Day celebrations in Beijing, Premier Wing had activated a battalion of overage reservists, something that wouldn't have been done for just a whim. If his battalion was to face the Soviet hegemonists, the situation was bad.

Hsin Piao had heard from the news that the Third Chastisement Campaign against the Vietnamese had been launched, and that the army was advancing rapidly, crushing resistance all along the front. The news had trickled down that the army was stalled on the approaches to Hanoi, and, since regular army units had been moved south, the fighting was much heavier than had been anticipated. The news had suddenly ceased to carry any information about the campaign, an even more alarming state of affairs.

Hsin Piao knew that his battalion, armed only with AK-47 assault rifles and RPG-4 rocket launchers would not stand a chance against the better-armed Soviets. Their only hope, he knew, was if the Soviets allowed them to escape into the hills, because only there could they use their weapons effectively against the much more mobile and better-armed soldiers of the Soviet army.

His thoughts were interrupted as the locomotive sounded its whistle, all too soon, telling the men that they had to board their trains; they had to clamber into the empty wooden boxcars which would carry them to the frontier. For once, Hsin Piao took advantage of his rank as he supervised the loading of the other men of his company. He held back and was the last to leave the platform, and therefore was able to board and turn immediately around to watch his wife fade from sight.

# TWO

## I

Jack Dawson stared in amazement at the sight of two trucks grinding their way up the steep narrow farm road. He knew that his brother was worried about something if he was going so far as to move everything the family owned up here to the farm.

As soon as the lead truck pulled up in front of the barn, the cab door popped and a bear-like figure leaped out. Jack was already running toward the cab. The two men came together like an irresistible force meeting an immovable object, until Jack, in better condition than his brother, swept Jim off his feet and spun him around, all the while pressing him close and pounding on his back.

"Jack, am I glad to see you!" Jim bellowed, "I finally decided to bring the family up to the farm and give them a taste of what real living is, not like back in the city."

Stepping back, Jim grabbed his brother's shoulders and held him at arm's length.

"Damn, but you look good, baby brother! The country life must agree with you! Come on over and say hello to the wife and kids."

Jack stepped close to his brother and hugged him, while leaning toward his ear, he whispered:

"What's up, Jim? I can't see you getting off your swivel chair just to come here. I'm not falling for that back-to-nature line, either."

"Just keep your lips buttoned, brother. I promise that I'll tell you the whole story as soon as I can. Things really look bad."

The two men separated, and Jim dragged his brother over to the second truck just as it rolled to a stop.

"There she is, Jack, my favorite wife, and see who's with her? Your favorite niece and nephew combination. Jean, just look at this guy and tell me that some time in the country wouldn't do that for anybody? Come on kids, come say hello to your Uncle Jack!"

After a few minutes of standing there, marveling over the size and accomplishments of his nieces and nephews, Jack turned to his sister-in-law for a moment.

"Jean, honey, I guess you and the kids are starved. I expected you yesterday, but I still have the food in the freezer, ready to go into the microwave. Why don't you go over and pop it in? While you do that, Jim and I'll back the trucks into the barn."

Jean, good army wife that she was, knew immediately that the two brothers wanted to talk. She gathered up her children and hustled them away from their father and his brother.

Jack and Jim climbed into the cabs of the trucks and backed them into the barn. Outside, the children were busy running around the barnyard and looking at all the animals and buildings they hadn't seen since their last visit. The oldest boy was already visiting a friend he had made among the employees' children.

Jack walked to the rear of the truck his brother had driven up and yanked the doors open. He saw boxes of household goods piled high and wedged into every place they could conceivably be squeezed. Jack's quick glance at the heavy-duty springs under the truck and the dangerous sag that had developed told him that there was more then mere clothing and furniture in the truck.

Before Jack could ask his brother what was going on, three small shapes dashed into the barn. Little Jimmy led the chase, with his two sisters, Melody and Carla close behind. As soon as the boy spotted his uncle, he began to shout.

"Unca' Jack, Unca' Jack, can I have a pony? Daddy promised that he'd let me ask you. I saw one out in your yard. Daddy said that he shared a pony with you when you were my age."

Jack scooped the running boy up and held him in his arms. The weight reminded Jack of the loss that he had suffered. The boy looked enough like his own dead son to be his twin brother.

"I think something can be arranged," he choked. "I think I'll let you kids have that pony, but you'll have to share him with your sisters. Is that all right?"

The shouts of childish delight that filled the barn told Jack the deal was all right. It also told him he still missed his family, more than he cared to admit. Jim saw the tears in the corners of his brother's eyes and shooed the children out of the barn.

"I'm sorry, Jack. I really didn't think. I haven't told the children what's going on, but Jean knows. I never could keep any secrets from that girl; besides, we've lived with each other so long, that she can almost read my mind. Look, we're going to be free from interference for a few minutes, so let me fill you in on what's happening.

"You know that Bad Boy Bryant's still my boss at the Pentagon, don't you? Well, the Boy tells me that there's going to be a full-fledged war between the Chinese and the Soviets soon, and we both think it's going to spill over into Europe. You know what the army's like today—they can't hold off some rebels in Puerto Rico, let alone a serious Soviet thrust to the Rhine.

"The general gave me a file on all the information he's taking to the president today, but he isn't too happy about the situation. He really doesn't think anything will get done, and neither do I. He wanted me to give you this stuff for safekeeping, just in case the war does start. He wants his ass covered if there is some sort of coverup, and he figures that we're the two people that he can trust in the whole world.

"I'll tell you, if he hadn't ordered me out of town, I would have left anyway after I saw that stuff, but he had already sent a truck over to the house to pick up what we wanted to take with us, and he had my truck packed as well. He even gave me some cash. Since I cleaned out my bank accounts, I have quite a pile to give you.

"I guess I don't have to tell you that I'm scared, Jack. I really am this time. If there's going to be an attack in Europe, I want my family clear of the prime target area, 'cause sure as I'm standing here, it will escalate into a full-scale nuclear exchange. I want Jean and the kids to live as long as possible, even if it only works out to a few hours more, because I know they don't have a chance for survival if they're on ground zero.

"The general must feel the same way, because he sent along enough M14s and M60s to outfit a small army, plus ammunition and grenades, dosimeters and mines; in short, everything you might need for defending the farm. Here's the packing list he gave me. You might want to check it out and add some stuff.

"Now, with the family safe, I'm going back to Washington. I want to make sure I get back there as quickly as I can, before I have to face AWOL charges. Seems somebody cancelled my leave and is looking for me. I got the word from a friend I called this afternoon. So, as soon as we can get the trucks unloaded, I'm heading for Boise and the airport to catch a plane for the Pentagon."

"Jim, you're crazy. Don't go back there, just hide out here. Bryant gave you papers, and no verbal order can cancel them. Just ignore that order."

"I can't, Jack. I'm still going back as soon as the trucks are unloaded; Bryant might need me. Oh—listen, the trucks are yours, he gave me the papers for them."

"All right, Jim. I'll watch out for your family, but I want you to get back here as soon as you can. Don't waste time!

"Tonight, we'll be the same happy family that we've always been. I just hope you get back here soon, so I can have the pleasure of laughing at you for getting everybody upset. . . . Dammit, Jimmy, stay here. Your prime loyalty is to us, your family."

"I can't do that, Little Brother. I'm just as much a slave to my duties as anybody else in the world. I gave my word, and if a man breaks his word, why, what else does he have? You're the same way too, come to think of it. Just be good to my family, okay?"

"I promise, Jim. You know, it's a good thing I tried for as much self-sufficiency as possible here. The electrical power plant and the alcohol still alone ought to give us quite an advantage when it comes to survival. What we can't raise or get from the land shouldn't be impossible to get before the crunch. With luck, we'll be able to live through an attack without much disruption."

"Well, that's true; but remember, no family, no matter what they claim, can be a hundred present self-sufficient for years after an attack, not unless you're willing to let your children inherit a constantly wearing out survival machine that they'll be forced to spend time and resources fixing until they can't fix it anymore."

"I know. Survival is a cooperative effort, and all I plan to do is give your kids enough of a boost to get them, and the rest of us, through the first couple of years after an attack. People are crazy to plan for decades in advance when they don't have the capital to finance half their program. It's not like the 'Valley Forge' project either. The politicians figure if they're safe, the hell with the rest of the country!"

"The only consolation is that the Soviets know where most of those installations are, and anybody in them ought to get a big surprise. I can't understand a government willing to spend tens of thousands of dollars to protect one politician, and which won't spend a few hundred dollars a person to protect its population."

"That's what we've had for thirty years, so why should we expect more? Look, I'll do the best I can, just don't worry."

"Yeah. Well, God knows what's going on in Washington, Moscow, or Beijing."

## II

The head of the presidential security detachment gave his report as he slumped comfortably in the chair which sat in front of the president's desk. He actually seemed bored as he reported.

"Well, Mr. President, your guest refused to talk, but I'm sure that he gave a copy of his papers to his aide, Colonel Dawson. We've checked him out and found that he and his family left home, and went to his family farm out west somewhere or other. I've already passed the word that his leave is cancelled and that he has to report in, and I've got a crew out looking for him. Oh, by the way, the general's heart wasn't what it should have been. He's dead."

"All right, thank you for the report. You may leave."

As soon as the agent left the room, the president bowed his head down onto the blotter for a moment. The general was the first man ever to die on account of his orders, and he was afraid that it would become a habit. He sat up suddenly and decisively, opening his desk drawer and drawing a fresh bottle out. Cracking the seal, he carefully poured a water glass full of the dark amber liquid.

Sitting there as he sipped his bourbon, Matthews looked out over the city from his window, wondering if all that he had done so far was really worth the cost. So far, it hadn't been.

Still, though, Bryant had died in the service of his country, just as he had sworn to do many years before, even if he hadn't perceived his duty as keeping his mouth shut and not rocking the boat. The boat would surely start to rock, though, if word of Bryant's death leaked out prematurely, so the president would order his people to keep quiet, at least until the Sino-Soviet war broke out. After that began, there was little worry that anyone would notice the death of an obscure general, especially with more important news filling the papers. In this case, he really would have to keep Bryant on ice up at the Camp.

The Soviet premier was stalling again abouthis trip to

visit with Matthews. He had apologized for keeping the president waiting, but he had had a plausible explanation for each delay so far. It was obviously all a put-down.

As for the Dawson matter, it might be wise to just order his men to leave the man alone, it made the president's own guilty feelings somewhat lighter. Even so, copies of the information might have been made, and nobody could possibly tell the difference. Since he wanted to keep the news secret that he had been told long before the actual war broke out, he would have to order Dawson's arrest anyway. Too bad.

## III

Senator John M. Howland was in a particularly foul mood. His wife was threatening to leave him again after catching him in a rather compromising position with one of his secretaries. On top of that, he had gotten word of the dangers of a Sino-Soviet war, and it looked as though the warnings were about to come true. That story worried him most, since he chaired a number of military oversight committees and knew just what the situation really was.

Just in case things did heat up, he was making his plans for a fact-finding trip over the next couple of weeks. The real reason was in order to get into one of the supersecret bomb shelters that he had convinced the other congressmen to fund. Buried deep beneath the mountains of the west, the shelters were designed to keep the deserving leaders of the United States safe against any possible threat. Never mind the fact that the rest of the people would be unprotected. After all, when you make omelets, you have to break eggs.

The shelters, all of which were named "Valley Forge," were stocked with the necessities and luxuries of life which no congressman could live without. In addition, a battalion of troops would be brought in to each shelter to help convince anyone so foolish as to resist the return of their leaders that such opposition was worse than useless.

The senator carefully formed a list of who would go with him. Obviously, several of the best looking secretaries would go, as well as a couple of his military aides. An FBI agent whom he knew and trusted would come and a half-dozen of his men. You could never be too careful about internal security. His personal chef was one choice that tore at the senator. There was nobody else whom a senator could trust to prepare his meals in just the right way, but the only drawback was, the man was a black. Of course, that problem could always be taken care of later.

One person who definitely wasn't going was his wife. Let her stay in the radioactive ashes in Washington.

The investment in the "Valley Forge" project had been worth every penny the unknowing American people had spent on them. Instead of wasting money on shelters for the whole population, the money had been spent wisely on the preservation of the elite leadership cadres. Instead of rancid crackers in a public shelter, each "Valley Forge" boasted its own supply of champagne, caviar, and all the good things no leader in his right mind would be without. No problem about rusted cans of water in "Valley Forge" because each had a well drilled a mile or more deep to fossil water, laid down before man walked in North America, and pure beyond belief.

The big problem had been power—how do you conceal the purchase and construction of small nuclear reactors? That problem was solved by tacking extra money onto the defense budget and using it for buying extra power plants that should have gone into submarines. The technicians involved had been somewhat of a problem, but by recruiting men without families and holding them in special camps, that difficulty had been overcome. Their natural death rate eliminated most of the problem, and that had been hastened along with deliberate programs of excess radiation exposure. The poor fools stayed on and worked all the harder because they were told that the work was immeasurably vital to American defense.

## IV

Mario watched with satisfaction as his troops spread out through the summer camp that he was taking over for a hideout. The men were from his *Ancien Garde.* Like Napoleon, he had formed his own special bodyguard, picking and choosing from the men he trusted most. Each man was bound to him by blood, and the knowledge that Mario held the man's deepest, darkest secrets ready to be used as a weapon against him.

The takeover was almost totally bloodless, since the camp was not yet open. The only person foolish enough to try to resist the capture of the camp had been a custodian. The poor man had fallen into the lake and drowned. Mario's men said that they had a hell of a time holding the old bastard under long enough for him to drown!

Mario went into the cabin he had selected for his headquarters while he and his men were on campaign. It had been the owner's own cabin, and was comfortably furnished. It was a change from the house that Mario was used to.

Tonight, Mario knew his men had planned to surprise him with a special gift. They had captured some farm girl and dragged her here. It should be interesting to have a woman who wasn't a professional, and his men could dispose of her in the morning when he was finished with her. If she lived, nobody would believe her anyway. His people would stick up for him.

Mario's thoughts drifted back to the mob ambush. His teeth began to grind together. *Try to kill me, will they,* he thought, *I'll show them they're not up against some punk!* He picked a vase up from the table and threw it against the wall, watching with mindless satisfaction as the water dripped slowly down the walls. In a moment of frenzy, he began to demolish the building, taking his anger out on anything that came near to hand.

An almost inaudible knock came at the door. Mario froze in the middle of his destruction, then opened the door. His men had decided to give him the girl now, rather than wait.

He grabbed the bound and gagged girl from his men and kicked them out the door. The girl's eyes widened as she saw the look on Mario's face for the first time. A strangled scream half-worked its way out from her gag.

*This is living,* Mario thought.

# THREE

## I

Jack sat with his brother's family around the big old oaken table that almost filled the huge dining room. It was a relic of their great-grandfather's trek west after the Civil War. It had been the wagon bed of the first Dawson wagon to come west, and had later been converted into a table for his family. The table was set in opulent contrast to the simplicity of the wooden table, because Jack had gotten out the best china and crystal for this farewell dinner.

Throughout the meal, the adults had managed to

avoid any hint of the subject that was uppermost in their minds. As soon as the meal was done, though, and they began to clear the table, their talk turned toward war.

"Jim, have you managed to tell Jack what you told me?"

"Yes, Jean, I did. He understands and knows what to do. Now, I want you to listen to me, honey. I want you to do what Jack tells you to do. He knows what's going on, and he can give the best advice possible about all this."

"All right?"

"Yes, Jim. But only if you promise not to go back to Washington."

"Jean, I've never given in to blackmail. I'm still going back tomorrow."

"Jean's right, Jim. I don't want you to go either. Look, just stay here for another day, then, if you still feel as strongly about this, I'll take you into Boise."

"No, no matter how much I want to stay, I have my duty. I'm going back tomorrow no matter what."

## II

Cal Lundgren was frightened for the first time in his life. He and his men had been in the White House when General Bryant was arrested, and now he was told by his boss that the general was so much dead meat in a freezer locker up at the Camp. Even worse, his boss had ordered him to arrest Jim Dawson on sight, because he was the only man who would know Dawson.

Jim had called the night before and warned him to get his family out of town as quickly as he could. Cal had told him that his leave was cancelled and the general wanted him back in town.

Cal knew that his phones were monitored, especially since his boss had ordered Dawson's arrest. Cal just hoped that Jim could read between the lines well enough to realize that he should do just the opposite to what Cal said.

Maybe the whole thing would blow over and everyone would forget what had happened. Cal knew he should do something positive, but he really couldn't decide what he should do. He had managed to get his boss to give him a presidential order to give Jim if he returned the papers intact. Cal hoped for the sake of their friendship that Jim would listen to reason.

As he sat there in the cafeteria, he mused on the reports filtering out of Asia. The Pentagon was denying reports that there was some sort of heavy fighting along the Sino-Soviet border. Cal knew from the way that they were denying it, the truth was there was heavy fighting.

That news didn't really concern him, though, since his office had just gotten another lead on an assassination plot against the president. This one might be the most dangerous one yet, involving a gang of militant anti-nukes and some other crazies.

The story was that they had built their own atomic bomb and were planning to demand the resignation of the whole government. If their demand was refused, they planned to blow up Washington.

## III

In the pearly predawn light, *Starshii Leitenant** Vladimir Kossov could plainly see the plume of smoke and steam that marked the route of a Chinese train, just across the border. He carefully focused his battery telescope on the train and saw that the wooden boxcars had their doors blocked open, a sure sign that it was a troop train.

*NOTE: Starshii Leitenant = ***Senior Lieutenant***

Since this was The Day, May First, Kossov picked up his telephone handset that connected him with his battery commander and carefully explained the situation. Even though they would be firing ahead of their plan, the target was worth the few extra minutes' warning that the Chinese would get.

Kossov waited as the message made its way up the Soviet command structure, from battery commander to battalion commander, and finally, up to the Marshal of the Soviet Union himself. Marshal Denisovitch was told of the situation at the front and he made the immediate decision: attack the train! The commands worked their way back along the chain of command with typical slowness, until finally, Kossov was told that his battery would have the honor of firing the first shots of the war.

The telephone crackled and a tinny voice spoke with Kossov.

"Starshii Leitenant, you will direct our fire on that Chinese train. We have orders from the marshal himself to open fire. When I stop speaking, you will be connected to each gun in the battery, and once we have registered our fire, the whole battalion will join in annihilating the train.

"Give your directions well, Comrade *Leitenant*, because Marshal Denisovitch himself will be listening!"

Without giving any sign of his nervousness, Kossov gave the orders for his battery and waited while the first rounds screamed their way overhead. The six shells exploded in a pattern behind the train and a hundred meters too short.

The explosions acted as a signal for the train crew, for barely had the sounds of the explosion drifted to Kossov, than the locomotive's stack began to belch black smoke and cinders as the crew frantically shoveled coal into the gaping maw of the firebox. Slowly, agonizingly, the train began to pick up speed.

"Up fifty and right three hundred! Fire for effect!" Kossov shouted into the field telephone. "We've got them now!"

The second salvo crashed into the ground just ahead of the train. With dirt and rubble raining down on the locomotive and the boxcars, the train sped through the curtain of fire. A moment later, the second salvo crashed to earth, backed up by the whole weight of fire of the battalion. A lucky round smashed the third boxcar in the train into fragments, flinging bodies and parts of bodies in all directions, all in the midst of a cloud of wood fragments thrown out from the suddenly blazing boxcar.

The locomotive with an animal-like shake, leaped ahead as the weight of the bulk of the train was suddenly taken away. Behind the locomotive, the boxcars had been riddled through and through by fragments from the shell, instantly converting the cargo of men into a twitching, screaming mass of wretches covered in blood. If the train could cover just another fifteen hundred meters, it would be shielded from view by the hills ahead, and the men would be safe.

Kossov screamed incoherently as the shells smashed home into the stalled train. A few of the Chinese could be seen leaping out of the boxcars and running into the trackside ditches in a vain effort to find some shelter from the sleeting fragments that tore through wood and flesh with equal ease. The men pressed themselves flat in the mud of the ditches, their hands digging into the dirt in an effort to pull themselves flat against the giant's fist that threatened to throw them into the air. The probing, searching shell bursts soon sought the men out and found them, throwing their bodies around like bloody rag dolls as the shell bursts threw them into the fragment-filled air.

Kossov got control of himself and requested that he be given the command of his battery alone, so that he could finish off the speeding locomotive.

The locomotive, steam leaking from every joint at the strain from the unaccustomed pounding that it was taking in its dash for life, was already disappearing into the shelter of the hills as Kossov stood impotently watching through his telescope and waiting for permission to fire.

The permission finally came through and Kossov almost simultaneously began to give the firing coordinates to his battery. They weren't aiming directly at the smoke that wafted up from the locomotive, but ahead of the train, so that the train would be unable to stop in time and would coast right into the fire from Kossov's battery. His planning was rewarded when a huge burst of steam rose up from behind the hills. A few minutes later came the dull explosion of the steam boiler as the shells cut it into scrap.

Kossov thought about the last few minutes of the train, as it slid helplessly into the shells that were pouring down onto the track. He could almost see the engine driver, frantically jamming on his brakes and pulling the reversing lever back to stop the train. Then, as the first shell struck the locomotive, the boiler would have burst, sending jets of live steam washing back over the engine driver and firemen, boiling their skin and cooking the men alive.

It was almost a mercy that Kossov allowed the battery to expend precious ammunition on the target. He sat back to enjoy the fireworks display in the valley below. He pulled a battered pack of cigarettes out of his tunic pocket, extracted one and lit it, drawing the foul smoke deep into his lungs, and violently exhaling. With a single command, he ordered the battalion to cease fire. Carefully, knowing that his ultimate commander was listening in, Kossov gave his report on the destruction of the Chinese train. A Chinese battalion had disappeared in the shellfire below, and only one man, Vladimir Kossov, had been responsible.

As he finished his report, he could hear other guns begin to fire, working over the Chinese positions below and beyond the hills. Kossov listened to the deep-throated bullfiddle roaring sound of the shells drilling their way through the air toward their targets. Kossov ordered his subordinate to take over command of the observation post and the direction of the battery.

The valley below was filling up with the smoke from the explosions of the Soviet shells, the chemical smoke that was being used to cover the advance of the Soviet troops, and the gas from the chemical shells that the Soviets were using to root the Chinese out of their bunkers. The valley was almost totally obscured, the smoke lit only by the intermittent flash of exploding shells.

Kossov could see the dark green shapes of the tanks and armored personnel carriers moving forward into the death-filled cloud across the valley. Behind them rolled men in trucks, clad in antigas clothing, that would prepare the way for the rest of the army that would follow.

## IV

*Podpolkovnik** Dmitri Vlasov, deputy commander of the elite *First Guards Tank Division* and his most trusted subordinate officers had successfully cleared the last and only fascist German checkpoint on the border of the Democratic Republic, and were laughing among themselves that their enemies were so stupid as to allow anyone free passage over international borders. Why, in the Soviet Union, a man needed more papers just to

*NOTE: Podpolkovnik = Colonel

travel from city to city! It was just one more clear sign of Western decadence which permeated all levels of their corrupt society.

This border crossing had been going on for years, but recently the number of crossers had been drastically increased. Before, officers had driven across the border disguised as truck drivers or flown across as *Aeroflot* pilots. Those days were past, because now officers were being sent across the border in increasing numbers to find out the lay of the land that they would soon be campaigning over.

The fact that the West Germans appeared to be reinforcing their border with some more border guards was interesting, but not really significant. Vlasov knew that his troops would brush the enemy aside as though they weren't even there. His division had been charged with capturing the vital bridge they were even then approaching.

Vlasov knew that the reconnaissance was vital, despite the studied carelessness his commander had affected as he stressed the need for speed as much as secrecy. That was why Vlasov had taken the chance of smuggling guns and ammunition along with his men. The biggest clue was the fact that his commander had ordered him to be back within a single day.

Vlasov knew that the day was fast approaching when the troops of the Soviet Union would finish once and for all the task their fathers had begun, and stamp out the nest of Fascists toads. The puppet German state would be eliminated and could no longer serve as a nest of spies and saboteurs for their raids against the peace-loving peoples of the Soviet Union and her allies.

Vlasov based his speculations on the fact that his division had been called forward from its normal bases in the Baltic Republics to participate in maneuvers. As the division rolled through Poland and the Democratic Republic, the men could see the huge quantities of supplies being moved forward, supposedly to support the maneuvers. His final confirmation came when Valsov met with an old friend, now a security general, who had told him in a moment of drunken confidence that the destruction of the American V Corps headquarters had been the successful culmination of one of his infiltration missions.

The general had gone even further, confidently telling his amazed friend about the massive infiltration of agents and special commando units into the West. Most of the men were ordered to go undercover until just before the attack, while the balance were to strike against the enemy's rear and stir up as much trouble as possible, softening the will to resist, so that on The Day, the regular troops would have an easy time of their victory.

Now, as they rode along, Vlasov and his men were studying their highly detailed maps, purchased from the West German government and reproduced in quantity for the use of the Soviet Army. The maps showed exactly what the officers could see as they rode along the *Autobahn.* The bridge that was the initial divisional objective loomed up ahead of the men, just three kilometers from the border his men would cross in a few days. Vlasov ordered the car pulled over to the shoulder of the road and got out. Across the river, he could see the squat shapes of British Chieftain tanks deployed in the fields on the other side of the river.

His eyebrows raised at the unexpected sight of the British tanks, but that did not cause him to hesitate for a moment, as he ordered his men .out of the car to examine the bridge and its approaches, and to check to see if it had been mined yet. One of his men, the chief engineer, slid down the steep bank of the river and disappeared, while he checked out the firmness of the ground.

As if the disappearance of the engineer was a signal, a West German police car pulled up behind the stopped Soviet vehicle, and one of the green-clad men got out, walking toward Vlasov and his men. Vlasov had ordered his men to stay silent in any such situation, since his German was the best of them all, having been polished by his years of service as a military attache in Bonn.

"Are you having trouble, gentlemen?" the policeman inquired, "I can have a repair truck here in a few minutes if you need it."

"No, no," Vlasov said, "we merely stopped for a few minutes to rest after a long drive. We are returning to our offices in Bonn. Everything is in order, officer."

"Ah, I can understand. Driving for a long time makes the legs very sore and tired. I often stop while on patrol to rest and walk around for a few minutes. Good driving and farewell, gentlemen!"

As the policeman turned around to return to his car, the engineer officer suddenly appeared over the embankment, his Stechkin machine pistol at the ready.

"I'll free you, colonel," he shouted in Russian, while at the same time, firing a burst at the broad green-clad back in front of him. The policeman was cut down almost before he realized that something was the matter, dangerously the matter. His partner in the police car could be seen fumbling the radio mike into his hand. Vlasov knew that if the man got a message out, they were doomed.

With the speed that marks the professional soldier, Vlasov and his men whipped their guns out from hiding and raked the police car with their fire. Through the disintegrating windshield, they could see the second policeman thrown backward in his seat, blood pouring from his numerous wounds.

Vlasov, a veritable bear of a man, grabbed the engineer by the lapels of his civilian suit and lifted him into the air, all the while raining a series of smashing backhand blows into the man's unprotected face.

"Fool, fool, fool," he shouted, "you have doomed us all! Do you know what will happen to us now?"

The two other officers pulled their commander away from the hapless engineer before he succeeded in killing the man, and pushed both men into their car. The only chance they had, they knew, was to recross the border and get to asylum in the East, before the border guards were alerted to the killing of the two policemen.

Gunning the car, they cut across traffic and bounced across the divider strip, U-turning in front of a speeding truck. In a few minutes, they were up to their top speed, and approaching the border post. Once they were across the border they would throw the engineer to the not-so-tender mercies of the army police.

Unknown to the Soviets, the first policeman wasn't killed by the engineer. He crawled, while the Soviets were fighting, over to his car and broadcast the story of the attack. As the Soviets sped away, he managed to gasp out the location of the attack, the description of the automobile, and the news that they were Soviet soldiers who had attacked him. As he finished his message, he collapsed onto the ground, unconscious.

The border guards, who had been monitoring all radio transmissions, and who had been alerted by the sounds of small-arms fire, heard the description of the car and realized that it matched the description of a car they had passed through the border just a short time before. Alerted, they ordered everyone at the border crossing to get away, then blocked off the border itself.

At the sound of the commander's whistle, the reinforcements for the border post, who were gathered in their tents, could be seen scrambling out into the open, pulling on equipment belts and weapons as they ran to their assembly point.

The border guards stood open-mouthed as the black Mercedes came roaring up to the barriers at full speed, bounced across the tire stops and slammed to a halt against the truck that had been parked across the border itself. The last of the civilians had prudently run away, abandoning their cars.

One of the passengers in the Mercedes leaned out of his window and began firing at the border guards. Once fired on, the men returned fire, raking the automobile from hood to trunk with their fire. The border guard's machine pistols made a carmine paste out of the imprudent man's head.

The other men leaped out of the car, crouched low, and ran toward the border, all the while shouting in Russian. The West Germans ran after them, ordering them to halt. When they kept running, a number of the guards dropped to one knee and aimed their rifles at the fleeing men. The burst of fire caught one of the Soviets across the legs, dropping him screaming to the ground. Almost as one, the other two Soviet officers turned and ran back to their fallen comrade, giving ample evidence of the man's importance. One of them began firing at the guards as soon as he flopped to the ground, while the other began to examine their fallen companion.

A stir at the Vopo checkpoint across the border announced their sudden interest in what was happening on the other side of the border wire. Men could be seen running from their bunkers and rushing toward the gate in the wire barricade.

In the meantime, the West Germans had closed in on the men surrounding the fallen Vlasov, and had driven them away with their fire. One of the men was killed just as he put the barrel of his pistol to the head of the wounded colonel. Vlasov himself was crawling feebly toward the border under his own power as the remaining Soviet officer leaped to his feet and ran toward the border.

As the man ran, he crossed the border itself and was

into East German territory, his head down and his arms and legs pumping as he ran, throwing his pistol away to speed his flight. The man carefully and skillfully zigzagged to avoid the West German fire, and had almost reached safety when he looked back for just an instant. That glance spelled the man's doom, because he stepped onto a partly concealed mine that catapulated him into the air and tore his leg off.

The mines that had killed and maimed so many other people, fleeing from the oppression in the East were about to claim yet another victim. If the man could have seen in that instant as he fell toward the mines, he might have appreciated the macabre joke about to be played on him. The mine that would kill him, had been manufactured in his own home town.

The West German border guards had not been idle while this drama was being played out, but had rushed forward to the wounded Soviet officer, grabbed the man, and were dragging him back toward the border. The sudden staccato hammering of a machinegun from the east showed just how much value the Vopos put on the prisoner. One of the West Germans was almost cut in half by the fire from the Vopo machinegun, while the other flopped protectively over his prisoner.

The rest of the West Germans had also dropped to the ground and were working their way forward, crawling from one tiny fold in the ground to the next, carefully taking advantage of even the slightest protection the ground offered them. All the while, they returned fire with their machine pistols and their automatic rifles, but the match with the heavy Vopo machinegun was almost totally onesided, especially as other Vopo machinegun nests opened fire. The West Germans began to withdraw, dragging their unconscious prize with them, just as the sound of an explosion announced that one of their men had blown up the Vopo machinegun nest with a lucky shot from a *Panzerfaust.*

With the sudden lull in firing, the two guards on either side of the prisoner rose to their feet, grabbed the man by his arms, and half-ran, half-crouched their way onward, toward the shelter of their concrete headquarters, their Uzi machine pistols slapping at their sides. For the last few meters of their dash, they were accompanied by the sounds of enemy slugs hitting the pavement around them and caroming off into space. Without breaking stride, they threw their prisoner into the back of a waiting car and leaped in on top of the man.

With a clashing of gears, the car pulled away from the border post, speeding toward a hospital.

# FOUR

## I

As true dawn illuminated the city of Harbin, the capital of the main oil-producing province of China, Heilongjiang, air raid sirens sounded. Their nerve-shattering, tooth-rattling wail echoing and re-echoing through the crowded streets.

In the civil defense headquarters, dug deep into the living earth under the city, word of the approach of Soviet aircraft had come in only minutes before the first of the attackers would appear over the city. The radar units that had been counted on to give advance warning of a Soviet attack had been destroyed by missiles that homed with deadly accuracy on the protective radar transmissions.

Even the network of ground observation posts which were supposed to back up the radar reports had been almost totally wiped out by a combination of enemy artillery fire and close attacks staged by enemy commandos who were infiltrated across the Sino-Soviet border days before the attack was supposed to begin.

The Soviets' efforts were well worth while, since most of the Chinese population was about to be caught aboveground in the face of the Soviet attack, and the civil defense command had no real idea where the attack was coming from, where it was going to, or how many enemy aircraft were involved.

Comrade Defense Commander Shin watched impassively as his subordinates indicated the known locations of enemy aircraft. Even without a complete picture of the attack, the ultimate target was quite clear. The enemy aircraft were approaching, like so many arrows shot at the enemy ready to plunge directly into his heart, into his city! *I must maintain control,* Shin thought, *I must divorce myself from petty worries and concentrate only on the defense of my city!*

Shin well knew what a tempting target his city made to the enemy, since it was not only a center of the huge refineries that supplied the bulk of China's fuel, but a great manufacturing center as well. Just as important was the fact that the city had nearby the largest rail yards on the main north-south rail lines. The enemy would have to take the city under attack to prevent its use in his own destruction.

Shin smiled at the thought. The tunnels under his city were numerous and deep, his people working like the humble mole to enlarge their refuges and seek safety in the very heart of the earth. His administration had made sure that the vast defense program was carried out, even at the expense of some production in the refineries and the factories.

Shin planned to make the city of Harbin the graveyard of any attacking Soviet army. His people would rise up out of their tunnels and strike against the enemy's rear. There would be no quarter in that desperate struggle in the ruins of the city. One of the two mighty communist systems would be destroyed in the coming struggle, and Shin knew that his people's indomitable will to survive would carry them through no matter what the cost.

Just as he had dreamed in the practice alerts that he had commanded before this actual attack, Shin pictured the scene as the Soviet troops advanced into a seemingly deserted and destroyed city. As the enemy dropped his alert, the Chinese people would surge up out of their shelters and attack the enemy, like a striking tiger! Again a smile played across Shin's face at the thought of the destruction that his people would make upon the enemy.

A subordinate nervously interrupted Shin's musings as he hand-delivered the report that the air raid sirens had been sounded, warning the people aboveground into their shelters, and also reporting that the antiaircraft batteries were ready to repel the attackers.

Shin studied the message and waved his subordinate away. The attackers should be over the city at that very instant.

As if in answer to his thoughts, Shin felt the ground around him tremble, and heard the sounds of distant explosions far above. Dust began to sift down from the ceiling, and Shin wondered if he shouldn't have had his command post dug deeper. It was too late to do more than speculate about that now.

The battle above the city had been joined.

## II

The Soviet aircraft which had been assigned to the first attack wave had already delivered their weapons onto their targets. They had been armed with radar-homing missiles, that had been locked on to the Chinese radar and then launched their missiles. The aircraft flew away from the launch site as fast as they could.

Moments later, intolerably bright flashes rose from where the missiles struck, and the dust and dirt on the ground was sucked up to form the characteristic mushroom-shaped cloud that followed the detonation of the ten kiloton weapons. The Soviets had planned to be absolutely certain that the enemy defenses were knocked out, and the bursts had been perfect in their execution of the plan. Detonating at ground level, they spread deadly radioactive wastes over the whole air defense complex, making certain that no man could use the weapons from that time on.

While the first wave of aircraft was taking out the defenses of the city, the second wave was forming up over the huge base complexes around Vladivostok, Charbarovsk, and other cities of Soviet Siberia, and turning toward the attack.

In deference to international feelings about using nuclear weapons against the hearts of cities, the Soviet aircraft had been loaded down with maximum loads of external fuel and "iron bombs" and rockets. As these airplanes made their way toward the target, their pilots could see the sun-bright pinpricks on the ground below that marked the detonation of more small nuclear weapons.

As the flights came into sight of the city, the pilots could see the first attack wave dealing with the few Chinese air defense batteries that had had the temerity to switch their radar on to track the Soviet aircraft. From the moment they warmed up their equipment, the men were doomed. Here and there across the city and in the surrounding countryside, the Soviet pilots could see the mushroom clouds rising over the graves of countless Chinese defenders.

Without any fire from the ground to disrupt their attack, the Soviet aircraft roamed freely over the city, bombing and rocketing at will, then returning to the city to strafe and kill wherever some Chinese huddled together to find protection from the attacks. The city caught fire as napalm poured down from the sky onto the wooden city. The smashed shells of buildings provided all the kindling that the attackers needed to reduce the city to ash.

The strafing pilots paid exclusive attention to their firing passes, since even the slightest miscalculation on the part of the pilot could convert his airplane from a shining aluminum shape into a blackened bit of twisted wreckage as it struck the ground. While his men finished off the helpless city, the Soviet strike commander orbited the city in his aircraft, waiting for the arrival of his top cover aircraft that had been supposed to rendezvous with his forces.

Finally, he acquired the image of a force of the proper size coming from the correct direction. Their IFF transponders gave back a proper response, even though he failed to get through to them by radio. With a shrug, he dismissed the problem and dove his aircraft back into the hell on the ground.

The enthusiasm that the Soviet commander felt would have soon disappeared had he known who the approaching aircraft were. The planes were a squadron of obsolete MiG-19s, suppled to China during a period of friendship with the Soviet Union, and now being directed to intercept the planes attacking the city.

The planes were returning to their bases near Changchun, navigating from burning city to burning city. They had already lost two-thirds of their number from accidents and Soviet intercepts. The only thing that was keeping them airborne was the fact that the Soviet IFF code had been compromised only hours before.

Now, as the MiG-19s returned home, they spotted the Soviet aircraft attacking the martyred city of Harbin, silhouetted against the flames below. Without waiting for orders, the pilots nosed their aircraft over, charged their guns, and made ready to attack. The Chinese had two advantages; first, they were attacking out of the sun, blinding enemy observers, the second, they would have their speed built up tremendously, allowing them to overtake and destroy the much faster Soviet aircraft.

Slashing through the sky at maximum dive speeds, the Chinese planes flamed enemy after enemy, sending their blazing wreckage tumbling into the streets below. As the enemy struck the ground, their fuel tanks ruptured, sending their vital fluids splashing outward in huge gouts of flame.

The Chinese didn't hold their advantage for long. Some of their planes, piloted by over-enthusiastic men, overshot their targets and spread themselves on the ground in flaming crashes. Once the Soviets were alerted, they slewed their superior aircraft around and counterattacked.

The aerial battle over Harbin ended as fast as it had begun, as a Soviet fighter regiment appeared in the skies over the city and overhauled the Chinese. Because their IFF was betraying them, the Soviet pilots were forced to close to visual range of their targets, rather than launch missiles at them from a distance. It was all the same in the end, as the MiG-25s casually brushed the Chinese from the skies, and converted their gallant attack from a heroic act to a useless sacrifice. Of the three hundred MiG-19s that had taken off from Chinese bases that morning, only three made a safe return to their dispersed bases. In a single blow, the bulk of the Chinese air defenses for the whole of Manchuria had been destroyed.

The third attack wave was already in the air, cutting

its' way forward toward Harbin even as the last of the Chinese crashed to earth. The pilots didn't have to depend on their navigational equipment to find Harbin. All they had to do was to fly toward the largest of the smoke columns that thrust up into the clear Manchurian air.

These aircraft were the true city-killers, carrying bombs beneath their aircraft, bombs whose contents sloshed ominously. These planes were loaded down with the deadly VX-7 nerve gas, a heavier-than-air gas specifically designed to flush the Chinese out of their tunnels or kill them.

The first attack had been planned to set the city ablaze to allow complete vaporization of the VX-7 and to drive the Chinese into their tunnels. The follow-up attacks would finish the Chinese off. A dose of VX-7 as small as one part of ten million would kill. . . .

## III

Shin sat frozen in his chair as the results of the Soviet attack were reported to him. He knew that the majority of his air defense batteries had been eliminated before the attackers even came into range of the defensive weapons; even deep in his command shelter, Shin had felt the shock wave from the explosion of the nuclear missiles. Thc worst news was the report that told of the destruction of all of the Chinese Air Force in Manchuria. That report sent a shiver of fear down his back because he had planned to wage an aerial guerrilla war against the Soviets and now, in the first few hours of battle, his entire air assets had been eliminated.

The reports also told Shin that his city was ablaze from one end to the other. There was nothing further that he could do, except wait for the Soviet army to enter the ruins of the city. Then they would suffer and die, just as his people had suffered and died.

The superior character of the Chinese soldier would once more show its merits. Stolid in defense, brave in the assault, the soldiers who had destroyed the Nationalists during the Liberation would again win the day, no matter how long it might take. Shin knew deep in his heart that the infantry would reign supreme. Men had character, while the tanks that Shin had seen crawled on their bellies in the dirt like some huge, obscene slugs. Nothing that looked like that, Shin reasoned, could conquer valiant infantrymen.

Shin snapped orders to his subordinates that they were to report the full extent of the damage to his people, and to whip them into a frenzy of revenge, so that they would be strengthened for their great efforts yet to come.

Shin ordered the reports carried by runners, since the telephone lines that had been counted on to carry messages from one shelter to another and to keep Shin in touch with the subordinate commanders in other cities had been cut. The radios were useless with the constant Soviet jamming. Shin had listened to the radios and heard the airwaves filled with Soviet war songs, completely drowning out all other communications.

The reality of Shin's isolation from the battle, even from the people he was responsible for, began to sink in. He had personally chosen all of his subordinate commanders for their leadership qualities and for their strong party loyalty. He knew that each man would conduct himself in a brave manner and face death with dignity. The only problem was that they were so much a part of the system that they lacked all imagination and Shin couldn't predict what they would do in the face of the unexpected. He suspected that they would simply freeze, unable to communicate, unable to do anything that didn't hew close to the party line.

They would have to face the consequences of their actions later.

His aircraft plotters alerted Shin of the approach of yet another wave of Soviet aircraft. The ground observation posts around the city had been manned, and the men in them were reporting, just as they had been ordered to report. Shin knew his time was limited. If this attack was as successful as the first, there would be no battle in the ruins of the city, for all evidence of the city's existence would have been wiped from the face of the earth.

## IV

High over the city of Harbin, the final Soviet attack wave formed up and dove toward the ground, releasing their load of black-painted cylinders. The missiles fell down into the flaming wreckage, while the airplanes pulled away from the city.

So contemptuous of the Chinese ability to interfere with the attack were the Soviets that the whole force was composed of flying antiques and trainers scrounged from every training base in the Soviet Far Eastern territories. Even so, these MiG and Tupolev aircraft were more than sufficient to carry out the attack.

In spite of the lack of sophisticated aircraft, there was an immediately observable difference between the two main attack waves. Instead of the bright flash and clearly visible shock wave racing across the surface, there was no flash, no shock wave, in fact, not the slightest hint that the bombs had even struck the surface. The difference in the attacks was much more subtle and more sinister in its effects.

In the rubble-choked streets below, the bombs split open as designed and spilled their contents onto the ground, and allowing the two separated liquids to mingle. As the heat of the fires boiled the liquid, an invisible gas was generated, a gas that spread through the city, hugging the ground. The streets were soon filled five meters deep with the gas as it flowed, like some invisible tide, downhill along the streets and alleys of the city.

Inside the buildings, animals died instantly. Inside the walls, mice suddenly convulsed and stiffened in death, their coats covered with bright red blood that flowed from their very pores. Even the humble cockroach, survivors of countless millenia, stopped moving and died in their tracks.

In the streets, some people, aboveground on official or unofficial missions died horribly as they walked unknowingly into the invisible river of death. In the high concentrations that occurred on the surface, the victims didn't even know they died, just like the mice.

The invisible river of death reached the first shelter entrance and rolled inside. The guards stationed at the entrance died where they stood as the gas washed over them and passed through the pitiful canvas curtains which were supposed to provide antigas protection. Within the shelters, people fell dead instantly as they breathed the gas.

As the VX-7 penetrated deeper into the shelter complex under Harbin, the gas became diluted in the volume of air of the shelters. Now, some of the people lingered long enough before they died to realize that they were victims of gas. They stood and tried to run for safety, but died instead, drowned in their own bodies' fluids as the gas triggered an automatic allergic reaction.

The Soviets continued to drop more gas bombs into the flaming city, intent on eliminating forever any resistance in China, made absolutely certain that Harbin was converted into a city of the dead. As the number of gas bombs increased, more and more gas flowed into the shelters under the city, until all life was eliminated. The Chinese, prepared for a nuclear attack on their cities had guessed wrong, and now the people were paying for the mistake.

Even the shelters with gas-tight doors were eliminated, since many had left their doors open to allow men to move back and forth with messages. Even if they had been closed in time, the people would still have been doomed, for the VX-7 gas was highly persistent, able to remain in enclosed areas for months and still kill. The Chinese, without the sophisticated equipment to defeat the gas, would starve or suffocate long before the gas was eliminated; they had the choice of rapid death from the gas or slow death from suffocation.

The peace of the tomb was spreading over the entire city of Harbin. The majority of the citydwellers had died in their shelters, and the few survivors were neatly locked and sealed into their own tombs.

In Defense Commander Shin's bunker, the doors had been sealed immediately, as soon as the approach of the third Soviet attack wave had been reported to him. Now, the huge vault-like door kept the defense command locked in their own tomb, since the antigas equipment that they would have needed to escape didn't exist in China. They knew that they were merely waiting for their own deaths.

While Shin sat in his command chair, brooding, one of the women aircraft plotters began edging closer to the door. Before anyone could stop her, she broke for the door and pulled the switch that began opening the door . . .

A guard shot her down with a single burst from his gun, while a second man ran for the door, trying to close it before too much gas leaked in. With a short, chopped-off bubbling scream, the man died, his skin turning red with blood from the hemorrhage of the blood vessels directly beneath his skin and his scream cut off by his own body's fluids filling his lungs, choking his breath off forever.

At the sight of the death that had crept into their shelter, the rest of the defense personnel panicked, trying to force their way back from the death entering their room. Shin watched as his people began to die, in a visible wave radiating out from the now-open door. Shin had enough time to pull out and cock his .45 caliber pistol, the one he had liberated from a dead Nationalist officer so many years before. He put the hugely gaping muzzle into his mouth and squeezed the trigger.

Above ground, the city blazed and crackled, the very asphalt of the streets turning into liquid and flowing, with tiny blue flames dancing over the molten surface as all that could burn burst into flames. The flames roared like something suddenly sprung into life and tortured beyond endurance. The flames writhed and twisted over the city, feeding ghoulishly on the rubble of the city.

The very air was heated beyond the temperatures that life could stand and rose up, drawing more and more air into the fire, fanning the dancing flames into feverish life. The smoke of the burning city rose high into the air, a black, contorted grave marker for the city.

Out in space, an American reconnaissance satellite reported the death of the city of Harbin as it probed the column of smoke rising over the city. A spectroscopic examination revealed the massive use of VX-7 gas against the unprotected city.

A frightened aide delivered the report to the president. He refused to believe that such weapons were used. He could have asked the survivors of Harbin, but there were none.

# FIVE

## I

Jack and Jim had spent a good part of the night explaining the situation to their hands, and giving the men purchase orders for the next day. Afterward, they had unloaded the guns and ammunition General Bryant had given them and carried all of the equipment into the basement of the house. In the morning, a dozen trucks of all sizes set out from the farm, to buy supplies from the feed and grain stores, sporting goods stores, and food stores throughout the area. Jim and Jack were ready to spend money like water to make sure that their family and their hands survived. Besides, as much of the purchases as possible would be simply put on the brothers' charge accounts.

Jack drove Jim straight to Boise. Nothing Jack could say to his brother seemed to convince him of the dangers that waited him if he went away from the farm. Jack knew Jim was as stubborn as he himself was and finally stopped trying to argue with him. Finally, they just spent their time talking about what Jack would buy in the stores.

Jack pulled up beside the telephone booth just at the edge of the shopping center and watched wordlessly as his brother climbed down from the cab.

"I'll be back, Jack, I promise. Just don't worry so damned much. I've always landed on my feet before, and I plan to do it again. Now get on over to the store and start buying!"

"Jim, I'm not going to ask you this time, I'm telling you: get back into the cab and come on back to the farm. Please!"

The anguished look and pleading tone in his brother's voice almost stopped Jim, but he turned away with a wave. Jack started the truck up and drove over to the food store. He went around back and backed his long trailer up to the loading dock and shut the engine down.

Hopping out of the cab, Jack walked around front and went into the store. He ducked under the divider and asked the cashier if the manager was around. Jack waited impatiently for the man to show up.

"Hi, I'm Fred Smith, the manager. What can I do for you?"

"Hi, Fred. I understand that you people sell things in case lots. Is that right?"

"We'll sell anything legal."

"Good. Take a look at my list, then start loading up my truck. I've got it backed up to one of your loading doors. Just total the cost up on a calculator, and I'll pay for it."

"My God, mister, there must be ten thousand bucks worth of stuff here! I can't sell you that much food."

"Look, Fred, do you want to call your district manager and ask him? You'll have a hell of a time explaining why you turned down ten thousand bucks worth of business."

"All right, if he says okay, I'll load you up. But you'll have to pay cash in advance for everything."

"No problem. Hold out your hand while I count out the cash."

The manager stared at Jack as he fished a huge roll of bills out of his pocket and began counting off hundred dollar bills. By the time Jack reached an even thousand, the manager's eyes were looking glazed.

"Now, everything is to be loaded in the truck so that I have some space at the rear. I'm going out front and do some more shopping, so I want you to send a boy with me to carry the stuff back and forth. I'll just pay for this at the front, if you'll have one of your girls just take care of my purchases."

"Okay mister. Look, with all this stuff you want to buy, why don't I just close the doors and take care of you?"

"Good idea. Let's get going."

Jack didn't waste time as he began loading cart after cart with food. Case after case of canned foods, spices, pickles, cake mixes, dried milk, and everything else in sight were loaded onto handtrucks and carried past the cashier. After every load, one of the other cashiers came to Jack for the money. His roll didn't noticeably shrink.

Jack stopped for a few minutes to rest and listened to the manager calling off the list of supplies that Jack had given the man. Hundreds of pounds of coffee, flour, tea, rice, salt, and freeze-dried foods were loaded into the truck. After the last of his buying in the store itself was done, Jack walked back to the manager and checked out the bill. While the two men stood off to one side, they talked for a few minutes.

"Mister, I hope you don't mind my asking, but what are you going to do with all this stuff?"

"Well, I have a large ranch, and I want to fill up my larder. Listen, while you load the truck, can I borrow a car to do some more shopping? I really don't feel like walking."

The man pulled a case of keys out of his pocket and handed it to Jack, after giving directions for finding his own car. Jack took the keys and walked off, whistling.

Jack drove over to the auto store and bought out case lots of antifreeze and oil, and tuneup kits and belts by the dozen, topping it off with twenty spare tires mounted on their own rims. Jack paid with his credit card and told the manager to have the stuff ready to load as soon as Jack came back.

A trip to the local department store netted extra clothes, blankets, pots and pans, canning and freezing supplies, and plenty of needles and pins. Someday, they might be scarce and worth their weight in gold. All these purchases went onto another credit card.

Jack walked into the drug store and gave the manager, a man he had gone to high school with, the list of things he wanted. The man balked at some of the prescription drugs, but gave in after Jack gave him the prescriptions for bottle sized lots. Jack combined these buys with others and paid in cash and on the credit card.

A stop at the sporting goods store gave Jack a big supply of .22 rimfire ammunition, loading supplies for other calibers, and a lot of field clothing for the children. He was also careful to pick up a lot of camping supplies, ranging from canteens to canvas tents. This stop wiped out almost all of Jack's remaining cash.

His last stop before going back to the food store was the local radio supply store. The manager recognized Jack as the man who had come in before and dropped almost ten thousand dollars on a computer system for the farm, so he approved Jack's line of credit immediately. Jack picked up pack after pack of rechargeable batteries, CB radios and walkie-talkies, and a complete backup short wave radio station to supplement his own unit. He also grabbed a dozen or so blank video cassettes; it might be wise to get a complete record of how the world ended.

Driving back to the food store, Jack cleaned them out of corn oil, vegetable oil, shortening, soaps of all kinds, candles, and multiple vitamins. The rest of the supplies had been loaded into the truck, so he waited just a few minutes while the last of his things were loaded. He flipped the manager his car keys and gave the man an extra five hundred dollars to divide up among the employees.

Everybody gathered in the loading doors to wave goodbye to Jack. After all, he had just dropped almost twenty thousand dollars in the store.

As Jack pulled away, he could listen to the reports on the local all-news radio station. They were reporting that the Soviets had launched a sneak attack on China. The Pentagon was denying the report, but also had stated that all the airlines had been militarized. It looked as though Jim was absolutely right so far.

## II

"Mr. President, I'm afraid that my report is most distressing. The Soviets have definitely attacked China. Our satellite reconnaissance reports show that virtually every Chinese city within a thousand kilometers of the border has been attacked. According to our reports, the Soviets have used mainly conventional weapons and a few dozen small tactical-sized nuclear weapons.

"Several of the cities have had firestorms started in their centers. Our satellites conducted spectroscopic examinations of the flames and we found that the Soviets have used VX-7 gas against many of the cities.

"In regard to the satellites, the Soviets have just presented us with an official note, stating that they consider the overflight of any portion of Soviet territory to be a serious violation of their airspace. They have stated that they plan to eliminate all such satellites. I . . ."

"Take out our satellites? Man, that's an act of war! Just what do you military men plan to do about this?"

"Do, Mr. President? We're going to let them take out our satellites. The previous administrations so emasculated our satellite defense program that we can't do much of anything. Frankly, sir, I doubt that there is anything we can do."

"What about the rest of the Armed Forces?"

"The ground forces are in such sad shape that they can't even meet the demands of the antiguerrilla campaign in Puerto Rico. The Air Force doesn't have enough trained pilots to man the airplanes that they do have, and the Navy, with less than four hundred ships, can't begin to protect the convoys that we'll need to ferry troops and supplies to Europe, let alone stop the Soviet missile subs from attacking all along our coasts!"

The general halted his tirade for a moment while he caught his breath. The president and the omnipresent secret service guard were both visibly stunned by the outburst. The general began to speak once more.

"Sir, I suggest that we keep out of this thing and pray that the Soviets bog down in China. That's about the only thing that will be able to stop them from attacking in Europe. If we ever have to fight a war, then God help us, because nobody will win that kind of war. My advice is, Mr. President, tell the Soviets that we'll give them a free hand in China, but we won't accept any threats to Europe."

The president jumped to his feet, spilling his coffee out in a light brown wave over his desk.

"Get out of here! Get out of here before I hit you! Dammit. I refuse to listen to what you say, you and all you other doom-crying generals. I DENY IT. We're not that badly off, I know. I'm officially ordering all of our troops to the highest state of alert.

"Damn you, damn you all," the President cried, slumping down into his chair, tears running down his cheeks, "I'll show all of you! I'll show all of you what I'm made of! Now get out!"

"Mr. President, I can't allow you to send those men to their deaths, not and be able to look at myself in the mirror ever again. Ever since that mess started in Puerto Rico, the Armed Forces have had a hell of a time getting men. An all-volunteer system always breaks down as soon as there's some fighting to do, and congress has only made it worse by refusing to approve even a tentative draft plan. We can't count on getting any recruits now, once they realize what's going on.

"We're forty percent understrength now, and the reserves are almost all overage for active service. We're going to be lucky if we can field the skeletons of a half-dozen divisions in Europe. The plan to take units out of Europe and put them into Puerto Rico blew up in our faces with the mutinies. For God's sake, Mr. President, forget the satellites, they're nothing more than a few hundred pounds of metal. The only striking force we have left is the bomb, and that isn't an option, only suicide!"

"General, I appreciate your revealing to me the true extent of your innermost thoughts, but I can no longer tolerate your presence in our Armed Forces. I accept your resignation for the good of the service. You are dismissed."

The president stomped out of the room, his anger building into a blazing inferno. As soon as he entered his private office, he began to take his anger out on the furnishings. His anger spent, he opened a bottle of bourbon, started to fill a waterglass, then with a shrug, put the open bottle to his mouth, drinking deeply. The stinging alcohol poured down his throat and began to choke him. As he gasped, it spilled over his face and ran down his throat.

As the uncontrolled coughing shook his body, he felt yet again the terrible pain from his cancer. Staggering across the room, he opened the case that contained his medicine. He spilled the bottle of pain killers out into his hand and put them in his mouth, washing them down with a flood of whiskey.

He fell to the floor, pulling his body tight around itself while he waited for the drugs to take effect. As he lay there, he felt the drug-induced numbness steal over him. In the silvery-rose glow that the drugs gave him, he could see his wife's face before him. She hung there in space, smiling at him. As he reached out his hand toward her, she turned away, her smile fading, to be replaced with a look of utter disgust.

With a sob, the President collapsed into unconsciousness.

## III

Cosmonaut Grigori Chuicov sat in his command chair in the Soviet space station *Cosmograd* and directed his laser rangefinder against an American satellite. The fools had actually believed the story that these stations were strictly scientific satellites. Now, they were finding out just how different the realities were.

Chuicov grunted in satisfaction as the laser intersected an American satellite's orbit and was locked on. Chuicov thumbed the button that fired the powerful charged particle beam weapon that followed along the laser's path. In less time than it takes to read, the satellite was vaporized.

Satisfied, Chuicov turned away from his console for a moment to pick up a squeeze bottle of the milky, heavily sugared tea that he liked so well. In that bare moment of distraction, Chuicov failed to notice that some object, identified long before as a booster stage from an American launcher, came into life, rockets flaring as it aimed itself in the general direction of the *Cosmograd.*

A tiny flash of flame jetted out of the launcher, with a puff of gases that almost instantly disappeared into the emptiness of space. A missile flashed outward toward the station, a "smart" missile that homed on any radar return that also leaked heat and oxygen.

This had been planned as the American answer to the Soviet Earth satellite system, the Misericordia II system of antisatellite weapons, which had been launched under the guise of weather reconnaissance satellites. The plan had been originally to establish a minimum of three Misericordia II weapons in orbit for each Soviet *Cosmograd* in orbit. The budget parers had reduced the number of weapons to one for every two Soviet *Cosmograds*.

Chuicov turned back toward the radar display just as the alarm sounded that an object was approaching the *Cosmograd*. The weapon closed the distance between the launcher and the target with an acceleration of almost a hundred gravities. Before Chuicov could do anything, the weapon struck and smashed its way through the boiler-plate shell of the Soviet satellite.

Before the air could rush out of the station, the second part of the warhead, a follow-through mass of twenty kilos of explosives, exploded inside the station, almost totally shredding it. In a matter of less than one minute, the entire *Cosmograd* was eliminated, its crew reduced to fleshy fragments that quickly froze in the hard vacuum and became mixed inextricably with the debris of the station.

In a few hours, the majority of the fragments would be consumed as they fell to earth, burnt into ash, but a few of the fragments would drift outward, past the planets, and into deep space, a macabre message to the stars.

There were no survivors.

## IV

As the presidential order was flashed around the world to alert American troops, the men responded in strangely different ways. Some of the men went about their duties slowly and languidly, stoned out of their minds while others reacted by mutiny. Most of the soldiers, though, went about their jobs as they had been trained to do, moving out to take up their positions to defend the world against the onslaught of Soviet troops.

The poor devils in West Germany never really suspected that their deployments were well-known to the Soviets, and each preplanned position was the target of heavy artillery, rocket, and missile fire.

Back in the United States, the units formally assigned to the REFORGER plan were assembling, or at least the orders had gone out; so far, less than ten percent of the men had bothered to report for duty. Naval units were putting out to sea, while airplanes shuttled toward their bases for flights across the Atlantic. The missiles in their silos were being brought up to their most efficient stage of alert. Some of the oldest models, since the MX project had been canceled, were unable to stay ready to fire for an extended period. They wore out the guidance equipment and there was no money left in the budget to buy replacements.

In Germany, the units were being moved forward according to plan. An American combat support unit of the Third Brigade, Third Mechanized Division, pulled out of its barracks near Aschaffenburg and rolled down the streets of the town toward the *Autobahn*. The troops were grumbling about their rude awakening. Most of them had just gotten back to their quarters after a long night in the bars around the town. Most of them sat with aching heads as they rolled forward. A few sat and smoked and tried to get an English-speaking station on their portable radios.

The story had been given out that they were being taken out on surprise maneuvers, but an even more recent rumor said that they were to take up defensive positions against a Soviet attack. The more alert members of the party realized that this might have something to do with the reports of a big fight up north along the border between the Germans and the British on one side, and Vopos and Soviets on the other.

Nobody believed the story anyway; it was just plainly

impossible. A few of the men surreptitiously opened their canteens and drank the whiskey they were carrying, passing it along to the worst hungover cases. The light ground fog that covered the area was cold and chilled the men to their bones.

The men felt their vehicles slow and bunch up as they began to climb the ramp onto the *Autobahn.* Most of them didn't see the first bright slash of flame spring out of the shadows alongside the road, but the nearly simultaneous explosion as the rocket grenade detonated was heard by every person in the convoy, as the lead truck exploded killing or wounding all its passengers, and blocking the road as it burnt. The trucks that followed slammed on their brakes and tangled into a traffic jam. A second rocket struck the rearmost truck and converted it into a flaming roadblock, neatly closing the other trucks and men between two sides of a trap.

In a perfectly executed ambush, the Soviets began to rake the trapped vehicles with fire from their machine-guns and with more and more rockets. Trapped in their trucks, the American troops first knew fear and panic, then death, as the deadly hail continued.

Luckily for the survivors, a patrolling attack helicopter was already in the air, the pilot anxious to beat any possible predawn attack, such as the Soviets preferred. As soon as the firing broke out and he realized what it meant, the pilot requested permission to attack, all the while turning his copter toward the ambush and readying his guns. The pilot had been a gunner in Nam and knew that if he didn't attack in the first few minutes of an ambush, there was no point in bothering. Now as a pilot, he moved immediately into the attack, to hell with orders.

The pilot immediately opened fire with his minigun, a rifle caliber gatling gun that could fire as many as six thousand rounds per minute. The slugs poured down into the Soviet attackers and literally turned the ground into a thoroughly churned mass of blood, flesh and mud. Knowing their only hope of getting away from that fire, the Soviet commandos climbed to their feet and charged the blazing convoy; they knew that the American pilot wouldn't fire into the convoy's wreckage for fear of hitting some of his own men. Once into the convoy, they could finish off the dazed Americans at their leisure, immune from the copter's fire. With shouts and whistles blowing, the Soviet commandos charged the trucks, their AK-47s tucked under their arms and firing from their hips.

Unfortunately for the Soviets, they were completely illuminated by the fires and easy targets for the survivors of the ambush who had recovered their wits. The results were slaughter as the Soviets were cut down by the copter and the fire from the convoy. Under the force of the fire, the commandos broke and ran, hotly pursued by the troops from the trucks.

Even though the commandos were in full uniform and threw their weapons away, there were no Soviet survivors. The support troops, mainly women, had been transformed into Valkyries by the deaths of their friends.

This wasn't going to be a gentleman's war.

# SIX

## I

Lying submerged to periscope depth, the ex-Soviet "W"-class submarine lurked in the rich shipping lanes off the coast of South Africa. The "volunteer" Cuban and Angolan crew stood ready at their battle stations as their captain tracked their target through his periscope.

For the last few months, these submarines had been the basis of the reports of "pirate" submarines that had conducted mock attacks against ships sailing these waters. Although officially there had been no completed attacks, there was a strong suspicion that at least one vessel had fallen afoul of the pirates. Of course, the report was officially denied.

Now the submarine had been lucky enough to be in the middle of a mock attack on an American tanker just as the radio crackled with the orders for the unrestricted attack on enemy shipping. After an hour of stalking, the target had finally turned, all unknowingly, into a perfect position for the sub's attack. The vessel was positively identified as the *Esso Chickamauga,* a two hundred thousand ton prize. During the Second World War, submarines had to sink many ships to match that tonnage. Now, they could beat the greatest submarine aces in a single day.

"Fire!", the submarine skipper shouted. The submarine's deck lurched under the release of the torpedo, then dropped down like a rollercoaster ride as water rushed into the now-vacant torpedo tubes, dragging the submarine's bow down. Eight silver-gray torpedoes leaped out and sped toward the target, leaving a bubbling, writhing wake behind.

A half-mile away, the tanker lumbered on, unconcerned about the dangers of the sea. All this was changed in a second, as four huge columns of water driven upward by the explosion of the torpedos, fountained at the ship's side. The greasy-black water had barely settled back into the sea and drained off the tanker's deck, when the submarine surfaced.

Aboard the tanker, the crew panicked and ran for the lifeboats, only to find their flight blocked by a hard-bitten mate armed with a huge wrench. The man had been a veteran of the rugged North Atlantic convoys, when he had sailed as a fourteen-year-old wiper. The crew turned tail and ran back to their stations, more terrified of the clear and present danger their mate presented, than the potential dangers of a sinking ship. All, that is, except one man who lay stretched out on the deck, his head having a strangely soft look. He had been foolish enough to pull a knife on the mate.

As the tanker's crew returned to their stations, their captain and his bridge crew watched incredulously as the sub's crew clambered out onto their deck and stood, cheering and waving their caps in the air. It seemed as if none of them realized that their sub was still underway and would cross the stricken tanker's path in a few minutes.

Despite their counterflooding of compartments and the antifire foam that was being spread, the tanker was sinking. The rich crude oil was already burning as the tanker took on an increasingly dangerous list.

"Try to sink me, will they," the captain rumbled. "I'll fix their asses!" Swiping the telephone handset off its cradle, the captain contacted the engineroom. The same mate who had stopped the crew's flight answered. He had jammed a fresh cigar into one side of his mouth, the only change in the man since the incident of a few minutes before.

"Chief, can you give me full power when I call for it?"

The telephone gave back a tinny reply, in a thick Scot's brogue.

"Aye, skipper. Full power 'ye'll get when ye needs it!"

"Then give it to me now!"

With a surge plainly felt on the bridge, the tanker came under way again, limping back into powered motion. Up ahead, the captain could see the submarine crew still on deck, cheering and waving. The captain pushed the helmsman aside and took the wheel to turn the tanker into the enemy sub. A look of intense concentration filled his face, with sweat popping out all over his body, his cording muscles telling of the struggle he was in to turn the tanker a little faster, a little more accurately, even by the force of his will.

With infinite slowness, the tanker's bow lined up in a deadly symmetry with the submarine while the tanker increased speed. The tanker captain could see the submariners as they realized that their target wasn't quite as helpless as they had assumed. The men were scrambling and fighting to get down the hatches now, and some of them jumped overboard, swimming for their lives. The submarine was dead in the water as it was neatly speared by the huge wave-breaking bow of the supertanker.

As the multi-thousand ton bulk rode over the submarine, the bridge crew could faintly hear the screams of mortal agony as the submarine crew was pulped between the hull of the tanker and the wreckage of their submarine. As the tanker recovered speed after striking the submarine, it tore the heavy pressure hull of the submarine open to the sea, filling it with tons of implacable water.

The wreckage wrenched off the bow of the tanker and was pushed downward by the weight of the tanker and the water that continued to rush into the hull. The ruined submarine bounced and scraped along the hull for a minute or two before it began its final dive to the bottom of the sea.

The crewmen who had leaped over the side of the submarine before the impact were swimming as fast as they could in a hopeless race for their lives. For them, though, there was no escape. The suction of the supertanker drew them helplessly against the crushing hull and swept their broken bodies through the house-high propellers, chopping them into still-living hamburger.

On the bridge of the tanker, confusion reigned as the crew cheered and pounded their captain on his back. The captain smiled and shouted to his cheering men.

"I knew I'd do better than my old man some day. He skippered a DE for the whole war and never got a sub. Now I'll never have to listen to his war stories again!"

The captain's words were cut off by an explosion from a flaming fuel tank, setting off still more secondary explosions. It was obvious that the crew would have to abandon their ship. With heavy heart, the captain gave the order to abandon ship and ordered his radio operator to continue broadcasting the report of the attack. Meanwhile, he turned the tanker so that the wind swept the flames off the hull.

In just a half hour, the men had all disappeared over the side with their boats while the captain stayed with his ship to take it away from his crew. Finally, even he called it quits and left the bridge, scrambling and sliding down the deck against the list.

With the tanker barely underway, the captain had no problem in launching his own boat. Starting the engine, he turned back toward the other survivors and sped off. Looking backward, he saw his command, listing badly to starboard and down by its head, limping off toward the horizon. Clouds of thick black smoke rose into the air, and flames were beginning to lick greedily at their base.

Just as the tanker began to disappear over the horizon, he saw his ship shudder, then blow up in a flower of flame as the bulk of the cargo was touched off. In a minute, the ship disappeared, leaving a pool of burning oil to mark its grave.

## II

Captain Fred MacKinnon, of the Forty-third Tactical

Fighter Wing, had been roused out of a sound sleep and ordered to lead his fight to Europe from their home base. He had barely enough time to kiss his wife and hug his kids before the air police jeep arrived and carried him off to the base.

From there, it had been a series of shuttle flights until they had their fuel tanks topped off and external fuel loaded on for their hop across the Atlantic. When they had set out, the forecast was for excellent weather. Now, with the peculiar perversity of Atlantic Ocean weather in May, heavy cloud cover and surface fog had dropped in, blanking view from the deck up to thirty thousand feet, and reducing visibility to less than a half-mile.

Now, the aircraft would be forced to depend on the voice of the midAtlantic air traffic controller and their own instruments to cross the ocean. The F4 was a fine all-weather aircraft, but this crossing was going to be a severe test on both man and machine.

Even as he listened to the traffic controller spotting their position, he heard someone in the background saying that one of the planes had just disappeared off the RADAR display. That had to mean that the man was down. Fred hoped that the crew was killed instantly in the crash, rather than be condemned to drift, without hope of rescue, in the freezing waters until the men were too numbed to stay afloat any longer. There was no chance that a rescue could be made; too many ships were trying to disperse over too much ocean to concentrate on rescue attempts for dead men.

Finally, the controller reported that they were over the friendly coast of Ireland. MacKinnon could imagine his plane passing over the startlingly green countryside. He knew that he was cleared for a landing at an RAF base up ahead, and was busily rehearsing the tale he would tell in the officer's mess about this flight. He heard the controller give the order to begin descent, and dipped his nose toward the earth.

It wasn't until MacKinnon saw the steel-gray waves looming out of the overcast and swallow him up that MacKinnon realized that he had been the victim of a Soviet spoofing operation.

The crew of the Soviet destroyer had received their orders to go to sea early on the morning of April thirtieth. For days, there had been mysterious comings and goings among the officers, and supplies had been loaded, most of them being ammunition and fuel.

As soon as they pulled away from the dock at Riga, their captain ordered them to stow or throw overboard all the peacetime gear on the ship. When he ordered them to strip paint from the ship, they knew what was going on. They were heading into combat.

The ship was barely underway when one of the sailors killed himself by jumping overboard and swimming into the screws. The petty officers drove the men back to work with shouts and curses, and the political officers watched the men with their little beady eyes to see who expressed the slightest sympathy for the dead man. Even when sailing into battle, the Party extended its attentions down to the very lowest levels.

Before dawn of May the first, the crew knew why they were at sea, as the loudspeakers announced the outbreak of war in China, then began playing patriotic songs. Those men who could bought alcohol from the torpedomen and drank themselves into unconsciousness. A few, mainly Ukrainians, plotted. These men had many traditional reasons for hating the great Russians, and especially the man who was their commander.

At noon, the Ukrainians mutinied, seizing the radio room, killing the radioman and taking the bridge with weapons stolen from the armory. In less than twenty minutes, they held the whole ship; all those who opposed them were killed and thrown over the side like so much garbage.

Ivan Popov, the man who had led the mutiny, took command on the bridge, ordering the men to man the guns and missiles and stand ready to repel either a surface or an air attack. As soon as the weapons were manned, Popov rang the engine-room telegraph to full speed ahead and began shaping course toward the West German coast.

The other vessels of the squadron tried to signal the now-speeding destroyer and then realized its true purpose, setting out in hot pursuit. Since the fleeing destroyer, the *Frunze,* had the advantage of being ready for battle, the engagement wasn't joined immediately.

Even as he conned his ship, Popov saw the waterspouts thrown up by the fire of the other destroyers. The ocean was stained by the colors of the rainbow, as each ship marked its fall of shot with dye-impregnated shells. Popov passed the order to return fire, then began a series of frantic evasive maneuvers to throw off the enemy's aim.

In the radio room, the reserve signalers, a trusted group of Ukrainians, tried to contact the West Germans, anybody, in their effort to find asylum. Popov could hear the men shouting excitedly in broken German to someone, as a blast of static from the naval jamming cut off the transmissions. Popov hoped that somebody understood the message.

The engines had finally wound up to their full revs, and the deck was shuddering and leaping underfoot as the ship leaped through the still waters of the Baltic. The shock was made all the stronger as the guns fired at their former allies.

Popov and the rest of the bridge crew flinched as a MiG-25 swept overhead, spraying their ship with cannon-fire and dropping bombs. Luckily for Popov and the rest of the mutineers, they had some armor protection on their ship, and only a few men were killed or wounded. The sound of the air defense missiles as they roared up out of their launchers drowned out all other sounds, let alone thoughts. A tremendous explosion behind the *Frunze* told them that at least one missile had hit its target.

Ahead of them, Popov and his men could see the West German coastline less than seven kilometers away. They were safe, inside West German territorial waters!

The Soviets, intent on capturing or eliminating their quarry continued to attack as the *Frunze* turned parallel to the coast to avoid grounding on the mudflats. The men could only hope that the West Germans would come to their rescue, because one of the other destroyers from the flotilla was already ahead of them and cutting across their bow. Popov and the other mutineers watched dumbfounded as the destroyer in front of them suddenly lurched to a stop. The water around the vessel was being whipped into white froth by something strange. Then the destroyer erupted into flames and exploded.

The cause became plain an instant later as a West German A-10 strike aircraft flashed across the sea at wave-top level. The A-10, equipped with a thirty millimeter gatling gun which fired depleted uranium rounds, had neatly cut the Soviet destroyer to ribbons. Further, the DU rounds had set the ship afire as they exploded into flames. As a bonus, they had acted as mini-neutron bombs, releasing huge bursts of radiation that eliminated the crewmen where they stood.

One of the MiG-25s splashed into the sea to port of the fleeing destroyer, the crash sending up a spout of white water, tinged with flame as the bomb load on the MiG exploded on impact. West German F4s raced over the destroyer and sent the rest of the Soviet aircraft racing back to safety on the other side of the border.

With a protective umbrella of airplanes overhead, the

*Frunze* and its survivors sailed into port.

## IV

Vladimir Kossov watched as his men packed up their observation post equipment and stowed it in their outpost vehicle. As soon as the gear was stowed away, Kossov called his battery commander and requested permission to go look at the wreckage of the train.

The commander gave his permission immediately and authorized Kossov to use one of the motorcycles attached to the outpost. After all, it cost the Soviet Union nothing to reward such fine service by allowing the man to see his handiwork at close range.

Kossov took the cycle, mounted it and kicked it into life almost before he had hung up on his commander. In a moment, he was rolling down the narrow footpath that led to the former border. As he rode down the trail, signalers assigned to pick up the telephone wires strung along the trail jumped cursing out of his way. Kossov laughed and continued to speed down the trail.

Still pursued by curses, Kossov crossed the former border without incident, although a shiver went up and down his spine. In fifteen minutes, he reached the train he had destroyed. Stopping his motorcycle, he climbed off the seat, fished around in the saddlebags for a moment, and pulled out a full bottle of vodka. After what he had seen as he pulled up at the wreckage, he figured he would need some fortification.

All that indicated the previous existence of a train here were the torn and twisted rails writhing up into the air, contorted into fantastic shapes by the force of the shells. Scattered along the tracks were the broken remnants of the huge bogies that the boxcars and ridden on, now scattered over the whole area. Everything else was mixed into a nauseating paste of flesh, blood, wood, and metal fragments. The smell of seared flesh and blood mixed in sickening combination with the smell of exploded shells.

Kossov walked through a ruin of boxcars and torn and mangled flesh. Bodies and parts of bodies lined trackside, while charred skeletons in the shattered boxcars gave mute testimony to the fate of their cargo. Kossov started to walk over to retrieve a souvenir rifle from the wreckage, but suddenly skidded and nearly fell. As he looked down at his feet, he saw what had almost knocked him to the ground, a blackened piece of human flesh.

Turning away, Kossov leaned on some wreckage and was overcome with vomiting. Even after emptying his stomach, he was racked with dry heaves at the sight of his day's work.

Kossov walked back, head bent, to his motorcycle, and remounted. As he began to start the bike, a figure, bloodsoaked and dragging a useless mangled leg crawled out of the ditch, leaving a snail-like trail of blood. Just as the cycle started, the wounded man fired a burst from his AK-47 into the back of the lieutenant, knocking him sprawling over handlebars.

Kossov rolled in an untidy bundle, all legs and arms, into a cluster of victims of his own artillery fire. Behind him, the bloodied survivor of the Chinese militia battalion stood up, using his rifle as a crutch. At that moment, rattle of a heavy machinegun sounded, sending the huge slugs from a 14.5mm gun smashing through his body and throwing him forward under the impact.

Comrade Company Commander Hsin Piao died alongside *Starshii Leitenant* Vladimir Kossov.

# SEVEN

## I

Sergeant "Ginger" Smith, Twentieth Armored Brigade, the Life Guards, of the British Army of the Rhine had sat the whole morning of April thirtieth in his tank turret, smoking and waiting for orders. Inside the tank, he could hear the low murmur of his men and their movements as they tried to find a comfortable position in a basically comfortless machine.

Smith and his company from the Life Guards had been sent out to provide a counterdemonstration to the Soviets busily maneuvering across the border. That the brigade had viewed the situation with alarm was shown by the fact that all the tanks had been issued live ammunition. Ginger had been in Northern Ireland and knew the value of carrying extras. He had thrown all of the personal gear out of the external carrying boxes and loaded them full of extra machinegun ammunition and a few more rounds for the main armament. The men hadn't protested too much.

As Smith loafed in the turret, he heard the sounds of distant small-arms fire for the second time that day. This was further off, but much heavier. It was punctuated by the *crump!* of an exploding rocket. Smith's intercom headset suddenly crackled as his radio operator spoke.

"Sergeant! The Old Man has just ordered us to move across the river. The Vopos are attacking a border post belonging to our Germans and are beating hell out of it! Ginger, he says some East German T-72s are moving up in support."

"Bloody hell! Always a muckup. All right, mates, let's fire up our engine. We'll have to pull the bloody German asses out of the fire once more. By the by, did the

Old Man say anything about returning fire, or are we just to scare the Reds off by showing our ugly selves on the battlefield?"

"You're on your own, Ginger. The radio's gone dead with Soviet jamming. All I know for sure is that we have orders to roll up to the border and give support to some West German border guards."

With a snort, Smith buckled himself into his harness and tested his intercom set's connections. Even if the radio wasn't working, his intercom was. A burbling roar announced that the Rolls-Royce diesel engine was starting up. Ever since the fuel embargos, the BAOR had to keep their vehicles shut down as much as possible.

Catching a movement out of the corner of his eye, Ginger saw his captain's tank already moving forward at a fast walk. *No warm-up time for that boy*, he thought. By that time, the captain's tank had lurched and clawed its way up onto the *Autobahn*, its treads spitting fragments of concrete and asphalt behind it as it rolled. *There'll be bloody hell to pay when Jerry sees how we've desecrated his precious Autobahn,* the sergeant mused. *Oh well, in for a penny, in for a pound!*

Smith gave the order for his driver to follow their captain's vehicle. As the driver engaged his engine with that particular neck-snapping lurch that marked all tanks, Smith signaled the rest of his platoon to form on him. The kidney-jolting, bone-rattling motion of a tank underway across a field began as the driver sped up to a fast walk. As they approached the embankment, he heard and felt the driver gun the engine and begin to climb the small obstacle. Once up on the road surface, the driver slewed the tank around and got into the proper lane to drive across the bridge. At the stately speed of twenty kilometers per hour, the tank rolled across the bridge.

"Exdigitate, corp. The captain's already up at the

post and he'll have somethng unpleasant to say to me if I'm not right behind! Speed it up!"

The tank stepped up its pace, amidst a cloud of black carbon blown out of the engine. The smoke was whipped up around Ginger Smith's head, choking him and almost blinding him. His eyes watering and his body convulsed by coughing fits, he almost missed the wrecked German police car on the opposite side of the road and the body inside it. When he did see it, his eyes widened in shock.

"Bloody hell! There's a Jerry police car all shot up on the other side of the road. There's a Jerry copper inside all covered with blood. I can see up ahead. There's heavy fighting going on up there, and the bloody fog's closing in again. You men stand ready to fire. Things look rather hot up there."

Even as he was filling his crew in on what was happening, Ginger could see his captain's tank as it rolled up to the border. Not just up to the border, but over it, and some stalled cars and trucks as well. Ginger ordered his men to stop as soon as he saw a half-dozen West German border guards waving to him.

One of the men, a *Hauptmann* in a mud-stained uniform, hopped up onto the road wheels and climbed up onto the tank's deck. In a moment, he had worked himself over to the sergeant and leaned over to him, shouting. Ginger lifted the earphone away and listened.

"Sergeant," said the German officer, speaking English quite well, "there were some men, apparently Soviet officers, who tried to fight their way across the border. The Vopos opened fire on us when we tried to take one of the men prisoner. Now you can see what has happened.

"Your captain wouldn't listen to me, but rolled off to silence those Vopo machinegun nests. I wanted him to take some of my men along as tank-riders to give him support, but he would have none of it. Let us ride your tank, you will need infantry support."

Smith hesitated for only a second, then spoke. "Climb on and welcome, *Hauptmann!* It looks like we have a merry ride ahead, and we'll want all the company we can get."

The rest of Smith's platoon caught up to him and stopped while the border guards clambered aboard the tanks. Once all the men were mounted up, Smith signaled the platoon forward. The West German captain shouted to Smith that he could direct the tank through the wire, so Smith got out a spare headset, handed it to the West German, and used hand signals to the rest of the platoon to form on him and maneuver with his tank.

An explosion and fountain of dirt announced the detonation of the first Vopo mines under the treads of the tank. Neither tank nor passengers were injured. Every machinegun fire hammered against the hull, with the border guards and the tanks returning machinegun fire. With a curt order, Ginger had the posts eliminated with a few well-placed cannon rounds.

Without pausing, the tanks crossed the border minefield and rolled up to the border wire. The tanks pushed up against the barbed fencing and kept moving. The wires were stretched to ultimate tautness and thrummed like bullfiddles before they sprang apart. With that simple act, Sergeant Smith and his platoon crossed into the German Democratic Republic.

Ginger and his men were greeted by the sound of exploding smoke shells mixed with high explosive. With a surge, he took his tank over the Vopo trenches and ordered the border guards off. If they had remained on the tank any longer, they would have been killed in the barrage.

As the clouds of smoke closed down, Smith could see

his captain's tank storming ahead, rolling over the confused Vopos with impunity. Then he saw the sudden flash as an enemy RPG was used against the tank, blowing a tread right off.

Smith ordered his tank forward into the thick of the action, hoping to rescue his captain. The rest of the platoon, lost in the fog, was milling about behind him. Through the smoke, Smith made out the shape of his captain's tank with Vopos crawling all over it. Smith sprayed the hard steel of the immobilized tank with machinegun fire, knocking the Vopos off. Unfortunately, he had failed, because one of the Vopos had planted a satchel charge under the turret ring and pulled the detonator cord, just as he pitched forward, dead.

With a deafening *clang!*, the explosion tore the turret away from the tank's hull and sent it spinning into the air. A cloud of dense black smoke rose up out of the shattered hull, accompanied by bright yellow flames.

Spurred on by their victory, the Vopos opened fire on Ginger's tank, hoping to make him button up, reducing his vision. Without waiting, he ducked lower in the hatch and charged the Vopos, sending them scattering in all directions. A few unlucky ones were crushed under his treads. Popping back out of the hatch, Smith scanned the smoke around him. Back in the rear, he could hear the detonation of more and more enemy artillery.

Suddenly, a bottle-green bulk loomed up out of the smoke in front of him, an East German T-72 tank, its main gun turning to take him under fire!

Even as he shouted the command to fire, he felt the tank lurch under the recoil. The sound of the two tanks firing mingled and the hammer-on-bell sound of an anti-tank round striking home came from the enemy tank. Without stopping, the British tank rushed past the enemy. Smith was soldier enough to know when to move and keep moving. He stood up in the hatch, swiveling his head from side to side to get a better view.

Another green shape appeared in the smoke, its rear turned directly toward his tank. A quick up-the-pants shot eliminated another enemy tank in a burst of flames. By now, the night was beginning to come on, heralded by the moisture of the nighttime fog. As the light disappeared, the battlefield was spotted by the burning wrecks of knocked-out tanks and resounded to the sounds of artillery fire.

Thoroughly disoriented by the fog and smoke, Ginger turned his tank toward the enemy's muzzle flashes, closing in on his artillery. Finally, ahead of him, he saw a cluster of artillerymen and their pieces setting up in the light from their headlights. With a whoop of joy, he ordered his tank to roll forward at top speed. Without warning, the tank burst out of the night, machinegunning the enemy soldiers and crushing their vehicles and guns under their treads. For the next few minutes, chaos reigned in the Soviet rear as Ginger and his men chased the enemy down and crushed them.

Spotting another enemy battery, Smith turned toward it, machinegun blazing. Before he could react, he saw another enemy gun aimed directly at his tank. With a close-range blast, the gun fired, throwing Ginger out of his turret and leaving him dangling in space, hanging by his intercom wires.

Struggling desperately to free himself from the burning hulk his tank had become, Ginger broke the wires free and, arching himself to clear the still flailing treads, fell to the ground. As he lay there in the tank's tracks, he saw the steel box, burning wildly, its ammunition cooling off, roll right over the gun that had done them in, then explode, its revenge complete.

Once he had caught his breath, Ginger heaved himself to his feet and started backtracking along the path his tank had marked out so plainly in torn-up sod and wreckage. Along the way, he picked up an assault rifle and spare magazines that the previous owner no longer needed. After rooting through the wreckage of the Soviet guns, he picked up an officer's stuffed dispatch case as a souvenir, then set out again on his way back to the border.

Up ahead, he could plainly hear the sounds of small arms fire and grenades exploding, mixed with the shattering roar of tank cannons. He knew that the sounds marked the actual border. All he had to do to reach safety was to march to the sounds of the guns.

Ginger ran forward in an infantryman's semi-crouch, dashing from cover to cover as he headed back toward the border. As he got closer, he could see the tracers from many weapons arcing out toward their targets, and could see individual muzzle flashes in the darkness.

All of a sudden, in the middle of one of his charges, he felt the ground disappear from under himself, smashing him painfully down into a hole. With the moon up, he could see that he had fallen into a Vopo machinegun nest! The Vopos still crouched over their gun, with bullet holes in their uniforms and dried blood on their tunics.

Ginger tried to climb out of the hole and fell back screaming with pain. His ankle felt as though it was broken. He began to curse, then stopped as he heard someone calling out to him in unmistakable English! Worried that it might be a trap, Ginger slowly peered over the edge of the pit and saw West German border guards crawling toward him. He threw his gun away and called out to them.

One of the men slid into the machinegun nest with the sergeant, his uniform torn and stained with mud and less pleasant materials.

"Well, sergeant, I see you have come home to us."

It was the West German *Hauptmann.*

## II

At almost the same time as Ginger Smith returned home, the war erupted in far-off China. The Soviet artillery, sited days before in prepared fire positions heaped high with shells and charges, opened fire almost simultaneously along over three thousand miles of front. The darkness was torn by the flash of fire, turning night into day, and letting the photographers take their pictures without flashbulbs, the light produced was so great.

In the firing positions, men were reduced to automatons as they served their weapons. Their whole world was reduced to carrying shells to their guns, shoving them into the breeches, firing, and starting the process all over again. In some surrealistic sense, the men resembled the pictures of the damned that a Bosch or Dore would have drawn had he known the depths of hell truly.

Closer to the front, the barrage was boosted by the fire of mortars, tank guns, machineguns and even rifle fire. Banks of rockets discharged into the air, trailing long streamers of flame as they hurtled through the night into the Chinese positions. Tracers cut a web of white, yellow, and red fire through the night, beautiful to behold, until it was realized that each round could kill without beauty.

On the Chinese side of the border, the soldiers were routed out of their bunks by the crash of exploding shells pouring down into their bivouacs. As the men scrambled for their trenches, they could see the whole arc of the horizon flashing with the fire of thousands of Soviet guns. The shells continued to crash home, squeezing the very breath from the defenders.

Under the weight of the Soviet fire, the Chinese trenches collapsed on their inhabitants, crushing them. Bunkers fell inward, burying the men inside them alive, and artillery pieces were swept from their dugouts and mangled with their crews. The ground trembled in revulsion to the incessant impact of the Soviet shells, rocking and bouncing the Chinese helplessly.

Even the Chinese far rear areas were open to attack as the Soviet deployed their FROG and SCUD rockets and missiles against preselected rail and road junctions and special troop concentrations. These areas were quickly flash-lit by the brightness of tactical nuclear weapons that burnt out unprotected eyes with nuclear fires, turning the night into bright yellow-white day. As the flashes faded, the land was lighted by the sullen red-lit mushroom clouds that the detonations left behind.

Worse than the use of nuclear weapons was the extensive use of chemicals against the unprotected Chinese. The Soviets were firing at least one round of chemical weapons for every two other types expended. Under the impact of high explosives, chemicals and nuclear weapons, the whole Chinese front simply vanished. For two hours, the firing continued, then with a horrible finality, stopped.

With the shout of *Urra!* Soviet infantry, clad in bulky antigas clothing, charged the Chinese lines. They might just as well have waited in their trucks. There was no resistance, only dead men in their path. Within an hour, the lead Soviet units had overrun their objectives planned to be reached on the night of May first. The destruction had been so complete that the Soviets would have no reason to expect serious Chinese resistance for days, perhaps weeks.

As the Soviet troops walked through the battlefield, the full horror of the scenes began to work on them. Worse, was the total lack of sound on the battlefield, with only the roar of Soviet vehicles moving along the roads or the brief rattle of machinegun fire and the *crack!-boom* of a tank wiping out some poor devil who survived the initial attack.

The Soviet troops mounted their vehicles and drove off in eerie silence past the churned and collapsed ground that marked a Chinese bunker or trench, where arms or other parts of bodies rose in contorted agony above the crushing weight of dirt. At intervals, they saw the twisted, burnt-out wreckage of Chinese trucks and cars which had been caught in their vehicle parks; more often, they saw the bloody wreckage of horse carts and their horses, torn by the shell fragments into horrid ruins. On some parts of the roads, Chinese guns pointed out, covering the roads crowded with Soviet traffic, the crew dead beside them, caught by clouds of choking gas.

The Soviets were rolling across the high desert of Inner Mongolia, a land dry and brown, barely graced with a touch of green even in the springtime. Now a tide of ugly green death rolled along the roads, crushing the clean green life out under its treads.

The land was crossed with deep, narrow ravines, and dotted with the poor huts of primitive tribesmen, their lives little changed since Genghis Khan surged out of this dreary land to conquer half the world. Now, a new conqueror was rolling forward across the land.

Already the primitive Soviet supply organization was feeling the pinch as the speeding lead units continued to outstrip their supply echelons. In the command bunker at Vladivostok, pandemonium reigned as the officers argued for a halt in the advance to allow the supply units to catch up.

Marshal Denisovitch cut the arguments short with the order for a general advance.

## III

Jack arrived back at the farm long after dark, to find the barnyard filled with light and the shapes of men, women, and children unloading supplies from the jam-packed trucks that were lined up. He spotted his sister-in-law trying to move a heavy crate of tools on a handtruck. She spotted him at the same time and waved to him.

Jean walked over to Jack, her finely chiseled features covered with sweat and dirt, and climbed up on the running board of his truck.

"Well, Jack, did you get everything we wanted?"

"Sure did, Jean. There's going to be a lot of happy store owners back in Boise tonight. Do you realize that I must have dropped fifty thousand dollars back there? I guess if Jim isn't right about his predictions, we'll both be in debt for the next ten years."

"Jim and General Bryant were right; haven't you been listening to the radio? The president has put all the armed forces on alert, and he's ordering REFORGER units to stand by for immediate movement to Europe. Even the airlines have been militarized. Do you suppose that means Jim's stranded somewhere?"

"If Jim is stranded, it doesn't mean that he'll try to get back to us here. He's a very stubborn man, and I think he'll keep on trying to do his duty, come what may. I think I heard something about fighting in Germany. What's going on there?"

"A Soviet destroyer mutinied and sailed into German waters, and the Soviets fired on it in violation of the West German border. The Germans struck back and sank one of the Soviet destroyers that was following the fleeing destroyer and shot down some Soviet aircraft that strayed into West German airspace. I also understand that there was some kind of an incident involving tanks and infantry on the border. I really can't figure that one out. The Soviets and the United States aren't saying much about that publicly. In fact, the censors have been at work already, and stopped most of the news coming through."

"Look, Jean, why don't you and the kids go into the house. The other big truck's unloaded, and that's all I'll need tomorrow. In fact, I think everybody ought to break for the night."

Jack called out to his men and told them to go home and relax. Everybody went as fast as they could. They were exhausted.

"Now look, Jean, I'm going to fix you and the kids some dinner. Before I left this morning, I took some steaks out of the freezer, so we'll have them and some potatoes. Sound good?"

"I'm so tired, I really don't know. All I want to do is to get into the house and get a shower and lie down somewhere. I feel as though I'm asleep on my feet. You kids get into the house and take showers. You've been great helpers, but now I want you washed up and ready for dinner. I want you at the table in half an hour, so run!

"That ought to get them moving," Jean said, turning back to Jack. "I'll tell you, we were really glad to see you had built loading docks in the barn. I don't think anybody could have unloaded the supplies that we brought in without them."

"Yeah, I figured that some day they might come in handy. Let me out of the truck so I can make sure that the other big truck's clean.

"Hey Sis," Jack said, taking his sister-in-law around the shoulders and pulling her close to him, "just relax now. We've got everything in hand. Jim'll be all right. If we got out of 'Nam together, he'll make his way back here from Washington without any trouble. Don't worry,

Jean, we'll hear from him soon.

"Tomorrow, I want to start early; just sleep in all day, because I can get my own breakfast. I want to shop early, so I can avoid the rush. I imagine that there'll be a run on the stores as soon as news of the war starts to soak in.

"By the way, is the TV powered up? I think we'll want to catch the late news tonight."

Jack felt Jean slump against him and had to catch at her to stop her from falling onto the ground. In an instant, he saw her face become deep-etched with lines of strain and exhaustion. She was obviously exhausted.

It was cruel to ask women and children to help unload the trucks, but it would be much more cruel to ask them to try to survive without what the trucks were bringing in.

Jack scooped Jean up in his arms and carried her into the house. The whole time, he focused his mind on the fact that the so-desirable woman that he held was his brother's wife.

It had been almost five years since had had lost Lori, and the time since then hadn't been spent in monk-like withdrawal from reality. Jim's taste in women was much like Jack's own, something that wasn't surprising because they were identical twins, and had spent their formative years together.

Jack thought back to the time when he and Jim were both unmarried; they had dated the same girls, gone to the same dances and movies, and, like most young men out in the world for the first time, experienced as much of life as they could. Jean had gone out with Jack several times, and seemed attracted to him, but Jim, always a little more fluent with women and less self-conscious, had married the girl.

In the years that followed, Jack always sensed a certain mutual attraction between him and Jean, yet it was something that was so subtle that he couldn't put his finger on any specific hint. His own marriage had pretty much put an end to the matter, and the different postings the two brothers had kept them all separate for several years.

Now, with a beautiful woman in his arms, Jack was tempted, very tempted, but held himself back. He still had his main loyality to his brother and his family.

## IV

"Mr. President, I know you were asleep, and that you left orders not to be disturbed. The problem is, sir, that the information that I have here is so important that it really can't wait. Sir, the Soviets are engaged in China just as we have been telling you, but without all the satellites that we had aloft, we can't get anything better than fragmentary reports at best. We do know, however, that the Soviets are meeting with almost no resistance and have penetrated almost two hundred fifty kilometers in some areas.

"We know that the Soviets mean business in these attacks because they have staged them on the first of May, and have used tactical nuclear weapons, up to a half-megaton, against selected Chinese targets. Even more important is the massive use of firestorms against Chinese cities, Beijing and Harbin most prominently, and the massive use of chemicals to exterminate the Chinese in the cities.

"We have been unable to penetrate the current Soviet codes and ciphers as yet; however, from radio monitoring and from clear-language broadcasts, we believe that we have worked out the Soviet plans.

"The main Soviet thrust is directed toward the sea, somewhere along the coastal areas opposite Korea. A second thrust is developing from Vladivostok through

Manchuria to eliminate or interdict Chinese industry. The Chinese will be forced to fight the Soviets, or lose all of their industry, and since the Soviets have superior weaponry, they will sooner or later eliminate the Chinese army. Once these objectives are reached, I believe that the Soviets will stand down in order to get the time to digest their conquests.

"Most of our information was, as I said, gained from intermittent satellite reconnaissances. Since the Soviets lost several of their *Cosmograds,* they seem to have lost interest, at least for now, in taking out our satellites. It is just as well, since our Misericordia II system is exhausted; we have no further weapons left.

"The rest of the information was acquired by flying air reconnaissance missions off the Siberian and Chinese coasts. Even then, we have managed to lose at least six aircraft 'accidentally' shot down by Soviet SAMs. Believe it or not, they even got some of our 'Blackbirds' at altitude.

"That was a summary of the information contained in the file marked 'One', Mr. President. That serves to bring us up to date about the situation in China. The rest of what I have to report, in fact the reason I had you awakened, is much more serious."

"Tell me honestly, General MacNaulty, what can be more serious than the end of peace in the world? The Soviets are showing what international criminals they are by their actions. Imagine, using chemical and nuclear weapons against the Chinese! Next, God knows, they might use biological weapons, and then where will we be?"

"Frankly, Mr. President, I doubt that the Soviets or the Chinese will deliberately use biological weapons; there's just too big a chance that the weapon will backfire and wind up decimating their own population. Besides, there is no evidence of any mass inoculation campaigns, and that would have been the solidest information that we could ever get.

"As for the use of chemical and nuclear weapons, the Soviets have confined their expenditures to roughly the same levels that we expect to face in a European conflict. The only problem is that the Soviets have about ten times the chemical warfare capacity that we do, ever since we unilaterally destroyed our stocks of chemical weapons.

"The point is, Mr. President, that the Soviets have sent us a series of very strong notes.

"The first involves that Soviet destroyer that had a mutiny and the crew sailed it into West German waters. As you'll remember, the Germans sank a Soviet destroyer and shot five or six MiGs down as well. The Soviets claim that we arranged to kidnap the whole ship and its crew by use of some sort of narcotic.

"The second incident is much more serious and involve a border crossing by West German border guards and British armored units. That was the one where the West Germans were trying to capture some murderers, and they turned out to be Soviet officers. The Vopos counterattacked, and called in some East German armored and artillery units, and the British arrived just in time to throw the attack back.

"To make a long story short, one of the British tankers penetrated deep into the Soviet rear and overran a number of Soviet artillery batteries before his tank was knocked out. Once his tank was destroyed, he set out on foot to the border, hoping to make it back across before the Vopos found him.

"On the way back, he found some Soviet souvenirs that he liked, and picked them up. Among them was an officer's dispatch case. At any rate, the papers were examined by the British and the West Germans as soon as they got them in their hands, and copies were given to us. What the tanker captured was the whole operational plan of an artillery division that is planned as support for a Soviet thrust across the border toward Hamburg! From the papers that we've examined, we believe that the Soviet attack will come sometime within the next seventy-two hours.

"The joint chiefs believe that you will have to put all of our strategic forces on full alert, airborne and ready, to meet any crisis. If the Soviets see that everything is ready for us to use nuclear weapons, we believe they will restrain themselves and keep any actions in Europe on a strictly conventional and tactical nuclear basis."

"How good is the information that you've acquired, general? Is it one hundred percent reliable?"

"I can't speculate about it being one hundred percent reliable, Mr. President. Nothing is that certain in life. All I can tell you is that the information is good and 'fresh'. A whole Soviet operational plan was recovered from an officer who died trying to burn the contents. The covers, as you will see when you examine the reproductions included in file 'two', are charred and blood-soaked. The West Germans believe that the threat is so serious that they have ordered a full mobilization and deployment of their army. The British are evacuating their families in Germany and are deploying their units forward as well."

"Is there anything else to indicate that the Soviets are actually planning some move in Europe?"

"Yes sir. That attack on the support unit of the Third Mech was definitely committed by Soviet commandos who had infiltrated the border just for that purpose. We have examined the bodies forensically and determined that all dental work is typical of Soviet practice; we know that they wore Soviet uniforms, and that they carried Soviet weapons. What is more important, we recovered the military pass that one of the men was carrying.

"As you undoubtedly remember, we have had a large number of merchant ships sunk off the coast of South Africa by 'pirate' submarines. One of them was sunk by the captain of a tanker that the sub attacked. He and his crew have all positively identified it as a Soviet 'W'-class submarine."

"Then I have no other choice, do I, general? You have my orders to alert all our strategic forces and the entire armed forces. Make absolutely sure, though, that word of the action gets back to the Soviets."

Snapping hasty salutes, the general and his aides grabbed their folders and almost ran from the room. As soon as they disappeared, the president ordered his guard out of the room and poured himself a glass of bourbon. After taking a small sip, he picked up his telephone and called a familiar number.

"Mary, I want you to get right over here to the office. I want you here in curlers or whatever, but I want you here as fast as you can get here. I'll send a car to pick you up.

"Once you get here, start canceling all of my appointments as soon as you get in. A matter of national security has come up. Also, I want you to collect a couple of secretaries that we can trust absolutely and send them to me immediately. As soon as you've done all that, come on in here to my office. I have a lot of catching up to do."

# EIGHT

## I

Half a world away, the battles in China continued with a one-sided savagery that has seldom been matched in all of military history, even by Genghis Khan. Soviet strength at the spearhead continually decreased as the units penetrated deeper into the Chinese rear, and the Chinese grew more numerous.

At first, the Chinese were mainly militia, poorly armed and trained, but driven to the heights of ferocity by the knowledge that they were defending their homes. In the first day or two, these units tried to fight stand-up, regular battles with the Soviets and were annihilated. In a short time, the soldiers who survived had retreated into the rough terrain where the superior Soviet mobility and firepower were greatly reduced in effectiveness. They had once more begun a long march and become guerrillas.

Most of the Soviet casualties had come from accidents and the strain placed on the tenuous Soviet lines by the incessant guerrilla attacks. As the supply lines were stretched out to their limits, the Soviets were forced to divert more and more of their manpower to guard their rear. These men assigned to convoy duty were lost to the attacking units as surely as if they had been shot dead.

Still the Soviet spearheads plunged forward.

## II

The flight of Chinese fighter-bombers was climbing high into the air to attack the Trans-Siberian railroad, the main supply line from European supply sources for the Soviet troops. As soon as they appeared on the RADAR display, the Soviets reacted by scrambling their interceptors.

On their airbase, pilots sat in their cockpits in their MiG-25s. The planes were dispersed into earth and concrete revetments, the ground crews ready to send the planes hurtling into the air to intercept the Chinese air force.

As the alert was sounded, the planes' twin engines

whined into life, then exploded into a deafening din as they came to full, roaring life. In a matter of a minute or two, the MiGs were airborne and being vectored toward their targets.

The pilots listened to their ground controllers as they directed the intercept from their nice, quiet bunker far away. The pilots merely followed orders as they flew, never thinking, never planning. The Soviet system discouraged any independent action, even on the part of their combat pilots.

Finally, the intercept controller announced to the MiGs that they were in the vicinity of the Chinese aircraft. After receiving their orders, the pilots began to scan the sky, looking for the Chinese. Finally they spotted the Chinese planes, their mud and green camouflage blending itself into the terrain below, racing at full speed toward the railroad.

Chattering excitedly, like schoolchildren playing a game, the Soviet pilots closed with the Chinese and wiped them from the sky; there were no Chinese survivors or Soviet losses. The Soviet pilots turned for home, leaving the wreckage of twenty Chinese bombers behind them.

As they flew along, the land in front of them was thrown into sudden high relief under the flash of an atomic bomb. A Chinese plane, flying nap-of-the-earth to avoid detection, had sneaked through under the cover of the deliberate sacrifice of the fighter-bombers to plant its weapon directly on the Trans-Siberian railroad.

Back in the valley where the bomb detonated, the railroad ceased to exist, its steel rails snapped like rotten string. Where the track once ran, a hideous coil of frozen steel snakes rose up into the air, the ends melted, then frozen, where the heat of the fireball had touched. At ground zero, the rails disappeared into a half-sphere, still glowing red, the rock and soil in the pit still running and melting with the heat. In the sky, the mushroom cloud rose up into the air and turned a dirty gray-brown as it drifted downwind, spreading death invisibly along its path.

The Soviet army in China would have to survive on the supplies on hand, or what could be brought in by sea to Vladivostok or by air to captured airports.

The Trans-Siberian railroad had been cut!

## III

The lead units of the Soviet *Sixty-eighth Guards Motorized Rifle Division* drove past the burning sites where Chinese gunners had placed their weapons to guard their home city. The guns had been flattened by Soviet fighter-bomber strikes.

The reconnaissance unit pulled to the top of a slight rise that concealed the city from the Soviets. Below them, they could see spread out a wooden city, with a few concrete apartment blocks thrusting up into the air. On the far side of the city, the men could see much hustle and bustle around the rail yards, and the movement of what had to be armored vehicles.

The reconnaissance unit was ordered forward into the city, and immediately ran into stiff resistance from Chinese regulars and militia units. In a short space of time, the men of the reconnaissance unit were calling for heavy artillery and air support.

As soon as the divisional commander arrived on the crest of the hill and saw the situation, he ordered his artillery to interdict the rail yards, and for the bulk of the division to move through the city to take the trains out. Driving around the city would allow the Chinese to detrain and dig in too deep for the Soviets to drive them out with minimal casualties.

The railroad yard erupted into a hell of fire from the

Soviet artillery, smashing the trains from the tracks and reducing their freight cars to flaming rubble. The Chinese continued to unload their trains, heedless of the death that was raining down on them from the hills above the city.

The bulk of the Soviet division advanced into the city after brushing aside the desperate Chinese infantry and militia. Once in the city, the resistance seemed to melt away. The Soviets advanced deeper and deeper into the city without seeing any Chinese.

Finally, near the city center, a T-62 tank erupted into flames as a Chinese soldier leaned out of a building window and let fly with his RPG-2. The rocket struck the tank's engine covers, throwing them into the air and destroying the engine. The tank was stuck.

Behind the lead tank, other grenadiers opened fire against the rear of the Soviet tank company, disabling another tank at the rear of the column and setting it afire. The rest of the trapped tanks suddenly began to spin in their own length as they tried to break through the buildings on either side of them and escape. More rockets made certain that they were unsuccessful. Once the tanks were immobilized, Chinese soldiers and civilians spilled out of the buildings and attacked the tanks, like ants swarming over a scorpion.

The Chinese pounded on the tank hulls with sledgehammers, stuffed the gun barrels with rags and rocks, and began prying at the hatches with crowbars. Finally, one of the tanks lost its battle as its turret hatch sprang open under the attack. The crew began firing upward into the Chinese clustered above, killing some, but not enough, as a flaming Molotov cocktail came sailing into their faces.

The Chinese cheers drowned the sounds of the Soviets screaming.

The Soviet infantry wasn't having an easy time of

their advance either. Most of the men were mounted in relatively soft personnel carriers, easy targets for a grenade or an RPG blast. The infantry had partially dismounted and was advancing along the streets, while Chinese snipers killed and wounded man after man.

Even the units in armored personnel carriers were suffering in the attack. As one APC passed under a window, a hand suddenly thrust a hose out of the building beside the vehicle, spraying some liquid all over the armor. The fumes carried into the APC before the automatic antigas equipment cut off the flow of outside air. As soon as the driver realized the danger, he speeded up his pace, plunging through a small rubble barricade in the road ahead.

The APC lurched as it hit an antitank mine, its front end being hurled up into the air, almost overturning the vehicle, then the gasoline that covered the vehicle began to burn. An RPG smashed into the stricken APC, setting off the magnesium alloy hull. The streets became lit by the harsh actinic glare of the burning metal and echoed with the screams of the crew trapped in their vehicle. In a moment, it was all over.

The Soviet divisional commander, told of the losses his men were suffering, ordered the division withdrawn from the city. He had another way to deal with the Chinese now, as a Soviet artillery division rolled up. The general watched as his men withdrew from the city. Isolated pockets of battle told of men trapped in the city and their eventual fate.

With muttered curses, the general gave the order to fire on the city, using mixed high explosive and gas shells. His men trapped in the city would have to get along the best way they could.

With a deafening crash, the artillery began to shift its fire, pouring dozens, hundreds of tons of death into the city.

One high explosive round, directed against a concrete apartment complex, exploded and set off a river of fire that flowed down the streets of the city, igniting all that was flammable in its path. More and more guns concentrated their fire on the bogus apartments, and the gunners were rewarded as more and more storage tanks concealed in the buildings blew up and scattered their contents through the city.

Soon, the small valley that cupped the Chinese city was almost filled with flames as the wooden houses all burst into flame at the dragon's breath heat of the flames. The Soviet artillery fire slackened, then stopped without orders as the gunners stood by their pieces and watched the city burn.

The men on the ridge above the town felt the breeze at their back pick up speed as it blew down into the city. In a matter of minutes, the breeze grew to a wind as the superheated air rose up from the flames and drew more air into itself, to be heated and thrown upward in its turn, until the process grew beyond control.

In a half-hour, the winds blowing into the valley were of almost hurricane force as the city blazed. In the streets, the winds whipped and moaned their way into the heart of the firestorm, and over all the pillar of flames danced and hissed and screamed like some giant torch gone mad. . . .

The force of the winds in the street swept the Chinese firemen and their primitive equipment from their places of safety and dragged them screaming into the center of the flames. In the narrow streets, the winds approached three hundred kilometers per hour, keeping everyone from escape.

In the shelters beneath the city, the people died horribly as the winds in the streets pulled the air out of their shelters, leaving near-vacuum behind. Other shelters were soon filled with the gases of the fire that choked out the people's lives, while in still other shelters, the heat became so intense that the people died of heat shock, and finally the fat from their very bodies melted and ran burning through the shelters.

There were no survivors.

## IV

The Chinese guerrillas waited in the ravines beside the Soviet supply road, just as they had been waiting, with growing impatience, since before the sun came up. They knew a Soviet supply unit was coming, but not when it would arrive at their ambush. Their plan: to let the first few vehicles pass, along with their guard of tanks and armored cars, then attack the vulnerable trucks that followed.

At last, the flash of a mirror from the distant hills told the men that the enemy was approaching. They checked their weapons again and crouched lower into the shelter of the ground.

Then they could hear the crunching sound of tank treads on packed gravel. The men held their breaths, knowing they would be wiped out without mercy if detected by the Soviets. At last the sound of tanks disappeared into the distance, and the sound of truck engines replaced the clatter of tanks. The men gathered their legs under them, ready to jump up and sprint out into the road to finish off their enemy.

The strident notes of bugles and the shrilling of whistles announced the attack, as the men rose up and overwhelmed the Soviet column. For a full two minutes, all their fire was concentrated against the convoy, everything from pistols up to 120mm mortars. The road was blasted and flayed by a whip of steel that tore the Soviet trucks and their human and material loads into bloody fragments.

As suddenly as the attack began, the Chinese withdrew, racing as fast as they could down into the ravines and grabbing hold of their tough ponies, like the ponies their ancestors had ridden to conquer half a world. They left behind them a road choked with wreckage where only minutes before a truck convoy rolled in blithe disregard for attack.

The mass of wreckage burned and fitfully exploded as some weapon was heated to detonation. Over a hundred trucks and their precious cargo had been destroyed.

Soviet infantry units remaining behind searched for their attackers and, when they were found, bloodily murdered them.

# NINE

## I

Jack Dawson dragged himself out of his bed long before dawn, dressed, and grabbed a sandwich to eat on his way to yet more shopping. He climbed into the cab of his empty truck and drove off toward town. As he steered his truck down the farm road, he mentally went over his list for purchases. Today was the day that he would go after the hardware stores. Today was the day everybody else would be looking for food.

His list ran from axes to wrenches, electrical supplies to paint, rope to hand tools; in short, everything needed to stock an extensive shop and provide Jack with back-up supplies if anything he already owned broke. One thing he wanted to be sure of getting was wire, lots of wire, fourteen gauge steel ought to do the trick. With smooth and barbed wire, he could rig an awful lot of trippers and traps for the unwary.

As he drove into Henderson's Corners, Jack saw a few

people he knew; they waved to him and he waved back, guilty at the thought he should warn them to get ready for the end of civilization. *I feel like a rat,* he thought, *letting them walk around all unknowing like that. Even if I told them, they wouldn't believe me. Who would or who could believe something like that?*

Jack drove by the half-dozen houses and small stores that made up the whole town. As he went past the bar, he could see several men inside, hoisting their beer. It was a hell of an early hour to be drinking. Past the bar, he pulled up in front of the big brick building that served as a combination county sheriff's office, meeting hall, mayor's office, and, most importantly, Adam Henderson's Feed and Grain Store. Shutting the truck engine down, Jack walked up the steps and into the store.

"Well, Jack Dawson, what brings you into town, boy?" Henderson said. "I never see you in town unless it's night and you're going into the bar with some of those hands of yours."

"Well, Mr. Henderson, my brother Jim sent his family out here for a while. He wants them out of Washington, what with the crime and pollution and all. He wants his kids to grow up knowing their roots and what it's like to live on a farm. So, I want to lay in some supplies and tools. He wants me to make real farmers and ranchers out of the kids, and I suspect that they'll get considerable use. Here's a list of things I want, sir. Would you have some of your people take them up to the farm? My sister-in-law will pay for them."

"My lord, Jack, it looks like you're planning to set a moon colony, not teach some kids about the land. I can let you have everything but the ten cases of dynamite. You know what the state laws are like. I can't sell you more than half a case at a time, and then only with a permit."

"Mr. Henderson, you know that I was a Green Beret. I know more about more explosives than anybody else in the whole area. I want to do some major clearing and I'll need the stuff on hand. Tell you what, how about if you sell me the stuff and just write it up as if I bought it a half-case at a time. Then you can just send the dynamite up in one lump. Okay?"

"All right, Jack. I guess you aren't planning to blow up the town bank, are you? Oh, by the way, Ginny's coming down to visit with me in two weeks. Are you going to be in town this time to see her? She keeps asking after you."

"Look, Mr. Henderson," Jack blurted out, "call Ginny right away and get her down here as fast as you can. Tell her anything you have to tell her, but get her back to town in the next day or two."

With that, Jack turned and almost ran out of the store, leaving Henderson looking quizzically after him. Jack was sweating. He hated to lie to Henderson, but he really couldn't bring himself to tell the truth. He had known the man all his life and respected him. Jack had even dated his granddaughter Ginny, until he went off to West Point and she went to Chicago and marriage.

If he had anyone in the world that he liked and respected outside of his own family, it was Henderson and Ginny. Now that he had told the old man to get Ginny back to town, a load seemed to lift from his shoulders. On the way back today, he would stop off and tell Henderson exactly what he knew. On the other hand, Henderson was pretty sharp, and would probably put two and two together.

Back in the store, Henderson stood for a minute, looking after Jack's truck. As he stood there rubbing his chin, he suddenly realized what Jack was hinting at when he told him to call Ginny. He picked up the phone and shakily dialed his granddaughter's private number at the office.

Henderson waited impatiently as the phone rang. On the third ring, although it seemed more like the three thousandth, Ginny's secretary answered the phone. He told the man that Ginny was in a conference and couldn't be disturbed.

"Dammit, I don't care where she is, get me Ms. Schroeder right away. It's a matter of life and death!"

Adam waited while the sound of music replaced the more traditional dead air of a telephone on hold. Finally a familiar voice interrupted the song.

"Granddad, what's the matter? Oscar said it was a matter of life and death!"

"Ginny, child, I need you home with me right now."

"Granddad, I'll bring the best doctors I can find. I . . ."

"Ginny, just get here on the earliest train you can get. I'll meet you at the station. Just get on that train now, don't bring anything from home but the kids and your checkbook. Now move it, girl. I want to see your smiling face."

Henderson hung up the phone, then sat at his desk, shivering.

## II

As soon as Jim Dawson walked out into the airport concourse, he knew that something was the matter. The buildings were deserted since the airlines had been militarized, but there was a welcoming committee waiting for him. He saw Cal Lundgren and decided to be dumb.

Jim waved and walked over to his friend.

"Hi, Cal, who are you waiting for?"

"You, Jim. I want you to come with us. Don't try to get away."

"What did I do, Cal? Did somebody see me picking White House flowers when I went home last time?"

"*No!* Look, Jim, you know that we're assigned to the presidential bodyguard, right? He wants to see you and your boss has been trying to get in touch with you for the last couple days, but you'd already left here. The general even called your brother on the phone and talked with him."

Jim was instantly alerted. His brother had never put a phone line in because the telephone company wanted too much money to install the lines. He always relied on his radio, in fact, even Jim had to call him by radio.

"Sure, Cal, I'll go along with you. If the general talked with my brother, then I guess it's all right. I'll bet you can't realize the trouble I went to just getting back here. The plane landed in Chicago to unload the passengers and they tried to throw me off! I had to flash my ID and my Pentagon passes to get a ride back here."

"Yeah, right, Jim, the general said you were flying back to Washington. Look, do you have some papers that the general prepared? He can't remember if he gave out a set or not. He said they were in a big manila folder, about a foot square and three inches thick. He said he needs your copies if you have them, since his got destroyed in an accident."

"Sure, Cal. The general gave me a bundle to take along on my vacation. Wanted me to study the papers while I was gone, but I left them behind. No sense in mixing business with pleasure."

Lundgren stepped in front of Jim and said: "You're sure you left them behind? Just wait a minute while I call your office."

"Sure I'm sure, Cal, but I didn't leave them in the office. I left them home in my secret hiding place. Come on, I'll get them for you."

The secret service men clumped themselves around Jim almost unobtrusively, as they made sure that he couldn't break and run without being grabbed by one of the men. They hustled him out of the building and into a waiting car. As soon as everybody was in, they drove off at high speed.

In a little less than an hour, they pulled up in Jim's drive and stopped under the big basketball hoop that Jim had put up for himself and his son. The house looked subtly wrong, like something had been torn up and put back in a place it didn't belong. Jim walked up to the door and pulled his key case out of his pocket. The secret service men were keeping so close to him, that they were almost walking on his heels.

Jim opened the door and looked around inside. He saw right away why things didn't look right. The furniture that they had left behind was overturned and slashed open, the rugs were rolled up and piled in a corner, and the curtains pulled down. Innocently, he turned to the secret servicemen.

"My God, the place has been robbed! Let's call the police. It's a damned good thing I got the family out of town when I did. Come on, let's see if they got the papers!"

Jim broke away from his guards and ran up the stairs two at a time. Behind him, he could hear the clumping of the agents running after him. He charged into his bathroom and dropped to his knees, fumbling behind the toilet tank. In a second, he started to pull something out. He felt one of the agents grab his arm and hold it in place, while another took the bundle out of his hands.

"Hey, what's going on here? Those are the papers that you wanted. Take a look at them, the seal's still intact."

Lundgren grabbed the bundle from his subordinate and peeled the plastic wrap over the envelope back. The seal was indeed intact.

"All right, Jim. I guess that this is all we need. The general told me to tell you to take the next couple of weeks off and go fishing or whatever and enjoy yourself. He'll telephone your brother when he wants to get in touch with you."

"That's great, Cal, but I'll have to have written orders to cover something like this. There's an alert on, and I don't want to get into trouble. After all, I'm the general's aide."

"I figured you'd say something like that, Jim. Here's a letter signed by the president himself. Now get out of here."

Jim blinked and studied his friend's face for a minute. The rest of the agents had already disappeared. Without another word, Lundgren turned and left, clutching the envelope tight in his hands.

Jim opened the envelope and looked at the contents. It was indeed on White House stationery and looked completely authentic. Without waiting for more than a moment, Jim walked over to the linen closet and started lifting out shelves. Behind the shelves was a panel, and behind the panel, a stairway up into the deserted attic.

Jim was up the stairs and looking out into the totally unfinished room, its bare rafters staring back at him. Jim stepped out onto one of the rafters and walked across to the old chimney on the other side of the house. Behind the bricks was an M16 that he had liberated while in 'Nam, plus a pouch of spare magazines and some handgrenades as well. Jim picked up the rifle, hefted it, put a magazine into the receiver, and cocked the gun.

He went back downstairs, carefully replaced the panel in the wall, and replaced all the shelves. He didn't neglect to scuff up the rug where the dust from his feet showed all too clearly where he had been. Jim walked into his bedroom and picked up the golf club bag, rearranged some of the clubs, and pushed the rifle down, muzzle first, and filled the ball pockets with ammunition.

Jim picked his bag up and walked back downstairs, out the door, and to the garage. He backed his car out and drove off. *With any kind of luck,* he thought, *I ought to be able to spot any tails and lose them.*

## III

Far out in the MidAtlantic south of Iceland, a huge, silent metal cylinder drifted free with the current, drifted ever southward. The Soviet submarine was silent, save for the hushed whispers of the crew as they walked about in felt shoes. The off-duty men were confined to their bunks, and were forced to lie in silence.

The submarine was a nuclear powered monster of the deep, built in response to the American Trident submarines. Strict secrecy had marked their construction, ranging from their fabrication under completely covered slipways in the naval yards at Archangelsk to their basing in the Arctic. After trials, the submarines had been based under a floating ice island that nominally was employed as a scientific station. In actuality, the island had been hollowed out to serve as a base for twenty submarines and housed over five thousand men and women and all their supplies. The submarines themselves docked at huge subsurface air locks that sealed directly to the submarine hulls.

Three weeks before, the submarines had been ordered to prepare to sail out into the Atlantic and Pacific. They were to be towed along the way by other submarines and released into currents that, ironically enough, had been charted by American oceanographers. On May second, the submarines were to warm up their reactors and turn their courses toward the American coastline, their deadly missiles with their high megatonnage warheads aimed directly into the heartland of America.

In the meantime, the crews could only sit and wait,

knowing that they were being exposed to excessive amounts of radiation because their government planners had decided that the weight of additional shielding could be better employed in carrying extra missiles. Now that they were setting out on a war cruise and knew that they would soon get to launch their missiles at the hated American enemy.

It was still not a thought to cheer them.

## IV

Far above the earth, a metallic cylinder aimed itself so that one end pointed directly at the earth below, specifically at the Atlantic Ocean. The object was an American ocean surveillance satellite, designed to track any vessel on or below the surface of the seas.

The satellite was equipped with standard optical scanners, as well as sophisticated magnetic and infrared detectors. It was equipped to detect metallic objects of as little as two hundred tons as they passed through the earth's magnetic field, even as many as six thousand meters below the ocean surface. The optical scanners were so sensitive that they could detect, after computer enhancement, the facial features of individual people on the decks of ships.

The information was transmitted in real time to the ground stations by a tightly beamed LASER amplifier to a small receptor located on the roof of an old building in Norfolk. The building was quaintly named the *United States Navy Motivational Development Center.* To keep the cover intact, an exceedingly boring course was given to select groups of sailors, assuring that word of the building's function would travel back to the Soviets.

Instead of being a mere training center, however, the building housed one of the most complex computer systems yet developed. It was capable of receiving and decrypting data from as many as thirty separate satellite systems at any one time, and by use of multiplex time-sharing, as many as three hundred separate inputs could be processed. This installation controlled the movements of the entire Atlantic fleet, while a sister installation in San Francisco controlled the Pacific fleet.

It was the proud and accurate boast of the men who manned these installations that they knew where every ship on the Atlantic Ocean was. They had been able to track the new Soviet missile subs that had been based under the arctic ice for over a year, and listened with scarcely concealed glee as one of the subs killed its crew when it broke up in a test dive.

Now, rather than sitting by tracking Soviet submarines, the controllers were directing their all too few antisubmarine aircraft toward intercepts of the missile-carrying boats. The budget cutters had managed to make sure that the Soviets would be able to strike almost unmolested at the United States.

In addition, the center had to cope with the increased numbers of Soviet ships at sea. The movements had been planned to seem as innocent as possible, but when the pattern was examined more fully, the dangers were obvious. The Soviet Black Sea fleet had passed through the Bosporus and entered the Mediterranean. Submarines were sailing from Murmansk, Leningrad, and Riga and dispersing into the Atlantic. The whole Soviet merchant fleet was either in Soviet or pro-Soviet ports, a clue that pointed more clearly than most to the real danger of another Pearl Harbor attack.

Since the president had approved the final alert stage, the navy had put all its ships out to sea and into naval staging areas for support operations. The American navy had much less strain placed on it, especially since the Soviets had three ships for every one that the United States navy could put to sea.

# TEN

## I

The Soviet units had crossed the high desert country of Inner Mongolia and were rolling directly toward the heartland of China, Hebei Province, in strength. Resistance from the Chinese was still light and scattered, but cost the Soviets more and more men each day. The loss of the Trans-Siberian railroad hadn't helped matters, by any stretch of the imagination, but the invaders still moved forward, using the supplies that each unit carried with it to the maximum.

The worst losses which the Soviets had suffered had been among their most valuable units, their armored vehicles. The tanks and armored personnel carriers that the Soviets had used in China were strictly their second line hardware, some of it, the T-54 tanks especially, was approaching its thirtieth anniversary in service. Under the strain of the easy advance, the tanks all began to suffer breakdowns as slipshod maintenance in the past and hard usage under combat conditions disabled vehicle after vehicle.

The situation was made worse by the Soviet practice of having the tank crew do all but the heaviest repairs to their vehicle, rather than the normal practice of keeping a special repair unit for the vehicles. As a result, the invasion was slowing down with many disabled vehicles simply abandoned as unrepairable. The armored units which should have formed the steel cutting edge of the Soviet advance were being constantly depleted and left in the rear.

The losses among the armored units didn't stop the invasion, only made it slow somewhat, as it brushed aside the feeble Chinese resistance. The Soviets were more hampered in the expenditures of ammunition than the losses in actual manpower. So far, their losses had been less than five percent of the men involved in the attack, while Chinese losses were approaching ninety percent. The Soviets were faced with the very real problem of running out of ammunition to kill their enemies with.

## II

General Feodor Yasnikov, commander of the elite *201st Guards Airborne Division,* which had been given the task of securing the city of Lanzhou, looked with contempt at the sea of Chinese prisoners being paraded in front of him.

Lanzhou had fallen to his troops in a matter of hours, and all the surface nuclear plants and laboratories had been captured by the end of the first day of battle. In fact, all of the Chinese nuclear capacity had been captured, except for the huge warren of tunnels that ran beneath the city. There, his engineers and infantry were pressing forward to eliminate the last vestiges of Chinese units. So far, his worst single group of casualties had occurred when a fully loaded transport had lost its brakes on landing and rolled off the end of the airport, exploding into a ball of flames.

"Look at them, Yakov Semyonovich," Yasnikov sneered, sweeping his hand over the wretched prisoners filing past him. "They are supposed to be the best soldiers in the Chinese army, yet three days after we wrested their only nuclear center from their grasp, they still refuse to fight and run away through their ratholes.

"I think . . ."

His second in command never learned what Yasnikov thought, because his commander was thrown off the reviewing platform by the impact of a sniper's bullet that tore through his chest. The Chinese army, after carefully reinforcing their units through the tunnels under the city, came surging out of their shelters, rushing through the deserted streets in an all-out effort to defeat their enemy.

The Soviet paratroopers, although lightly armed by European standards were still better armed than their much more numerous opponents. Bitter street fighting erupted through the entire city as Chinese soldiers tried to wipe out isolated Soviet units. House-to-house fighting grew in ferocity, often developing into room-to-room combat in the stone and concrete apartment blocks and municipal buildings of the city center.

In one building, the Soviet sappers blew a hole into the outside brick wall of a building, then rushed through the breech they had opened, spraying the room with their assault rifles. There was no one inside.

As the sappers prepared their charges to enter the next building, a Chinese machinegun poked through a hole in the wall and opened fire, slaughtering the trapped Soviets. One round from the machinegun struck the back-pack flamethrower that one of the engineers carried, exploding the napalm that turned the room into an instant inferno, complete with the screams of the damned.

In another section of the city, a Soviet self-propelled gun rolled along through the streets, supporting paratroopers as they mopped up the remains of a Chinese unit that had been foolish enough to charge across open ground to attack them. As it entered the alleys, heavy machinegun fire drove the paratroopers to cover. As the self-propelled gun moved to take out the hidden enemy gun, a Chinese soldier threw aside the rubble-strewn canvas that covered him, rushed over to the gun, and slammed an antitank mine against the hull. Both attacker and self-propelled gun disappeared in the cloud of dust and smoke raised by the explosion of the mine and the ammunition the vehicle carried.

At the vital airport, a team of Chinese infiltrators had penetrated into the control tower building itself, and were clearing the building of Soviets in hand-to-hand combat in the semi-darkened rooms. Rifle butts, knives, shovels, and even fists were used to maim and slay the enemy. While this drama was being played out on the ground, the aircraft of a back-up Soviet division circled impotently overhead, awaiting orders. Finally, the Chinese sappers blew the steel door that protected the control tower itself and machinegunned the men inside.

Deep underground, the struggle for the interlaced network of nuclear plants, mines, and weapons vaults was heating up as the Chinese fought back. In the hell of darkness, the only light came from the flash of weapons fire and the explosion of demolition charges and grenades. A deadly, blind battle was fought out between the paratroopers and the Chinese infantry.

The image of hell was made even more appropriate by the poor radiation security that the Chinese tolerated. The air itself was contaminated with drifting radioactive dusts, deadly to invader and defender alike.

As the Soviets made more progress into the tunnels, the Chinese resistance grew more fierce and desperate. The Chinese knew that if the Soviets broke through to the vaults themselves, the bombs that they guarded would be detonated, taking Soviet and Chinese alike out in the blast. The Soviets knew that their enemy was quite capable of doing just that and were pushing forward regardless of cost to capture the bomb vaults before the weapons could be detonated.

One of the Soviet engineer parties attacked a Chinese force holed up behind steel blast doors. Under cover from the Soviet machineguns, an engineer suddenly bolted forward, a smoking satchel charge in his hand. With a heave, the charge disappeared through the vault doors and the man fell to the tunnel floor to protect himself from the blast.

The satchel charge slid under one of the fuzed weapons and exploded, with just enough force to drive the two polished hemispheres of refined plutonium together with enough force to initiate a "squib" explosion.

As the weapon detonated, the air within the cavern was turned into the substance of the sun itself for a microsecond, as molecules were ripped apart under the impact of immense energies. The Chinese in the room were vaporized before the image of the exploding satchel charge could register in their brains.

The Soviet paratroopers lived a few microseconds longer as the thick rock walls between the blast and themselves turned to vapor from the sun-like heat. The rock vapor was blown down the tunnels, dissolving men in its path. Further down the tunnels, the sun-hot tongues of gas and rock vapor, channeled by the rock walls, reached out and charred into blowing ash attacker and defender.

Above ground, the ground shook, then bulged upward in a dome over the site of the explosion. From cracks that opened in the soil, jets of flame sprang out and a bright light that was beyond light showed fleetingly in the gaps. At last, an obscene mushroom shook itself free of the ground that tried to contain it and rose up out of the earth, dragging tons of radioactive materials after itself.

Even as this was happening, the rest of the Chinese nuclear weapons detonated simultaneously.

Suddenly, the ground around the entire city heaved and buckled and rose up into the air, turning to instant vapor from the heat. The whole area was made bright by nuclear fires such as can only be found in the heart of stars, for a mini-sun grew into harsh life in what was once the city of Lanzhou.

Another, immensely larger, mushroom cloud leaped up out of the glowing hell-pit that had been the city of

Lanzhou, punching its way upward through the air and out to the very fringes of space itself. The young sun that lay in the pit shook itself free of its womb and jumped upward into space.

Below, in what used to be the city of Lanzhou, the rocks and soil of the ground shook and shivered as the force of the explosion slammed downward against the surface. The force shattered the rocks into dust and broke through the earth's mantle and released native magma to flow into the hole.

Throughout the entire continent, the mountains and hills shook and groaned aloud as geologic faults, long dormant, came to life and shrugged off their burden of rock. Tons of rock slid down the mountainsides everywhere, sweeping the works of man into their stony flood and grinding them into unrecognizable powder.

Volcanoes rumbled and belched out molten lava under the impact of the explosion. Mount Etna overflowed and wiped away generations of labor as its contents burnt the grape vines into cinders.

In Washington, the waters of the reflecting pool rippled then spilled over the banks onto ground once despoiled by angry farmers. In the Great Lakes, the huge waters slopped sideways, surging up and over the coastlines, drowning thousands.

Where Lanzhou once stood, a glowing wound had been opened into the very earth itself, twenty kilometers across. A raw ragged wound that glowed with the red-yellow color of hell itself. In the very center of the hole, the rock and debris heaved and rippled under the thrust of magma bubbling up from beneath the earth's surface. In a matter of hours, a volcano grew where man had detonated a thousand megatons of nuclear weapons.

Those who had the misfortune to live in the city itself were, perhaps, the luckiest of all, for they died instantly, not really knowing they died. Further from the center of the explosion, the ground shook the buildings that grew out of it into tumbled heaps of rubble, which the heat of the nuclear sun set into instant fire.

For kilometer after kilometer, radiating out from the center of the blast, buildings were smashed flat and set ablaze. Whole forests were flattened as if by a giant hand, and turned into blazing coals that flew ahead of the wave of death.

The heat of the flash burnt unprotected skins far out from the city of Lanzhou, and even on Mount Everest, the snows that perpetually wrapped the mountain melted and ran downward in a torrent.

Worst of all, the blast had been extremely dirty, throwing immense quantities of highly radioactive debris high up into the atmosphere. A wave of death spread downwind leaving only the dead behind it as it rolled toward the sea. The Chinese provinces of Xi'an and Zhenzhou died, and the cities of Nagasaki and Hiroshima were once more visited with nuclear death.

Throughout the lands of Asia, the knowledge of the events in China spread as the ground shook underfoot. The people would soon know just how deadly an event had occurred.

## III

Jack returned to his farm just in time to see the truck from Henderson's store pull away from the front of the barn. Jean came out of the barn and waved to him to stop.

"Jack, you can't back into the barn. It's full to the top with the supplies that you bought.

"Have you heard what happened in China? The news reports say that there was an explosion of at least a thousand megatons in west China! The seismographs at Upsala reported that the shock went right off their scale, beyond nine on the Richter scale."

"Omigod, I wonder what target was worth a planet-buster like that? Are you sure that's what the radio said?"

"Yes, Jack. Didn't you see any landslides? The whole road near town was supposed to be blocked by a slide in Winston Canyon."

"I must have gotten through before the slide."

"I guess everybody on the farm believes you now. Did you have to explain it to anybody?"

"Yes, but some of them took off for the hills and wouldn't listen to me. The rest, mostly the people with families, are staying."

"By the way, did you pay the feed and grain men in advance? They wouldn't take any money, but they left a letter for you. Here, take it."

Jack took the letter and tore the end off, shaking the note out into his hand.

*Jack,* he read, *I know what's happening to make you so worried. You told me the moment you said to get Ginny back here.*

*I want to buy a place up at your farm for Ginny and the kids with all of the supplies that I sent up there today. If you agree, please come into town tomorrow with me and we'll pick them up at the train station.*

"Do you know what this says, Jean?"

"No, but I can guess. There must be twenty tons of seeds and tools and everything else I can think of in the barn. If the men wouldn't take cash for all of it, I imagine the owner is trying to buy a place up here with us."

"Not for himself, but for his granddaughter and her kids. I used to date Ginny before I went off to the Point. I had planned to marry her as soon as I graduated, but she found somebody else in Chicago. We wrote back and forth for a few years, but then the letters tapered off until we stopped everything except Christmas cards. Henderson wants me to go into town tomorrow and help him pick them up. I'm going."

"I would never try to stop you, Jack. Are you going to go armed?"

"Better believe it. I'm going to carry a shotgun and my .45. They ought to keep prowlers away. I'm going down and tell Mr. Henderson that I'm coming with him. I'll catch some food along the way, OK?"

Jack walked over to his four-wheel drive and drove back to Henderson's Corners. He could make a lot better speed now than with his big truck. As he drove, he tried to remember just what Ginny looked like. It had been almost fifteen years since he had seen her, even though she came to visit her grandfather. It always seemed that she came at a time that Jack was too tied up on the farm to get away or when he was away on business. Jack really couldn't form a clear picture of the girl, even though he knew her well, very well. After a certain amount of time, even the best memories fade.

With an almost visible jolt, Jack remembered Ginny, very clearly. It had been during that last summer before he and his brother went east to the Point. Jack and Ginny had spent their time exploring the countryside, and exploring their relationship with one another.

The very first time they made love was during a trip up into the woods, to a beautiful blue lake set in the middle of a green mountain bowl. After lunch, they went for a swim in the icy water, then sat together, shivering, under their blankets. What followed seemed the most natural thing in the world.

When the time came for him to leave, Jack almost refused to go. He couldn't care less about college or an education, or anything but Ginny. Finally, she promised him she would wait until he graduated from school, and in the meantime, they should think about what their future would be like, and remember what they meant to one another.

The very last image of Ginny Jack had was of her standing on the train station platform, waving goodbye. She looked so *tiny* as the diesel pulled out.

Jack brushed at his eyes as he sat in front of the bar, then got out of his truck and walked in, his pistol slung low on his hip, the holster flap securely buttoned down. This was now, and not a time for memories, not when a war threatened.

The place was almost empty, except for about ten noisy strangers sitting off to one side. All the locals were home trying to plan their futures in a very dangerous time. Jack wolfed down his sandwich and followed it with his beer. As soon as he was done, he walked away and drove his car over to Henderson's store.

Henderson was waiting just inside the door.

"I knew you'd come, Jack."

"I was coming to tell you about tomorrow, sir."

"I figured that. Come on in out of the dark and have a cup of coffee with an old man. That's about all I have left in the store. It was the best business day I've ever had.

"People bought everything that wasn't nailed down and paid off in hard cash. They're scared, Jack, and working themselves up into a panic. When people act like that, Jack, they can't reason. Things are starting to get ugly, even here.

"That's why I sent all of those supplies up to you, and I'm sending a couple of tank trucks full of diesel oil up tomorrow. Have I bought Ginny and the kids a place there?"

"They had a place up there if they wanted it, even without everything you sent up. Look, let's go over to your house and get your clothes together. I want you up to the farm."

"I'm too old, Jack. I'll be seventy-three this November, if anybody lives that long. If things happen as I suspect they will, there won't be any room for the likes of me. Just take Ginny . . ."

"Bull. You're the youngest old man I know. You're coming along with me if I have to pick you up and throw you over my shoulder. Now, let's lock up here and get moving."

Henderson turned away, but not quickly enough to hide the tears that filled his eyes from the younger man. Jack walked over to the doors and made sure that they were locked tight, and the windows, behind their metal bars, were shut. A few minutes later, Adam Henderson appeared with a suitcase in hand.

"I'm ready, Jack. I've been living in the store for the past few years, except when Ginny and the kids come to town. That big old house of mine is too empty for me to live there. Let's go before somebody comes in looking for some feed."

The two men left the building, locking it behind them, and got into Jack's truck. As soon as Jack started up, two men appeared out of nowhere, grabbed the sides of the truck and shoved pistols in the windows. They were two of the strangers that Jack had seen in the bar.

"Let's have that money, old man. You had a busy day."

Jack threw his door open, catching the man on his side in the pit of his stomach and spreading him on the ground. At the same time, he jammed his foot down on the gas and backed up at top speed, scraping the second gunman off on the steel sign that Henderson had put up in front of the store.

Without stopping to see what kind of condition he was leaving the men in, Jack shifted and sped out of the parking lot in a cloud of dust. Behind him, in the glare of the lights, Jack could see one of the gunmen shaking his fist after them.

"That was close, Jack."

"Punks like that couldn't fight their way out of a

paper bag, Mr. Henderson. They're too used to preying on people who are too civilized to fight back, even when they're threatened with death. The punks also know that if their victims do fight back, the courts will jail the poor guy for having the guts to fight back.

"Look at this gun! A .22! Hell, if I wanted to tickle my target to death, I'd use something like that. Unless you practice every day, you have to be damned lucky to kill somebody with one of these."

"What are you carrying?"

"My .45. Tomorrow, we'll both carry one, plus a shotgun each and lots of ammo. I think that the scum's starting to float to the surface, and we owe it to ourselves and to Ginny and the kids to have some protection. I'm going to pull over to the side of the road here and let you drive. I think I ought to ride shotgun for a while. By the way, were your trucks locked up tight?"

"Yes, I figured you could send some of your hands back to get them in the morning."

"Right. Now, let's go home."

## IV

In the cavern that had been hollowed out of a solid granite mountain, the people in charge of America's defense against enemy attack sat in front of their radar displays and satellite reconnaissance televisions for the slightest indication of an enemy attack. Ever since midnight of May the second, they had been losing their satellites.

Most of them had been picked off by Soviet ground-based lasers that formed the backbone of Soviet antimissile defenses. Now, over seventy percent of the satellites that the defense depended on to identify a Soviet attack had been eliminated, and others were being taken out moment by moment.

The command fell back on the obsolete equipment that ringed the northernmost parts of the continent. For years, the number of men at these bases had decreased, as had the number of operable stations. Now that the need was really here, the majority of the stations were out of action.

Not that it really mattered. There were no surface-to-air missiles available, nor laser antimissile batteries, or even enough interceptors to seriously contest a Soviet attack. The last of the antique interceptors which were planned for such an interceptor role had been retired years before as too costly to maintain. They had been replaced by other aircraft, worn out and badly maintained to boot. No more than three hundred aircraft were assigned to defend the whole continent against a Soviet attack.

Against the defense forces, the Soviets deployed a force of over a thousand Backfire bombers and over five hundred Tu-160 superbombers. The Soviets planned to hit every worth-while target in North America.

The defenders knew just what faced them, so they made certain that careful attention was paid to all their information-gathering devices. Finally, the inevitable happened, as a force of Soviet aircraft, headed for an attack in South China, flew well out to sea beyond Japan and dove to approach their targets from the sea.

Norad command flashed the report of the immediate attack to the White House, and the president, after a few minutes hesitation, approved a full-scale alert!

# ELEVEN

## I

The president was presented with the information that

a Soviet attack was apparently aimed at America as soon as his men could get the message to him. Luckily, one of the generals, MacNaulty, was in the room as the message arrived.

"Well, General MacNaulty, what do you recommend?"

"As harsh as it sounds, Mr. President, I recommend that we don't alert the people."

"What!"

"Sir, nobody we alert now could hope to get more than a mile or two from home at best. They have perhaps fifteen minutes to get moving, if we're lucky. They have no place to go to when they get out of town, if they get out of town, and there won't be enough food or gasoline to do much more than prolong their lives a few days or weeks at best. Besides, if this is a false alarm, thousands of people will be injured or killed for no reason. I say you should just ignore the alert."

"I'm sorry, general, but I must tell the people to get away as soon as they can."

People were sitting in their living rooms across the nation with the multicolored glow from their televisions illuminating their rooms. Without warning, their televisions suddenly told them one thing:

EVACUATE!

People poured out of their homes and fought their way to cars that carried them out onto the roads away from their cities.

Minute by minute, the roads became more and more jammed with cars filled with terrified people seeking escape, somewhere, anywhere. Few listened to the directions that flooded the airwaves, and few of the people who did could understand them.

In a half-hour, most of the roads in most of the cities

of the United States were packed, bumper to bumper, with cars blocked by broken down or wrecked cars up ahead. In the crowds of people who sat, frustrated and frozen into unthinking immobility, a rage was beginning to grow.

All across America, the cars devoured the last few drops of gasoline in their tanks, and in an almost symbolic act, sputtered to a stop.

Some of the people, more alert or more terrified than their neighbors, set out on foot, pushing their way through the crowds of people waiting to have something done for them. All along the route of march, people could be seen stealing from one another, fighting and killing to escape the danger that lay behind them. Scene after desperate scene was repeated with monotonous regularity and increasing bestiality all across the land.

As dawn stole across the wreckage, the all-clear sirens sounded, while the radios announced, in suitably mellifluous tones, that a mistake had been made. The dead really didn't care.

## II

The president was presented with a preliminary casualty list, the death toll of the "simple error in judgment." The number of dead and injured exceeded the losses of all the holiday weekends combined together and was climbing by the minute. People had been killed in automobile wrecks, trampled in the panicked flight of mobs, robbed and murdered, and even killed for the crime of running out of gas and blocking some other person's flight.

Police and fire departments all across the country had seen that there was nothing that they could do and deserted *en masse,* preferring to go home and protect their loved ones to guarding another man's property.

The hopeless, trapped in the heart of the target, turned to riot and drunken revels to lessen the fear of death. The city centers burned to the ground in a frenzied orgy of destruction.

The flight of the lucky few who had led the pack ended as soon as their cars ran out of fuel, stranding them in totally unknown surroundings. An unlucky few had run afoul of towns which were determined to protect what was theirs and had been shot dead by the fearful townsmen, while others took their revenge on the rural people by looting and killing their way across the nation.

In that short space of time, less than six hours, all plans for orderly evacuations had fallen apart, leaving everybody in the same disastrous situation. The roads all were so tightly blocked, that there was no hope of ever getting back into the cities if necessary, let alone escaping from them if a real alert was sounded.

## III

Mario Ginetti and his men had watched the flow of traffic past their hiding place with amusement. They had been keeping themselves hidden and hadn't heard about the evacuation until late on the morning after. By then, everyone knew that it had all been a costly mistake.

Mario and his men had enjoyed the whole thing. They had simply stopped the largest and most expensive cars and robbed and murdered their drivers. That is, those that they didn't decide to keep for their own use or for trade.

By noon, Mario had collected several dozen luxury cars, some more guns, and a couple of voluntary recruits for the Demons. Mario was getting ready to set out to the north, then turning west along one of the old trails. Mario had had a dream where he became a cattle baron, like the ones on TV. Now was the time for him to do it and steal what he wanted, just like they did in the Old West.

## IV

Jim Dawson had stopped at a car lot after losing his tails in the twisting suburban streets. After a quick deal, he had traded in his car on a diesel powered compact and a hundred gallons of fuel. It was going to be a long drive back to the farm.

In a couple of hours, he had topped the Blue Ridge Mountains and was driving down the road from Rockfish Gap into the Shenandoah Valley. He thought about his brother's passion for this great battlefield out of American History One; now, it looked so peaceful, almost sleepy.

Back in 1862, Stonewall Jackson had earned military immortality when he led his forces, always badly outnumbered and outgunned, against the Union troops which milled around trying to catch up with him. Jack had become so fascinated with the man that he studied his campaigns and wrote a number of published articles about each one of them. Jack had come to the conclusion that Jackson's victories were the result of a sophisticated understanding of the relationship between terrain and mobility to keep the Union army off balance.

Now Jim was rushing past the sites of some of these very battles, trying to get to the bridge at St. Louis. He heard something about an alert, but the poor reception in the hills blocked it out.

# BOOK TWO: BELLUM

## PROLOG

The facts of the matter are these. The targets of a major nuclear exchange are divided into five distinct sets of potential targets: population, military, industrial, communications, and biosphere. From the outset, it must be assumed that, contrary to dire warnings that state otherwise, no combatant will be able to totally eliminate any one category of target, although there will be considerable attacks directed against the available targets in each category. It is further assumed that there is a point where further expenditure of nuclear weapons against a target category will not be effective to a degree commensurate with the cost of the expensive weapons.

Certainly at the head of any target list will be the urban centers, since they tend to contain several target categories within their boundaries; that is, population, industrial, and communications targets. Attacks on centers such as these will have the collateral effect of disrupting or destroying the military and/or political command structure.

Military complexes will be subjected to a certain degree of attention, especially strategic force bases, with their concentrations of missiles and aircraft. Here, though, the weapons employed will be relatively small, since the bases are generally "hardened" or protected under covers of earth and concrete or will have their aircraft aloft, and hence safe from an attack on their bases. Certainly it is naive to suspect that these bases will remain unattacked. It is probable that they will receive some attention in order to prevent their owner from using them to launch a second strike against the aggressor.

Other types of military targets are much too diffuse to be attacked effectively with any but the largest weapons. Obviously, these weapons could be more effectively used against concentrated targets. As a result, a nuclear war may well be the first war in which a nation's youth is not sacrificed in vain battles, but rather would survive to help in reconstruction. Perhaps this is one of the best reasons to support a sexually integrated military.

In any case, the urban centers will be prime targets, perhaps attracting half the total megatonnage expended. In such a case, the weapons will be multiple targeted, first, to lessen the effects of interceptions or accidents, and second, because the effects of a number of nuclear blasts are greater than if the same megatonnage was expended in one blast.

Attacks on urban centers will have a number of immediate effects: blast from the explosion itself, which can flatten buildings many kilometers from the center of the blast itself; radiation from the materials of the weapon itself as well as materials irradiated by the detonation; and heat from the explosion that can erase people as if they never existed, leaving only macabre photographs of their end etched on walls of rubble.

Such attacks on urban centers are often the cause of firestorms that can so burn out the hearts of cities that only a calcined shell will remain, useless, uninhabitable monuments to the essential destructiveness of war.

Industrial targets will be hard hit by nuclear attacks, even if the plant itself is not destroyed. If for no other reason, the strikes against the urban centers will eliminate much of the trained personnel in the factories or so disrupt the flow of materials into the plant that they would be abandoned.

Outside the urban center, oil fields, mines, chemical plants, and power stations will be targeted for some sort of attack.

Since oil fields represent a widespread target, they would probably be hit with a very dirty weapon, designed to simultaneously destroy surface installations and interdict the area to people with a desire for survival or normal children.

Power stations will certainly be hit, especially nuclear power stations. Even though a direct hit will not breach the core, the support equipment will certainly be destroyed. Other types of power plants, including hydroelectric plants, will certainly be attacked. Success in this attack would have the effect of "turning off" the whole country.

The communications net, that is, the sum total of all roads, railroads, waterways, harbors, radio, and telephone centers, will be hard hit by the strikes against urban centers, since these tend to concentrate in such areas. However, most of the damage inflicted will be temporary in effect. There is no way that the Mississippi River can be stopped from flowing, although the canal locks that serve the traffic on the river can be eliminated. Roads and railroads can be repaired and maintained by relatively unskilled labor in a short time, especially if salvaged materials are used.

Biosphere targets would probably be limited to strikes against concentrations of agriculture, fisheries, and possibly forests. Because of their diffuse nature, attacks against these targets would probably be limited, since the weapons used against them would be better employed against the sources of fuel for the harvests or the roads and railroads that carry the food to market.

The whole world biosphere effects would be relatively small, since the worst fallout would sink to the ground within twenty years. Only carbon-14 and tritium would remain in the atmosphere as, respectively, carbon dioxide gas and water vapor.

Effects on the ozone layer from the high altitude injection of nitrogen oxides are more difficult to estimate, especially since the exact thickness of the layer is unknown. Certainly after twenty years, the ozone layer will recover to within five to ten percent of prewar levels.

The dangers of heating or cooling the world's temperature levels due to matter injected into the atmosphere will not be a significant factor, since nuclear weapons are most effective when detonated at high altitudes, rather than as air bursts.

It can be assumed that the use of approximately ten thousand megatons of strategic nuclear weapons will serve to "win" a war for one side or the other, but will not destroy the world as so many novels and movies of the fifties and sixties contended. Certainly the greatest effect of the use of nuclear weapons will be on the fabric of society and the attitudes of the survivors.

# ONE

## I

In the hidden Chinese missile base, buried deeply under the mountains of Manchuria, the final IRBMs available to the Chinese government were being readied for launch. The Soviets had eliminated all others by their attacks.

The missiles were being readied, a long and dangerous task, in which the slightest interruption or error could eliminate a significant portion of China's nuclear might. In the hardened launch site, the Chinese missile crewmen, clad like monks of some obscure order in their protective clothing, moved about as they finished fueling the weapons with kerosene and liquid oxygen. The lines were disengaged and stowed in their holders.

The bird was ready to fly.

The countdown resumed at the base commander's orders. The missile was relatively small compared to the Soviet giants, but still could destroy a city.

With an explosive shudder and deafening roar, the missile was hurtled upward into the sky. The Chinese crew cheered, doubly proud that their bird was flying, and in memory of their families in Harbin and Beijing. The base's radar was warmed up and ready, so in a matter of only a minute or two, everyone knew that their missile was in the groove and racing toward its target, the Soviet city of Irkutsk.

The crewmen knew that they had only a few minutes left of life, and climbed upward from their shelter, preferring to die above ground to being smashed by the retaliatory Soviet missiles. One of the men happened to be looking directly south, just in time to see the appoaching Soviet missile that destroyed the base.

In the city of Irkutsk, the population went about its day to day tasks. The railroad yards were crowded with loaded freight cars destined for the troops in China. These loaded cars had come into the city in just the last few hours, after the special repair crews, made up of convicts, had finished reconnecting the railroad. The survivors, of course, were to be pardoned if they survived their radiation sickness.

The city's factories were busy producing munitions, replacement parts and new vehicles, as well as overhauling the damaged equipment that was being shipped back into the city. Out on Lake Baikal were huge rafts of logs, destined for the mills that lined the shore around the city.

At the airport, the last paratroopers of the *231st Airborne Division* were being loaded into the Anatov transports that would carry them westward. The rumor was, that they would soon see action against the West German fascists.

In the homes and schools, women and children worked and played as they did any other day.

Soviet radar detected the Chinese missile almost as soon as it cleared the silo launch site. It tracked the missile as it lifted up into the sky, and American computers predicted the fall of the weapon, even as the warhead was heated into a hot yellow glow. People in the city looked up and saw death approaching, a yellow flaming arrow trailing a black shroud of death.

From the hills that surrounded the city, antimissile missiles shot into the air and blasted for their target. The ruby pulse of lasers waving through the air showed clearly, as the weapons attempted to lock onto the plunging warhead and eliminate it.

Even as the warhead entered the atmosphere, it began a series of maneuvers, bouncing and tumbling across the sky in its cold mechanical efforts to escape death.

The first ABM exploded less than a kilometer from the warhead, but from behind; it had no effect. The warhead split without warning into ten separate sections, each like the other, each of which could contain a small nuclear weapon. The defensive system was suddenly strained far beyond its planned capacity, because each of the targets had to be eliminated, or the results of their failure would be too horrible to think on.

The lasers did their job, illuminating the warhead fragments in an eerie red glow, then vaporizing them. All but one of the segments had been eliminated in the five minutes since the launch of the Chinese missile. That fragment disappeared below the hills, effectively masking it from attack. There was nothing more that could be done.

The fragment impacted less than a hundred meters from the main plant of the Red Banner Tractor Works Number 27, smashing a wooden shed that housed the worker's cafeteria into splinters.

It was a decoy.

Less lucky was the city of Vladivostok.

Of the three missiles targeted for the city, two were launched from such short range that they were impacting in the city before the defenders could react.

The first missile struck just on its target, the port of Vladivostok itself, the funnel through which almost fifteen percent of the supplies used by the Soviet Army in China were being poured. The fireball melted and twisted the dockside cranes and the blast threw them far beyond the dockyard. Warehouses were smashed flat and incinerated leaving only an outline where their foundations remained.

The water in the harbor itself boiled, then vanished as the heat flashed it into vapor, leaving the ships stranded, to be tumbled about by the blast and to have red-hot fragments torn from their structure and hurled far and wide, to set more and more fires. A merciful tidal wave roared back into the harbor basin as the fireball waned in strength and covered the shattered wreckage.

The second Chinese missile, after suffering a catastrophic guidance failure in midflight, crashed to the ground near the Soviet command bunker just outside the stricken city. The people inside the blastproof bunker had just a few seconds to wonder what had happened before the very tunnels beneath their feet began to crack and crumble as the bombproof bunker collapsed in on them. The contractor for the shelter had sold the reinforcing steel to another company for use in an apartment complex.

The blast that destroyed the Soviet command in the Far East also had the effect of setting the pine forests ablaze. The heat from the blast dried the gums and resins in the trees and set them ablaze. The pine torches set still more trees afire, and soon, the blaze spread throughout the area.

Far out over the Pacific Ocean, an American reconnaissance plane, flying an intelligence gathering mission, saw the smudges of smoke and the leaping pillars of flame that announced the birth of two new firestorms, this time in the Soviet Union itself.

Like two giants locked in a *danse macabre*, each determined to kill the other, the Soviet Union and the Chinese let fly with all their missiles. The exchange totaled approximately two thousand megatons, and was painfully one-sided. In exchange for a dozen Soviet cities, China was eliminated for all time as a world power. Over sixty percent of the population outside the invasion areas died immediately from the attack or slightly later as all communications broke down.

In berserk retaliation for the death of thousands of Soviet citizens, the Soviet forces unleashed a hail of conventional explosives, incendiaries, and chemical weapons against the Chinese that exceeded in ferocity any air attack ever waged before. In less than twenty hours, every major Chinese city had been eliminated, and more than half the other cities converted into blazing charnel houses, inhabited only by the dead and the dying.

Target classifications ceased to exist in those mad times, as everything that moved in China was subjected to the lash of Soviet revenge. Even the dikes, raised after years of unremitting hand labor, disappeared under the attack, letting loose the age-old curse of China, its rampaging rivers.

Outside China, the nations of the world protested the use of so many weapons, but were curtly reminded that the Chinese had launched the first missile attacks. Carpets of death and suffering were reaching out again from China and drifting across Asia.

North and South Korea became united in their hatred

of the Soviets and attacked against the Soviet rear. The battle raged for a few days as the Korean peoples packed up bag and baggage and marched northward through their bare mud-colored hills to some safety that they were never to know.

Taiwan, already in secret contact with the People's Republic, offered its aid in attacking the Soviets. An expeditionary force of three divisions was hurriedly ferried across the Straits of Formosa, while the Taiwanese marines stormed ashore in the great Soviet base at Cam Rahn Bay.

Even Japan, pushed beyond endurance by the deaths of hundreds of citizens in the radioactive hell that all of southern Japan was becoming, struck back. As jets struck at low level against Soviet bases, Japanese paratroopers, true knights of Bushido, landed in exposed Soviet airbases and gave back red death in revenge for their countrymen killed yet a second time by nuclear weapons.

The war in Asia was running wild.

## II

In Eastern Europe, the situation worsened as the Soviet satellites saw their masters in their true guise, ready to pull the whole world down into ash if they were blocked in their advance. The people revolted and rioted in the streets, but were bloodily put down by Soviet army units, just as had happened so often in the past.

In Poland, the Polish army was disarmed and confined to its barracks, guarded by a gang of traitor-soldiers, while on the city streets, Soviet soldiers had to go about in groups of at least ten; otherwise they would be attacked and killed for their weapons.

Czechoslovakia, still restive after the brutal Soviet occupation of only a few years before, reacted with violence to the presence of Soviet troops. Grenades were thrown into bars filled with Soviet troops or into their barracks. Sentries on guard duty were run down by speeding cars or trucks, and their weapons pulled from their still-warm hands. Arsenals were broken into and looted before the Soviets could arrive to scatter the crowds.

In Yugoslavia, occupied and administered directly from Moscow ever since the death of President Tito and the subsequent invasion of the country by Soviet troops, boiled over. The people who had liberated their country from the Wehrmacht a generation before took to the hills to drive their latest invader out.

Even the Soviet Army itself was not immune to the disruptions that wrecked the satellite armies, especially as the word of the debacle in China spread through the ranks. The Soviet minority problems, carefully hidden for many years, began to erupt. The Ukrainians, the Moslems, and all the non-Russian peoples began to grumble. Some deserted to the rebels who attacked their posts, while others decided to destroy their army from within.

The Soviets responded to the problems with their typical ruthlessness, arresting and executing all their opponents in a series of bloody, lightning raids. The KGB hadn't spent all the interwar years developing the largest domestic spy network in the world for nothing. The swath that the KGB cut through the ranks of the dissidents was so wide that effective resistance all through the Soviet state and its satellites ceased, freeing the army from worries about rear area security. In the meantime, the loyal satellite troops had their divisions disbanded and the troops incorporated directly into Soviet divisions.

With their rear secure, the Soviets began rolling their units into their forward positions, ready to attack. Each of the units had been provided with two weeks supply of fuel and thirty days issue of ammunition, more than enough, even without drawing on stocks in East Germany, to reach the Rhine and beyond. Chemical and tactical nuclear weapons were stockpiled, along with more conventional ammunition, beside the weapons that would soon pour death onto the Western Allied troops.

Ten Soviet artillery divisions were deployed along the West German border to back up the fire of all the Soviet assault divisions that would move forward as soon as the attack orders were issued. Each artillery piece in the border zone had been issued a detailed fire plan that listed targets, the number of rounds to be expended against each target, and the time the fire would take.

## III

Senator Howland watched with satisfaction as the last elements of the army battalion which had been assigned to his shelter filed into the barracks and settled down. They were an elite unit, drawn from the most politically loyal units in the armed forces, and would be used as the core around which a new United States army would form. The troops supposed that they were going to be used as a guard for the republic; instead, they would be surprised to learn that they were to be the new Praetorian Guard.

Howland and the other congressmen were already jockeying for positions of power within the shelter, but Howland had the advantage of being the man first on the site and to whom the others deferred when he spoke. Having arrived long before the fiasco of the false alert, he and his secretaries and staff had simply taken over all the positions of power within the shelter, and had established a neat little political police force in the bargain. Once the troops arrived, Howland took them over formally, activating his reserve commission.

Unfortunately, Howland was already bored. There wasn't much that he could do about running the shelter, since everything was controlled by a preprogrammed computer which controlled everything from the airconditioning to the nuclear power plant nestled in the bowels of the complex. With all the knowledge that was encoded in the computer, from the entire contents of the Library of Congress to the top secret documents that the government accumulated, ever since the development of the photoscanner, the process had raced ahead; after all, the stored knowledge would be enough to rebuild a world.

The Senator had asked the computer for an inventory for the complex and was rewarded with ten kilograms of printout. As he flipped through the information, he found that there were at least a hundred kinds of oils stored in the complex, ranging from a hundred gallons of sesame oil up to five hundred thousand gallons of diesel fuel. There was even immense cryogenic vats that contained eggs and sperm from every important animal, including man.

Huge supplies of metals and special alloys filled the store rooms buried inside the mountain, enough to get an economy back on its feet after a devastating attack. Ingots of precious metals—gold, silver, and platinum—were stacked like cordwood in the vaults of the shelter; they would serve to buy a senator or member of the house anything he wanted after an attack had destroyed the United States.

What was stored in the other vaults, though, would guarantee the owner the control of the whole local economy. An arsenal of weapons, case after case of M16 rifles and M60 machineguns, along with piles of ammunition which towered above the custodians up into the blackness of the unlit ceiling of the caverns. Every weapon of destruction was stocked here, from rounds of ammunition for the rifles up to artillery ammunition for the 155mm howitzers that sat toad-like covered by their protective plastic cocoons. In an ultimate betrayal, the ammunition vaults held nuclear artillery shells, put inside the fortress to be used in stopping an enemy attack, whether that enemy was foreign or domestic.

Senator Howland had already made his decision about how he would run his new army. The politically reliable troops would be purged once more, just to make absolutely certain none of them would pose a threat to his government. They would be used like the British had used their European troops to control India for so many generations. They would control the artillery and armor, while the mass of the army would be drawn from the natives. If they revolted against the beneficent reign that Senator Howland planned, they could be eliminated under the crushing treads of the tanks or armored personnel carriers that were stored in the shelter's garage.

Just to make certain that the soldiers didn't revolt, Howland planned to set the former federal agents he had brought into the shelter over them the guardians who would guard the guardians of the new republic. Howland had always had a sneaking admiration for the Caesars, but they had fallen because they failed to control their Praetorians—Howland and his cronies wouldn't make the same mistake.

Control of the "Valley Forge" complex would mean immense power to whoever held it, both during the period of reconstruction and afterward, and Howland was determined he would be the one to emerge in control of everything as far as his army could march. If it meant using nuclear weapons against people who stood in his way, well, that was a terrible thing, but unavoidable in the long term.

## IV

Despite evacuation warnings in West Germany, the majority of the population still had been unable to leave their homes, and the few who had gotten away were blocking the West German roads in much the same manner as the roads had been blocked in the United States. In the confusion, the Soviet agents infiltrated days, even weeks, before, were able to move about freely through the German rear.

It was only by accident that a man was caught in the main Hamburg waterworks with a sealed container he was about to throw into the system. A quick interrogation told the police all they needed to know. The saboteur had been given a bottle of botulin toxin, as had many of his fellow agents, and ordered to dump the bottles into the West German water systems. The result was the whole population of West Germany was in imminent danger of poisoning. An immediate guard was placed on the reservoirs and water works to protect them from such an attack, but the damage was already done.

Within hours, the hospitals were filled with people dead and dying from the effects of the botulin toxin. Radio warnings had gone out in the middle of the night, when too few people listened to save them from death. Even in areas not affected by poisoning, the people went thirsty, afraid that their water was or would be poisoned.

In Hamburg, the policemen decided that the long niceties of a civil trial would be wasted on their prisoner and drew lots for the duty of executing the man. Just before dawn, the commando was led, screaming and pleading for his life, out into the courtyard of the police headquarters. Far off in the distance the sound of firing could be heard as the Soviets attacked.

The man pointed up into the air and screamed.

"Look, they are my people. Paratroopers coming to

your city. Don't kill me!"

"Do you seriously believe that the attack was staged just to rescue you?" the policeman said, as he pulled the trigger of his pistol.

# TWO

## I

Jack and Adam Henderson had set out long before dawn to drive into Boise to pick up Ginny and her family. The news, despite the rigid clamp of censorship that the government had imposed, was bad. Asia was almost totally at war, with major exchanges of nuclear weapons on both sides. The radioactive materials carried by the winds would soon reach the United States, and Jack wanted to get back under cover as soon as he could.

The reports of the false alarm had been suppressed also, but the wreckage along the roads and the heavy car traffic away from the cities, as well as the hopeless, dispirited columns of refugees marching stoically along both shoulders of the road told more eloquently than mere words of the sorry state of American morale.

Most of the escapees were doomed, whether they realized it or not, since they had no skills that would be of value in a post-war society, save their untrained labor. The majority would die of exposure or starvation when winter came, or be turned into bandits.

Jack pulled up to the train station, a converted house trailer up on blocks that had been erected a couple of years before. Jack and Henderson got out of the truck and made sure it was locked up tight, and that they could see it clearly from the station. Nobody seemed surprised to see both of the men so heavily armed in the heart of a supposedly civilized city.

That the trains were running at all was testimony to the resilience of the railroads. With the increasingly more difficult fuel situation, aggravated by the OPEC embargoes of the last couple of years, the airplane had been eliminated as a means of long-distance transportation for all but the very rich or the desperately needed specialist traveling on a government pass.

The passenger load had to be absorbed somewhere, and the railroads were the most likely candidate to carry the flow of people. Despite the years of bad press, just two years' time had been enough to see every city in America with a population of fifty thousand or more served by some sort of rail traffic.

Because of the false alarm, Henderson was careful to question the ticket agent to find out if his granddaughter's train was on time. Jack kept a careful watch on the people on the platform, just as careful as the watch they kept on him.

The train would be on time, and arrive within a half-hour. Jack and Henderson walked back to their truck and stood guard.

Finally, far off in the distance, Jack could hear the moan of the diesel horn as the train rolled into town, and then the sound of steel grinding on steel as the brakes were applied. The pair walked past the locomotives, huge diesel monsters which sat and throbbed with power as they waited to pull away from the station.

"There they are," Henderson shouted, "I see them right there! Come on, let's get them!"

The older man pushed his way through the crowd toward the train, ignoring the stares of the other people. Jack followed somewhat more circumspectly.

"Ginny girl!" Henderson cried as he swept her into his arms, "your old granddad's missed you, honey, and you kids too! God, I'm glad to see you!"

"Granddad, are you all right? After I got that call

from you, we got right on the train to get here. Now, I see you running around like a kid and looking like a gunfighter. What's going on?"

"Look, Ginny, don't ask questions for a little while. I promise I'll tell you everything."

"Say, do you recognize who brought me here?"

"Yes, granddad, I sure do—Hello, Jack."

Jack stood there for a long moment, looking carefully at the girl he had left behind him fifteen years before. She hadn't changed a bit; if anything, she'd become more beautiful and more polished than she had been. Her perfectly tailored gray suit was obviously expensive, and even though it was rumpled and stained from her trip, was worn as if she were one to the manor born.

"Ginny, I'm glad to see you again. You look more beautiful now than when I left for West Point."

"Thank you, Jack; I can always count on you to know just what to say to a woman to make her day. Thanks too for bringing my granddad to me."

"I'd have never let him come alone anyway, what with the situation the way it is. Besides, this is the easiest way for us to get you back to my farm. That's where you'll be staying for a while."

"Oh, really? Granddad, I thought you wanted us down for a visit. Tell me right now what's going on!"

"We'll tell you what's happening as soon as we can. Just wait until we're on our way home. First though, we want to stop off at the store and get you and the kids some clothes. I think you'll need them. Kids, I want you to meet Jack Dawson," Henderson said, leaving his granddaughter speechless. "He's a good friend of your mom's and mine. Now, we're all going to go shopping."

With a minimum of protest, Henderson dragged his daughter off the train platform and over to Jack's truck. Jack and the kids followed with the baggage.

After a ten minute drive, they pulled into the parking

lot of the department store where Jack had done his shopping a few days before. In a few hours, the trim, elegant executive from Chicago was transformed back into the farm girl that Jack had grown up with. Henderson was supervising the outfitting of his granddaughter and her family from head to toe, for summer or winter, for the next ten years. Jack and the oldest boy, John, had been given the job of carrying the clothes out to the truck. The parking lot was guarded by a dozen men with weapons at the ready as a service to customers.

The two men loaded the cartop carrier and the back of the truck with their purchases and finally leaned back against their truck to take a break.

"Well, John, what do you think's going on?" Jack said.

"That's easy. There's going to be a war and granddad wants us in the safest place he knows of. God, you should have seen what happened after that phony alert! We had to force our way through crowds of people all over the tracks. They climbed up onto the car roofs, hung from the handrails, everything. It looked like those magazine pictures of trains in India, you know, with the people looking as though they're glued all over the train. People were fighting for seats and throwing other people out of their compartments. I saw them beat one man to death because he wouldn't open his compartment door. We were lucky, 'cause I had just bought a new rifle and was taking it to granddad's to try out. I'm on the school ROTC rifle team.

"That kept them away, just waving the gun around. I had just five rounds with me, but they never tried anything. I hope we never have to go through something like that again. The people were like animals; you could smell their fear."

"I can imagine how it was," Jack replied. "I saw a lot of that in 'Nam, just before the collapse. You were pretty brave to stand up to a mob. I guess you get that from your dad?"

"Mom always says I'm just like my father. She thought the world of him, I guess. He died when I was six, so I don't really remember too much about him. Uh oh, here comes my sister. I'll bet she has something else for us to do."

The appearance of the girl was a signal, because the other boy, Ginny, and Adam Henderson all came out of the store, their arms loaded down with clothing. Jack and John went over to help carry the load and, in a short time, with a minimum amount of pushing, shoving, and shouting, everybody and their clothes were loaded into the truck, and they were driving off toward the farm.

"Ginny," Jack said as he drove, "have you and the kids had anything to eat?"

"No, and we're starved."

"I sort of counted on that. Kids, open up that ice box beside you and hand out the food. The brown thermos has coffee in it, and the red has milk, so help yourselves."

Conversation died away in the truck as the kids and their mom reduced the food in the box to crumbs on the floor and a full feeling in their stomachs. It had been almost two days since they had had anything to eat. Finally Ginny brushed the crumbs from her lap and turned to her grandfather.

"All right, will you please tell me what's going on? I get a call from you that you're dying and I rush down here to find you in top condition, as always. Then you introduce me to Jack, whom I haven't seen for fifteen years and tell me that we're all going to live on his farm, and then to top it all off, you drag us to the department store and buy us all kinds of clothes. Now what's going on?"

"Uh . . . Mr. Henderson, I think I can tell the story

better than you. Let me explain it to Ginny and the kids.

"Ginny, I'm sure that you know what's going on. I know that John does, so I'll lay it all out for all of you. You remember my brother Jim, don't you, Ginny? Well he has a job in the Pentagon in military intelligence. He and his commander have come to the conclusion that the war in Asia is going to spill over into Europe. He believes that there is a good chance that it will become an all-out Soviet effort to wipe us out once and for all.

"You've heard what's going on in West Germany? Well, we've been monitoring the short wave frequencies, and things that are coming out of there make it look pretty bad. Only part of the story is leaking out to the American people.

"Your granddad tricked you into coming here because he's worried about you and the kids. He wants you here where he can keep an eye on you, and besides, it's a lot safer here than back in Chicago on ground zero."

Jack fell silent, and Ginny turned her head to look at the columns of refugees lining the road. In the back seat, the girl, Virginia Marie, sobbed as she realized what was happening to her world. John and the other boy sat silently.

"Then John was right?" Ginny said.

"Ginny, I would never have sold out my store in one day, nor would Jack have spent thousands of dollars getting in supplies if we didn't believe the same thing as John. Jack showed me the papers that his brother brought back and they would have convinced me even if I hadn't been a believer already," Adam said.

"Your graddad's right," agreed Jack. "We'll be all right. I produce all of my electric power on the farm myself, with a hydroelectric dam and some windmills. We grow all the grain we need to make alcohol for the tractors and trucks; in fact, we're running on green fuel right now. About the only thing I don't make on my own farm is the fuel oil I use in the back-up heaters and generators, and your granddad shipped a lot of that up to me."

"Then I guess I ought to listen to you two. Tell me, straight out, don't lie to me now after all these years. Do we really have a chance to survive. Can we live on after a nuclear attack?" Ginny asked.

"There aren't any absolute guarantees of anything," her grandfather said, "but if it comes to a nuclear war as we expect it to do, we stand our best chance of survival up on Jack's farm. He's got almost everything you can think of that'll make getting through this disaster a little bit easier."

"Your granddad's right. My family's been trying to make the farm self-sufficient for generations, but now, all the work that all the Dawson forebears did over the years is paying off.

"We're guaranteed fresh, uncontaminated water from our deep wells. We're into water strata that were laid down when the dinosaurs wandered through these uplands. We've got our own power plant that gives us all the electricity we'll ever need, and we've got windmills to keep the line shacks and wells out in the field operating. We produce all of our own food and all of our fuel. Even if we're cut off for ten years, we'll make out okay."

"What about looters and robbers? You know what happened on the roads around here and everywhere else, what happened on the train. Will we have to live in fear for the rest of our lives, like animals, never knowing when somebody'll try to kill us for what we have that they want?" worried Ginny.

"My farm stood off a major attack by a motorcycle gang just a couple of years ago. With the mass unemployment we've been having, the streets haven't been safe for years. I'll tell you this, though, anybody who tries to raid my farm'll have one hell of a time getting in. I've put in barbed wire entanglements all around the farm buildings, and we've built mini-blockhouses like we used in 'Nam. I've had the buildings banked with earth where wood was exposed, and covered the roofs with sod. We even have the farmyard criss-crossed with a network of slit trenches and covered firing posts. Nobody's getting in without a fight. As your grandfather said, I can't guarantee anything, but I can promise that I'll do the best I can. Will that do?"

Ginny leaned over and kissed Jack on his cheek, then said: "I always knew you to keep your word, Jack. For what you and my grandfather are doing, I thank you, I thank you both. I hope I can help you in everything that's about to happen, but I hope even more that you and everyone else is wrong about the future."

## II

Jim Dawson had run into trouble almost a hundred miles from St. Louis. He had been caught up in the flow of refugees from that city and the others around and forced to drive further and further north, trying to find a way across the river. He had been forced to run through most of his precious fuel, but had managed to find a station where the owner sold him all the diesel he wanted. The man thought he was being crafty in charging Jim ten dollars a gallon. Jim had gotten even by putting it all on his credit card.

He had found an old bridge just south of Chicago that had been posted as condemned. He had crossed anyway and was soon speeding south and west, trying to avoid cities, and yet still trying to move as fast as he could. He had been stopped a few times, but either his military passes or the M16 had gotten him through.

Hopefully, he would be a survivor.

# III

Long before dawn, the Orion patrol bomber crews had been roused from a sound sleep and ordered to get themselves into the air. After a hasty breakfast and an equally hasty briefing, they found themselves in the air and heading out for an intercept of a Soviet submarine. It had been with but mild surprise that they saw the heavy weapon load they had been issued.

Now two hours later, they could see the sun coming up over the horizon, and looked for the green flash. They didn't see it. As the plane entered its final approach leg, the pilot paged the navigator.

"Will, are we still on course to that sub? Have you gotten a satellite fix yet?"

"Be cool, skipper, the sub's going to be there when we get there! He ought to show up in about fifteen minutes. Look, I don't know what's the matter with the satellites, but we'll be over him, just as planned, no sweat."

The plane was fully illuminated by the sun now, even though the ocean below was still as black as liquid pitch. The Orion seemed to drift, suspended in midair as it flew along its course. The intercom buzzed once more.

"Skipper, this is Sparks," the man said, his voice choked and almost impossible to understand. "I just got a message from base. We're to take out this sub. The Soviets are attacking all along the West German border, skipper. It looks as though we're at war!"

"Did you get a formal confirmation? I don't feel like dropping our eggs into the wrong basket."

"Yessir, skipper. The word came through the AN/SVR-14. Ain't no way the reds can fox that baby! The rest of it I got by eavesdropping."

Switching on the general intercom, the pilot spoke to his whole crew.

"Guys, it looks as though we're going fishing with live bait. That sub we were supposed to shadow will be our first target. I want all the weapons ready to go when I give the word. SONAR, I want you ready with your buoys to track that bastard. We're going to put him down!"

The crew went about their jobs confidently; they were professionals and every move they made showed that. In a matter of a few minutes, the plane had been transformed from its sleepy peacetime routine to utmost readiness for war.

Deep beneath the surface and almost fifty kilometers from the speeding plane, the Soviet submarine captain finished reading the orders for his attack on the United States. At his command, the engines began to turn the sub's propellers, giving him headway for the first time in two weeks. The helmsmen began to shape course toward the distant American coast.

In the Orion, the first reports from the passive sonobuoys were being processed through the on-board computer system. As the SONARmen released their pair of active buoys, the sea was illuminated as if by a giant searchlight. The water was nearly flat, with only a whitecap or two here and there, that showed the sea was actually in motion. Conditions were almost textbook perfect for an attack on a submerged submarine.

Far off on the horizon, a trawler passed unknowingly about its business. A freighter came into view, its phosphorescent wake trailing back over the horizon in arrow straightness. The peace of the scene was about to be interrupted.

"Skipper, we've got him! We're feeding data into the weapons computer now. He gave us the best fix we could ever hope for. He started his engines just as we dropped the active buoys. Just keep right on, as you are now, and drop down to attack altitude."

"Rog. Will do. Make sure that we just have to make one pass. I'd hate to be overhead when that sucker lets loose if we set off his bombs!"

The huge airplane had descended to a height of about a hundred meters as it dashed over the wavecrests, bearing down on the submerged Soviet sub.

Below the surface, the submarine picked up speed.

"Torpedo away, skipper!"

With a slight lurch, the pilot felt the torpedo rocket away from the plane, leaving its zero-length launch rails in a burst of flame. It was one of the new Mark 63 antisubmarine homing torpedoes, and had a range of almost fifty kilometers under rocket power. Once the torpedo was in the water, it would circle until it had a positive SONAR signature of the ship it was supposed to attack, a signature that was programmed into the torpedo just before launch. Once the torpedo was on target, there was very little that would keep it away from the kill. Even as the torpedo was splashing into the water, the pilot was turning away from the area, anxious to avoid being too close to possible nuclear explosions.

"Comrade captain, we have the sounds of an object entering the water! Now there are screw noises; we are under attack!"

The captain calmly gave the order to release a spoofing torpedo.

"High speed screws approaching. The torpedo is in full motion."

The captain snapped the order for the sub to shut down completely, after an abrupt turn to starboard and to dive. Hopefully, the spoofing torpedo, carrying a tape of the sub's own screws and amplifying the sound, would draw the Yankee torpedo off course. In a matter of a minute or two, the crew would know if it would live or die.

"Dammit, skipper! They've shut down and launched a

Fox. I think we might lose them!"

"Like hell! Ready the depth charges, I want that sub and we're going to get it!"

Below the surface, the American torpedo detected the Fox and began to alter course away from the sub. Unfortunately, the submarine passed directly below the torpedo, just at the extremes of the range of the torpedo's magnetic detectors.

Just two years before, the torpedo would have been an impossibility, its electronics too complicated for even the American manufacturers to duplicate in quantity and small enough to fit into the hull of a torpedo. However, a special chip, designed for a child's toy, came onto the market, and a naval engineer just happened to see it in action with a nephew's toy. Within a year, the first issues of the weapon to field units were made.

The Soviet soundman heard the screws suddenly shift in pitch as they changed direction and screamed the word to his captain. The captain immediately ordered the submarine to full speed, hoping to outrun or run the torpedo out of fuel. As he stood there at the con, he lapsed back into the prayers of his childhood. Even seventy years of Soviet rule had failed to totally erase the faith that had helped to shape his childhood.

Before the submarine could do more than start its maneuver, the torpedo struck home, detonating a half-meter from the submarine hull. A lance of flame licked out from the shaped charge warhead and melted through the hard metal. In a bare second, a hole the size of a man's head had been cut through the sub.

As soon as the flame cut its way into the submarine, the pressure of the sea took over, sending a steel-hard rod of water into the hull, smashing through internal compartments and flooding the submarine. The crew rushed away from the impact point and tried to seal the waterproof doors or get through them before they slammed automatically and trapped the men in a watery tomb.

Their efforts were in vain, because the torpedo had struck the engine room, flooding the turbines and shutting them down. Without power, the lighting failed, to be replaced with the red glow of the emergency lights. The submarine could no longer remain afloat and began to sink, stern first, under the weight of the water that poured into the hull.

As the water poured into the stricken submarine, the weight of the water pulled it deeper into the sea, making even more of the ocean pour into the hull. With fiendish cunning, the sea was claiming its own.

The submarine captain, braced against the almost forty-five degree pitch, watched the depth gauge with fascinated dread, knowing that the hull would soon give way under the remorseless pressure of the depths.

He could hear the groaning, grinding sounds that told of the imminent end of his ship echoing through the sub, as the hull was squeezed ever tighter by the sea. Then with a bone-chilling sound, the bulkheads gave way, sending a tube of water as thick as the submarine roaring upward, compressing the air trapped in the hull, pulping the crew, and finally bursting out the very bow of the submarine.

Aboard the Orion aircraft, the crew listened eagerly to the sounds of the torpedo's detonation, then to the sounds of the Soviet submarine settling into its lightless grave. At last, they heard the sounds of the bulkheads blowing out and the ship shattering. The plane erupted with shouts of joy, even as the pilot turned it toward the next target.

On the surface of the sea, the water writhed as bubbles from the submarine popped to the surface, carrying with them the pathetic debris of an undersea wreck. A lifejacket here, a broken wooden case there, and a film of oil that melted under from the force of the wind. In an hour, all trace of a submarine and its crew had vanished.

There were no survivors.

## IV

Above the North Sea and the verdant fields of England, a far different battle was being fought out. On the ground, onlookers could see white contrails tracing their way across the sky, to suddenly intersect and be replaced with the bloom of black flames. In the sky, men fought and died at speeds approaching three times that of sound.

As had been the case with their ancestors of the Battle of Britain in 1940, so again was so much asked of so few, for the Soviets unleashed a force many times in excess of the estimated strength of the enemy, strengths guaranteed by treaties. Overwhelmed, the British defenders were simply swept from the air, though not without taking many of their enemies with them. Even so, some of the attackers got through.

Pure terror attacks were delivered against defenseless cities throughout Great Britain and all of Western Europe.

Coventry was once more destroyed, its monuments to the attacks of 1940 melted into useless lumps of metal as a twenty megaton bomb detonated and leveled the city and the countryside around it.

Rotterdam, rebuilt after its accidental destruction in the Second World War was again set afire as another twenty megaton bomb struck and vaporized the port.

Brussels, Lille, Den Haage, Dunkirk, Versailles with its irreplaceable palace and art treasures, all were hammered flat under the blow of Soviet nuclear weapons. Only Spain and Italy in all of Europe escaped attack.

Even Switzerland was attacked, as was Sweden; there were no neutrals in this war.

The terror attacks that had been intended to break the will to resist in the European nations and to warn America away from the continent failed. Instead, just as in the Second World War, the people were hardened in their determination to carry on. The "decadent democracies" realized the bloody nature of Soviet expansionism and countered it as best they could. In the towns and villages, even as fallout drifted down on the people, prominent communists and their sympathizers were dragged from their homes and murdered.

Few European communists survived.

# THREE

## I

Before dawn the East German border erupted in flames as thousands of guns, rockets, and missiles were fired into the west. Just as in China, the night was made bright by the explosions of thousands of weapons, weapons directed with great skill against the Western troops in their shelters.

They had no better luck than their Chinese counterparts as the enormous weight of shells crashed into their bunkers and collapsed them. Here, also, gas was used in huge quantities killing the unprotected military men and civilians as they stood awaiting the attack.

The huge expenditures of ammunition, easily as great as those in China, but on a front a tenth the length, pulped the Allied defense. Men and women manning the forward outposts were chopped into living hamburger by the shell fragments, then mercifully buried by still more shells. Even armored vehicles were destroyed by the force of the barrage that churned the earth into mud and stripped trees of their limbs. In just four hours, a strip over twenty kilometers wide along the border had been turned into a lunar landscape, pocked with craters, its atmosphere unbreathable.

Finally, the curtains of fire lifted and the stunned defenders came out of their few surviving bunkers, clad in bulky antigas clothing, their faces made hideous by their gas masks. Already some of the units were suffering from the body heat trapped in the suits and the fogging of the gas mask lenses because the antifogging gel didn't work under European conditions.

In front of them, the men could see the green shapes of Soviet tanks moving forward across the churned and torn ground. From forward outposts, the LASER rangefinders reached out to "paint" their targets for the follow-on "smart" shells. The number of shells which crashed onto the advancing Soviets was small, since many of the artillery pieces and their crews had been destroyed or killed in the whirlwind of steel that descended over Germany.

Even so, some of the Soviet tanks had their treads knocked off. Yet another storm of Soviet fire poured down on the Western outposts who had the temerity to show themselves. The survivors looked on with dismay as the "smart" shells bounced off the advancing Soviet tanks like spitballs.

The Soviet tanks were T-80s, made invulnerable by their version of Chobham armor, a composite of metal alloys and ceramics that defeated all conventional shells. Now the problem was simple survival for the advanced Allied units.

The assault streamrolled forward, crushing resistance under its steel treads wherever it was found, and rolling unopposed into the Allied rear. Sporadic fire from the defenders announced that resistance had not been totally eliminated, but even this desperate resistance was smothered under the weight of Soviet artillery and infantry.

The Allied artillery had been reduced to shoot and scoot tactics and strewing the path of the Soviet advance with minelet shells in the hope that they would blow off enough enemy treads and wheels to slow the advance. Unfortunately, because so many of the Allied guns had been destroyed, the number of vehicles damaged remained small.

In the immediate rear of the battle, the Soviet tanks ran wild, crushing and shooting up Allied artillery units, command posts, and supply dumps. The Allied self-propelled artillery was a prime target, because even though the vehicles looked like tanks, they were not tanks, and were easily destroyed by the T-80s.

Further in the rear, immediate attacks had been launched against all the prepositioned equipment depots for American units, against the "igloos" that contained the tactical nuclear warheads, and against the almost unprotected airports. With a single series of attacks, all American reinforcements were disarmed, their tactical strength taken away, and the air cover for every Allied soldier seriously reduced.

In the north, the units under command of NORTHAG were exposed to the Soviet attack, and the Dutch and Belgian Corps simply disintegrated under the steel flail of Soviet artillery. The remainder of the forces, the British Army of the Rhine and the West German I Corps, retreated and extended their flanks northward to guard against Soviet flanking attacks. The retreat was to stop on the banks of the Rhine.

In the far north, the Danish Army, such as it was, had become so deeply involved in defending itself against Soviet amphibious assaults that the units promised to aid the NORTHAG command never arrived. The whole

Soviet weight fell on the West German Sixth *Panzergrenadier* Division; without some support, the West Germans were brushed aside by the torrent of Soviet troops which rushed forward over its positions.

In a matter of hours, a gap over two hundred kilometers wide opened in the Allied lines, a gap that was soon filled by rushing Soviet columns.

In the area controlled by CENTAG and SOUTHAG, the Soviet attack eliminated the American advanced units, leaving only covering forces available to the commanders. Even the West Germans in this area were thrown far back.

By dusk of the first day, the Soviets had penetrated over fifty kilometers deep into West Germany in the south, while in the north, they were driving straight for the Rhine, with nothing able to stop them. Even at night, Soviet units rolled forward.

## II

The war at sea had raged from the instant of the Soviet attack. Submarine hunted submarine beneath the seas, and thousands of men disappeared into black watery graves, their only tombstone a froth of bubbles on the surface which was blown away in the winds.

The American aircraft carrier *America* was steaming at full speed through Atlantic waters, simultaneously launching and landing its aircraft, and keeping a constant barrage of electronic countermeasures protecting its charges. On deck and below, aircraft were being refueled and rearmed, and thrown back into the air. The constant effort had paid off so far, for although the *America* had been exposed to a half dozen Soviet attacks that day, the enemy had never managed to penetrate the defensive ring that surrounded the ship.

The most dangerous threat had been a force of

Tu-160 maritime control aircraft that had left Murmansk hours before and refueled over the Atlantic. The aircraft had approached the carrier under the cover of heavy jamming and, without the satellites that had been lost to Soviet attacks, the *America* had taken a chance and scrambled its combat air patrol to an interception north and west of the fleet. In the attack that grew out of the intercept, half of the Soviet bombers had been downed and the rest sent streaking for home. Unfortunately, the bombers had dropped their cruise missiles which were flying directly for the fleet.

Jamming and interceptor attacks managed to destroy or misdirect all of the cruise missiles, putting them into the sea so that their weapons detonated far from the fleet. The only casualty of the attack was the escorting destroyer *Kelley*, which had been battered into uselessness by a blast from the Soviet weapons.

Now, late in the afternoon, a Soviet "Papa"-class submarine, hidden from detection by a combination of thermal currents and the total loss of American ocean surveillance satellites, crept toward the fleet. With much careful maneuvering and some luck, the submarine came to firing depth well within easy launch distance of the fleet.

As soon as the submarine released its cruise missiles, it dove back into the sheltering depths of the sea, but not before it had been detected by an antisubmarine helicopter. Even as the pilot reported the launch of the cruise missiles, he was attacking the Soviet submarine. A Mk. 63 torpedo was dropped and successfully attacked the submarine.

Alerted by the reports of the helicopter, the fleet made radical alterations in its course, trying to avoid a cluster of ships that would be easy to destroy, and at the same time trying to remain under the protective umbrella of the *America's* electronics and aircraft. In spite of the warning, the *America* risked launching its remaining ready aircraft and then sealed itself off from attack.

Out on the edge of the protective ring around the carrier, the destroyer *Momsen* had the misfortune to turn its gun control RADAR on while it was in the path of a homing cruise missile. Before the single five inch gun on the ship could fire more than a few rounds, the missile passed over the *Momsen* and detonated, high in the air.

The explosion slammed downward like a giant fist against the sea, crushing the unarmored ship under its force. The crew was already dying from the neutron flux that the explosion put out. Before the shattered *Momsen* could sink beneath the surface, the heat of the blast melted the aluminum plates of the superstructure and made them flow like water. The sea began to boil as the hapless ship sank beneath the waves.

The aircraft which formed the bulk of the fleet's defenses attacked the cruise missiles with their own snapdown missiles, striking against their enemy even as they dropped down to wave-top altitude. The two surviving cruise missiles continued to rocket toward the American fleet.

As the two surviving missiles closed in on the fleet, the aircraft carrier directed all of its jamming capacity against the approaching enemy, filling the air with jamming and, as the missiles streaked closer, with chaff rockets fired by the protective screen of ships. One of the missiles flew near a burst of antiaircraft fire from a Mark 71 eight-inch gun, and, as it passed beyond the cloud of smoke that marked the burst, watchers could see the missile wobble erratically, then suddenly plunge into the sea.

The final missile was far too close to the *America* for any normal effort. One of the F-14s from the carrier, piloted by Lieutenant (JG) Ann Brewster, began a long, hard tail chase with the missile, her ammunition expended in downing another of the dodging missiles. Observers in the *America's* combat information center reported that, two minutes from impact on their ship, the two blips on their display merged, then disappeared as a gallant flyer sacrificed her life for her shipmates.

## III

The Soviet Indian Ocean fleet made the mistake of bunching far too closely together as it assembled after leaving its base at Bazarute, off the coast of Mozambique, for strikes against the American base at Diego Garcia.

Guided to the assembly of Soviet vessels by a long-range patrol bomber which shadowed the Soviet fleet, a series of cruise missiles were launched from the American base and directed toward the Soviets.

Without air cover, the Soviets were forced to rely on their own RADAR, and that RADAR was swamped under the jamming from the shadowing American patrol bomber at just the right moment. By the time the Soviets made visual identifications of the approaching missiles, it was too late to do anything, their countermeasures taking out only three of the missiles.

The other four American missiles reached their designated target area and detonated. The four hundred kiloton blast from the weapons wiped most of the Soviet threat in the Indian Ocean from that sea.

Elsewhere, though, the battle wasn't going nearly as well.

## IV

Under the Pacific Ocean, now so tragically misnamed, dozens of Soviet submarines sailed boldly toward their designated launch points for an attack on the American west coast. As they sailed, they unknowingly entered the area protected by the American Trans-Pacific Defense Line.

The defense line consisted of twenty deep submergence installations planted years before by the *Hughes Glomar Explorer* under the cover of a recovery operation on a sunken Soviet sub. In actual fact, the cranes on the *Explorer* were far too small to lift the submarine, but they were large enough to plant the twelve-hundred ton installations accurately on the ocean floor.

Each of the units had been designed to give fifty years of service, and drew their power from a powered-down nuclear reactor. For years the stations were designed to wait until they were activated by a coded signal. Until that time, they listened to the ocean around them and released buoys that drifted far with the currents, then transmitted their data, and received new programs by very low frequency transmissions.

The presidential order brought them to full alert and in just a few hours, the installations were ready to deal with any enemy vessel within their hundred kilometer range.

The Soviet missile submarines cruised unknowingly into range, and, as they crossed the deadline of each unit, torpedoes were launched that destroyed over three quarters of the Soviet subs. The remainder escaped and continued on toward America.

## FOUR

### I

Night in Europe failed to bring peace anywhere in the continent. Battles still flared around the airports that Soviet paratroopers had seized on their morning jumps on the first day.

On the main battlefields, patrols from both sides probed through the darkness, trying to find their opponent's positions and his strength. Sensors would be planted all through the area, by hand where possible, by artillery fire when they were available.

The battles that raged that night were short, sharp, and bloody as the patrols from either side, clad in their heavy antigas equipment, met and fought to the death.

A unit from the First Battalion, Argyll and Sutherland Highlanders, probed northward in the darkness to try to link up with the remains of a Belgian battalion supposedly somewhere in the area. The night was broken by the crack of artillery and the sudden harsh light of flares, as the Highlanders walked into a Soviet ambush.

In a matter of minutes, the surprised Highlanders had joined in the firefight with their traditional gusto, all the while attempting to turn the enemy flank. The sudden detonation of a grenade in one of the enemy machinegun nests sent the men forward, ducking from cover to cover, alternately running forward and hiding behind cover supporting their mates with their fire.

In a matter of minutes, the Highlanders could see the Soviets breaking and running across the battlefield, pursued by the bright tracers from the captured machineguns. Their triumph was short lived, though, as the crash of 120mm mortar bombs sounded throughout the area they had just captured. The men withdrew in what order they could, taking most of their dead with them.

To the south, Soviet units moved forward into the area defended by the American troops with relative ease. The men who should have arrived and been armed from the prepositioned stocks were unarmed, because their weapons stores had been eliminated by the Soviets. With the destruction wrought on the green American troops, there were very few coherent units remaining.

The men at the front were beginning to melt away under cover of darkness and walk into the rear, heading for some place that would hide them from the battle.

In Austria, the brutal Soviet occupation forces were once more in the country, indulging in their customary looting, raping and murdering. The Austrian Eastern Division had attempted to hold on the line of Vienna, but had been eliminated under the assault of five Soviet and Hungarian divisions. Soviet marines had even stormed the city of Vienna itself, sailing up the Danube and capturing the vital bridges. The remains of the army had retreated north and west, toward the West German border where, after linking up with a West German mountain brigade, they dug in to secure NATO's flank.

## II

Long before dawn on the second day, Soviet units were storming ashore from their assault boats in the cities of Venice and Bari, crossing the Adriatic from their bases in Yugoslavia. North of Venice, the poorly equipped and badly trained Italian army melted away under an attack that would make the disaster of Caporetto resemble a children's game.

The men were gassed and blasted into flight, and kept moving by the lash of Soviet ground attack aircraft that seemed to roam freely over the whole front. Without antigas equipment, the Italians were doomed.

In the city of Venice itself, marine fought to the death with marine, as the crack men of the Italian *Lagunari* Regiment fought in the collapsing ruins of Doge's Palace and slum apartment. No matter how bitter the resistance, the end was clearly in sight, because the Italians were outnumbered, outgunned, and exposed to almost unopposed air attack.

The *Ariete* Armored Division, descendant of the unit

that fought alongside the *Afrika Korps* so well for so long, was pushing its way through passes and roads choked with refugees, civilian and military, who blocked its route. The *Ariete* had already taken heavy losses from Soviet aircraft, losing a third of its strength, including most of its artillery, after downing only two Soviet planes. The *Ariete* had been ordered into the battle in Venice.

As the division broke out onto the empty plains that surrounded the city, it began to deploy, and was immediately attacked by swarms of Su-25 Stormovik aircraft which shot the tanks into shreds. On that open ground, in the dash to the city, the *Ariete* was reduced to barely three battalions.

The attacking Soviet aircraft disappeared as suddenly as they had appeared, and were replaced with huge transports, loaded with paratroopers from Irkutsk. As the planes passed overhead, the drone drowning out all hopes of normal speech, they began to spill out hundreds of camouflaged parachutes with men and cargo attached.

With the shout of "*Avanti Ariete!*", the surviving men of the division surged forward and planted themselves in the very center of the Soviet dropzone, and waited. As the paratroopers descended, the Italians began blasting them from the air, partial revenge for all the losses they had suffered.

Even with the slaughter, the Soviets never stopped their drop. Parachute after parachute fell downward with men dangling at the end of the shrouds. Some of them survived to reach the ground, and as the paras gathered their wits and their weapons, they counterattacked against the battered armored division.

The battle surged back and forth across the dropzone, an area a little more than twenty kilometers on a side, as each side tried to eliminate the other. By nightfall, the

*Ariete*, reinforced by some of the *Lagunari* that had managed to break out of the city of Venice, held its final muster. One tank, three APCs, and 215 men responded.

All around them, waiting for the dawn to attack, was a force made up of a Soviet parachute division, a marine brigade, and the bulk of a motorized rifle division. There would be no Italian survivors.

## III

In Siberia, an infiltration battalion from the People's Liberation Army was fleeing north under heavy Soviet pressure, after their attempt to sever the Trans-Siberian railroad had failed. Now, all the men cared about was finding a place where they could make a final stand and sell their lives dearly.

One of the reconnaissance patrols reported they had detected a heavily defended Soviet installation right on the line of march. Taking only a minute to make his decision, the Chinese commander ordered his men to attack, reasoning that if the Soviets were guarding an installation out in the wilderness that heavily, it must be valuable, and therefore if he could destroy it, he would have dealt the Soviets a serious blow. Certainly, if nothing else, the men would earn a worthy death attacking it.

The troops, hungry and exhausted after days of harrowing flight through the pine forests of Siberia, fanned out through the trees and crawled toward the barbed guard wire. The two surviving mortars were set up to breach the wire obstacle, and, with the tinny blare of the commander's bugle, the attack began. The sound of bugles echoed eerily through the trees, accompanied by the sound of squad leaders' whistles and heavy firing. The flat *crump!* of exploding mortar bombs announced the elimination of the barbed wire.

The Chinese rushed through the remains of the fence, machinegunning and grenading the Soviet soldiers who stood in their way. Their mortars were now attacking the entrances to underground Soviet bunkers, smashing them open. The battle was over in a few minutes as the desperate Chinese shot, stabbed, and clubbed their enemies to death.

The sounds of battle slowly died away as the last of the Soviet troops were routed out of their shelters and killed. The Chinese commander was already looking at the smashed entrance to a concealed installation, as his engineers were already pulling the twisted door open so he could go in. One of the men pulled a metal plaque off the wall for a souvenir. His commander took it to show his superiors what he had eliminated. Perhaps, had he been able to read the cyrillic characters on the plaque, he might not have been so eager to enter the shelter.

The sign read: *State Biological Warfare Station Number 45.* In the now half-blackened corridors below, the Chinese looked with curiosity into laboratories behind now-shattered glass at racks filled with nutrient solutions that contained all the plagues known to man, and some that weren't. Had they known, they would have seen the signs telling them of the dangers of cholera, Lasa and Magdeburg fevers, anthrax, and a deadly new agent, Bubonic-X.

Bubonic-X was a product of Soviet biotailoring, and combined all the deadliness of normal bubonic plague with a deadly new twist. The victim could be infected and not show any sign of it, walking about, spreading the germs, until twelve hours later, he fell over, dead. Mortality, as tested on convicts, was one hundred percent, even with the best of medical care. The only saving grace was, that if the disease couldn't find a host within a half-hour, it died.

Back on the surface, the Chinese soldiers had found a

helicopter. Bundling himself and the political advisers into the copter, the commander said farewell to his men. He ordered the pilot to keep low to the ground and head for China as fast as he could.

As they flew, they could see, rising over a range of hills that protected them from the blast, a mushroom cloud rising from where the Soviets had eliminated a possible epidemic.

## III

"Mr. President, we've finally contacted Premier Davidov on the hot line. Do you still want to speak with him?"

"Yes, I do."

The president picked up the telephone and listened to the sounds of electronic hissing and crackling.

"Davidov, are you there?"

"Yes, Matthews, I am," the premier replied, with a chuckle in his voice. "Are you still on ground zero?"

"Davidov, you bastard, why are you attacking us? What can you hope to gain? You know you can't win a clean victory now. I . . ."

"You have made the same mistake that so many other presidents have made, Matthews. You believe that we will keep the letter and the spirit of our agreements. You were wrong. Communism is destined to expand into the vacuum that will result from the elimination of the decadent democracies, and we shall emerge from our shelters to extend our domination over the entire world.

"You, poor fools that you are, believed us and believed that the very concept of nuclear war is too horrible for us to even contemplate. You were wrong, because we believe we can strike now, before either the West or the East is strong enough to resist us, and strike with a reasonable chance of success. We are willing to sacrifice ninety percent of our people, provided the ten percent who survive are the most loyal and fanatic communists we can find.

"You have one option. Immediate, unconditional surrender and occupation of the West. Otherwise, I will not call back the bombers that are even now streaking across the North Pole to deliver your deathblow, nor stop the launch of our missiles. You must answer right now, or I shall order the launch of our strategic missile forces.

"*Answer!*," Davidov roared.

"I refuse your despicable terms. If you threaten us with destruction, I also threaten you with destruction. The Soviet navy is being wiped from the seas, the air force from the skies, and army from the land. You, sir, must capitulate!"

A strange sound came from the telephone. The president listened for a moment before he realized what the sound was. Davidov was laughing!

The president resumed speaking.

"History will be a harsh judge of your actions, Davidov, because the guilt for thousands, no, millions of deaths, now and in the future will be placed squarely on your shoulders. How can you accept the horror of this?"

"You are being both stupid and ignorant, Mr. Matthews. The great Stalin did not hesitate to excise twenty million people in the purges, nor did he shrink from the loss of another twenty million people in driving out the Nazis. You forget that history is written by the victor, not the vanquished. You will have no historian left to recount your final minutes. Goodbye, *Gospodin* Matthews."

The telephone on the other end slammed into its cradle, leaving the president with a uselessly buzzing handset emitting a whining, buzzing noise. With shaking hands, he dropped the telephone and picked up the red phone that instantly connected him with every nuclear-armed part of the American arsenal. In a calm, almost detached voice, he gave the order to fire all missiles and launch the bombs, then, gently, he returned the telephone to its cradle.

The president slumped back into his chair, knowing that he had just pronounced the doom of the world as he knew it. He picked up the bottle of painkillers that he had saved for the last few weeks. He knew just how many would be a fatal dose. He carefully lined up the pills in soldierly, precise rows, then filled his waterglass with bourbon, picked up a handful of pills, and washed them down with the whiskey.

He collapsed across his blotter before the last pill was consumed.

## IV

With the confirmation of their authority to attack, the huge, obsolete B-52 bombers turned away from the holding patterns and streaked for their launch points. In a matter of a few hours, hundreds of cruise missiles would be flying through Soviet airspace, each tipped with a deadly two hundred kiloton warhead. The problem was that the bombers had to get into position for the launch.

Far from the rendezvous points, a horde of top-secret Soviet Su-30 Backfire fighters waited for their authority to use their increased avionics and snap-down missile capacity to kill the enemy bombers threatening their homeland. Even before the premier had slammed his phone down, the planes were released.

A swarm of missiles, like deadly bees, flew down at the rendezvous points and detonated in the midst of the circling bombers. Few of the planes were even damaged by the bomb itself, but the shock wave that boiled outward from the explosion was an entirely different matter. Bombers were slapped from the sky like some noisy mosquitos, splitting open and spilling their contents and crews into the empty sky as wings were torn away.

Aircraft commanders on the fringes of the attack nosed their aging hulks over into high-speed dives in an effort to escape the shock wave, trying to lose themselves in the protective shelter of ground clutter which would confuse the Soviet RADAR defenses. A few of the planes actually made it to their launch points, almost twenty percent. None of them came home.

# FIVE

## I

Aboard the Backfire and Tu-160 bombers which were approaching the still-frozen coastline of North America, the crews relaxed for the first time since their takeoff. Their flight paths were now cleared of interceptors, ever since RADAR-homing cruise missiles had taken out the last vestiges of the NORAD RADAR line. Loaded to the maximum with weapons and fuel, the bombers would strike against the enemy's heartland with impunity. The great American population centers were spread naked to the attack, especially since the false alert had trapped most of the people in the cities. Soon, the city would be a cenotaph for the vanished American people.

The first attacks had been pressed home successfully by bombers and intermediate range missiles operating from their bases in Cuba, their bases secured by the troops of the "training brigade" the trusting Americans had allowed to remain in Cuba.

In an arc that extended as far north as Atlanta and as far west as Houston, city after city paid for allowing the budget cutters to work freely in removing defenses that "might never be used, and are therefore not cost effective."

There were no surface-to-air missiles, no flak, and no antiballistic missile defenses. There were just 267 aircraft to defend a whole continent, and there were but eighty crews to man them. The rest of the men whom the air force had counted on were being shipped to Europe. The men left behind were appalled at the condition of the overage, virtually condemned aircraft they were given to fly, but still launched themselves into battle, downing dozens of Soviet aircraft, until they were themselves eliminated.

Within the space of a few hours, all American cities with populations of more than fifty thousand had been attacked with nuclear weapons. The Soviets didn't hesitate to use their fifty or even hundred megaton bombs against the American megalopoli. They wanted to make sure that there would never be any serious American resistance again.

American units had not been idle. As soon as the missile bases received their orders, they had launched their Minuteman missiles into screaming flight against the Soviet Union. As the missiles leaped out of their underground silos, they were washed with bright yellow flame from their own exhausts, showing the shimmering metal plating that covered them and protected them from the Soviet LASERs. The Soviet missile defenses had already been eliminated under the crush of incoming cruise missiles.

In Europe, the militarily bankrupt Allied forces used their remaining tactical nuclear weapons in desperate efforts to stop the Soviet steamroller, while the Soviets responded in kind and dumped thousands of tons of more and more deadly chemicals into the European theater.

In Asia, a helicopter-load of death made it back to a Chinese base against all odds, where the contagion spread out like wildfire, affecting Chinese and Soviet alike, spilling over other national borders as though they never existed. In a day, half the population of Asia was affected; in the next twelve hours, the population of Asia was dead, and the plague was spreading through Africa and war-torn Europe.

In sixty hours, the war came to a halt, both sides too exhausted to do more than launch spasmodic attacks against one another. The Soviet hierarchy had been almost totally eliminated when their shelters became prime targets. The people in the cities had been attacked, but not wiped out. Instead, their leaders had died.

The plague which raced around the world killed everyone who survived the bombs, horribly. Even in Africa, untouched by either side, millions died as the plague caused the people to sicken and die. Most died fighting, releasing old tribal hatreds, and in-fighting against the oppression of hundreds of years of exploitation.

All along the Mediterranean littoral, the two sides fought, the restraints of the superpowers removed, as the plague killed their people. The remaining Arab nations struck with all their might against the Israelis and the Egyptians, even using their few precious nuclear weapons. Both Israel and Egypt responded in kind, and launched their dying armies against their killers.

Man and his permanent works was disappearing from the earth.

## II

Jack Dawson had made his home as fallout-proof as possible. Like all the houses on the farm, furniture and beds had been carted down into the basements, while everything else had been cleared out of the first floor. Plastic sheets had been spread on the polished wooden floors, and dirt, tons of it, moved in and spread out on the floors until it was two feet deep. Below, timber props reinforced the floors and held the protective soil from crashing through onto the people it was supposed to protect. Even the outsides of the houses were protected with earth banks that shielded against fallout.

In the ill-lit basement of their home, Jack, his family, and his friends listened in as the world ended. Someone once asked how the world would end, and answered his own rhetorical question by saying with a whimper. He was wrong; the world ended with screams and sobs.

In Paris, the Seine flowed into a cauldron where it boiled and hissed, and around the charred chancre on the earth's face, tumbled heaps of masonry, ruined parks, and even the half-melted, twisted remains of a great iron tower thrust upward precariously against the gravity that threatened to pull them down.

London had been spared the horrors of a ground burst weapon, and the survivors managed to avoid being choked to death on the clouds of dust thrown up by the explosions. Instead, London cooked in the flash of nuclear disaster fires which kindled in the ancient heart of the city of London; fires which, unlike those of the blitz, raged out of control in a matter of hours. The close-packed wooden houses and housing estates began to crackle and burn, and the winds howled through the streets. Those few people who sought safety in the subways crouched lower and prayed as the howling winds rose into the demonic shrieks of a crazed god, a god of destruction bent on leveling all of man's works. For some, the flow of carbon dioxide brought a swift, painless death as consciousness slipped away, while others, closer in, exploded their lungs as the firestorm pulled the air out of their shelters. A firestorm raged over London, just as firestorms had raged over Occupied Europe, and nobody really gave a damn.

Moscow, long prepared for attack, was in its shelters or evacuated. In the great tunnels of the Moscow subway, specifically designed to protect against attack, some of the people managed to live for as long as three weeks before hunger and thirst drove them out into a devastated city, where radiation and man-made plagues took their toll. Few of the survivors would remember the great victory of Socialism.

Jack and Adam Henderson were the only ones who watched as the world died before them in the television screens. The signals, carried by satellites, lasted long enough for them to videotape what was happening; the rest of the horror was recorded on tape recorders. The cities of the United States died, in no particular order, as the Soviet missiles descended. For an hour or two, one would survive, its missile either impacting far from the target, or having been lost in the launch process or whatever quirk of fate driven by a capricious god kept some people alive while their neighbors died. But these cities weren't spared for long. As soon as the Soviets had reloaded their launchers (something the SALT negotiators had gotten the Soviets to solemnly promise not to do), these cities died.

Pity the poor people downwind of the missile fields, for they died smothered like the people of ancient Pompeii in the dust of their world's end. The only effective method of taking out a buried missile silo is to detonate the nuclear weapon at or below ground level. The result was a volcano of dust, some of it, most of it, radioactive, that drifted downwind; a thousand missile silos, a thousand Mt. St. Helens of dust.

Most of the stations faded from the air as the day wore on, replaced by silence as the stations were vaporized, or because the surviving operators realized their transmissions made them prime targets. Most of the people simply walked off the job and drove to their homes, to die with their families; why stay at a radio or television station when, in a few hours, there won't be enough power to transmit, or enough of an audience to listen. This was one time when audience share ceased to have meaning to the executives.

A few radio hams remained on the air in unlikely spots. One man up on the North Cape of Norway transmitted for nearly a year before his supplies ran out. No one paid attention to him because he was stark, staring mad. One man stayed behind in the suburbs of Los Angles because he couldn't have gotten away in any case. He was paralyzed from the waist down. He stayed at his transmitter continuously, for nearly fifteen hours, before the constant internal hemorrhage killed him. Some people even found out that their familes survived the initial attack, small comfort that that was.

Finally, the air waves quieted, with only the sounds of military transmissions, most in code, that rattled like hail on a metal roof through the night. A few stark messages came across, like the air base commander whose aircraft had all been destroyed on the field, who kept begging a non-existent Pentagon for new orders.

More poignant were the transmissions from the men manning a RADAR station on the far north coast of Canada. They were sending their last messages to families who had, in all probability, preceded them in death.

Jack sat as still as a statue in front of his radios, but statues don't cry, don't send streams of salty water down their cheeks. With a snarl, Jack shut the radios off with a slap of his hand, and, standing up so quickly he knocked his stool over, stumbled off to his cot.

# III

Jim Dawson had heard about the bombings over his car radio as he drove toward the farm. There was nothing he, nor anybody else could do to reduce the human misery that was spreading across the land.

He saw a smudge far away, up on the horizon, where the road disappeared into some hills. As he drove closer, he saw the burnt-out wreck of a car with a bus beside it. As he came closer, he saw the cause: a motorcycle gang had ambushed a school bus. The young girls were running for their lives across the fields. Some of them had been caught and Jim could see what was happening to one of the prizes.

Hitting his brakes and killing the ignition, Jim leaped out of the car as it rolled to a stop, his bag of ammunition in one hand, his M16 in the other. Dropping the bag to the ground, Jim took aim and casually blew the skull off the nearest biker, collapsing the body onto his victim, whose incoherent screams, if possible, grew even louder.

With the skill of the practiced marksman, Jim began to kill the bikers around him, cursing his rifle all the time, since it didn't give him enough range to do a proper job. Some of the men began to return fire, so Jim scooped up his ammunition and ran into the cover of a roadside ditch.

Finally, after much firing back and forth, Jim was hit in the left shoulder and thrown back into the ditch. Gathering up their courage, the bikers charged Jim, their hobnailed boots ringing on the concrete.

Jim couldn't have wished for a better situation. He listened to the sounds of racing footsteps as they crossed the first concrete lane, then disappeared as they went out onto the grassy divider. As soon as Jim heard them step out onto the second concrete strip, he stood up and threw his grenades out into the road.

The explosions and scything fragments cut the gang to ribbons, slicing through flesh as easily as through the filth-encrusted colors the men wore. The gang broke and ran back to their bikes and roared away.

A wave of giddiness washed over Jim, and he slid back against the side of the ditch. Here and there, Jim could hear the crack of guns as the schoolchildren, suddenly thrust into a terrifyingly adult world, gathered up the fallen biker's guns and finished the men off. Jim tried to stuff a clean handkerchief into his wound to stop the flow of blood. All the strain of pulling the pins on the grenades had torn his wound open even further.

A shadow fell across him, and Jim looked up, startled. A woman stood over him, her clothes torn and blood-stained, with a pistol in her hand. The look of pure hatred and rage on her face froze Jim onto the spot.

"You're the one who helped us, aren't you? I really don't know how to thank you. Let me help you," she said, sliding down the bank into the ditch, "that wound looks bad.

"By the way," she said, smiling and holding out her hand, "I'm Janice Wilson, of the Wilson School."

Jim knew that the woman was in deep shock; he'd seen it before in combat where men had been stressed beyond their capacity and the pressure suddenly let up. They acted almost normally, until you looked into their eyes and saw the boiling insanity that was just below the surface. The facade that the young woman was showing the world could collapse without warning into blazing action.

"My name's Jim Dawson," he said, reaching out to the girl's hand. "I was driving back home when I saw what had happened. Did we get rid of them all?"

"Oh, were you speaking to me? I think we saw them all go away. What happened, Mr. Dawson? We heard about bombings and then the radio cut off . . ."

"Ms. Wilson," Jim said gently, "the world we knew just went up in smoke. The Soviets attacked us with nuclear weapons and apparently took out most of our cities."

"Impossible!" she snapped, "everybody knows that if there was a nuclear war, we'd all die instantly."

"Not quite. We're still alive."

That stopped the girl for a minute, she sat back against the side of the ditch in silence. After a moment's thought, she began to rearrange her clothes. Jim looked at the girl carefully. Her face was too strong to be called beautiful, yet there was a certain attraction, even in his condition, in her dark beauty. She couldn't have been much more than twenty-five, and had just gone through some of the worst experiences that any woman could face. Small wonder she was confused.

Jim pushed himself upright and tried to climb the steep dirt wall. Janice stood up and helped him up to the top.

"Listen to me, Janice," he said, speaking slowly and clearly so that she could understand. "I think I can get the bus out of the wreckage. If I can, you can drive anywhere you want, even come back home with me. Just stay out of the open air for a couple of weeks, that's all. Now go out and gather your girls up and try to get them straightened out. I've got some clothes and some medicine in my trunk. Just take my keys and get them out, okay?"

The girl nodded, as if in a dream, then took Jim's keys and walked off toward the car. Jim watched to make sure she was all right, then turned away and walked over to the bus. Inside the doors, he saw the driver, an elderly man, slumped over the wheel, his chest a bloody ruin from a bullet that had smashed through the windshield. Jim put down his rifle and started to drag the body out of the seat. As he did, he heard a soft cry for help from a very young voice. Looking around, he saw a girl, no more than twelve years old, lying in a pool of blood under the seats. She looked just like his Melody.

Jim picked her up and looked at her. A slug had clipped her head, knocking her out and making her bleed a lot, but not killing her. Jim held her as he wiped the blood away with water from a half-broken picnic cooler on the floor.

He put the girl down on one of the seats and went back to his grisly task of moving the body out of the bus. He finally managed to get the man under the arms and begin to drag him out. Just as he stepped to the ground, Jim saw a biker standing alongside the bus, his chest covered with blood and the white ribs showing through the tatters of flesh. The man was aiming a pistol at Jim. Even as he lifted the man's dead body up as a shield, the biker fired.

Jim watched in wonder as time seemed to telescope. He could see the muzzle belch flame and even the bullet as it crossed the short space between the two men. The slug hit Jim in the chest and threw him backward, sprawling into the road. *Funny,* he thought, *it doesn't hurt a bit!*

Blazing pain cut through his body and centered in his torn chest. Jim turned his head toward the biker just in time to see the man topple forward toward him and fall into the dust like some giant redwood. Jim could see a little girl standing behind the biker, her pistol smoking. He chuckled and then winced in pain. He looked back toward his chest and saw the blood pouring out.

The little girl walked over to him and looked down. Jim could see tears appear for the first time that terrible day and run down her face. He tried to speak to her, to reach his hand out to her, but his body just wouldn't respond.

*I'm dying!*

His vision faded, like looking through the wrong end of a telescope. Janice Wilson's face appeared in front of him, swooping closer to him with lightning speed. He could hear her whispering to him and tried to tell her to speak up.

Janice had heard the pistol shot from over near the bus and ran over as fast as she could, her own gun firmly clasped in her hand. Before she got to the bus, she heard a second shot and ran up just in time to see a blood-dripping biker fall forward, almost on top of Jim Dawson, as little Sue Johnson shot the man.

Janice ran to Jim Dawson's side and stared with horrified fascination at the wound in his chest. The blood was beginning to fountain out of the wound, jetting up into the air with each beat of his heart. She thrust her fingers into the hole, leaned close to Jim and shouted into his ear.

"We'll get you a doctor! The State Police will be here soon, I know it! We'll help you."

She looked at Jim's face, now a dirty gray color, beaded with icy sweat, and knew that there was no hope for the man who had given his life rescuing her and the girls. She saw his lips move and leaned closer, pressing her ear to his lips to catch every word.

"Map ... car ... way home," he gasped, "tell 'em ..."

His voice trailed off, even as his heartbeat stopped. Janice blinked away a sudden rush of tears and pulled her bloody hand away from Jim's chest. Her clothes were covered with blood, mostly the blood of a perfect stranger who didn't stop to ask questions, but helped her and the girls. Now he was dead and instinctively Janice knew the truth, the world had really come to an end.

While she sat sobbing beside the body, a police car,

its sirens whooping and lights flashing, roared past the girls who tried to flag it down. Their only answer was an empty scotch bottle thrown at them.

Janice vowed then that she and the girls would survive.

## IV

The guards at the training base stood in their sentry boxes forlornly, in shock ever since the news had come through about the devastating attacks on America and the Soviet Union. As the story spread, some of the men went over the hill, trying to get back to their homes and find their families. Most of the men were from the cities.

The general had ordered the men confined to their barracks or locked into shelters, and gave the guards strict orders to shoot to kill any person who tried to get away. Then he countermanded his order and had all the men assemble on the parade ground. They listened as the general rambled on and on about duty and staying on the base. He began to rave.

Finally, the colonel stood up and tried to take the man's arm. The general pulled away and shoved the colonel back into his seat. Then he tried to pull his pistol out of its holster and began screaming about deserters and traitors and shot his pistol into the crowd. The colonel stepped up behind the general and shot him dead. He reached down and pulled the mike out from under the body and spoke calmly into it.

"Go home now, kids. There's nothing left for you to do here anymore."

The young men and women stood there and watched while the colonel from Chicago put his pistol into his mouth and pulled the trigger.

# FIVE

## I

In Europe, the survivors of the two armies fought on in the chemical-laced radioactive fog. Neither side had anything left to fight for, except to make sure that the people who killed their homelands died.

The nuclear exchange had been relatively light, but the wide-spread use of chemicals and the sudden appearance of bubonic plague had finished off the survivors. The Black Death once again stalked throughout Europe, and this time there were too few people left to bury the dead. There would be no fortunate fire to save the people this time.

From North Cape to Good Hope, from Portugal to Japan, the stillness of the grave settled over the land, the population killed in an accidental loosing of the plague.

## II

Far below the surface in the former *Bundesmarine* command bunker, a motley assortment of men in stained and worn uniforms gathered. They were survivors from all nations, gathered in here just before the biological weapons had been used.

Most of the men knew that their shelter had been breached by a lucky detonation of an enemy missile. The result was that the concrete had shattered, and despite the best efforts of the repair crews, the exterior air was leaking in unless the shelter kept a high pressure inside to force the outside air out. The result was that the men could calculate, almost to the hour, when their reserve pressurizing air would be exhausted.

The admiral walked up to the podium and addressed the men.

"Most of you men know that we will all die within the next few days, either from the plague or from the fallout and gas that fills the air. You also know who released the plague into the world when their invasion of China failed.

"Most of you are not Americans; even though I am the senior officer present, I have no authority over any of you. What I have to propose is, therefore, a suggestion, and every person present here has the option to volunteer or not as his or her conscience dictates. We have detected radio signals from the Soviet city of Leningrad, as well as from Riga. We know that the enemy survives in these cities.

"What I propose is that we take some of the nuclear weapons stored in an undamaged 'igloo' near here, place them aboard a ship, and deliver the weapons to our enemy's heartland.

"Those of you who do not wish to participate in this action are free to go to the dispensary and be issued pills that will put you to sleep. The rest, those who will take part in the attack, will remain here and listen to the attack plan."

No one left the room. Everyone listened to the admiral as he detailed the plan of attack, then broke up into small groups to begin detailed planning for their particular part of the operation.

## III

The Soviet weapons officer listened as his commander detailed the second strike his ship would launch against America. Unnoticed, he edged out of his station and walked aft to the weapons lockers. Using his keys, he broke into the locker and took an assault rifle and plenty of ammunition with him. Then he walked aft to the engine room, where he closed and sealed the watertight doors.

In the next few bloody minutes, he hunted down and killed the entire engineroom crew, then turned to the control panel. He had listened to the reports of plague and knew it was a Soviet weapon; his brother-in-law had worked on the project. He also knew the Americans had not launched the attacks that devastated the world, and had sworn that he would be responsible for no more deaths.

At the control panel, he used the controls that pulled the moderator rods out of the reactor core, causing the reaction to speed up and release much more radiation. Even though the reactor would not explode, the radiation would be enough to kill everyone on the submarine.

Even as he worked, he could hear the sounds of the other crewmen as they pounded on the sealed doors. He opened the valve on one of the air lines, raising the pressure in the engine room to the point where, even if the others managed to unseal the door, they could never push it open against the pressure. He yawned and his ears popped as the pressure built up.

As soon as the rods had been fully withdrawn, he shot the controls into sparking rubble with his gun and walked over to the reactor fueling hatches and the inspection hatches. These gave direct access to the reactor, and could also give the radiation access to the interior of the submarine itself.

He could feel the radiation passing through the thin shielding, striking his skin like the sun on the Black Sea beaches near his home. He knew that this sunburn was going to be the last he ever felt, especially as the fierce blue glow from the radiation bombarding the air itself appeared as a shimmering curtain that covered everything as it burnt out his optic nerves.

He had just enough time to set his explosives over the motors that opened the reactor doors and string the detonator back to a place behind a huge piece of machinery before all his vision disappeared. Feeling his way back to the doors, he started the motors that swung them open, then crawled back behind his sheltering machinery. Absently, he rubbed the back of his hand to stop the itch, and felt the skin slicken as the blood from countless burst vessels oozed through his skin.

He heard the sound of a high-speed drill over the noise from the door motors. The fools had finally figured out how he was keeping the door closed. He knew that the metal of the bulkhead hatch would hold them back until he finished his job. He heard the change in pitch of the door motors as they strained to force the doors open beyond their stops, then pressed his detonator. With a satisfying *whump!* the explosive wrecked the motors beyond repair.

The sounds of his missiles being launched reverberated through the hull. He listened as the missiles popped out of their hull cylinders and the motors failed to ignite. Even his sabotage of these missiles had remained undetected. As he waited to die, he thought back to his home by the sea, now reduced to ash, and the wildflowers that dotted the fields in the spring, just like the first day he met his wife.

The sudden hiss and the popping of his eardrums told him that the crew had penetrated the door, as it sprang open and machinegun fire smashed through the air, bouncing off the machinery.

The man returned the fire, catching one of the men in their bulky antiradiation suits as they rushed into the room. He continued to fire blindly, sweeping the gun back and forth across the engine room, hearing the screams as he hit another man. A moment later, a grenade put an end to his fire.

In a matter of hours, the rest of the crew would be dead as well.

## IV

The Orion bomber had left its alternate base in the Azores after refueling and rearming. They had taken off just ahead of the Soviet cruise missile that incinerated the base.

After a long, fruitless flight, the pilot opened the intercom and spoke with the crew.

"Well, we've got a choice. We have enough fuel left to just make it to America or Europe, if we have a lot of luck.

"I guess you know what going back home in either case means, or we can stay out here and hunt some Reds.

"What do you say?"

Nobody objected, since the alternatives were all equally grim. Besides, with luck, they might be able to take some more of the enemy with them.

# SIX

## I

"Jack," Ginny asked, "why didn't you bring some of your neighbors into the shelter yesterday? Couldn't you have helped some of them?"

"I might have been able to bring some people in here, sure, but what would all of us have done? This basement's crowded already, and there's only ten of us and two dogs. Imagine what it would be like if there were forty or fifty more people in here. The facilities couldn't stand it. Remember, the only reason we're not using a chemical toilet like the people in the other basements here is that I always did a lot of work in the basement and hated walking upstairs every time nature called. My employees have it a hell of a lot worse!" Jack replied.

"Yes," interrupted Jean, "but what about your neighbors, couldn't you have sheltered some of them?"

"Jean, it all boils down to this: am I my brother's keeper? The answer's yes, obviously. I have my brother's family here right now, and Jim'd be here too, if he wasn't so stubborn and anxious to get back to Washington.

"That's the literal answer, though. I know what you mean—don't I have a responsibility to the community? I can only help so many people, Jean, and then the food, and the water, and the light, and even the air run out. The only reason why I don't have this basement sealed up tight is that there weren't any nuclear strikes close enough to bother us. Remember, the heaviest, most contaminated fallout is dropped within a few miles of the target area, while the rest is carried up so high, and broken up so small, that I know it won't begin to come down until it's well mixed in the whole atmosphere of the planet.

"Adam, shut off that fan for a few minutes, and let's see what happens."

The people looked at one another curiously. No one could figure out what Jack was up to. Within a half an hour, they found out, as the smoke from Jack's pipe mingled with the odor from the burned pan of food cooked on the electric hotplate, and the temperature, even buried in the cool earth, rose and the humidity increased.

"Well, Jack," Adam said, "do you think you've proved your point?"

"Yeah, the point is that with two or three times as many people in here, we wouldn't be able to breathe, it's as simple as that. We just don't have enough air circulation.

"Besides, do we owe shelter and aid to people other

than our friends and families? If I brought in twice as many people as we're sheltering right now, our food reserves would be cut in half, and I'd have to cut back on everyone's food rations to survive. Double the numbers again, and we reduce our survival margin to a quarter of what it once was. Do as the government planned to do and dump thousands, even tens of thousands of people on areas where the people aren't expecting any guests, and everybody starves.

"If I can't take care of everybody, then I can only take care of a few people, and those few people will be made up of my family, my friends, and my farmhands. I owe everybody here whatever I can give them. I don't owe safety to anybody else."

## II

Jack rolled over in his cot, and grunted and flailed wildly as he almost fell off the bed. He lay flat again, staring up into the blackness; without lights, the basement was as dark as a tomb. As he lay there and sleep began to steal over him, he realized that something wasn't quite right; he stayed still for a moment then realized what was the matter. The fan wasn't working.

Jack slipped on his boots and picked up his flashlight as he went over to see what was the matter. The fan was turned on alright, but it still wasn't working. Jack swore under his breath and flicked the light switch on at the foot of the stairs.

Nothing.

He began to swear in earnest.

"Jack, what's the matter?" came Ginny's voice.

"I think we've got a problem here. Want to hold that flashlight while I check the circuit breakers?"

"Sure, Jack, just a minute."

Jack and Ginny walked deeper into the basement, past

the silent rows of food freezers where food for two years was stored.

"Dammit, if we don't get those freezers started soon, we're going to lose a lot of food here. I hope everybody's not in the same shape, or we're going to go awfully hungry until the next harvest."

Ginny followed the bear-like man and watched the play of his muscles under the surrealistic light and shadow of the flashlight. She saw scars from old football injuries, scars she remembered from their last summer together, before Jack and Jim went off to West Point, and new scars, the pockmark of holes the size of quarters that clustered high on the left side of his back, and a huge, nasty scar with torn, puckered lips that circled around his stomach.

Finally he stopped, and opened an electrical panel.

"Shine that light in here," he said, "while I flip the breakers. Sometimes, they'll trip and cut out the electricity, but not go all the way over. You have to reset each and every one to see which one was out."

While Ginny focused the light onto the panel, Jack snapped each breaker back and forth. In a few minutes, he was done.

"Damn, it looks like everything's okay here. I'm going to go through them one more time, hopefully, I just missed the right one. Old wiring like we've got here in these houses'll fool you sometimes. I hope that's all that's the matter."

It wasn't. The freezers remained obstinately silent, the lights stubbornly dark.

"Well, it looks as though I'm going to have to go out there and see what's the matter. It's either our bank of batteries on the fritz, or something's the matter with the hydrogenerator."

"Jack, you can't do that! What'll I . . . we, do if you get killed?"

Too wrapped up in his plans to catch the slip, he answered.

"Don't worry, Ginny. The army planned to fight in a nuclear environment for years. With proper precautions, I can get out of here, check out the batteries and the generator, and get back before I get anything like a harmful dose of radiation. Remember, honey, that I spent a lot of time training to fight in Europe. I can improvise some protective gear without any trouble."

"God, Jack, what if you breathe some of that fallout, you'll catch radiation sickness and die!"

"It's not like a germ or virus. I can protect against fallout with a pollen mask, and I can make up my own protective suit out of trash bags and tape. Listen, I want you to wake up everyone else and explain what happened while I get dressed. I'm not going outside in just my shorts like this. OK?"

While Ginny explained the problem to the others, Jack got out his oldest pair of jeans and pulled them on. The smooth surface would reduce the danger of fallout particles getting stuck in the fabric if he brushed against anything. He then pulled on a T-shirt. Now was the time to start getting ready to go outside.

Jack opened up a box of plastic garbage bags, and shook one out and laid it aside after testing the strength of the plastic. He wrapped his heavy boots in several layers of cloth towels to prevent them tearing through the plastic, then pulled the garbage bag over his leg, carefully taping it to hold it in place. By the time he was done, each leg was swathed in a half-dozen bags. Next, a rubberized poncho was shaken out and put on. That would prevent anything from sticking to him. By this time, Jack could feel the rivulets of sweat pouring down his legs and starting to gather under his arms as well. The outfit was hot.

"Well, everybody, wish me luck," Jack said, as he

pulled his pollen mask on. "See you soon!"

He staggered up the steps, then out of the house, his legs so deadened by the wrappings that he had to watch to make sure his feet touched the ground each time he took a step. He kept a careful eye on the radiation survey meter; so far, he could stay outside for a couple of hours without danger.

At the battery house, Jack checked the precious power cells, bought surplus from a submarine salvage operation. They were flat, no charge whatsoever, but nothing appeared to be wrong. Staggering from the heat, Jack went outside the small shelter and picked up the hose after checking for radiation. He jammed it under his clothes and turned the cooling water on, then quickly took a deep drink of the icy water, and replaced his mask.

A fifteen minute walk was stretched into nearly three-quarters of an hour as he staggered to the dam. Nothing was the matter there, either. Now Jack had to make a decision and choose what to do in a hurry. If he stayed at the dam, and the problem wasn't there, or couldn't be corrected in time, he would be overstaying his time outside, and that could cause problems. Jack mentally flipped a coin and turned back toward the battery house, hoping the problem was there and could be fixed in a hurry. The one big advantage of going to the battery house was that the building was made out of stone, and like all other buildings on the farm, was covered with earth and banked high against fallout, blast, or marauders.

The return trip under the hot noon-time sun almost finished him off as the black plastic and rubber suit was converted into a steam bath. Somewhere along the way, Jack dropped the survey meter, letting it slip from exhausted hands to fall onto the path. Outside the battery house, he stopped to wash the suit down carefully, then peeled off one set of garbage bags to keep contamination outside the building; he tossed them in the general direction of the first set he had discarded.

Once inside the cool building, Jack stripped off his poncho and poured water over his whole body. The shock of the cold water almost knocked him out, and he slumped to the floor of the building, panting, while he tried to catch his breath. For nearly an hour, he sat in a stupor, then finally roused himself enough to check the building out once more, paying closer attention to everything that he could check. Finally, about half-way through the checking process, a brainstorm hit.

He walked over to the far wall, where an electric meter was installed; it ran in reverse normally as he sold excess power to the electric company. Between it and his generator was an automatic cutoff switch that was guaranteed to transfer all his electrical current to his own use if the main power line failed; otherwise, the power Jack put out would be "lost" into the main line.

Popping the cover off the switch, Jack took a look and found that his guaranteed switch had failed; he quickly flipped it over to prevent any further wastage of his power.

"Well," Jack muttered to himself, "look's as though I'll have to get to that manufacturer and convince him to give me a new transfer switch. Only problem is, I don't think I can contact him too easily: his factory's located in Newark."

## III

Time passed very, very slowly in the basement shelters. Jack and his group spent much of their time reading or playing games. Jack and the two women exercised until they were exhausted, and he and Ginny taught Jean the rudiments of karate. Adam Henderson lost almost consistently to his grandson John in their chess marathon. The rest of their time was taken up eating, cooking in turns and cleaning up, and keeping the shelter neat.

It wasn't the most inspired method of keeping busy, but it worked. The boredom and cabin fever that normally accompanied long stretches enclosed in a single room were staved off, although nothing could prevent the realization that the whole world outside their sheltered basement had been changed, radically, for the worse.

Jack and the rest of the people in his farm staff kept in touch via CB radios, their antennas poking out of the soil that covered their windows. Contact between the groups helped, but didn't solve the problems that everyone faced shut up: never to see the sun for two weeks.

Unknown to Jack, problems had been stretched to the breaking point in one of the shelters, where one of his hands, always an outdoorsman and a heavy drinker besides, went berserk and began shooting up his family.

By the time Jack and some of the other men could force their way into the basement, three people, including the gunman, were dead, and one of his small children was so badly wounded that he died the next day.

The only piece of good luck for the people in their shelters that day was that the radiation level, which Jack had been monitoring for the whole two weeks, was low enough that everyone would be able to come out of their basements without special gear. The only thing they would need were rubber boots to prevent carrying the tiny amount of fallout materials that were still dangerous into the shelter.

## IV

At last, the day arrived. Jack announced that everyone could leave their shelters!

# BOOK THREE: POSTBELLUM

## PROLOG

Since the main effects of a nuclear exchange would be directed against the urban centers, we should examine the effects of such attacks on a hypothetical target.

A typical near-ground burst of a ten megaton weapon would completely destroy any buildings within approximately ten kilometers of ground zero, with progressively lesser effects out as far as forty kilometers from the center of the blast. The heat from the blast would instantly reduce everything flammable on or near ground zero to ash and could cause second degree burns on exposed skin as far as thirty kilometers from the blast.

Initial radiation at ground zero would soar far beyond the lethal level of 650 rads, and would inflict an almost immediately lethal dose of radiation out to some four or five kilometers. Residual radiation, caused by contamination of ground materials by the material of the weapon itself, could extend downwind from ground zero for as many as three hundred kilometers. While not fatal to people under cover, the residue would have the effect of contaminating the ground for a long period of time.

From this description of the effects of a moderate-sized weapon, it becomes obvious that the best strategy for "city-busting" would be to place a series of weapons that, when detonated, would have overlapping circles of total devastation. Note also, that the Soviets have long had fifty and even hundred megaton bombs.

It can be assumed that mortality rates in the urban centers would be well in excess of ninety-five percent; the survivors in the urban center would be exposed to high initial radiation and would probably die within a week of the attack. A few, a very few, people would be lucky enough to survive even this, but would be exposed to the further dangers of blast effects, fire storms, and later cancers which can be directly traced to the exposure from the explosion.

The people in the suburban areas not immediately affected by the detonations would be exposed to the same dangers of blast and fallout, but the effects would be lessened to the extent that they would have a greatly reduced mortality, approximately on the order of fifty percent.

The biggest danger in the suburbs will be from fallout. This can be reduced by remaining under cover for a certain period of time. One rule of thumb is that for every seven hours after the initial detonation, the amount of residual radiation decreases by a factor of ten. In theory, everyone should remain in shelters for certainly the first forty-eight hours, but since the blast effects would damage or destroy shelters over a wide area, such protection can very well be hard to find.

The danger of later thirst and starvation would certainly face the survivors. Fresh foods would disappear or be made useless within a matter of hours as refrigeration fails. Even stocks of canned goods would not last for a long time, since there would be relatively few major stocks of such goods on hand.

Communities wishing to survive would be faced with the immediate problem of finding shelter and food, and will probably be forced to roam far and wide to find them. The people who have shelter and food will want to keep them, and clearly there is a potential danger of further fighting to secure or hold these supplies.

The basic fabric of society would have been ripped asunder and the new society that would replace the old would be strikingly different. Certain classes of people would almost certainly disappear in the aftermath of an attack, especially in the hard-pressed cities. Those with severe handicaps, chronic non-fatal diseases, and possibly the elderly will die unless they can contribute more to society than they consume. In the rural areas, this effect will be much less obvious, since the supplies of shelter and food will be relatively unaffected.

Genetic effects will be extremely important, since the production of obvious non-survival and esthetically displeasing mutations can not be tolerated, either in livestock or humans. This fact, coupled with women being inherently better protected against radiation effects than men, may very well lead to a situation in which men who can produce genetically acceptable children will have multiple wives, while the radiation-damaged male will be ostracized. The situation among domestic animals is somewhat simpler; the defective male will simply be slaughtered and processed for food.

In spite of the problems which will face the population in the microcosm, the effects on the whole human race will not be exceptionally serious. A rise of cancer rates, for example, of twenty percent in the whole population would mean that if the chances were formerly one in a million, they would increase to 1.2 in a million.

The icecaps would not melt, nor the earth heat unbearably, nor ice caps march south overwhelming the country. There would be certain minor climatic changes, but no serious effects. Probably the climatic effects would be no worse than the "Year Without Summer" that everyone survived.

Of course, on the local level, the survivors would have to make great efforts to stay alive.

# ONE

## I

After two weeks of enforced imprisonment, Jack and his family and friends were stretched to the breaking point. Now that it was relatively safe for them to go outside, they could finally do something that would relieve the pressures.

First, Jack and his crew surveyed the whole area for radioactivity, using a pair of geiger counters that he had bought. They went over the farm and marked out "hot spots" with warning flags. So far, there were few dangerous areas, and most of the crops Jack had left unharvested could be gathered in, with precautions, as they ripened.

The next job was to get some more, and heavier, weaponry. Jack and his family had listened as more than one ham or professional radio station reported the attacks of starving mobs which overran them. The fate of those people had not been something that Jack would like to expose his people to in any case.

The nearest armory was over an hour's drive away, so that would have to wait for a while. With luck, Jack would get all the equipment for a whole mechanized infantry battalion. As soon as everything else was done, he and the other men would go over to pick up the weapons. Meanwhile, he and Adam Henderson would drive into the Corners and scout out the town. There hadn't been any reports of the plague for almost a week, so it was probably safe to go out and meet other people.

The two men drove down the deserted highways and into the town. The only sign of life was in the bar, and that seemed to be doing a land office business. The church was deserted.

Jack and Henderson drove over to the store and

looked it over carefully. It was still locked up tightly, as they'd left it. Henderson opened the garage and drove the truck inside, while Jack walked off after making sure the older man had locked the door securely behind him.

He walked around front to check out the mayor's office and the sheriff's office. The first thing he saw was the sheriff himself, a man he had known all his life, Frank Janus. He was sitting back in his swivel chair, a cigar in his mouth, and a half-full bottle of cheap whiskey on the desk in front of him.

"Well, if it isn't Cowboy Jack Dawson, the great landowner! Come on in and have a drink with poor little me. I was just getting ready to close the office and head up into the high country with the wife and kids. First, though," he said, picking up the whiskey and waving the bottle around, "I wanted to finish off my duties."

"Frank, I've known you since grade school, and I never expected you to run away and hide when the chips were down."

"There's a crisis, don't you know? The world just came to an end and you expect me to stay here? Every city in the world's gone with the bombs, and a plague is killing off everybody else." the sheriff protested. "Stay, bullshit! The mayor loaded his family into his car and hauled ass up into the hills after the guys over in the bar raped his wife. I couldn't do a thing about it, nobody'll back me up. What am I supposed to do?"

Jack looked into the tormented eyes of his friend and quietly said, "I'll back you, Frank. In fact, I'd better take care of the whole thing. You're too drunk to do much of anything. "Stay here!"

Jack walked out of the office and jacked a round into the chamber of his shotgun, then loaded an extra into the tubular magazine. Holding the shotgun in his left hand, he tucked back the flap of his pistol holster and opened up his spare magazine pouch. He took off his coat and dropped it in the street, making sure that he had lots of freedom in his movements.

Jack knew the bar like the back of his hand. He had been in there for his first drink when he was fifteen, when he'd taken a prime buck while hunting; his dad had bought the whiskey. He'd also spent a lot of time in there since. He walked behind the building and crept up to the kitchen door. From inside, he could hear men shouting and singing and the occasional scream of a woman.

Jack eased the screen door open with his left hand, holding the shotgun vertically in his right hand. He leaped in, covering the whole room. The only person in the room was Marty Dennis, the owner. He wasn't going anywhere with a butcher knife between his ribs and a bloody rose spread out from the wound in his chest.

Jack crossed to the window, closed now, between the kitchen and the bar itself, and peered through the crack at the bottom. Inside the bar, he saw a dozen men, all drunk and all armed, as well as some women. It was obvious that they all had been beaten and raped repeatedly. They huddled off in a corner of the bar, as far away from the men as they could get. Jack memorized the positions of the men.

He walked over to the swinging door and stood there for a minute. He took a deep breath of the stale air, then kicked the door open with his heavy boot. He followed the door, firing in a half-circle from left to right.

The shotgun belched flame and lead into the men clustered around the bar, dropping eight of them almost immediately. The last sight some of the men ever saw was a gigantic maniac who charged into the room, screaming and cursing wildly before he shot them. The other men tried to pull their guns and shoot, but before they could get off more than one or two rounds, he had thrown his clubbed gun at them and pulled his own pistol, cutting them down.

In the space of less than a minute, the room suddenly became quiet. The men, all strangers, were down on the floor in pools of blood. Some of them were moaning and calling for help. Jack calmly shook the empty magazine out of his pistol onto the floor and replaced it with a fresh magazine. He cocked it and walked over to the screaming men and shot each of them in the head. The *berserkergang* was on him and he had no time for prisoners. Jack picked up a fresh bottle, ripped off the top, and put it to his mouth, letting the harsh wash of whiskey flow down his throat as well as over his face and chest.

Slowly, Jack's eyes came back into focus as the whiskey warmed him. He was standing in the middle of a room filled with the acrid stench of powder and the smell of blood. He looked at each of the dead men in turn, kicking them to make sure that none was playing possum, then walked over to the women.

"Are you all right? Were any of you wounded? You'll be safe now, they're all dead."

Weeping and sobbing, the women got to their feet and tried to kiss him, just as the front door opened. Frank Janus, weaving from side to side, stood in the doorway.

"Frank," Jack said, "go get the doctor and some clothes. Move it!"

Jack untangled himself gracefully from the women and walked through the rest of the building. There were no survivors. He stood off to one side as the doctor and some of the women from town came in to help the terrified victims of the strangers. Frank stood off to one side, his chin down on his chest. The sight of the slaughter in the building had sobered him completely.

"I'm not much of a man, let alone a sheriff, am I, Jack? I let you do my job after I got too scared to do it myself."

"Frank, I've been trained in just what I did to this

slime, you haven't. Nobody could expect you to go up against these guys alone." Jack walked over to his friend and grabbed his shoulders.

"I did the job because I was the only man in town with the experience. Now snap out of this and give me a hand."

Jack bent over and picked up his shotgun. He snapped it a few times, and began to reload.

"Frank, you know I'm a colonel in the army, right? Then I'm going to exercise my authority and take over. I'm declaring martial law in the absence of the mayor or other civil authority."

"Do you have that power, Jack?"

"I think I do, and that's what counts. There's never been a situation quite like this one, so I'm going to play it by ear as I go. Will you back me up?"

"Hell yes! Whenever we played in school, either you or Jim were the leaders. Might as well let you take charge now. Here, shake on it."

"Frank, I want you to send somebody out to find all the old gang and get them here. I want them deputized and ready to move as soon as possible. Also, have people spread the word that there'll be a meeting at Henderson's tonight at eight. In the meantime, I'm going over to the mayor's office and try to get something done."

Jack went back to the office and cleared away the evidence of the former mayor. He carried in several files of notes that he and Henderson had compiled while they were under cover. His duel with the men in the bar was reduced to two laconic sentences.

By the time Frank Janus came into the office, Jack was all set with lists of supplies and the people who sold them for miles around. They carefully examined the lists and made their plans for getting the supplies. As their old friends filed in, they filled them in on the situation.

Finally, Jack deputized all of them and they set off for the armory.

## II

In the cities, the mob had taken control, stealing and looting for the basic stuff of life. In bestial rage, they destroyed, and many died. Still more people, without any chance of medical aid, died from relatively minor injuries, and many more died of the plague.

Within a week, the plague disappeared as it ran out of hosts.

## III

In the Soviet Union, the last of the great fallout shelters was under attack by the desperate survivors trapped outside the bunker. Everybody in the area knew the purpose of the shelter, and they wanted to get in.

The survivors of Uralsk had gathered around the old mine shaft that disguised the entrance to the fallout shelter and had tried, time after time, to storm the blast doors. Hails of machinegun fire had driven them off with heavy casualties.

Finally, one of the dying crowd outside the shelter hit on an even better idea. They carefully pried the protective screens off each air shaft and lovingly filled them to the top with concrete, while other people threw explosives into the tunnel, bringing down the room, while still more people poured more concrete over the rubble.

Their work was in vain, because the people in the shelter could always dig their way out. The guards laughed as the valves of the pressure tanks that held their air supplies were opened. They didn't laugh as nitrogen gas poured out, and choked the life from everyone in the shelter.

## IV

In Valley Forge, Senator Howland was coping with the traitors who threatened his regime. The soldiers who had mutinied were holed up in their barracks and resisting all his efforts to drive them out. In return, Howland sealed off the barracks area and filled it with Soman gas. In a matter of minutes, they were all dead.

# TWO

## I

Jack and his men had pulled up to the National Guard Armory, expecting to find somebody had beaten them to the weapons cache. There were no signs of life as they stopped in front of the building and walked in. There was no one inside, and the equipment bins and weapons lockers were still intact. Within a matter of hours, the men had loaded their loot into the M-113A armored personnel carriers, fueled them, and driven the supplies home. All along the way back to Henderson's Corners, the men saw no signs of life. It was as if everyone had simply gone into their homes to die.

## II

In and around the cities, a few people gathered together to defend what they had. Usually, these groups started as families stuck together. A few friends joined with them, and soon, there was a speck of order in a disordered world. Most of these specks were washed away under the tide of lawlessness that swept through the land, but some survived, and, surviving, flourished.

In a few weeks, order began to appear out of chaos.

## III

Deep in the heart of Leningrad, on the Neva River, the freighter nudged against the riverbank and unloaded an APC. The men drove off with their cargo of death, clad in bulky respirators and antiradiation clothing. The city looked dead, just like Riga, yet the men knew that the Soviets were still here and were determined to eliminate them, just as they had done in Riga.

All during their voyage here, the men had seen no signs of life, except when a submarine, nationality unknown, surfaced off their starboard side. As the sailors watched, the crew came scrambling out of the conning tower and tried to get into rubber boats. They had listened dumbfounded as the sounds of a pitched battle erupted.

Finally, the submarine shot flame from its conning tower, split in half and sank out of sight, taking the few men swimming in the chilly water with it.

When they reached Riga, it was easy for them to find the source of the radio transmissions that had led them here. Inside a huge concrete submarine pen, some of the Soviet personnel from the base had set up a temporary refuge. The Allied soldiers had gone ashore and hoisted their weapon right up on top of the bunker. One of the sickest men stayed behind to detonate the weapon when everyone was clear. After an hour, they saw the mushroom cloud rising high into the sky behind them.

Only a few hours later, they entered the Gulf of Finland and sailed toward the fortress island of *Kronshtadt.* Nothing blocked their way. In the harbor, they saw the melted and sunken wreck of the *Aurora,* the ship that launched the Bolshevik Revolution, and passed it, their wake lapping over the rusting hulk.

Once unloaded, the men would drive to the Soviet

bunkers and wipe them out, while the rest of the sailors would go through Lake Ladoga, up the Archangel Canal, and destroy the naval base there.

In the whole of untouched South America, revolution after revolution flared up and died away as the people struck out against their repressive governments, started war, or indulged themselves in their traditional pastime, the coup.

Chile and Peru, traditional enemies of long standing, went to war against each other. The armies melted away and headed home as the supplies of ammunition were exhausted. The hell of the Gran Chaco resounded with the sounds of weapons again, and the soldiers prudently deserted rather than continue the war. All the while, El Salvador and Nicaragua, enemies since the Great Soccer War of 1969, unleashed their respective might against one another. In two days, ammunition was exhausted and the soldiers went home.

Throughout the whole world, fallout-laden winds carried their load of death around and around, but even as they traveled, the heaviest radioactive particles disappeared, carried to earth by their own weight. Only dust remained in the sky, turning the sky red, morning and night, in a fitting protest to war.

# THREE

## I

Right from the beginning, Jack had taken charge of the meeting he had called for. Long before the scheduled hour, the building was crowded by everybody who could get to the meeting house. Jack had watched the people as they arrived, and recognized most of them. They were people he had gone to school with, as well as relatives, close and distant. There were some strangers among them, their fine clothes rumpled and stained from work. Long before dark, Jack had started a portable generator and hooked it up to the store. There would be light.

By eight o'clock, the building was bursting with people who wanted to hear what was said, and the parking lot outside was jammed with still more people who would hear the meeting through the windows or over the loudspeakers that had been set up. Jack walked over to the microphone and began to speak with the crowd.

"I think most of you recognize me, but for the benefit of those who don't, I'm Colonel John Dawson, US Army. I have called this meeting under my authority as colonel, and have declared a state of martial law throughout this area.

"I have ordered the stores closed and guarded . . ."

"Yes, damn you," a man screamed, leaping to his feet and pushing his way toward Jack, "you've closed my store and thrown me out into the street! How dare you! I was making the best profits I ever expected, especially since that old fool Henderson sold out his stock at cost."

"Frank, restrain Mr. Morlee. I think the shock has gone to his head.

"Of course I ordered all the stores closed. Henderson sold his stock out to those who needed it or could use it. You're selling your stock to outsiders and charging them ten times the going prices."

At these words, Jack saw some of the strangers shift uneasily as they listened to him. Some of them began to edge toward the door.

"These outsiders you're gouging are ordinary people we want to take into our community. Many of them have arrived here with nothing, and need shelter and food, but not at the price you've demanded. These people who want to work along side us are welcome to the community. We need outsiders. None of us are teachers or engineers or machinists. Hell, we even need just plain old dirt labor now to help us with the crops and set aside food for the winter.

"You outsiders," Jack said, turning to a large knot of people by the door, "are welcome if you want to become part of the community. We don't need anybody here like the men from the bar. All of us are going to find the next years tough, tougher in many ways than anything we've ever known, but just like our grandfathers and greatgrandfathers who first wrested a living from this land, we'll come through.

"To make sure that our resources are used efficiently, I've ordered Adam Henderson here to form a committee which will gather up supplies from all around us and make sure they are distributed fairly.

"To keep us safe from marauders like those men from the bar, I've ordered Frank Janus here to train a group of deputies. We'll need a lot of volunteers if we're to make certain of our survival. Are there any objections?"

Nobody objected and Jack's ultimate authority was confirmed. After that, he threw the meeting open for nominations of men to head the health, education, and construction committees. Jack's men in the audience called out the names of his choices and their election went through without trouble.

After the speechmaking was over, the people drifted over to the bank of coffee machines Jack had set up and gathered into groups to talk about the new government. Jack and the committee heads went off to his office to map out the plan to make their community safe.

The first, most important part of the campaign, was to map out a way of joining the outsiders into the community and helping them get under shelter. Jack knew from the deserted condition of the country that he had driven through that food supplies would be more than sufficient for everybody. One thing they had to do was conduct a census and a survey of resources available in the town. That way, they would know who they had with them, their skills, and what use they would be to the community.

The needs of the defense force could be easily met. Most of the men were hunters in season or out, and knew the land like the backs of their hands. Since they had acquired a lot of military weapons, there would have to be some training for the men to learn to handle the new weapons, not to mention the APCs. Jack knew from his time as a Green Beret that the men would be best trained for combat. No fancy parade ground nonsense, since if they were needed, it would be for a fight, not a parade.

## II

The last fifteen men defending Gitmo against the combined Cuban-Soviet troops which had overrun the base after the war were getting ready to die. They had retreated into the base's main magazine and had successfully defended it against anything the Cubans had thrown against them. Now, the Soviets were taking over, and the end was near. They had wired the ammunition in the building to explode on command and were waiting for the last attack.

Most of the rest of Cuba had been buried under an avalanche of American weapons, but the counterattacks were too late. The Backfires that the Soviets had put into the country had struck the American cities the missiles hadn't before their bases were eliminated.

Naval air units from Jacksonville and a few other bases had struck at Cuba and eliminated the Soviet second strike wave of aircraft, and setting off many secondary explosions, including at least one nuclear explosion, in their attacks on the hidden missile silos. Unfortunately for the people who lived in the cities within a thousand kilometer radius of Cuba, the attacks were useless. Even as the planes had returned to Jax, their bases had been eliminated by a Backfire.

Sailors and marines sat exhausted behind the barricade they had thrown up across the entrance to the magazine and relaxed as much as they could. Fatigue lined each young face after two weeks of hard, unremitting combat. The men were filthy dirty and hungry, covered from head to toe with mud, stinking of sweat, and sometimes covered in blood from their wounds. One could only tell black from white by the clean circles under their eyes.

They relaxed and smoked their cigarettes, waiting for the next wave of Cubans the Soviets herded into their machineguns. Most of the bodies piled up in the heat and sun outside had once been Cubans, led into the assault by the Soviet "noncombatants" who had been allowed to stay in Cuba. There were a lot of bodies out there, because they had to cross over five hundred meters of open ground to reach the bunker.

There was no way to tell which of the bodies belonged to a Cuban and which to a Soviet. The bodies had been burnt black by the sun and made to swell as they decomposed; some had burst open. The Americans had been forced to put on gas masks to shield them from the stench. Now they had run out of filters and were forced to breathe the stench.

Dotted here and there across the field were the burnt-out hulks of some Soviet T-64 tanks, destroyed by alert TOW and Dragon crews in the earliest Soviet attacks. Now the enemy seemed to have run out of tanks, and the waves of infantry had also thinned considerably.

A marine lieutenant covered the field with his binoculars. He could see the enemy getting ready to attack. The enemy was safe, because the Americans didn't have weapons heavy enough to reach them. The magazine they were in was for naval eight inch guns, not thirty caliber machineguns.

"All right, here they come again. Johnson, I want you back there with the detonator. As soon as they get into the magazine, I want you to set off the whole mess."

Johnson, a wounded sailor, crawled back to the rear of the magazine. He had been wounded in the arms and couldn't handle a machinegun, so he would have to be the backup, the failsafe for the demolition of the magazine.

The Cubans came charging in, crouching low to make as small a target as possible, and covered by the heaviest fire that the Americans had yet been subjected to, with even heavy mortar bombs exploding in front of the bunker. The Americans held their fire until the last moment. They had gathered up six machineguns and a lot of ammunition and set them up to cover the whole field in front of them. The almost solid wave of fire that these guns spat out seemed to sweep the attacking Cubans from their feet and shred them. In a moment, the surviving attackers had gone to ground, crawling their way forward through the grass that covered the field.

The Americans relentlessly probed the ground where the Cubans were hiding, killing dozens, wounding many more. At last the Cubans got up and ran for cover. A few of them even stopped long enough to pick up a wounded companion. Another attack had been beaten off.

Just as the last of the Cubans disappeared around the corner of a nearby bunker, the Americans heard the clanking and grinding sound of steel treads on concrete. A tank came lurching around the corner of the building!

It had been hit and knocked out before, as shown by the scorch marks and the hold gouged into the armor on the turret. Somehow, the Soviets had gotten it moving. As soon as they saw the tank, the Cubans rallied and began walking behind it, sheltered from the American fire.

The Americans concentrated their fire on the tank turret and tried to get some rounds into the hold, hoping the richochets would kill some of the crew.

Still the steel monster rolled forward.

The lieutenant dropped his machinegun and ordered the men to retreat into the depths of the magazine. With any kind of luck, he would lure a large number of the attackers after them, then set the explosives off. One of the men had been badly wounded by the mortar fire, almost losing his left arm from a fragment that had sliced into it. He had wrapped the wound in rags and tied it tight to stop the flow of blood. Now he waited while his companions got away, then turned back to his gun.

The Cubans, assuming that the Americans had abandoned their guns, rushed out from behind the tank and charged forward against the bunker. Once they were well away from the shelter of the tank, the wounded marine opened fire. The Cubans fell like wheat before a harvester as the bullets cut into them. With a roar and a puff of black diesel smoke, the tank rolled up onto the barricade.

Far back in the tunnel, the other Americans heard the rattle of the machinegun and checked to see who was missing. In a moment they knew. The sound of the tank filled the tunnel with deafening sound as it crushed aside the barrier. The machinegunner never stopped firing until a choked-off scream sounded. The lieutenant turned to Johnson and nodded.

The effect was like a gigantic shotgun as the explosion, channeled by the heavy bunker walls, slammed into the enemy tank and troops, leaving red smears behind. The explosion finally tore through the bunker roof, sending up a huge pillar of dark brown smoke that marked the grave of the last fighting men in Cuba, sacrificed to a Soviet "training brigade".

## III

Senator Howland and the surviving congressmen managed to put down the rebellion against them quite successfully. Now all that remained was for them to sit out the worst of the fallout and then emerge, to be greeted by their people with joy.

The Senator was already planning how he would divide up the country after the restoration. Each section would be allotted a specified sector of the country to rule, while Howland himself retained overall command. The rest of the congressmen had grumbled, but knew all too well the fate that awaited them if they spoke out.

## IV

Mario and his people had managed to outrun the plague and had even managed to find shelter from the fallout. Now they had gathered up a large number of prisoners for slave labor and had taken many weapons from a convenient National Guard Armory, including several tanks.

All the equipment was coming in handy as Mario and his men overran several villages for food, shelter, and women. Never before had Mario had such a good time, not even when he was battling against the mob.

## V

Life at the farm was slowly running down, as Jack took his men out on salvage missions. Most of them and their families had moved into town because they simply didn't want to be left alone.

Jean and her family stayed behind. She wouldn't leave the farm because it was too much a part of her husband's family, and she knew that he was never coming back to the farm now; he was dead, but to Jean the farm became a symbol. So long as she held on there, she wasn't admitting Jim was dead.

In the meantime, she supervised the work that she and the two families which stayed behind had to do, and kept the house cleaned and polished. She fell into bed every night, exhausted, because she couldn't stand the thought of staying in the house at night, awake and alone in her bed, and wondering where her husband was, and what had happened to all her friends.

# FOUR

## I

The last two weeks since he had come out of his shelter had seen Jack almost living in the mayor's office as he supervised the gathering of food and other supplies from all over the area. The two stores had been filled to overflowing with supplies that had been gathered in forays into other towns.

During some of the trips, the salvage parties had found people dead in the streets. Those towns Jack would leave alone for a year, then enter. So far, Jack had not lost a single man.

The census that Jack had ordered had proven a blessing, although it showed that about a third of the people in the immediate area had simply taken off into the hills after the attacks. The empty houses and barns were put to good use by the outsiders who had agreed to stay in the town. Most of the strangers had been ordinary working people and were ready to learn what was needed to develop a farm and keep it running as the townspeople showed them how to survive in a totally strange environment.

The best find so far was a surgeon and his family, who had been driving north toward Boise when the war broke. He was carrying much of the equipment that he would need to set up practice in town. He had been put in charge of a special five man team that was responsible for gathering up medical supplies. Doctor Johnson would be a welcome addition to the community.

A genuine machinist had driven into town just a few days before. He and his wife had loaded his camper with all his supplies and driven south, hoping to find somebody who could appreciate his usefulness. John Gomez had planned to make his considerable talents available for the best and highest offer. Jack was willing to meet his demands and settle him into a house in town.

The inventory of supplies was going well, with most of the people cooperating. A few people had refused to let the inventory crews onto their property. Jack had ordered that they were to be left alone and that they were not to be given anything from the community's supplies that they didn't pay for.

One of the biggest needs for the whole community was fuel, and Jack had supervised a crash program to build alcohol stills. There was plenty of fuel around now, but when the day came that the salvaged supplies ran out, then Jack wanted to make sure that his people would have something to run their tractors on.

Some generators had been found and brought into town. They would be used to power the refrigerator units that were being set up and to keep the battery sets charged for all the radios that were in town and on the farms. Eventually, Jack planned to replace the generators with something similar to his setup on the farm. For now, the generators would have to do.

Large barracks had been set up in town, built of concrete and stone. They would be used as warehouses as soon as the people sheltered in them were assigned to a farm of their own. Other construction crews were busy building other shelters centering on the town. As soon as the community's needs were met, the excess manpower would be used to build homes for all the people in town.

Almost everybody who could carry a gun was being subjected to military training. They were working under the pressure of an attack on one of the outlying farms.

The night before, Jack's guard station to the west had reported the sounds of heavy firing and then flames about a mile away. Jack, the sheriff, and a half-dozen deputies had gone out in an APC, in time to rescue the last two survivors of the farmhouse from a gang of bandits. Most of them had been killed, but not before they burnt the house to the ground and killed the farmer and most of his family.

The surviving attackers had been captured and taken back to town and imprisoned while the community debated their fate. The debate which followed lasted for only a few hours. The evidence was clear, the men had been caught barehanded after killing and robbing the Frank family; there were no mitigating circumstances and the whole community voted Jack their permission to deal with the men as he saw fit.

Before the whole community, Jack pronounced the sentence.

"You men have been found guilty of multiple murders and robbery. There is no defense. You are sentenced to hard labor to rebuild all that was destroyed in your attack and to work in the forests harvesting timber. When your task is done, you will be imprisoned until dawn of the following day, when you shall be taken from the jail and hanged by the neck until dead. Take the prisoners away."

"You can't do this to us, man, we're deprived! You got no right to make us work and then kill us. We're victims of circumstances . . ."

Before he could continue, Jack stood up, walked over to him, and lifted him by his lapels. For a moment, he stared into his eyes then, with a snort, threw him to the ground.

"Punk, you killed five people I knew last night, and you wounded three of my men besides. Your kind counted on that psychoanalytical crap to protect you before, but that was in a different society. Before, you could get away with murder by going before a judge and crying about how you suffered all your life. At the very worst, you'd do a couple years of easy time, then be turned out on the streets to do the same thing time after time.

"This is a different society. We recognize the duty of society to protect its people from people like you, and this society will do more about that protection than just pay lip service to its people.

"You are going to rebuild what you destroyed and you are going to do work that can replace that lost to us by the wounding of our men. Then you will be removed from society, since you have proven that you can't exist in any community. I'll be damned if I'm going to let you go somewhere else and rob and kill again."

The four captives looked at one another and walked out of the building under the guard of a deputy. The spectators cheered their approval.

## II

Senator Howland relaxed in his bed, covered by silken sheets, and ate the meal that his chef served. In his luxury, he couldn't fail to think of his colleagues who hadn't made it to their posh shelters, as well as the men who had been killed when their shelters were attacked.

The senator had never regretted the pressure that he had used to get the shelters built and stocked. As long as his "Valley Forge" was safe, he couldn't care less what happened to anybody else. It had been regrettable that the troops which had been stationed here had turned out to be disloyal; they would have to be replaced.

Now it was enough for him to remain undercover and save himself from the dangers outside. There was no need for him to expose himself to radiation. After all, he was going to take over the presidency as soon as he emerged from his cocoon.

The senator cursed as his naked blonde secretary crawled into bed beside him; she spilled his Blue Mountain coffee.

## III

In the city centers, volunteer squads of men and women probed the ruins of their homeland. Careful use of geiger counters and dosimeters let them wander around in relative safety. One of their goals had to be the recovery of food from the air raid shelters in the town centers.

By tunneling through the debris and avoiding the worst "hot spots", they finally managed to reach their designated shelters. Most had been placed in the basements of old buildings, in subway tunnels, or even in the corridors of schools. In the shelters, the survivors found a few people dead of blast effects, many more dead of radiation, and the boxes of supplies intact. As they opened up the packages, they found the cruel joke that had been played on them. The tens of millions of dollars squandered on civil defense preparations had bought boxes of rat and mouse infested crackers, rusty cans of water, and some medical supplies that had expired years before. It appeared the government had never planned to protect its people.

## IV

Stillness finally settled over the ruins of Marsh General Hospital. Days before, the story was quite different.

The hospital had been built to serve the burgeoning suburbs and had been located far enough from ground zero to survive the attacks by the Soviets. After the raids ended, the hospital had been swamped by the flow of injured and dazed people who needed some sort of medical attention. Within hours, shelters had been set up on the hospital lawns and parking lots, and even these helped but a few of the worst cases. Long before the day of the attack ended, medical supplies had completely run out, the supply of water had stopped, and the food stocks had been exhausted. Scenes of horror had never been seen outside a medieval hospital; operations of all sorts, from treating second and third degree burns up to amputations were completed without any anaesthetic save a blow to the head by a sandbag. With antibiotics or even clean bandages completely used up, wounds became infected, then gangrenous, and nobody could take the time to help the victims.

Once the people on the lawns, the least injured cases, began to suffer from lack of food, they began to grumble. When rumors started that the doctors and nurses were secretly eating in the cafeteria, they decided to go get what was due them.

When one of the wretched people saw a nurse pouring sucrose solution, the starving survivors charged into the laboratory and spilled the solution on the floor, to be followed by the sugar that was being used. The civilized veneer of the people crowding into the room slipped away as they dropped to the floor and scrounged for a single grain of sugar. Other people rushed to the laboratory and fought for the privilege to hunt for the spilled sugar.

By the time the food riot died down, the hospital was in flames, the patients inside trapped and roasting alive. The mob left the torn and bloody remains of the staff behind. There were few survivors.

### V

Jack stopped back at the farm only long enough to pick up some clothes and other things he would need. Jean, and everyone else, was out on the farm, taking care of the animals, and working with the crops. Jack had warned them a thousand times not to leave things empty when they went out to work, that somebody ought to stay around to guard the buildings, but there wasn't too much point in trying to talk to Jean anymore. She was always right, no matter what.

Jack looked through the house to pick up a few things he could use. He stopped for a moment and picked up the gold-framed picture of his wife and family, and looked at it for a long, long time. He carefully put it back on his desk and left it behind. It was a symbol of another life, a life that he had passed through, but he was going onward to a new life; it was time to put the momentos of the past where they belonged.

## FOUR

### I

In the months that passed since the war, Jack and the rest of the community had worked to build the shelters and gather the supplies which would carry them through the winter. They had grown from a small town of less than five hundred to a full-grown farming and ranching community of over two thousand as more and more people came into the town and still others came down from the hills.

The energy problem had been almost completely solved, at least for the most important uses. Several of the small rivers which flowed through the valleys north of the town had been dammed off, flooding them and creating enough of a head to allow a waterwheel-powered generator to be installed. The power from that was used to keep the refrigerators and freezers in the warehouses going, and to provide some lights for the central offices. Otherwise, everybody simply did what their ancestors did, go to bed with the sun and rise with it as well.

The harvests had been generally successful, even allowing for the fact that sunlight was radically decreased by dust. Most of the food that had been gathered would be used for seed for the next crops. The hybrid varieties were going to be used up immediately, since they could never breed true. Luckily for Jack and the rest, many people simply stuck to the old, familiar crops, rather than the new versions.

Fertilizers and pesticides had been gathered in and stockpiled for next year, and seemed to be abundant enough to last through the next several years, perhaps long enough to let them set up some sort of manufacturing facilities.

One thing which had been greeted with little enthusiasm was the reopening of the schools. Jack had managed to find several teachers among the refugees who settled in the town and had drafted every skilled worker as well to provide the children with a practical, as well as theoretical, curriculum for everybody of school age. There had been strong, almost fanatic, resistance from the most conservative people in the community against teaching anything beyond the "three Rs". It had finally been solved when Jack simply ordered that all students had to attend school and get good grades or their families would get no help from the community. That stopped the debate.

About the only thing that Jack had been overruled on had been the defense plans. He had wanted to construct a series of watchtowers which would guard the town and be a rallying point in case of attack. Everyone else argued that there was no need for the defenses, since there had been no attacks. With that defeat, almost everyone stopped going for militia training and the town's defense program came to a grinding halt.

In spite of the one setback, Jack had made the most of his time, personally supervising almost all of the projects in town, as well as acting as the central coordinating authority. He had lost weight until he appeared almost gaunt, and had taken to staying in the office almost all the time, even sleeping there. Both Jean and Ginny tried to convince him to come home and relax, but they had had no luck.

He was sitting in his office going over the latest reports on the crops when Frank Janus rushed into the room.

"Jack, come on down to the radio room, quick. Something's happened to our foraging party up in Boise!"

Jack leaped to his feet, his chair falling backward to the floor, and ran down the stairs to the radio room. As soon as he went into the room, he could hear that something was indeed the matter.

The foraging party was under attack, heavy attack, that much was clear from the sounds of a heavy firefight that came over the radio. The man on the other end was screaming and crying for help into the mike.

Jack picked up his own microphone and cut the man on the other end short with a curt command.

"Shut up and listen to me!"

"Report exactly what has happened. Don't spare the details."

Another voice answered Jack.

"We were coming into town, heading for the big shopping center, when all of a sudden, the lead truck blew up. Before we could do much of anything, somebody was blasting away at us with really heavy riflefire.

"We're pinned down in one of the stores and can't get out. What can we do?"

Jack thought for a minute. There was nothing he or any of the others could do, since they were over a hundred miles away from the battle. The only chance for the men was to try to break out of the building they were trapped in and head back to town.

"There's nothing we can do for you from here; you'll have to get out of this mess the best way you can. How many men are left?"

"Maybe a dozen of us."

*A dozen out of a party of fifty!,* Jack thought. A low whistle came from Frank Janus.

"Then you're going to have to fight your way out of there to the nearest truck and haul ass out of there. Try to get everybody together and make a break. Whatever you do, don't come directly back here. Go some other way, then sort of circle back here. Make sure that you aren't followed, no matter what you do.

"Also, before you leave, make sure you destroy all the gear you can't carry. We don't want to be attacked by our own weapons. Now get moving and get out of there!"

He cut the mike and shook his head. So many men dead and all the trucks destroyed as well. Both men and trucks were irreplaceable.

"Frank, I want to see the scouts we sent into Boise right now. Get them here as soon as possible. Something went badly wrong, and I want to know what it was.

"I want you," Jack said, turning to the radio operator, "to contact the jeep patrols we have out and call them in."

"I already did, colonel."

"Good girl. Keep a radio watch for reports from the Boise party and tell me as soon as anything comes in."

Jack double-timed up the stairs to his office and got out the maps of the whole area. It was obvious that someone was probing into the countryside, and Jack didn't like the way they operated. Jack carefully studied the maps to see how he could have his scouts find out where the strangers came from. As he sat there, Carl Bonner, the head of the whole scouting force, walked in.

"Well Carl, what happened?"

"Damned if I know, Jack," he replied, "Frank told me what happened, and I really can't figure out what started the whole mess. Christ, my brother Roscoe's up there too."

"I know, Carl. You've done a great job so far, so I can't believe that it was sloppiness on your part that caused the problem. Do you have scouting parties out around Boise that we can divert to scout out the route the strangers took to get into the city?"

"I have two jeeps north of the city. They reported in this morning right on time. They were supposed to sweep east of the city and head back here in the next couple of days. I imagine we can contact them by radio and have them change their course south to us."

"Okay. As soon as you can contact them, tell one of the jeeps to march east and south, just as they had planned, but have the other jeep retrace its steps and head west. This way, we ought to be able to have somebody cross their path and find out where they came from. Now get downstairs and get in touch with them, Carl."

"I'm on my way, colonel. Good luck!"

"Frank, I want you to alert our force of trained deputies and have them ready to move out as soon as I give the word. We might just have a fight on our hands soon, and I want to be ready to meet the enemy somewhere other than here in town."

"Right, Jack."

Jack picked up the maps and began to plan his campaign in detail.

## II

The foraging party had managed to break out of the shopping center, but not before they lost six more of their men. Even so, they had managed to take a prisoner before they had fled. They couldn't tell Jack about the captive, since the heavily-burdened radioman had been shot down by the enemy and nobody had been able to recover the set.

They planned to drive as far west as they could before they turned south on one of the old forestry service roads. Nobody was following them; that was certain. In the meantime, they planned to question their prisoner.

The captive was little more than a boy, perhaps fourteen or fifteen, who crouched in a corner of the truck bed, fear filling his eyes. He hadn't looked so scared just a few hours ago, when the escapees had overrun his riflepit. They had been forced to shoot another boy down, and then to club this one. The boys had accounted for four of their casualties in the breakout.

"Where are you from, boy?" Roscoe Bonner asked.

The boy sat in silence.

"I'm talking to you, boy! Speak up!" Roscoe punctuated his question with a stinging slap to the boy's face. Roscoe's brother-in-law had been in the lead truck, and Roscoe had seen him leap from the flatbed, his clothes ablaze, and run across the empty parking lot until he could run no more.

"Back east. I'm from Kansas City."

"How many of you are there? How many guns?"

"There's more of us than there are of you, you stinking farmer. We've all got guns and we're going to take everything you've got. How do you like that?" he shouted, spitting in Roscoe's face.

Roscoe leaped on the teenager and began pounding his head against the side of the truck. The other men pulled Roscoe away and held him. They knew Jack would want the prisoner alive and well.

## III

Back at the shopping center, the gang which had ambushed the foraging party was busy stripping the bodies of the men they had killed. They also found two wounded men who had been left behind; they dragged them, screaming and pleading, into the parking lot. As a horrified survivor of the ambush who had hidden himself in a drainage ditch looked on, the gang members poured gasoline over the wounded and threw a blazing pack of matches onto the pile of bodies, living and dead.

Lee Tanner cupped his hands over his ears and pressed himself into the mud of the ditch, anything to shut out the sounds of men he had known all his life as they were burnt alive.

Mercifully, it was over in a minute or two. The screaming stopped and the stench of burnt flesh drifted away on the breeze. Lee almost sprang to his feet then and opened fire, but he stopped himself. He had to get back to the Corners and warn them what was coming.

## IV

Mario Ginetti watched as the men from the enemy

party burnt on the parking lot. They had been stupid enough to let themselves be captured and were paying the penalty. Mario looked the men and women over and pointed to several of them. They clutched at his pants leg to beg for their lives as they were dragged off. They knew they would be left to die and that no one would have the guts to bring them help.

Mario was proud of his expertise in conducting the ambush. He had learned much in the last few months since the war ended. During his march, he had learned how to capture a city with minimum casualties, and had gathered together a force of over three thousand soldiers and almost ten thousand slaves.

The best part of all of this was that Mario and his people still had two of the tanks they had captured still in running condition.

Mario knew from the way the men they had fought had struggled and the way they were equipped, that they had come from an organized community. All Mario and his people had to do now was to move in and take over. His empire was already established and waiting for him.

## V

For Jean, the farm had come to mean almost everything to her. It was her home and her refuge against the world that held all too many terrors. She could hide here forever if she had to, and lose herself in the mindless round of working, eating and sleeping. She wouldn't have to think ever again, because that only stirred up bitter memories of the past, when she had another home where she and her husband lived.

The harvests had been magnificient, and even now, weeks later, she was still busy processing the bounty of the farm, setting aside the food that would carry everyone on the farm, and many others, through the harsh winter which was coming.

Jack had stopped by the house several days ago, or perhaps a week or so ago, it was so hard to remember these things clearly anymore. Perhaps it had been Jim, but he wasn't coming home anymore.

At any rate, Jack had told her that the snows would be extra heavy this winter, because so much dust had been thrown up into the atmosphere during the war. The dust made the nuclei that caused snow. It was easy to believe him. The skies were heavy all the time, with clouds pregnant with moisture. Fall had been wet for the last week or two, wetter than most people even remembered.

Remembering, that was the problem. Jean had almost walled off the corner of her mind where Jim still lived.

# FIVE

## I

Jack and the rest of the council sat around their conference table and listened while Roscoe told them what he had learned from the prisoner. The words Roscoe spoke cut deeply into each man as he catalogued crimes that would make any normal man sick. That a seemingly innocent young boy could be guilty of such dreadfulness seemed beyond belief. That it was all too true was shown by the way the boy laughed as Roscoe told of some particularly disgusting crime.

"Take that little bastard out of here and lock him up," Henderson shouted. "We'll take care of him in the morning!"

The guards dragged the struggling prisoner away. As soon as he was out of the room, Roscoe finished explaining what he had learned from the captive.

"As I was saying, that gang has managed to rob and

pillage its way here from around Kansas City. It was really unbelievable what we learned from him. He told us about things he did that I could hardly believe were humanly possible. I guess that's really the answer, they're not human. What that kid told us was so disgusting, we almost killed him before we got back here, but we figured that you'd want to hear for yourselves just what kind of an enemy we're facing.

"He said that they have over three thousand soldiers and even have a couple of tanks operating. I guess if what he said is true, we're pretty much out of luck, Jack. He said they plan to march this way soon, and when they find us, they're going to kill us. I guess that's about all I can tell you."

"Roscoe, thanks for bringing that kid in here alive. I think he has shown everybody here what kind of danger we're in. I want to put him on display so everybody in the community will know what's facing us. I don't want anybody to ever say 'you're killing kids'."

"What are we going to do?"

"We're going to have to take advantage of our knowledge of the terrain to beat them. The first thing we're going to do is to try to draw them up into the high country and get them snowed in good and tight. If we can do that, we'll let General Winter finish the job for us, then finish off the survivors in the spring. With any kind of luck, we'll gain enough time that we can fortify at least part of the town."

"We'll use jeep patrols to try to draw them off. From what that kid said, they don't have any powered vehicles, except for their tanks and a few motorcycles. The jeeps will be armed with machineguns and should be able to give better than they get.

"We'll operate from out of the west, assuming that they realize that was the way our foraging party escaped. The big advantage is that we know the country all round here, plus we have detailed maps for the whole country.

"Now, while our patrols attack them, we have a lot that the rest of the community can do. I want everybody we can spare from the harvest, and all the construction crews as well, to start building fortifications—the kind I wanted built before, when we weren't under pressure. I have a series of drawings here that show just the kind of wire traps that we can build from the things we have right here. I've brought samples of the entanglements from home, as well as models for the large obstacles.

"Remember, this isn't some novel where the cavalry will come charging over the horizon or where we can produce clouds of poison gas to wipe out the enemy. We've got a long, hard struggle in front of us, and if we win—please note I say 'if'—it can only be at the cost of some of our people. The alternative is, of course, death as our little friend told us a few minutes ago."

"Jack, do we have the right to assume that these children are all that much different from ourselves," said the Reverend Gillespie. "There is a moral issue here, do we have the right to kill just because these people are acting differently from us?"

"If it wasn't for the fact that I'd be sending you to your death, reverend, I'd let you go into that boy's cell and debate the merits of the case with him. I really can't see how you can suggest negotiations with people who did what the kid told us they did. Do you seriously believe that anybody can negotiate with that kind of person?

"Look, if I see a mad dog running down the street and about to attack some children, don't I have the duty to shoot that dog down out of hand to protect the lives of the children? Do you think I should negotiate with it?"

"Dogs are different from children, Jack."

"Granted, but are these children? That kid was

responsible for killing three men in our foraging party before he was captured. Was that the act of a child?"

Silence reigned for a moment, broken only by the sound of Jack tapping the dottle out of his pipe. A few of the men shifted uneasily in their chairs.

"Jack," Gillespie said, "I have known you and your family for many years, and I fear for your sanity. I think you ought to step down now and let the community be run by a more humane committee . . ."

"Like hell, reverend," Roscoe shouted, "these kids as you call them are nothing but a gang of killers. If we're your flock, your duty as shepherd is to protect us from the wolves.

"Instead, you're trying to set yourself up as our leader. You ought to be supporting Jack and his plans, because if it hadn't been for you, we would have had something that could stop them, instead of having to make them up in a hurry! Why don't you . . ."

They never found out what Gillespie should do, as a car pulled up in front of the building and the drivers dragged a man into the meeting. Under the blood and mud, they saw that he was Lee Tanner, one of the men who had been with the foraging party. The man was half-raving as he was carried in.

"We found him up on the north road, Jack," Les Niemann one of the deputies, said, "driving like the devil himself was after him. He stopped at our barricade, started to get out of the car, and collapsed."

"Damn, I hope he didn't lead that gang from Boise back to us," Jack said. "Take him over to the hospital and get him patched up and calmed down. We'll want to question him as soon as possible."

Jack turned back to the committee heads and stared at Gillespie.

"I think we should start making our plans now. Reverend, if you want to do some good, why don't you go over to the hospital and see if you can help with Lee?"

## II

The city of Boise was burning.

The fires lit the sullen lead-colored skies with a surrealistic splashing of reds, oranges, and yellows and the smoke stained the dark clouds even darker.

The Demons were setting out on a march to the south. The city had begun to burn after a slave looting party had set a small fire to keep warm. The survivors had been thrown into their funeral pyres, kicking and screaming.

They had been attacked time after time over the last month by the people out of the west, and the subordinate leaders had been straining to go after the enemy that cut and tore at them, then sped away. Mario refused, and when the protests became too loud, killed the men.

Mario's patience had been rewarded a few days ago, when one of his patrols had ambushed the ambushers and captured one of the townsmen. A few hours of torture gave them all the information they needed. The attackers were based to the south, in a little town called Henderson's Corners.

Now the townies would learn what it meant to attack Mario and his men.

Mario and his people had set out, trudging south toward their goal. The column stretched out along the old state highway and was dominated by three tanks which led the march and towed gasolineless cars for the Demon leaders. The third tank had been repaired and returned to the group by a party of Demons left behind just for that task.

The slaves had been hitched to carts and sledges that

pulled the loads of guns and ammunition. There was little food, even for the Demons, let alone the slaves.

The cold weather had set in with a vengeance, the thermometer falling from a relatively mild forty to a bone chilling ten, accompanied by high winds, that made the weather even colder. Few of the people had bothered to equip themselves for the cold. At best, they were wearing blankets wrapped around themselves and around their feet. For the last two days, they had had no shelter, and the cold was beginning to take its toll of both Demons and slaves.

Anyone who couldn't march was simply left alongside the road being stripped of whatever pitiful belongings they still had. Marchers looked at their friends with a dull-eyed stare of broken men, especially among the slaves.

Up at the head of the column, Mario and his staff planned their operation against the town they knew was to their south. The plan was simple: They would attack with the tanks in the lead, crushing any barriers that the enemy could put up, then finishing off the survivors with a charge by the Demon infantry. Since there was no ammunition left for the tank guns, that would have to do.

Marching behind the tanks, the bulk of the Demon infantry shivered under their blankets and softly cursed their leader for getting them into this mess. Everybody could see that the weather was turning bad, and that they had to get under cover for the winter. Everybody, that is, except Mario.

To make matters worse, about half-way to the town, it started to snow.

## III

Deep in the bowels of Valley Forge, Senator Howland watched the reports from the radiation monitors up on the surface. The reports showed that he and his people would not be risking their precious skins, let alone their genes, if they went up to the surface now.

Howland decided that they might as well wait until the spring, then stage a lightning campaign to overrun the country. He had spent an awfully long time unpacking some of the armored personnel carriers and tanks, and wanted to put them to use. The fact there were barely one hundred people still alive in the shelter didn't really matter, so long as they had the better weapons.

The strain of being locked up for so long underground was beginning to tell, as some of the weaker members of the select band committed suicide in their desperation. Worse had been the mutiny which swept the battalion sent into the shelter. They had all died.

The survivors were planning to make certain of their success.

## IV

Outside the ruins of the cities, the survivors had developed some form of government and had formed communities to protect and expand their interests. Most of the rump governments had solved the problems of food and shelter for the short term, and also planned to solve the problem for the long term as well.

The wisest governments were already planning for their expansion into the countryside as soon as the weather cleared. They planned to take over the towns they had been trading with as soon as the spring crops were planted.

# SIX

## I

Jack supervised the fortification of the approaches to his town with a single-minded determination to succeed. The town was lucky in that the ridges which ran from east to west across the whole countryside tended to channel any advance from the north into one of three possible approaches.

The first way into town was via a deep, narrow valley. That had been closed off by blasting and flooded by the construction of a power dam. Nobody would be coming in that way. The other two entrances weren't as easy to defend.

In these areas, Jack and his people had constructed many passive defenses, designed to break up an attack or to channel it through "killing grounds." Primarily, they had taken advantage of the heavy construction equipment they had salvaged to scout the valleys to make sure neither tanks or men, once committed, could get away.

Trees were cut down and dropped so that they fell into the direction of the advance and interlocked their branches into a wild tangle, impossible to remove. To make certain that the trees just couldn't be pushed aside, the stumps were wired to the trunks with barbed wire.

The many telephone poles which surrounded the whole area, since they were of no further use, were cut down, and the poles buried at a forty-five degree angle, pointed toward the route an invader would have to take to reach the town. They would also serve to keep the enemy tanks away.

Even so, the whole area wasn't sealed off. Jack still kept his jeep patrols out to cover the enemy advance and keep the townspeople informed of the enemy's movements. With any kind of luck, Jack and his people would be able to lead the enemy directly into the traps they had prepared.

Snow began to fall, covering the traps that Jack and his people had installed better than any manmade camouflage could have hoped to do. Now all the townsfolk had to do was wait while their enemy wore himself out in a march in the snow.

## II

Mario watched and cursed helplessly as the townies stood off and machinegunned his people. Over fifty of his soldiers had been killed outright by the huge slugs that could tear a man in half. Many more had been injured in the rush to get into cover and had been left behind. So far, the attacks had cost him less than five percent of his soldiers, but the cost in morale was high. Already some of the men were grumbling out loud, and their mutiny had been put down only by using the most loyal of his troops.

The snow still poured down, making the tanks hard to steer as their steel treads slipped and spun on the icy surface of the roads and sent them slithering off into the ditches. Because the tanks were uncontrollable, the cars they had towed had been mostly abandoned, and now Mario's officers had to march like their men. They didn't like that.

If it hadn't been for the fact that Mario knew there was little behind them in Boise, he would have turned back rather than risk his force. At it stood now, they had to win in the battle ahead or freeze and starve to death.

Even the pace of the march was slowing down, as Mario was forced to spread his men out on the flanks to keep the attackers away. The men on foot were becoming exhausted by the strain of pushing through the snow that came up to their waists. The constant wind was a curse, because it cut right through the clothes his men had with them, freezing them in their tracks. In a way, though, the snow was a blessing, since the attackers couldn't see any better than his own men. Mario knew that as soon as the snow stopped, they would be back.

The slaves were beginning to fall out of the march deliberately, sensing that their guards were too few to watch them all. A few of the slaves had even turned on their guards and killed them!

Mario dimly sensed that he was being made to dance to his enemy's tune, but he lacked enough command experience to realize that he and his men were being channeled to their doom. Instead, he was already making plans about what he would do when he captured the town up ahead.

## III

The jeep crews had been constantly harassing the Demon column, striking at them as soon as the snow cleared and roaring away, leaving their dead and wounded targets writhing in the pink-stained snow. The cold that was working for the townsmen was proving to be a capricious ally. Just the night before, contact had been lost with one patrol. When the scouts went out to find out what happened to the men, they found that the jeep had broken down, and the men were frozen to death.

The cold was doing much more to the enemy. The ragged enemy soldiers were stealing whatever clothing they could get from their slaves, leaving them naked in the snow. A few of these poor people had been picked up by the jeep patrols and told their story before dying.

The snow clutched at the marchers' feet, pulling boots

away as easily as the crude blanket wrappings that became encrusted with ice and slowed a man even more. The path the enemy followed was stained red with blood from their frozen and slashed feet. Nameless lumps alongside the path told of people who had fallen out and died.

Roscoe Bonner had a personal reason to lead the attackers on the Demon column. He reported what was happening to the enemy back to town; he was especially moved by the fate of the slaves.

"They're falling out of the march like flies, mostly their slaves. The Demons are taking their clothes and leaving the slaves to freeze to death. We've managed to pick up some of the slaves, but it seems hopeless that we'll rescue any more of them. What should we do?"

"Roscoe, I want you and most of the other patrols to drift back into the enemy's rear. Try to pick up as many of the slaves as you can and get them into one of your supply trucks.

"I'm going to send out a truck-load of food and blankets and a couple of nurses to help with the slaves. As soon as they meet up with you, break off the attacks and just try to rescue as many people as you can. Come what may, we can't stand idly by and let the prisoners die."

## IV

Senator Howland was enjoying his swim in the Congressional pool. It was warm almost to blood heat and relaxing after a hard day of planning.

He had heard from one of the servants that the temperature outside was down to -10° and the wind chill was making it like fifty below! It was nice to be safe.

# SEVEN

## I

Jack had taken a chance and divided his forces up to cover the two unblocked entrances into the town. He had taken command of about two-thirds of the force and had taken them up onto Blackman's Ridge. The rest had been placed under Frank Janus' command and sent to cover Schneider's Valley.

Jack and his men could hear the sounds of firing off to the south, punctuated by the sounds of mortar bombs exploding in the valley and echoing off the cliffs. Jack knew that everybody there was busy, and that he would have to wait for a report. There simply wasn't enough time for the men on the other end to waste in telling him details.

He and his men had watched the enemy patrols that probed into his valley. They had been clearly visible as they dashed into the open ground, but nobody had attacked. Jack wanted the enemy drawn into the trap so that he could spring it shut, wiping them out.

As the enemy scouts disappeared, Jack could hear the sounds of battle taper off.

## II

The Demon's attack had been a disaster from the beginning. Mario had led off with his tanks, just like he had planned.

The first tank had rolled up to a log barrier in the road and pushed against it, its treads spinning and clattering on the hard-frozen ground. The enemy had apparently poured gallons of water onto the road in front of the barrier, enough to make it impossible to knock the barrier down. After a minute or two of trying, the tank backed off and turned away, the crew planning to drive around the barrier. As soon as they got off the icy road, they smashed through ice that covered the wide ditch, and sank until the turret was almost completely hidden by the black water.

Mario sent his infantry in to drag the barrier away and let the other tanks through. As soon as his soldiers showed themselves, the enemy opened fire with mortars, cutting his men to ribbons.

In desperation, Mario sent in a second tank that managed to knock the log barrier aside. As soon as it moved forward, a tremendous explosion lifted the tank into the air and blew its treads off, stranding it. The crew tried to run, but was cut down.

Within minutes, Mario decided that the best way to get into the valley was to have his infantry cross toward the hills on the other side. He sent his men out in groups of one or two, knowing that his enemy wouldn't waste a mortar round on so few people.

Instead the men fell afoul of the same ditch that trapped their tank. The ice had been shattered by the mortar fire, and the infantry simply floundered into the water as it cracked beneath their feet. The few men who had managed to get across tried to run into the valley and were thrown to the ground, to be impaled on stakes set into the rock-hard ground. They had been caught up in the loops of wire that Jack had ordered strung. They were the lucky ones, since they were simply killed where they fell.

A half-dozen men had managed to work their way through these obstacles and began running across the open ground toward the enemy positions three kilometers away. As they ran, they disappeared as they fell, one by one, into the spiked pits that had been dug over the whole area.

Without orders, the men withdrew from their assault.

Even Mario didn't stand in their way as they escaped the hell-fire that they had walked into. Mario and his men were beginning to realize that this was no chicken-stealing expedition, but rather that they had walked into a lion's den, and an angry lion at that!

## III

The defenders held their fire as they allowed the enemy to lose his first tank all by himself, then waited as the enemy infantry came forward to unblock the road. As soon as they appeared, the defenders wreaked stern justice on the men. The bombs from the mortars had exploded just at surface level, sending their fragments spraying out to cut the legs from under the enemy. They had watched and waited while the second tank came forward and managed to maneuver itself almost directly over a charge of twenty-five sticks of dynamite, then had carefully set the explosives off under the vehicle.

The enemy infantry attack was the most interesting of all, because the Demons had managed to walk right into the same ditch that had claimed their tank. They fell into the freezing water and struggled for a few minutes, trapped in the barbed wire that Jack had coiled in the ditch. In a few minutes, they stopped fighting as the chill of the water froze them into unconsciousness and death.

The men who had managed to get across the ditch had run full tilt into the wire network that Jack had built up, stringing plain wire from stake to stake in a triangular pattern almost ten meters wide, and filling the inside of the pattern with loosely lying barbed wire and sharpened steel stakes. Those who survived the stakes would die from the cold before nightfall.

A few had been unlucky enough to make it through all the wire barriers, only to fall into the Wolfpits that had been dug throughout the entire field. They had fallen into the inverted cones and been impaled on stakes as their companions had been.

Under the pressure of the barriers and the deadly sniper fire from the concealed sniper posts that dotted the fields, the enemy broke and ran back into the shelter of the hills on the other side of the valley. Almost eight hundred enemy soldiers died in the valley. The worst defending casualty was a broken arm, suffered when one man jumped up to cheer, and slipped on a patch of ice.

The bodies left behind made red and black dots on the snow-covered ground. A few of the wounded tried to crawl off, but alert snipers finished them off before they could get safely away.

There was no mercy to be had that day in the blinding snow glare. Some of the slaves had been brought back into town, and the stories of rape, torture, murder, and other crimes so horrible that they were too sickening to repeat, had been spread throughout the community. Nobody planned to take prisoners or be taken prisoner.

From behind the hills, the sounds of heavy machine-gun fire drifted as the jeep patrol attacked the enemy again.

Mario had been smart enough to stay behind and keep to the safety of his remaining tank. From safety inside the heavy hull armor, Mario ordered his men to begin to retreat from the battlefield.

## EIGHT

### I

Jack cursed as the snow started up again. With any kind of rotten luck, the Demons could infiltrate the valley in front of them, overrun the sniper posts, and be up into the trenches before anybody knew they were coming. He turned to one of his subordinate commanders and ordered him to gather up a dozen men to come along with Jack on a dangerous mission.

"Dave, I'm going to go down there with a couple of the wrecked APCs and dump them in the middle of the road. That ought to stop them from bringing up tanks. Maybe it'll hold them up long enough for us to find out what they're doing."

Dave Schorner disappeared ghostlike into the snowfall, his white camouflage smock blending right into the falling snow. Jack made sure that somebody was in each APC to use the brakes as they descended the hill.

Once they got to the designated roadblock, Jack signaled to turn the APCs sideways, and as they slammed together, had each one chained to the other, and the pins pulled out of their treads, making them almost impossible to move.

Back up on the ridge, the defenders set up a guard rotation by the alarm wires that covered the hillside. The guards would be relieved every half-hour before they began to suffer too much from the cold.

The men sat huddled around the fires in their shelters, some smoking and talking, the wise ones with their socks and boots off to dry. Everyone had left his or her gun outside the shelter, since the condensation that would form when the weapons were brought into the warm shelters would freeze up the guns when they were most wanted.

Jack climbed into his command APC and listened to the report that was coming in about the battle his men had just fought.

## II

The snow fell in blinding waves, blown by the strong

winds into unprotected faces with enough force to feel like thousands of knives slashing at the skin. Even this feeling disappeared as the faces froze.

The Demons were marching toward the sole remaining way into the town, their only hope of finding the warmth and shelter that they needed. The slaves had been left behind to fend for themselves. Most of them escaped when the Demons opened fire into their ranks. A few of them would probably survive, making their way into the valley that had claimed so many of their captors and reaching safety at last among the townsfolk.

The unprotected Demons had set out to march almost ten hard kilometers through the snow, knowing they had to fight a pitched battle at the end of the march. Mario had been wise enough to have ropes rigged behind the tank, so the men could hang on to something as they struggled through the snow in the wake of the lumbering steel monster.

When the march started, Mario had almost a thousand soldiers remaining to him. By the time they reached the gap, they would be reduced to less than six hundred men.

As they moved up to the valley, the snow stopped as suddenly as it had begun. The sentries that Jack had placed on the forward slopes above the road the enemy was following reported in, then fell silent as they watched and waited.

## III

The cold had exacted a terrible price from the surviving Demons. Almost eighty percent of their manpower had fallen in this expedition, leaving a bare six hundred men to make the attack. They were warm, clothed in the blankets and jackets stripped from fallen companions. Now, most were almost equipped to survive in the cold.

The exhausted foot soldiers moved off into the snow. They failed, some falling into the sterile white embrace of the drifting snow to die where they fell, unmourned and unaided by their friends.

Most of the Demons gathered in the shelter of the tank as it rolled forward, content to let it break a path for them and half-drag them in its wake. Inside the tank, the crew strained to see through the snow-blocked episcopes and vision blocks, anything to remain in the warmth of the hull.

The tank commander finally decided that he had better clean off the vision blocks, and opened his hatch to climb out. As soon as he was a knee exposure, a single shot rang out from the hillside, catching him in the side and spilling him down in front of his tank. The tank, uncaring, rolled over his screaming body. As the tank lurched to a stop, the Demons opened fire against the hillside, trying to root out the sniper.

He was safe in a nice warm concrete sniper's post.

Finally, under cover of the barrage, one of the crewmen crawled out and wiped off the snow that blocked their vision. Mario, smarter than the crewman, slid out the escape hatch and joined his men. In a moment, the crewman had nimbly scrambled back into the tank, and it was again rolling forward.

As it entered the gap, it accelerated to push its way through the snow. Those who could let go of the rope they held, while others watched their frozen fingers being cut off, as the rope ran through them.

The tank rolled up the drift that marked the location of the two wrecked APCs and slowed, wary of meeting the same fate as its two brothers.

The turret swiveled as the crew strained to see any sign of movement or attack from the hills. With a sullen roar, it came forward and pressed against the linked APCs. The treads spun on the hard-frozen ice, sending chunks spewing behind it as it pushed against the vehicles.

## IV

Back in town, Reverend Gillespie watched as the surviving slaves were brought into the hospital. Of over ten thousand slaves who had been marched out of Boise, only seven hundred had survived long enough to reach safety here, and of these, most would die from the freezing cold and pneumonia.

He had seen what had happened to the Demons who had entered the valley in the first attack and had reeled back half-fainting as he saw the bodies of the men sliced open by the mortar bombs.

In that moment, something in the man snapped, and grabbing up a fallen Demon's gun and ammunition, he rushed off into the gathering snowstorm to join Jack and his men.

# NINE

## I

Jack waited for the enemy tank to back up enough to clearly fill the sight of the single TOW launcher that he had recovered. The launcher held one of the three precious missiles ready for launch. Jack had not been able to bring himself to trust anybody else for this job, and for good reason. The use of these weapons was not something that could be picked up in an hour or two of lectures on a Sunday afternoon.

Jack squatted beside the launch tube and watched the Demon tank through his eyepiece. As he watched, he heard one of his men shout out loud.

"Look down there! Some fool's got a jeep and he's charging them. It's Gillespie!"

The sounds of shots echoed from in the valley as the Demon infantry scattered and dove into the ditches, ditches that Jack and his men hadn't had time to booby-trap. At the same time, while Jack was distracted, the tank backed up and charged forward, brushing the linked APCs aside and off the road. Without stopping, the tank gathered speed, seeming to flash over the snow-covered road, straight for the jeep.

In a moment, it had rolled over the vehicle, leaving smashed and bloody wreckage in its wake. Still the tank rushed on as it climbed the road. Jack knew that he had only a few minutes left to stop the tank.

Returning to his weapon, he centered the Demon tank in the eyepiece and made ready to fire, only to have his view blocked as the tank disappeared behind some pine trees. Jack turned his weapon until the sights found the road beyond the trees and waited.

"Get ready to reload!," he yelled to his crew. All along the ridge his men began to open fire on the enemy below. The noise level rose as the sound echoed back and forth in the narrow valley.

Just as Jack had planned, the Demon tank appeared suddenly from behind the screen of trees. He fired and continued tracking the moving tank through his eye-piece. As long as he kept the tank centered in the sight, the missile would automatically adjust its course to strike the tank. Jack realized with a sinking feeling that the missile was out of control. He turned the whole tube bodily in an effort to pull the missile back on course.

It was over in a matter of a few minutes. The missile continued to curve off to the right, away from the tank, and nosed into the ground. The explosion sent a geyser of dirt and flame into the air, alerting the Demons to their danger.

In back of the tube, the two-man crew reloaded and secured the second missile's control wires. One of the men patted Jack's head to signal that the round was loaded.

If anything, the tank had increased its speed up the icy road, as it sped up to avoid the weapon that could kill or cripple it. Jack centered it in his eyepiece and pressed the firing button.

Nothing happened.

He pressed it again, and again had the same result. He quickly checked the missile and found everything in order.

Cursing, Jack yanked the wires from the control box and signaled his men over to remove the missile from the launcher. Just as one of the men crossed behind the launcher, the missile suddenly launched itself out into space, the deadly backblast cutting the crewman down and sending him flying backward into the snow. The unguided missile flashed off toward the opposite hill-side, and finally disappeared over the opposite ridgeline.

Without stopping to help the wounded man, Jack and the surviving crewman reloaded the launcher and, as the crewman stepped away, Jack sat back down to track the tank. As he tried to center the tank in his crosshairs he saw the turret as it rotated and pointed in his direction. *If they have a few cannister or beehive rounds, we've had it,* Jack thought. At last, the tank was centered and Jack fired, the missile heading directly toward the tank.

Jack watched as the tank slewed around to face directly toward the missile, presenting the smallest possible target. With a metallic *clang!,* the missile glanced along the turrent and slithered up and over it, to explode a minute later in the rocks behind the vehicle.

Frustrated, Jack picked the launcher up bodily and threw it off the ridge into space. Stopping just long enough to grab up a canvas bag, Jack went over to where his wounded crewman was sprawled.

The wounded man, incredibly enough, was still alive, even though the backblast had burnt through the flesh on one side of his body exposing bare and blackened bone. The man turned his ruined face to Jack and managed to gasp out a few words.

"Jack, God it hurts! Please stop it!"

With tears brimming in his eyes, Jack fumbled in the man's pocket for a moment and pulled out his pistol. Even with the best of medical care in a modern hospital, the poor devil would probably die. His whole side was cooked.

Jack took the man's good hand and placed the pistol in it and wrapped the loose fingers around the butt. He guided the muzzle up the man's forehead and held it in place while the man pulled the trigger.

Jack stood up and walked away, down the slope. He signaled his men to stay behind while he took out the tank. By now, he was pretty sure that the tank was out of ammunition. Even so, it was too formidable a weapon to let untrained farmers and ranchers try to take out.

## II

As the tank nosed its way past the roadblock, the driver spotted the jeep floundering toward him, its driver firing a rifle from behind the wheel. With a grin, the driver gunned the engine and rolled right over the jeep, grinding the car into twisted and mangled wreckage under the pressure of its flailing treads.

Seeing a rise in the road up ahead, the driver kept the tank moving forward at speed, but as it passed behind the screen of pine trees, slowed down as the road leveled out. As he emerged from the cover of the trees, the new tank commander yelled that somebody was firing at them. The sound of the TOW crashing into the ground nearby reverberated through the tank.

Without hesitation, the driver again gunned the tank into motion as it roared ahead, its speed its best defense against attack. The commander screamed the news of a second missile flashing toward them a few minutes later. Everybody heaved a sigh of relief as it passed overhead.

This time, the tank commander had spotted the flame of the launcher as it sent the missiles winging toward their vehicle. The gears creaked as the turret was turned toward the launcher, hoping that the sight of the gun aimed down the antitank crew's throats would shake their aim.

Once more, the launcher spat flame, and the driver turned toward the launcher and waited. Through his vision blocks, the driver watched as the missile approached. At the last minute, as the tank rolled forward, it suddenly dropped down into the bed of a creek, hidden in the snow.

With a sound like that of all the bells in the world simultaneously ringing in their ears, the missile grazed the turret and bounced off. The crew shouted their thanks, but couldn't hear a sound. They were deafened, at least for the time being.

With much clashing of gears and roaring of the engine, the tank laboriously backed up out of the creek bed. With a bounce and a roar, its rear end slammed down onto the road, and the driver pointed it up the road toward the townsmen who had tried to kill him and his men.

Behind the tank, the sounds of a major battle erupted as the defenders poured a river of machinegun and mortar fire into the ranks of the Demon infantry. The only hope the Demons had was to get the tank up among the enemy as soon as possible.

With that in mind, the tank resumed its crawl up the hill.

## III

The snow in the valley was being churned into a pink-splashed mess as mortar bombs and machinegun slugs pummeled the floundering Demon infantry. Most of the Demons had gone to ground in ditches and behind other shelters as the townsmen kept up their fire. Some of the Demons panicked and tried to run. Those who weren't shot down by their officers were hit by the snipers Jack had placed on the hillsides.

The Demons could see their tank had survived the best the enemy could throw at it. As the defenders' fire slacked off, some of the Demons stood up and cheered as they charged the hillside in front of them. The rest, seeing that their friends seemed to be safe as they crossed the snowy field, rose up and followed.

The Demons made good time through the snow, driven by a combination of fear and blood lust. Even so, some were cut down by the finger-sized .50 caliber slugs that plucked men from their feet and threw them, in bloody tatters, to the ground.

Despite the protective shelters that the townsmen were fighting from, the enemy was starting to hit and wound or kill some of the men. Now the townsmen knew fear in their turn as a seemingly invincible horde of enemy soldiers charged across the field below. In a matter of minutes, most of them had reached the shelters of the trees at the base of the slope.

A few of the townsmen thought of their families and stayed. The rest thought about themselves and fled. Their friends and neighbors, left behind to fight and die, couldn't bring themselves to shoot them down.

Below them, the remaining defenders could hear the sounds the Demons made as they gathered themselves for the storming of the bluff. The yipping, yodeling sounds the Demons made sounded hauntingly like a hunting wolfpack. Down below, the townspeople knew that the Demons were assembling for their final attack.

## IV

The Demon infantry knew that they would die in their ditches if they stayed where they were for a moment longer, so, as the enemy fire slackened, some of the platoon leaders and company leaders stood up and charged the enemy, cheering as they ran.

With a shrug, the rest of the men climbed out of their ditches and charged forward into the enemy's fire. Some of the men were knocked right back into their shelter, but the rest were up and moving. A freak of the winds had blown all but the thinnest cover away from the field they charged across, so they made it into the shelter of the trees at the base of the hill with few casualties. A force of about three hundred men assembled in the shelter of the trees and made ready for their attack.

The survivors of that charge gathered together and collapsed onto the snow, panting and gasping for breath. Some of them gathered up handsful of snow to quench their thirst. A few of the men patched up their wounds and sat while they caught their breath, while others sat numbly and let the blood freeze on their skin.

When enough men had gathered together, Mario signaled the charge up the slope. The Demons got stiffly to their feet and moved out.

# TEN

## I

Jack watched helplessly as the defensive fire slacked off and his men broke and ran. In some ways, he couldn't really blame them, because if the tank wasn't taken out, the enemy could literally roll over any resistance. Even so, their cowardice could cost the lives of many people.

Jack pulled the white snow smock over his head as the tank rolled up the slope. It had been slowed down considerably by the slope and was coming on at a slow walk. In a few minutes, it clanked and clattered past Jack's shelter.

As the tank passed by, he threw his snow smock aside and ran after the tank, slipping and sliding on the ice as he ran. In a few minutes, he had overtaken the tank and grabbed onto a handrail to pull himself up onto the vehicle.

He slipped and was dragged for a few hundred feet as he struggled to pull himself onto the deck. Finally, he yanked himself up onto the rear deck.

The stink of burning diesel oil and the clouds of carbon flying out of the exhausts told of the bad maintenance the tank had been getting. While Jack caught his breath, he unslung his M16, cocked it, and climbed up onto the turret.

He felt along the hatch covers. The gunner's hatch was closed tight, but the commander's hatch was raised about an inch.

Jack worked his fingers under the lip and jerked the hatch open, pushing his rifle muzzle into the opening and squeezing the trigger. The thirty high velocity rounds that poured into the hull were devastating. Bullets and fragments bounced around inside the hull, cutting and killing as they flew about. A second magazine was fired after the first. Jack could have saved the ammunition.

Gingerly, Jack peered over the rim of the hatch as the tank drifted to a stop. Inside, he could see one of the Demons, the back of his skull blown away, and his shirt covered with blood, hunched over the breech of the main gun. Another was splayed out in messy abandon on the turret floor, lying in the center of an ever-spreading pool of blood. The third Demon was slumped over in the driver's seat, his head and back covered with blood.

Just to make sure, Jack carefully took aim on the man on the floor, then the driver, and shot them once more. It never paid to take a chance on possum players.

He quickly lowered himself into the turret and began the stomach-wrenching task of dragging the bodies out of the tank. In a matter of minutes, the bodies had been stuffed out the escape hatch, but the abundant evidence of their presence remained underfoot.

Jack slipped into the driver's seat and put the tank into gear, moving it slowly up the road. He hoped that he wouldn't cause too much of a panic when he appeared behind his men.

## II

The Demon tank crew never heard the sound of Jack's arrival on the turret. Before they knew what was happening, they were dying as bullets tore into their bodies.

## III

The Demon infantry was working its way up the hillside, spread out and howling their warcries. The enemy above them was silent, a silence made all the more terrifying by the fact that they had superior firepower. In a rush, the Demons overran one of the machinegun nests, its sole occupant too busy trying to clear a jam to notice the enemy until it was far too late.

The Demons turned the gun around and opened fire on their enemies, pouring fire into the townsfolk in revenge for their losses in crossing the fields below. Everywhere the townsmen broke and ran, especially with the sounds of the tank rolling up the road at them.

### IV

The farmers and ranchers who defended the hillside successfully when the battle was at long range could not stand a close attack. In the fury of the hand-to-hand battle that raged for a few minutes, many of the men were killed, and the others ran away. A few of the men, mainly the deputies whom Jack had trained, withdrew in fairly good order toward the town.

Nobody on either side noticed as the tank stopped and a man got out. Nobody saw him pick up boxes of ammunition and lower them into the tank. As soon as the Demons reached the road, they saw their tank moving toward them and cheered. The town was theirs for the taking!

## TEN

### I

Jack had been careful to lock each hatch in the tank as he rolled up toward the Demons. Now he stopped and forced his body into the contortions required to get out of the driver's seat without leaving the tank. In a few minutes, he was free and loading his machineguns.

As the Demons sauntered toward him, Jack opened fire, sweeping the coaxial machinegun back and forth, tearing gaps in the Demon's ranks. Jack continued firing as the Demons broke and ran, leaving fifty bodies behind them.

The survivors ran down the slope, throwing their rifles

away and fleeing for their lives. Jack continued to fire long after they were out of range. Perhaps two hundred survivors made it to safety.

## II.

The Demons had won the battle and knew it as soon as the townsmen broke and ran away from them. The fact that they had won without their tank made them all feel better, and the sight of the tank lumbering up the hillside cheered them even more. Now they would be able to crush any opposition they met. Best of all was the fact that they wouldn't have to share the loot with as many people. Most of the men gathered around and congratulated themselves on their victory, sharing their cigarettes as they bunched together. The comradely feeling was brutally ripped aside as the tank opened fire on them.

The Demons stood, shocked, for a fleeting instant, then they themselves broke and ran away, followed closely by the slugs from the enemy machinegun.

When they gathered together on the other side of the ridge, the Demons mustered one hundred ninty-three men under Mario's command.

Ahead of them was their march back to Boise.

Mario and eight-six men would make it back to safety.

## III

Under the cover of their machinegun fire, the deputies made good their withdrawal, carrying most of their weapons with them. Carefully, skillfully, they broke contact with the Demons and retreated toward the town.

As the men withdrew, they gathered up as many of the fugitives as they could and whipped them into the last defense lines, right on the outskirts of the town.

## IV

Jack clambered out of the tank as the last of the Demons disappeared through the gap and fled the lash of fire that Jack used to hurry them along their way. He walked over to his gun positions and looked for his own dead and wounded. As he passed the bodies of fallen Demons, the flat *crack!* of his pistol announced that he was still taking no chances. None of his men was alive, and most of the bodies had been mutilated in the few minutes that had elapsed since the Demons took over the hillside.

As he walked among the bodies, Jack was totalling up his own losses. Including Reverend Gillespie, his people had lost almost twenty-five men in this battle, plus however many would die during their flight to safety. On the other hand, the enemy had lost three tanks and perhaps ninety percent of his forces. The battle had been a lopsided victory for the defenders, but still, the cost to Jack's men was great, too great, even if only one of his men had died.

He walked over to his command bunker, which had been built into the hillside. He stopped for a moment to light his pipe. As the match flared, and he drew the flame into the bowl, a single shot rang out. The slug struck Jack high in the back, knocking him face down into the snow. He tried to get up, pushing against the hard ground, then fell forward.

A man in camouflage clothing came down out of the trees and walked over to Jack's body. He kicked the fallen man in the side and turned him over. As soon as the sniper recognized his victim, his face blanched.

He quickly stuffed a handkerchief into Jack's wound and dragged him over to a jeep. With a whirr from the starter, he drove off down the road as fast as he could go.

# BOOK FOUR: RECONSTRUCTION

## ONE

### I

The chill March sun shone down on the man in a wheelchair, sitting in the glassed-in porch of the hospital. The man was gaunt and pale, his skin stretched tight over the bones of his body. A nurse came out onto the porch to take him back into the building.

"Come on, Jack," she said, "let's go back in now. Doctor Randolph says that you're doing so well and we don't want to take a chance of getting pneumonia."

"Yeah, Ginny, all I'd need is another dose of that. Get me back inside so I can rest. All this moving around is more exhausting than working on the farm. Are you sure that Jean and the kids are doing all right out there?"

"Of course, Jean just plain took over. She and her kids and my kids are getting everything ready for spring now. They're doing fine."

"I just feel so lazy sitting out the winter here, Ginny."

"Jack, you must be a compulsive about working. You were shot in the back, operated on, got a post-op infection, then pneumonia. What do you expect except to sit here and rest? Besides, just think, you've been the only patient in the hospital, and without you as an excuse, Doc Randolph and all the other nurses would have been out of a job."

Ginny and another nurse helped Jack into his bed,

carefully tucking the covers around him. The wound that had nearly killed him still wasn't fully healed due to the infection that had developed and the pneumonia that weakened him so badly.

Jack was extremely weak and badly wasted, looking more like a skeleton than the man who had led the battles against the Demons. In the last few weeks, Jack had definitely turned the corner and was beginning his recovery. He was gaining weight and beginning to take an interest in the world around him.

During the recovery, Adam Henderson had taken up the reins of government and was leading the community with much the same ability that Jack had shown. Besides making sure that everybody would be ready for the spring plantings, Adam was already planning the implementation of the fortification program that Jack had laid out.

People were already being notified of their duties under the program, and plans were being issued to each of the construction crews. Henderson had it easy with this job, since Jack had prepared the plans and set up the hour schedules in advance, then filed them after his plans were blocked by Reverend Gillespie and his people.

The plans were extensive, and laid out in a logical sequence, starting with the fortification of the most exposed areas of the community and working inward. Most of the plans had been designed around the exploitation of natural obstacles to channel enemy movements, the erection of concrete shelters on each farm to protect its owners, and the construction of large concrete watchtowers that would serve to protect the people against an attack by a force armed with more than simple weapons.

Even the town was to be converted into a sort of fortress, with the town center, its warehouses, offices, hospital, and school fortified as a last-ditch defense against attack.

Ginny suggested to her grandfather that, as soon as Jack was better, he report to Jack what had been done so far, and the plans for the future. He was also to ask his advice about the future direction of the community.

## II

The work on the first watchtower was finally finished and the crew assigned to the job stood back and watched with satisfaction as the last of the forms were pulled away.

The building stood thirty feet high, with walls that increased in thickness from one foot to four feet at the bottom. The smooth concrete offered an attacker no handholds or openings, since the entry was up at the top. Steel combs, sticking out and down and sharpened to a fine edge prevented any unauthorized climbing. The four rooms inside the tower would provide cramped shelter for about forty people for the time needed for the mobile forces from the town to arrive and drive off the attackers.

Around the base of the tower, a series of antipersonnel obstacles, ranging from barbed wire entanglements on up to a dry ditch presented passive barriers to any one coming close to the tower. In addition, the shelter was liberally stocked with light infantry weapons to fend off an attack.

The value of the plans was demonstrated after the raid on the Kingman farm, south of the town. The enemy had attacked in overwhelming force, killing many of the people on the farm in the first wash of fire. The survivors retreated into their basement and fired back, turning the farmyard into a charnel house as the attackers were cut down. Jeep patrols had been sent out to attack the invaders and had successfully driven them off. Unfortunately, two of the jeeps had been cut off and their crews killed, with the ambushers making off with both jeeps and weapons.

The only reason anybody survived at the Kingman farm was that their shelter had been partially completed and stocked. It had allowed the survivors to fight off the immediate danger of attacks, while waiting for the mobile force from town to finish the job. The only real failure with the system was the loss of the two jeeps.

The result was that Frank Janus was spending more and more time trying to train an effective militia, but he really didn't remember much about drills, nor did he know how to operate some of the weapons that Jack had recovered. He spent most of his time hoping that Jack would come back and take over the training schedule.

## III

The surviving Demons had settled down in Boise and had simply absorbed everyone who came into the city to find shelter. After much purging of undesirable elements, they had built up a force of almost two thousand infantry, and had found supplies to last them well into the next year. Most of what had been destroyed by their careless slaves had been purely residential areas.

The winter had been hard for the surviving Demons, since there was no power and therefore no heat. No one in the gang, nor any of the people who joined them later, knew how to produce any power, and the only heat that kept them going through the winter was the heat from burning wood and the heat of the hatred they felt toward the people of Henderson's Corners.

Mario and his leaders planned their campaign for the coming summer. They would wait until the farmers got their first crops harvested, then strike. This time, they would have their main attack directed against the southern outskirts of the town, over ground that was gently rolling and covered with patches of woods. With any kind of luck, they would be able to overrun parts of the town itself before they could be stopped.

They would wait until August, getting themselves ready for the attack. In the meantime, they would keep up the attacks on the town, just like the one that had netted them some jeeps, machineguns, and lots of ammunition.

Mario planned that since his troops were almost as strong as they had been when he first attacked the town, and the fact that the first attack had undoubtedly inflicted heavy casualties on the townspeople, he would be able to swap off his people at even a two for one ratio and have enough men left to take over the town.

## IV

Janice Wilson and her girls had survived the winter by holing up in a vacation hotel. Some of the girls had died from starvation and the cold, but now Janice and the eighteen survivors of her school class were setting out to fulfill the debt they owed to Jim Dawson's family.

Janice and the girls had survived by trapping other people, like the motorcycle gang that had ambushed them. They had attracted their victims with the hint of sex and food, and killed them. Some of the gangs had prisoners with them, and they were allowed to live, but were kept separate from Janice and the girls.

As soon as the weather broke, Janice and her girls would set out on the five hundred mile journey that lay ahead of them. Without trucks or busses to carry them, they all knew that the journey would take at least two months of hard marching, especially since they would have to first become toughened for the march, then would have to forage for food along the way.

With any luck, they would keep their promise by September.

# TWO

## I

Jack listened carefully as Henderson explained what had been done in the community after the winter ended and they were passing into spring. As each point was carefully explained in detail, Jack nodded his head and told Henderson to go on.

One of the most important things Jack learned was that the town had been monitoring the radio transmissions of a number of other communities. There were other bands of survivors in the world and they were also striving to build up a civilization. Almost all of them were short on food, but long on other supplies. Finally, as Henderson wound down, Jack began to ask him questions about other things.

"What about the tanks? Has anybody been out to salvage the two wrecks yet?"

"No, we thought they were useless. Besides, the one that you captured lost its tracks when we tried to bring it into town and we can't seem to be able to get them back on."

"That's okay. Just get both wrecks towed into town if you can. If not, strip them of everything that you can get off them, clean off any rust and pack them in oil. As soon as I can, I'll supervise their repair.

"Now, as for the tank that lost its treads, from what you said, it sounds like somebody gunned the engine from a standing start and the track torque snapped some of the pins. Take the pins out of the other two tanks and try to put the treads back together. If you can't get it done, tell me, and I'll come out to tell the crew what has to be done.

"Adam, what about the raid on the Kingman ranch? Did you ever find out who did it?"

"No, but we believe that it might have been some of the survivors from the Demons who escaped us last fall. We've been probing north toward Boise, and have run into some pretty heavy battles. We've lost a half-dozen men and had two jeeps wrecked as well."

"Well, the answer is to get in there with something heavier than a jeep. We'll cut back on sending patrols north until I can sketch out some plans for improving our APCs. Once that's done, we'll send them out. Until the conversion of the APCs is finished, don't send any jeep patrols out to the north.

"Also, try to impress on our people that we want to get ourselves a prisoner or two. The more we have, the better off we'll be, since we can cross-check their stories.

"From what you say, everybody is ready to plant their crops as soon as they can work the ground. Once that's done, we can finish off the fortification program, as well as build a lot more storage space for our crops. If things look as good for us this year, we ought to have a bumper crop, much more than we can ever use.

"What I want to do is to try to open up communications with some of the nearby cities and start trading our food for their supplies of things we can't make. We're going to have to expand our farmlands as much as we can, since as soon as the fertilizers run out, we'll start getting decreased yields. We'll have to find some substitute for manufactured fertilizers, since just manure won't do the trick. Also, I want . . ."

"Jack, you don't want anything! Granddad, I'm surprised at you, keeping him up like this. It's time for him to get some rest! Now scoot!"

Adam got out while the getting was good, knowing full

well what his granddaughter was like when she was mad. For a few minutes, Ginny fussed around, tucking the covers back around Jack and fluffing his pillows.

Finally, the flurry of work was done, and Ginny sat down on the edge of the bed. Reaching out, she rubbed Jack's hair.

"Jack, I think you look better right now than when I brought you into the bedroom. Do you feel as well as you look?"

"Sure I do! I feel as though I could eat a whole horse. Listen, Ginny, could you try to sneak me some real food? I want some red meat and lots of potatoes. I want to get out of here as soon as I can. Will you give me a hand?"

Ginny smiled and leaned over, kissing Jack on the forehead.

"I'll bring you some food later today. I'll talk to Doctor Randolph about starting you on solids as soon as I can."

Ginny stood up and started to walk out the door, then turned and started to speak. After a moment's hesitation, she walked back out the door.

As soon as Ginny was out of sight, Jack dropped back into the pillows, exhausted. He wouldn't let Ginny or anybody else know how tired he still was. His town needed him, and would need him all the more by the harvest. He was sure that the Demons wouldn't be planning to harvest anything, so they would wait until the harvest was in before they attacked.

By that time, Jack wanted to be up and back to normal.

## II

Adam Henderson returned to his office in a very good mood. It had been a long time since Jack had looked so well or was so interested in what was going on around him. Even Jean had stopped visiting him, because she couldn't bear to look at him the way he was. Ginny had given up her job in the town's administration to nurse him back to health and stay beside him.

Adam had figured that Jack would approve what he had done, and knew that the community was well prepared as far as food was concerned, but he also realized how woefully unprepared the town was for an attack. Once more, he indulged himself by wishing that Jim Dawson was here also, but everyone, even his wife Jean, had pretty much given up hope for Jim. Some of the other men had been in the service, but few of them really remembered too clearly what they had done or how they had been trained, at least not enough to set up a coherent training plan.

Henderson sat down at his old desk in the store. He couldn't bring himself to move into Jack's office, it would be too much to expect that. He looked over the reports on his desk and studied them. Most showed the work crews were on schedule or ahead of schedule. Only the work of drilling new deep wells on the farms was dragging, mainly because there weren't enough materials around to build windmills or pumps.

Jack might know some way of getting water out of the wells or perhaps to conserve materials; he would make certain to ask him in the morning. In the meantime, Henderson studied the plans for the old-time wood-fired fireplaces that were to be built into all the houses over the summer. Each was a big cast-iron unit with a heat-holding compartment and was specifically designed to keep a fire going for a long time. They ought to do to keep the use of fuel down this winter.

Alcohol production was up, using a process one of the teachers had developed for using weeds and clippings to supplement the precious grains that they had been using. The process worked well on a small scale, and now it was time to approve the full-scale use of the process. So far, the stills were producing a little more than eighty percent of the fuels that were consumed in the town, but that was proving to be enough to supplement and stretch the existing stocks through the summer, allowing them the time needed to build still more stills to keep the vehicles running.

Drastic fuel conservation programs had been instituted, and the bicycles that Jack had ordered brought into the town were beginning to show their value. Everybody who had a horse was especially lucky, and the town committee had been forced to place controls on their sale and use, especially since it took a long time to breed and train horses.

Adam Henderson had already made up the plans to breed the horses to the point where, in ten years, they would have replaced powered vehicles in almost all jobs around the town. Most people were cooperating with him, all except Herb Jaczech. He owned a horse farm and had completely refused to allow anybody to buy or breed his prize Arabians. Adam was using all sorts of friendly persuasion, but was out of luck so far. The man completely refused to cooperate in that way.

The electrical supply was proving to be one of the real bright spots in the community. Copies of the installations that Jack had built on his farm were beginning to appear on every farm with a stream and everywhere the wind blew with some regularity. The town was well on the way to having a surplus of electricity available. Once that occurred, they could begin some of the other projects that Jack had laid out.

Yes, the plans Jack had made up and rammed through the opposition of the committees were showing their worth. Too bad Jack wasn't in a condition to appreciate it.

## III

One of the two-man jeep patrols had been sent far to the south on a scouting mission. Along the way, they had met a fairly large number of people who were hanging on in their homes and on their farms. They had eagerly questioned the men on where they had come from, and many made plans to contact the town. The patrol had driven up into the high country, planning to go overland and across the hills to save some time. Now, they were thoroughly lost. Overcast prevented them from taking a fix from the sun, and the maps they had were so old as to be useless. Therefore, they had spent much of their time driving around and around in circles, trying to find their way back to familiar territory.

Finally, they came out into a mountain meadow and saw a huge flight of crows and vultures rise up into the air as the noise of the jeep frightened them off. The jeep bounced across the field to the body. Bodies, rather, because there must have been fifty bodies scattered around the field, almost all of them in fine suits. Around them, were the tumbled ruins of some tents that had been blown down in a windstorm. The men who were in the field had died from exposure when they couldn't set their tents up again.

The jeep crew left the bodies where they lay. After seeing a world die, they had grown callous in the treatment of mortality. As they drove across the meadow, they saw what looked like a road in front of them. They stopped and looked at the carefully rolled stone and oil surface, and at the chemically trimmed weeds that lined the road. Overhead, the trees had been cut back to completely conceal the road from the air.

The two men looked at one another as they checked the road out. It was obviously something other than what they had expected. A lot of money and work had gone into building a road like this up on top of a mountain, and it sure didn't show up on any map they had!

As they drove around a curve, they saw the bulk of an APC squatting in the road in front of them, its left-hand tread broken and snarled around the drive sprocket. They climbed up onto the vehicle and looked inside. There were no bodies, but all of the weapons were intact, and the interior was piled high with boxes of field rations. The men helped themselves to what they needed and drove on.

They almost drove past the opening in the rocks, and would have missed it completely if a chance ray of sunshine hadn't reflected off some metal object. They stopped and looked, and found that they could pull the mountainside away. As they tugged at the door, for that was what it was, they marveled at the sheer size. An opening fully twelve feet high and as wide soon gaped blackly in front of them. The safe-like door was over four feet thick!

They looked down a huge corridor, that stretched off into the distance, the rays of light from outside swallowed up long before they reached the end. One of the men went back to the jeep and brought it over, shining its headlights into the tunnel. They showed nothing. The men turned on the searchlight mounted on the side of the jeep. Faintly, far away, they could see what seemed to be a gray reflection.

Excitedly, knowing they had found something extraordinary, the men took a navigational fix on the noon sun and warmed up their radio.

## IV

Mario and the surviving Demons had made themselves the unquestioned leaders of their gang through a reign of fear and terror among their recruits. Now they were busy taking over the whole area around Boise, capturing more slaves and finding, in the extremes of hunger, more and more recruits.

The campaign of raids against the townsmen was coming along quite well, effectively forcing them to fight a war on many fronts, and spreading their troops consistently thinner and thinner. Soon, the time would come for the Demons to attack.

## V

For Jean, the coming of spring was the opening of a new life. The blackness and depression that had haunted her all through the winter, isolated as they were up at the farm, almost cost her her mind, but she had pulled through. The news that Jack was still alive, after the first stories about his being killed during the battles with the Demons, was welcome.

As soon as the weather let up enough, Ginny had managed to come up to the farm in a jeep loaded with some surprises for the kids and Jean herself. The biggest gift, though, was having someone whom she could talk to, someone to whom she could poor out the grief that had paralyzed her mind for half a year. By the time Ginny went back to town Jean felt more human than she had for months, and more like living than she had ever felt since the attack.

What was past was past, and now the future beckoned to her and her children and Ginny's children as well. She owed it to all of them, and to herself, to stop being a fool. There was so much constructive work that she could do now, there wasn't any point in worrying herself to the point of insanity over something that couldn't be changed.

It was hard to think, let alone say, but let the dead bury the dead. Jean and the kids had a lot of living to do!

## THREE

### I

Jack was up and around on the late May morning when Adam Henderson came running over to him.

"Jack, I've got to talk to you about something. One of our jeep patrols found something that you ought to be interested in. It was a huge tunnel drilled into a hillside and closed off by an enormous vault door. They think it was some kind of military installation, although they found a lot of bodies all done up in fancy civilian suits. What do you think we ought to do?"

"Frankly, Adam, I don't know what to do offhand. The place the scouts found probably wasn't a missile silo or a command shelter. If it had been, it would have been surrounded with fences and guardposts.

"I think it might be one of the top-secret government shelters that the *National Globe* was always blathering about before the war. Looks like they're right. If that's the case, the scouts found themselves a real treasure trove.

"What I think we ought to do is to have the patrol go in on foot, one man well in front of the other, say, by a hundred meters. That way, if the tunnel is booby-trapped, only one of the men will be injured.

"By the way, are the men broadcasting continuously? If they are, we'd better order them to keep their transmissions to a minimum, because somebody else may decide that the supplies in that shelter belong to them, and try to take them away from us.

"I'm going to get one of the APCs fueled up and drive down there to check it out myself."

"Jack, you can't do that, you're still pretty sick!"

"Look, Adam, this is just the sort of thing that I'm here for. Everything is running smoothly without me, you've done a beautiful job managing the town. The only thing we really have to do is to write up some sort of drill manual for the militia, and the training schedule I've already set up takes care of that. That means that nobody really needs me around here, so I'm going."

## II

In his headquarters in Boise, Mario and his officers gathered to discuss their plans for the attack on Henderson's Corners. It wasn't too early in the season to start planning a major campaign, especially with the memory of their last attack on the town firmly in mind.

Their plan had evolved from what had originally been thought out, but was still kept quite simple. The attack would consist of two parts: the first attack would be made against the same two gaps that had claimed so many of the original Demons. These men would have the job of drawing off the majority of the defenders and keeping them pinned while the second attack went in. The second force would march by night until it was in position to attack through the vulnerable flatlands south of the town.

Mario had been crafty enough to work out a plan where the majority of his raids were directed against the northern hills, while only light and seemingly ineffectual probes were used in the south. With any kind of luck, the townies would fall for the plan, especially since the northern attacks were scheduled to begin hours before the southern attacks.

That was one of the problems that faced Mario and his officers, the lack of communications. Except for a few battered CBs and some other radios they had salvaged, there was no way for the two forces to communicate. Everything would have to be done by prearranged plan, and since that could mean a security leak, nobody but the top twenty officers in the whole Demon force knew that the northern attacks would be no more than a diversion.

The time between the planning and the attack on the town was going to be taken up in attacking the small family groups and tribes that surrounded the city. They would be taken and made into cannon fodder and slaves. The slaves would provide the Demons with all the transport capacity they needed to execute their sweep around to the south of the enemy. In the meantime, the Demons would sharpen their skills at murder, torture and rape.

For sheer terror, only Genghis Khan or Attila matched the Demons.

## III

The jeep patrol was waiting for their orders, sitting in their jeep, eating their captured rations and smoking liberated cigarettes. Just a few feet away, the tunnel mouth opened into blackness. After searching for a while, they had finally found the man-sized hinges that the door swung on. They had finally seen through the camouflage, but only because they knew exactly where to look.

After nearly an hour, their radio crackled into life. In a short time, they had been given their orders and sent on their way. In silence, one of the men fished in his pocket and pulled out his wallet. Opening it, he pulled out a worn silver dollar and flipped it into the air.

"Heads!"

"Tails, you lose!"

With a sigh, the loser picked himself up and got out of the jeep. With a wave and a shrug, he disappeared into the tunnel. When the other man figured that he had walked far enough into the tunnel, he started the jeep and drove it into the tunnel. As he rode along, his jeep bounced over the massive tracks that still more blast doors would slide on; he could see their foot-thick sides drawn back into the walls.

Almost a kilometer into the tunnel, the driver saw that there was an abrupt turn, and he carefully followed it. Ahead of him, he could see, in the otherwise blank wall, the ball-and-socket fittings for machineguns, and the much more massive mounting for an artillery barrel. Again the tunnel turned, and again it was heavily defended.

As he drove up to the end of the tunnel, the lights flashed on in a huge cavern. The man was out of his seat and diving for cover before he realized that the sounds echoing from wall to wall were not the sounds of machineguns, but of his partner's laughter.

"Gotcha!," he chortled.

"Goddam you, Lee! You scared ten years life out of me. What's it look like in there?"

"I'm sorry, Mark, but I just couldn't resist. The lights flashed on when I came into the motor pool and I couldn't resist trying them out on you.

"Well, I only got as far as this motor pool. There are over a hundred APCs and maybe half that number of tanks all sitting here, wrapped up in plastic cocoons. It looks like somebody planned to do a lot of fighting.

"Over there are what look like helicopters all wrapped up neatly and put away, and back here is a whole shop for the tanks and APCs. Somebody used it to get the one we found on the road fixed up.

"Christ, I think we found out where all our tax dollars have gone, right down the hole, just like we always figured!

"I found a wall diagram over there, just beside that airlock door. Mark, this place is spread out over kilometers and dug deep into the ground as well, with at least a half-dozen levels. This place could hold our whole town in safety and without squeezing. Let's take a look around."

The two men wandered around the shelter, from room to room. They found the shelter was piled high with rack after rack of boxes, neatly labeled, of everything from anchovy paste to zithers. The quarters all ranged from magnificent to totally luxurious.

Finally, they found the soldiers' quarters. A look through the sealed doors made up their minds for them. They left the door sealed and continued on. Finally, they came to a door labeled, in neat simulated walnut, as the "Main Control Room". They went in and found why the door had been slightly open. Inside, an old man in a silk leisure suit was slumped over the control panel.

Both men walked back to their jeep to report the whole find to their home base.

Back in town, the process of assembling an expedition to the shelter was well underway. Two APCs with fuel and supply trailers, as well as about two dozen men, were ready to set out for the south.

This group was assembled from the various experts that Jack felt he would need to evaluate the contents of the hoard, as well as the men that he might need to defend it. Most of the men moved about excitedly, knowing that the expedition to the shelter was a change from their routine. Jack was busy checking to make sure that all their gear was loaded.

At last, with a clatter of tracks, the expedition moved out.

# FOUR

## I

As the beginning of September approached, Jack

regained more and more of his strength, until he was almost back to normal. He had returned from the trip to the shelter complex in much better condition than he had gone in, and was soon swept up in the problems of contacting nearby governments and making arrangements to sell off the surplus crops that his farmers were gathering in.

All the while the delicate negotiations were going on, Jack was checking out the reports of his salvage crews at "Valley Forge". Almost three months of work had barely put a dent in the mountainful of supplies that the scouts had discovered.

Most of the supplies that Jack and his men had removed consisted of medical supplies, enough to set up a proper hospital for Doctor Randolph. Spare tractors and other agricultural machinery were brought out of storage and brought to town, since the custom harvesters hadn't been through last year, and wouldn't return for the foreseeable future.

The military supplies had been carefully examined, and the weapons removed to provide everybody with a single caliber of weapon, and weapons capable of automatic fire. The probes toward the north were running into the fiercest resistance the townsmen ever encountered, so tough that two of the APCs had been destroyed. Finally, Jack had approved the activation of five tanks. That was proceeding as rapidly as possible in the shelter shops.

One project that Jack was trying to rush to fruition was the assembly of a small, ten-man transport plane that they had found in the shelter. Jack planned to use that as a courier plane to carry emergency supplies to the people he was in contact with. The survivors in Spokane were especially in need of antibiotics, and a mercy flight to that city would be well worth while.

Throughout the summer, Jack's recovery had seemingly gone as well as the town's bumper crop of food. His sheer enthusiasm rubbed off on everybody whom he came into contact with, because at last, they were building for the future and reaching out to their fellow men to trade food for other goods.

Most of the watchtowers and the outlying farm buildings had been connected into the telephone network that had been constructed. The use of the lines was, however, kept strictly to business. Many of the farms had been re-equipped with electricity, most of it generated on their premises. They would need every watt to preserve the harvest.

The salvage of the harvesting machinery from "Valley Forge" had freed most of the people from a large portion of their normal work load. The extra time had been well-spent by developing a series of courses in agriculture, mechanics, and the cottage-industry skills that the people would need to survive. Especially important were the first aid courses given to everybody in the town. The doctor and his nurses couldn't be everywhere in an emergency, and the people would have to learn to deal with their own problems.

The flow of refugees increased all through the summer, with an average of two or three people per day passing through. Most of them were so exhausted that they joined up with the townspeople at once. A few, the most incorrigible, went on their way. Significantly, most of them moved north, toward Boise.

The refugees who stayed were gaunt survivors of a whole winter of the hardest scrounging, just to stay alive. They told stories of walking through towns and villages whose streets were white with the skeletons of the people who had lived there. They told stories of roving bands of men and women—the children didn't survive—that made travel very hard, if not almost impossible. Their stories were enough to let everybody in the town know exactly how lucky they had been to survive so long.

The wanderers were nursed back to health, taught some of the skills they would need if their former jobs were useless, and parceled out among the farmers as an extra pair of hands to lighten the load. A few families had arrived intact, and these were especially welcome, since they were the core around which the community would form. Most of the wanderers were young, male, and friendless strangers who created a serious problem with an imbalance in the sexes.

Despite the lessons of the past fall, the townsmen were again beginning to neglect their military training, although many of them did so well that they were almost as good as the old paratroopers. Most had received their training with their personal weapon, as well as cross-training on at least two other weapons they would normally find in their units. A small armored infantry unit was formed around a core of fifty deputies who would man a dozen APCs and their one tank.

All the training seemed to be wasted, especially since the Demons had abandoned Boise and headed west.

## II

The Demons moved out of Boise, carrying all of their ammunition and looted food with them in slave-powered carts. Behind them, the city burned, completely this time. There could be no turning back for any of them, since there would be nothing to turn back to.

Mario led his band off to the west, into the forests, where they soon lost or ambushed all of the patrols that Jack sent after them. Finally, they turned south, marching by night and sleeping by day to avoid any patrols from their target. Finally, they reached their jumping off points and made ready for the attack.

The attack force on the northern section of the front was accompanied by an improvised flamethrower. Some unknown genius among the Demons had designed a combination of fuel tank and high-speed pump, that was ignited by waving a burning propane torch over the stream of gasoline.

As they waited for the word to attack, the Demons rested. In two days, no matter what, they were going to attack at dawn.

### III

George Johnson and Wilson Good, the leaders of the community of Spokane, had discussed and finally approved the plans to meet with Dawson and his people. In one week, they would arrive at the town, with some of their bodyguards.

### IV

Janice Wilson and her girls were approaching the town of Henderson's Corners. That very day, they had crossed the path of a large body of people marching southward. They were about a day's march ahead of the young women, but had left macabre mileposts behind themselves. The path was marked with the torn and mutilated bodies of people.

Janice and the girls stepped up their pace, determined to reach the town and get their job done with.

## FIVE

### I

Jack was awakened out of a sound sleep shortly before

dawn as one of his aides shook him awake.

"Colonel, the northern outpost line is under attack. We just got word from the woodcutters that the Demons are coming into the valleys!"

"God damn! What happened to our scouts out to the north?

"Sound the air raid siren and have the combat team gather in the assembly hall. As soon as they're ready, we're moving out.

"Get hold of Frank Janus on the phone and tell him I want to talk to him. I'm going to get dressed."

The officer went to the emergency phone while Jack pulled his clothes on. Just as he was lacing his boots, the man handed him the telephone.

"Frank, it looks like we're under attack up on the northern ridges again. I want you to gather the militia together as they come in. Send half the men up to me on the ridges, and keep the rest here, buttoned up in their APCs and ready to move out. I may need them on a moment's notice, so be sure that you keep control of them. Got all that? Good, see you soon."

Jack dropped the handset back onto the cradle and pulled on his boots. It looked like he was going to get another battle, but he wondered if his people were ready for it. He knew that most of them weren't.

The weird ear-shattering warbling of the air raid sirens blotted all thought away as they sounded from the roof of the administration building. Others, placed on various watchtowers, took up the call. Jack knew that a good portion of the men would answer the call, but he wondered how many would actually turn out.

As the sounds of the sirens died away, Jack could hear the diesels of the tanks and the APCs as they hammered into life. At least his maintenance crews knew what they were supposed to do. Jack ran down the stairs from his office-home, buckling his pistol belt around his waist.

In a matter of minutes, he had crossed the distance to the tank park and was checking out his vehicles. Already some of his combat team was arriving and waiting for orders. Jack watched as others rode up on bicycles and horses. Short greetings and orders followed as each of the men checked out their vehicles and their ammunition loads. The maintenance crew was topping off each vehicle's tanks with more fuel. In less than a half-hour, the whole combat team was assembled and ready to move out.

The news from up north was grave. Most of the outpost line that had been set up was already in the hands of the enemy. The jeep patrols which had been counted on to provide information about the enemy's movements had been apparently wiped out or were pinned down under heavy fire. Only two wood parties, each defending one of the ridges, were holding the enemy back.

Jack ordered the men to hold at all costs.

As soon as his whole group of soldiers was available, Jack moved out at top speed, not knowing just what kind of dangers he faced.

The past year had shown Jack that there were more heavy weapons around than he had suspected. The survivors in San Francisco had been almost wiped out by a roving gang which had recovered a heavy howitzer and some ammunition.

To add protection to his equipment, Jack had ordered metal racks and skirting bolted to the APCs and the tanks. Both of the vehicle types had been improved by the addition of bare copper wire mounted on insulators and attached to a spare alternator. Anybody who tried the same trick that Jack had during the past winter would be in for electrocution.

The APCs had had metal plates fitted around their heavy machineguns, in effect forming a turret, just like Jack had seen in 'Nam. Firing ports had been cut into the hull to let the crew inside fire out.

As they rolled along, Jack ordered part of his force to move out and support one of the wood parties that was only lightly engaged. The rest stayed under Jack's command and went up onto the ridge that he had fought from last year.

In a little more than an hour, Jack and his unit were heading into the battle zone. Ahead of them they could hear the rattle of small-arms fire and the louder tearing sound of the .50 caliber machineguns. Jack signaled the men who were riding on top of their APCs to get under cover, and ordered the lead tank to pull over so that he could take the lead.

As Jack's APC edged past the tank, he could see a man step out of the woods up ahead. The whole column stopped as Jack leaned over, recognizing his cousin Linc, who had been in charge of the wood party.

"Hi, Jack, 'bout time you guys got here. I think that they're those damned Demons again, you know. There must be a thousand of them out in the woods below us, and all trying to climb up the hill to get at us.

"We've been using the weapons we brought with us, and we're keeping them pretty much away, but now they're beginning to slip through. They're across the obstacle line down in the valley and into the trees. I'm glad you got here, Jack."

"I am too, Linc. This is a job that's been waiting too long for finishing. I wanted to get it over with a long time ago, but I got overruled every time.

"Linc, I'm going to spread my infantry out among your men, set up a couple of mortars here and let them have a few rounds, then send one of the tanks and a couple of APCs down the road and see if we can flush them out from behind. I want you to wait here and intercept the militia as they get up here. As you get them, send them into the line. I'll be watching the rest of the battle."

With that, Jack dropped out of sight into his APC to pass the orders along via radio. In a matter of minutes, the tank and two APCs disappeared down the road and the four mortar carriers had parked themselves over their surveyed firing points while the infantry dismounted and joined the wood party in firing into the enemy below.

The sounds of battle raised perceptibly as the newcomers added their weapons to those of the wood party. The sounds rose to a crescendo as the 107mm mortars began lobbing their bombs into the trees below.

At the foot of the cliff, trees shivered and disintegrated into flying splinters as the high explosive bombs struck the ground and detonated. In a matter of a few minutes, the Demons were eliminated as an effective fighting force.

Jack was watching the progress of the tank and the APCs as they worked their way down the road. The APC crews were using their machineguns to slash at the enemy, and the tank was rolling over the barriers that the enemy had put up. The tank was already positioning itself in a nice, clear fire position, ready to blast away with its 120mm gun and finish off what the mortars missed.

The Demons broke faster this time than they had the year before, and ran much harder. Most of them withdrew in good order, although the mortars were able to take out a number of them.

As Jack swept the area with his binoculars, he could see a stream of liquid suddenly spurt out and spray over the tank. Grabbing up his microphone, he shouted out a warning.

"Get out of there! Back up, they're spraying you with gasoline! Get your asses out before they fry you!"

Before the final words had passed Jack's lips, the gas ignited in a terrible fireball, leaping upward from the stricken tank like the fireballs that had destroyed civilization. The tank continued to roll backward, trailing streams of fire, then clattered to a stop.

The APC crews reacted to the stream of gasoline by backing clear of the tank, then, as one of the APCs stayed on the road and sprayed the ditch with fire, the other vehicle bounced over and straddled the ditch, the gunner pumping round after round into the strange flamethrower. In an instant, the tank of gasoline was split open, and the fuel ignited by the tracer rounds from the machinegun. The tank crew watched where their accompanying APCs fired their weapons and added their machinegun fire as well. Since the crew was almost blind inside the tank, they relied heavily on their supporting vehicles to direct fire.

At last, they reached a point where the fire from their cannon could do some good. The driver halted to provide a better firing platform, and the gunners opened fire. The men quickly slammed round after round of high explosive ammunition into the breech of their main gun and jumped out of the way of the spent rounds ejected from the weapon. A dozen rounds did the job, then the tank displaced and moved slowly down the road, planning to cut off the enemy's retreat.

As the tank rolled forward, the radio operator heard the warning from Jack and passed it to the driver. With clashing gears, the driver brought the tank to a halt and began to back up.

With a blowtorch roar, the gasoline erupted into flames.

The APC crews reacted just as they had been trained. Their response was almost textbook perfect, as one of the vehicles covered the advance of the other by fire. Now they were backing hastily up the road to avoid the river of flame that was pouring out of the Demon machine.

At the sight of their flamethrower bursting apart, the nearby Demons went berserk, charging the APCs and firing wildly in their direction. Like ants swarming over a scorpion, the Demons clambered up onto the side of the vehicle. An alert member of the crew threw the switch that sent current through the wires, electrocuting many of the attackers.

The Demons backed off, frustrated, as the soft lead of their bullets splattered harmlessly on the vehicles' armor. Instead of standing, they began to retreat. Sensing the enemy's demoralization, the APCs began to advance, their gunners back in their improvised turrets and blazing away at the enemy. Breaking through the enemy ambush, the two armored vehicles raced toward the gap that the enemy would have to pass through to escape. Even before they reached the gap, the crews could see and hear the explosions from dozens of mortar rounds that smashed into the ground up ahead.

It was all over but the mopping up.

## II

The Demons who had been thrown into the northern attack didn't know that their assault on the enemy was a diversion. They only realized it when their top leaders disappeared from the attack waves. Now they were stalled at the bottom of a steep slope, and the enemy up above was dumping thousands of rounds of machinegun fire into their ranks.

As soon as the mortars began to drop their bombs into the woods which sheltered them, and the enemy began to send armored vehicles down to rout them out, the bulk of the leaderless Demons simply ran away, back across the open fields and away from the death that was being heaped on them.

A few reached the gap just as the tank burst into

flame, but that couldn't hold them back. The constant enemy fire was increasing all the time, and the Demons could see single black dots from the ridge rise up and run down the slope, hunting them.

The few Demon survivors didn't live long enough to appreciate the fact that the arrival of the militia meant that the townspeople could take their time about hunting them down.

Jack watched helplessly as the tank was enveloped in a ball of fire, then turned back to his main job, finishing off the enemy below the ridge. Steady heavy fire was directed against them without mercy. This time, Jack wanted to make sure that no Demon escaped to rebuild the gang again. The militia was already beginning to filter into the front line and support the firefight.

Jack contacted his men who had been sent up along the line and found that they were no longer needed. The wood party commander had greatly exaggerated the trouble. Jack ordered his unit back to join him, while the militia was to finish off the Demons who were trapped in the valley.

As Jack stood there on the back of his APC, another one of the vehicles rolled up beside him, and Frank Janus called out.

"Jack, I couldn't stop them! The whole militia is coming up here with everything they've got!"

"Goddammit, can't these fools ever learn? Have my men and the wood party try to stop the militia from going over the ridge. Have them try to hold 'em back until I can impress them with a little bit of order. Don't those idiots realize that there were over twenty-five hundred of these bastards? Where do they think they went—into thin air?"

Jack dropped down inside his APC and passed his orders to his men to try to collect the militia and hold them in place for a little while.

Then he ordered his APC to go down the hill to check on his knocked out tank. The fire had done little real damage to the tank, since they had been designed to survive near-misses from nuclear weapons. As Jack's vehicle pulled up alongside the tank, he could see the tank commander perched gloomily in the turret hatch.

"Bill, are all of you guys all right?"

"Yeah, colonel, but the tank's had it. The fire burnt up the batteries and the electrical system. The engine died and we can't get it restarted. The whole thing's ending up on one hell of a note."

"Well, Bill, just relax. We'll have a repair truck down here as soon as we can and see if we can get you back under way. Can you manage without my help?"

"Yessir, don't see why not. Where are you going now?"

"I'm going to see if we can run down some prisoners. I want to question them about where the rest of their men disappeared to. See you later, Bill."

With a wave, Jack drove off down the road, past the blackened spot where the Demons had torched the tank. After a minute, his driver slowed down as they approached a ditch filled with Demons trapped by the fire from above. Jack ordered his driver to turn the vehicle and straddle the ditch.

Once in position, a quick burst from Jack's machine-gun stopped the pitter-pat of enemy fire against his armor. A second burst got their attention while he talked to them over the loudspeaker. "All right, you know you're trapped. Who wants to live long enough to get out of here?"

Most of the Demons sat in place, their mouths shut tight. Finally, one of the men stood up, only to be shot down by a companion near him. Jack walked a half-dozen rounds across the killer's chest.

"Now that you've gotten that out of your systems,

who wants to live, or would you prefer that I just kill you now and find somebody else who wants to stay alive?"

A Demon stood up and threw his pistol off into the brush.

"I want to live," the man said, "I want to see that the guys who left us here to die get theirs. What do you want to know?"

"The deal is," Jack said, "that you move up onto the road, one at a time, and pile your guns and ammunition up over there. As soon as I hear what you have to say and if I like what I hear, I'll let you go. How about it?"

The leader nodded, climbed out of the ditch and dropped his weaponry into a pile in front of the APC, then backed away, his hands raised. In a few minutes, the road was covered by twenty Demons, guarded by two of Jack's crew.

"Let's hear your story. Better make it good!"

"Well, I guess you know that after we lost your scouts, we marched back here. We were told we were the main attack, and that the rest of the men would be marched east to make a diversion.

"We found out we were the diversion when our leaders left us behind as we attacked. They must be chasing after the rest of the men, maybe two thousand of them, and the slaves. We should have killed them as soon as they left us, but we didn't think of it. I hope you kill those bastards just like you killed all of us!"

Jack pushed back his helmet and scratched at his head for a moment, then leaned forward.

"I believe you. Now, take your men and get out of here while I'll still let you go. I don't want to see any of you ever again, because if I do, I'm going to hang you to the nearest tree and let you kick your life out at the end of a rope. Now get moving!," Jack yelled, punctuating his sentence with a burst of fire from his machinegun. The Demons ran off as fast as they could, herded along by the APC. As soon as they ran through the gap, Jack turned back to see if he could get some more prisoners to talk.

On the other side of the valley, he could see what looked like hundreds of men walking down slope, firing as they came. The militia still wasn't listening to orders. As the mortar fire ceased, Jack used his radio to contact his men.

"Colonel to company, are you there?"

"We're here with our ears on, Jack."

"Good. Did you cease fire because you didn't want to hit any of our men or because you're out of ammunition?"

"Both. We've got maybe a dozen rounds left between us, and the infantry and the wood party are almost completely out of ammunition.

"Say, did you order the militia to move out? They just took off, yelling and firing as they went."

"No, they went on their own. I want you and the wood party to mount up and go back to town, reammo and overload your vehicles, and wait for me to get there. I'm afraid that our hardest battle is still ahead of us. Are you rolling?"

"Right now, Jack. It'll take us about twenty minutes to drive into town, another half-hour to load up and catch some food. Figure we'll be ready in about an hour. Do you think we ought to clean out our weapons?"

"Yeah, but don't break them down too far. We might have to have them ready for use at a moment's notice. I think I found out where our friends disappeared to, but I'm not going to send the whole force out on a hunch. As soon as you get to town, report to me. Out!"

Jack rolled off across the battlefield and captured a few more Demons. The story was the same, the bulk of the soldiers had gone off to the east.

Now Jack was really worried. Somewhere out there

were almost two thousand soldiers, heavily armed and spoiling for a fight. He had to find them soon, or his town stood a good chance of being wiped out, or worse, enslaved.

## III

The Demon initial assault teams had crept into the isolated farmyards, armed only with knives, and waited for the people to get up and about. By dawn, the selected farmhouses that barred their way into the town had been captured. The few women survivors of the attacks wished they had died, rather than captured.

By noon, though, the word was out: the Demons were coming!

Virtually the entire militia force, without orders, had marched north in response to their orders, instead of going to their assigned watchtowers. Only a very few of the men and women who remained behind were armed, and when they saw the seemingly endless stream of Demon's marching along their roads, fled, spreading panic wherever they went.

A few of the people stayed behind in their fortified farmhouses and fought back against the enemy, blasting down dozens of the Demons as they tried, time after time, to storm the fortifications. After delays of an hour, maybe two, most of the farmhouses had fallen to the Demons, their owners too badly wounded, or dead, to resist any longer. The loss of the militia was felt strongly that day.

## IV

In the town itself, the warning about the approaching Demons came much too late, since the militia which was planned to guard the town had disappeared northward to join in the fun. The townspeople were worried about the attack, but no panic had yet appeared. After all, one of the APCs had been left behind.

Adam Henderson decided to act on his own and gathered up a force of about thirty overage members of the militia, left ten of them behind to guard the town, and set out in trucks and the APC to help get the trapped farmers and ranchers into town.

## V

Jean, like everyone else in the community, was working in the fields to get in the last possible ounce of food from the harvest. Without the rich manufactured fertilizers, without the insecticides that were normally used, the crop this year had been very disappointing. Food supplies were disappointingly low this year, perhaps so low that the food wouldn't carry everyone through the winter and on to the next harvest. There would be a real danger that, unless massive use was made of the stored food from the Valley Forge complex, people would starve.

Jack had decided that the food would be kept as an emergency reserve against a real crisis. The stocks of food in the government shelter had been huge compared with the small number of elite people who had to be protected from the effects of a nuclear war, but when the number of people to be fed ran into the thousands, as they did in this community, they were far too little to feed everybody.

Jean and the rest of the people living on the farm were out in the fields harvesting the crops, or up in the hills tending the animals. Nobody was back at the farm buildings to see the ragged band of men that came into the compound, ducking behind cover and running in short bursts from building to building as they went forward. Nobody was there to see how heavily they were armed.

Scarcely an hour passed before the strangers found the people working in the fields.

With savage shouts, the men opened fire on the helpless farmers, cutting them down even as they tried to pick up their own guns to defend themselves against the vicious attack. Almost as quickly as the attack began, it was over, with almost all the casualties on the part of the farmers. One or two of the Demons had been lightly wounded, none killed.

The murderers walked through the field, poking each body with their rifles to see if there was any sign of life. Those who moved were shot in the head—this time, there would be no survivors to carry a warning back to the townsfolk.

Off to one side of the field, a woman stood up with a rifle tucked neatly at her side, clamped under her right arm to steady it as she blazed away on full automatic fire at the men so casually engaged in murder. It was Jean Dawson, and in a moment, all eyes were focused on her as she evened the score with the Demon's in a last suicidal effort. She was shot down in a moment or two, but not before she had killed two Demons and wounded another.

None of the Demons could understand the smile on her face as she died, but then none of them had seen the little girl who ran into the woods while everyone was distracted by her mother.

# SIX

## I

Jack and the crew of his APC broke for lunch about 11:30 and sat down in the shade alongside their APC as the sounds of battle tapered off into nothingness. The last of the Demons were being hunted down and killed by revenge-seeking townsmen. Many of them had seen the remains of the two jeep patrolmen and few would ever forget the sight.

Before they had been trussed up by their heels, the men had been tortured and mutilated. The remains, hanging head down and spinning in the wind were enough to make a Mau-Mau sick with revulsion. The men who had found the bodies had spread the word and others had come and looked and gone away steeled for bloody vengeance.

Some of his men had even chased the Demons that Jack had let go. They found their bodies where their slaves had caught up to them. They had died to a man, unarmed and unmourned.

In the meantime, Jack had ordered the militia to gather together and return to town. About half of them had already disappeared over the hilltop, close behind his combat team. They would arrive back in the town in about ten minutes, and start loading up on ammunition. In the meantime, Jack and his crew could afford to take a break.

While they sat in the shadow of their APC, their radioman interrupted their lunch with a startling message.

"Jack, the town's under attack! They say that the Demons are moving up from the south and overrunning the farms along the way!"

He threw his lunch bag away, climbed into the APC and started to question the man on the other end. In a few minutes, Jack's worst fears were realized. The Demons were on the move while his force was scattered all over the north and out of ammunition. Meanwhile, Jack was told that the enemy had overrun his own farm, and was advancing all over, driving hundreds of refugees ahead of them.

Jack hid his personal losses well, and began to give orders.

"Listen carefully. Get all the ammunition you can out and ready for loading into the APCs. As soon as they come into town, load them up, overload them if you have to, and feed the crews. Hold everybody there, even if you have to shoot somebody. Have them wait until I get there to take charge.

"Try to contact all the watchtowers in the south and have them report what they see. The number of Demons, their weapons, and the direction they're marching in.

"Keep me informed with all the information as soon as you get it."

"As for the town, order everybody to stay put and wait until we get there."

"But Jack, Henderson and some of the other men are already gone. They said they were going to cover for the refugees as they marched back here. Should I tell them to come back too?"

"Damn. Yes, order Adam and his men back at once. As soon as you start getting in information, contact me."

Jack switched over to the loudspeaker and tersely told the militia what was going on, ordering them back to town as fast as they could go. Two-thirds of his troops were out there scattered around and useless. The two hundred fighting men he had left were going to have to fight one hell of a battle.

## II

Adam Henderson and his men were already too deeply involved with heavy fighting to get away. They had managed to ride directly into a Demon ambush. The enemy had hidden himself in roadside ditches and clumps of trees, waiting. As soon as the trucks drew up level with the ambush, the Demons cut loose with everything they had. Over a dozen men were killed outright, including most of the men they had picked up along the way to the front.

As the ambush victims tried to get their wits about them, the enemy started to throw molotails onto the road, soon covering the APC in a wash of flaming gasoline. The trapped men squeezed as many of the wounded into the APC as they could, but their band, that had grown to over fifty, was too large for all of them to find shelter. Now, with the APC dripping flames, it suddenly pulled away, leaving the trapped men behind. The men knew they were as good as dead when the first molotails began to fall onto their trucks. They crawled out, stood up and leveled their rifles and charged their enemies.

In the blaze of fire, all but three of the men were cut down. The three survivors leaped into the ditch with their enemies, firing for all they were worth. A Demon officer eliminated them by throwing a molotail into the knot of townsmen and Demons.

It was much simpler that way.

## III

The tide of refugees washed over the town. People desperate to find some safety didn't stop, but paused only long enough to snatch some food as they passed through the town. They cursed the men loading their APCs who refused to move out to attack the Demons. Under the guard of Jack's deputies and the threat of instant death, the militia stood firm and waited for orders.

By one o'clock, the first APCs were loaded and ready to move. Less than one hundred effectives were ready to take on over two thousand of the enemy. Jack was forming his task force around his sole remaining tank, and trying to sort order out of the chaos that the town had become.

By three o'clock, Jack was leading a force of three hundred men out of the town. All were mounted in APCs and given strict orders to remain buttoned up, no matter what happened. Everyone had heard the story of what had happened to Adam Henderson and his men. Fewer heard or understood that Jack had had his whole family wiped out.

## IV

The Demons had done well, although they had lost almost two hundred effectives in their attacks on the isolated farmhouses. They had driven the fleeing ranchers and farmers ahead of them into the watch-towers and into the town itself. Now they were attacking the watchtowers that dominated the roads they would have to use to attack the town itself.

The watchtowers were proving to be very hard targets. Attack after attack was beaten off, with high casualties to the Demons. Each attack left a few more men, dead or dying, locked in harsh embrace with the barbed wire that ringed the towers. Still more men littered the open ground with their bodies.

Inside the towers, things had not been going as well as planned. People had been killed or wounded by rico-chets, and ammunition supplies were beginning to run low. A few of the towers had been hit by molotails, and only the screen netting over the windows had prevented them from going into the tower and exploding.

Furthermore, the people inside the towers were not the ones for whom the defense was planned. They were wives and mothers, the old, the sick, and the injured who couldn't make use of the equipment.

With the desperation born of the sure knowledge that they would suffer more if they were captured than if they fought to the death, they struggled on. They got the word that a relief force was on the way, and it made them happy. A few minutes later, they would know black despair and defeat.

Mario had studied the situation and come up with a foolproof plan to take each watchtower. The Demons simply herded their prisoners and slaves in front of them and walked up to the towers. The people inside could see their friends and neighbors and didn't fire for fear of hitting them.

In a few minutes, it was over, and the defenders butchered. Now the Demons had the keys that they wanted.

# SEVEN

## I

Jack and his armored taskforce had an easy time sweeping through the enemy patrols as they ran across them, machinegunning and overrunning them whenever they attempted to stand fast. By seven o'clock, Jack and his men had killed at least a hundred Demons and had put militia units and their weapons and ammunition into watchtowers all along the way.

Finally, they fought their way through to where Adam Henderson and his men had died. The bodies lay where they had fallen in the road, stripped of their weapons and ammunition. Jack and his men stopped to remove the bodies.

A couple of the men called Jack over to the ditch where the last of the men had died. Below him, he could see the bodies of his men, locked in permanent embrace with their enemies, the bodies too charred to identify. There were a large number of enemies around the area. A gratifyingly large number.

Once that job was done, Jack moved off to reinforce some of the other towers. At each, he unloaded ammunition and some of the militia to defend the place against further attacks. He was especially careful to unload flares, because this was to be a moonless night.

Finally, as the sun sank over the hills, Jack ordered his men to return to the town, unable to complete their mission without sun.

"Why don't we just keep going, colonel?"

"We can't fight the Demons if we can't see them," Jack snapped. "I'll be damned if we're going to lose any more people than we absolutely have to. Rather than keep going, we'll go back to town and pick up some more ammunition, some more militia, and some rest. Tomorrow, before dawn, I'm going to be out hunting Demons."

## II

The Demon leaders had survived the battles by the simple expedient of hiding when the going got tough. Now, they were whipping their men and the slaves forward, taking tower after tower as they advanced. There were just about nine hundred Demons left to take out the town, and they were on the town's outskirts long before dawn.

## III

As night darkened the whole area, the sounds of battle died completely away, save when a nervous sentry fired off a flare, then the distant *pop!* and sudden glow told the story. Spotted widely around the countryside were the flaming ruins of farmhouses torched by the Demons.

In the town, lights glowed brightly as the crews worked on their APCs, loading them up for the next day's action. The soldiers and militia lay where they had fallen, most too exhausted to stay on their feet. Few had taken time for more than grabbing a few bits of food, then went off to sleep. All were still covered with the grime of combat and looked like piles of old, dirty clothes as they lay beside their vehicles.

A few of the men and women, too charged with adrenalin to sleep paced nervously through the town, weapons at the ready, looking for rest. A very few sat in the town bar and drank themselves into a stupor.

Unlike any of the rest, Jack stayed in his office, planning the next day's operations. His combat team, newly promoted to officers in the militia, sat around and took notes as the orders were passed out.

In the hospital, the wounded screamed and groaned in their pain. The hard-pressed staff could only treat a small number of the wounded, and then only the people with the best chance of survival. Some of the victims were sedated and pushed off to one side; with only one surgeon available, the luxury of adequate medical care for everyone was impossible.

In the refugee barracks, the people sat around, glassy-eyed and helpless. Some walked through the rooms looking for friends and neighbors, but most were far too stunned to care what was going on around them. Many of the people had walked their roads so well known in far happier times for over ten hours to reach the shelter of the town, only to find no trace of their family. Exhaustion and fear cut deep valleys into the faces of the dispirited refugees.

A few of the refugees gathered together in the immemorial fashion of all people under pressure to criticize Jack's handling of the battle. If they had been in charge, they would never have allowed any of the militia to run off to the north, but would have simply marched south, since it was obvious that that was the way the Demons were coming. Facts meant very little to such people, especially when the man they were slandering wasn't around to hear about it.

## IV

Under the cover of darkness, some of the slaves and prisoners slipped through the loose Demon guards. Many just ran away, leaving behind friends and family, but a few made their way through Demon patrols and past trigger-happy militia units, to warn the town.

The story that they told Jack and his officers was very frightening, especially the story of how watchtower after watchtower had fallen without a shot to the Demons. All of a sudden, Jack's plan for the defense of the town were radically changed.

Dismissing all but the men he could trust, the men of his combat team and the wood party that his cousin Linc had commanded, Jack began issuing new orders.

# EIGHT

## I

Before dawn, the townspeople heard the cries of the slaves being forced toward the town walls. Jack stood on the wall and waited while the predawn light showed the sea of human misery that stood before the wall.

The Demons had planned well, driving their victims up against the wall, then gathering in their rear, safe from fire from the town's defenders. As Jack and the citizen's committee watched, a short, arrogant teenager pushed his way through a crowd that melted away from his path. Though Jack didn't know it, the man was Mario Ginetti.

"Do you see 'em?" Mario screamed. "We're going to start killing them if you don't throw down your guns and open the gates. We're giving you five minutes to make up your minds, then we start killing them."

Mario turned and walked back into the crowd. The town council dissolved into panic, as, without Adam Henderson's lead, they began to dither and blather about how the gates had to be opened, that perhaps the Demons might see reason if the townspeople cooperated with them. Jack snorted in disgust and told the men to get off the wall.

"If you can't think of anything better to do than to surrender, get the hell off the wall! I'll take care of the problem, just leave me alone!"

Jack didn't even bother to make sure the men left the wall, but immediately picked up his .30-06 rifle and scope, threw it to his shoulder, and squeezed the trigger. The one soft lead slug did its job well, exploding Mario's head like a watermelon dropped from a skyscraper.

Almost immediately, machineguns began their deadly chatter, the sounds coming so fast that it was as if a crazed giant was ripping and tearing a cloth that never ended. The sound reverberated from the buildings and grew until it seemed to fill the universe with its clatter.

The slaves watched with dull incredulity as Jack killed the Demon's leader. They realized an instant later that the death was the signal for their own end. With an animal-like moan of pain and terror, the slaves broke and ran away from the guns leveled on them.

The Demons saw their leader shot down and hesitated for a moment, before they brought their weapons up to their shoulders, ready to fire into the mass of slaves in front of them. They could see the slaves were well aware of the fate that waited for them as they broke and ran away.

Jack's combat team had been waiting for the signal to attack the Demons, and as soon as they saw the Demon leader shot down, they opened fire with a dozen machineguns.

The night before, they had crawled out of the town and worked their way into the buildings that surrounded the square that had to be the ultimate destination for the Demons. Each of the guns had been placed so it could sweep the whole square and kill anyone who stood there.

The plan was that if the Demons pushed their slaves up against the town wall, the machinegunners were to wait until they had clear shots at the Demons and had gotten their signal from Jack. The ambush was sprung in a moment.

The Demons trapped in the town square fell in clusters as the slugs tore into them, passing through one man and striking another. A rain of over a thousand rounds a minute was poured in its leaden deadliness into the enemy ranks. In minutes, most of the Demons had been killed, their bodies torn and torn again as the gunners lashed the square with their blazing whips.

The slaves, fleeing from the death that they knew was waiting for them, ran from the square and gave the people who lined the walls a clear field of fire. In seconds, everybody with a gun was firing into the bloody mass of dead meat that sprawled in the square.

As the bullets continued to tear at the bodies, the mortar crews opened fire, mashing the enemy bodies into a bloody paste.

The battle ended.

# NINE

## I

The campaign was over two days later as the last of the Demons was hunted down by the townspeople and killed, without mercy. Most of the people had seen what was left of their families or had heard the stories that the slaves told of the degradation and barbarity that the Demons subjected their slaves and prisoners to and could not be held back.

One of the militia units ran into a heavy battle to the east of town and was thrown back with heavy casualties before it could be established that the people they were attacking were friendly. It was Janice Wilson and her girls. They were sent back to town under heavy escort by Jack's combat team. Jack himself was out of the battle. He had withdrawn into his office and locked himself inside.

The girls had disarmed with obvious reluctance and only put down their weapons on the insistence of Janice. Janice had carefully explained her mission to the men from the combat team, and they had contacted the town, telling Ginny to meet them.

Ginny walked into the sheriff's office and looked at the dark-haired woman sitting on the desk. She was heavily tanned and clothed in worn camouflage fatigues. A long, narrow scar sliced through her left cheek.

"Hi, I'm Janice Wilson. Can you tell me where Jack Dawson is?"

"Hello, Janice, I'm Ginny Schroeder, a friend of his. I don't think you want to see Jack just now. He locked himself into his office this morning and refuses to come out. His whole family was wiped out yesterday, except for his little niece Melody. Why do you want to see him?"

"I guess to bring him even more bad news. Jim Dawson sent me and my girls here before he died."

"Jim's dead? Are you sure?"

"Yes, Ginny, he died in my arms. He rescued me and my girls from a motorcycle gang, just after the bombing. He was the only person who tried to help us, and he died for it."

"When he was dying, he asked me to come here and tell his family how he died. I guess you folks don't really need any more bad news, do you? We'll just march on out of here."

"Janice, we need all the people we can find. The men we killed today managed to wipe out almost a third of our people, and the slaves that they took are all too scared to stay around here. They're all marching south for the winter. We're giving them food, and all the weapons that the Demons carried, but they're still going."

"If you and your girls can march here to carry a message, I suppose that we can't very well send you back. I know Jack wouldn't hear of it, and he's the leader here.

"Listen, Janice, you come home with me, you and your girls. We'll talk and get to know one another better. When Jack's ready to come out, he'll talk with us. Meanwhile, let's let him struggle with his own problems, and not add to them any more than we have to."

"All right, Ginny. I think my girls and I could use the rest. We've walked almost five hundred miles so far this year, and we're getting tired. It'll be nice not to have to forage for our food for once."

## II

George Johnson and Wilson Good arrived on the outskirts of Henderson's Corners just about on schedule. Instead of a welcoming committee, they found the road into the town covered with bodies. More bodies lined the road and were scattered over the fields, some flat on the ground, others crucified in coils of barbed wire. The road was even blocked by a badly burnt and abandoned tank.

Johnson and Good had their guards dismount and spread out. It wouldn't do for them to get killed in a forlorn attempt to reach a dead community. There were altogether too many dead men as it stood.

## III

The people of the Henderson's Corners community gathered together in the store to talk about the future. Most of the people had lost some member of their family to the Demons, and all had been affected by the battle that followed.

Where once the community numbered almost two thousand, now there were less than fifteen hundred men, women, and children gathered around. They had been called together to speak with Jack Dawson. Everyone wondered what he had in mind.

Everyone was tired, worn out by the struggle to stay alive.

Jack sat at his desk, an unopened bottle of cognac salvaged from Valley Forge sitting in front of him. Jack had been in the room for several hours, the only sign of his presence the pile of burnt tobacco ash in his ashtray. At last, he picked up the telephone and dialed Ginny's number at her grandfather's house.

"Ginny, it's Jack. Listen, I'm sorry I locked you out of my office, but what I had to think about was best done alone. Do you forgive me?"

"Jack, I've always forgiven you. I'm afraid, though, I have some more bad news. A woman just got into town and told me that Jim was killed on the first day of the war."

"I've always figured that he was dead, Ginny. At least now we know for sure. I want to get our whole community together as soon as we can. There's something we all have to talk over and get straightened out. I'll take care of that later."

"Ginny, I don't know how to ask you something like this; you'll have to forgive me for being a little clumsy about this. I want you to think about marrying me, Ginny. I should have done this years ago, but I could never get my nerve up. It's not too late for either of us to start another family, you know."

"Jack, you already have a family. There's your brother Jim's little girl, there are my children, and there's your son, John.

"Jack, that's something I never told you. I wanted to let you go through West Point before I told you, but then I found a man I loved as much as you, and I heard you were married yourself, so I just kept quiet. Now is the time for me to tell you, Jack.

"Yes, I've always loved you. I'll marry you tonight, tomorrow, any time you say."

"Ginny, I never knew. If I had, I would have married you. God, if only I had known!"

"Jack, it was better this way. Neither one of us should have any regrets about the past, it's the future we have to think of, the future of all the children we have now, and the children who will come."

"You're right, Ginny. I'll be over to talk with you as soon as I can get this meeting set up.

"I love you very, very much, Ginny."

## IV

By pure luck, one of the men from Spokane found a man from his town. After a wary exchange of greetings, the two men went back to pick up the rest of the Spokane party. Everyone was going to Jack's meeting.

By seven o'clock, eveyone in the town knew that the people from Spokane had arrived. Most of them were waiting for Jack to begin his speech. They all hoped that it would start on time.

Jack stepped up to the podium, closely followed by the two men from Spokane. A hush fell over the crowd as Jack began to speak.

"My friends, I had planned to make a speech to keep us all together and to try to bring our community out of the terror and horror of the last few days.

"The arrival of our friends from Spokane has changed all that. I could stand here and tell you about the wonderful future that we'll all have, now that we have contact with the outside.

"Well, it just isn't so. We have a long, hard road ahead of us, all of us, the people of Henderson's Corners and the people from Spokane. I've told our friends about the cache of supplies that we found in Valley Forge and have made a deal to share the wealth that lies in that mountain.

"In some far off time, perhaps a thousand years from now, a world made better than the old will ask what kind of people they were who founded their society. I know the answer, and it is one that we all can be proud of.

"I want them to say, they were survivors!"